EVIDENCE
of GRACE

Books by Teresa Slack

A Tender Reed

The Ultimate Guide to Darcy Carter

The Jenna's Creek Novels:

Streams of Mercy

Redemption's Song

Evidence of Grace

EVIDENCE
of GRACE

Third in a series of
JENNA'S CREEK NOVELS

Teresa D. Slack

Tsaba House
Reedley, California

All scripture quotations, unless otherwise noted, are taken from the King James Version of the Bible.

Cover and text design by Bookwrights
Senior Editor, Jodie Nazaroff
Author Photo by Andrea Lundgren

Published by
Tsaba House
2252 12th Street, Reedley, California 93654
Visit our website at: www.TsabaHouse.com

Printed in the United States of America

First Edition: 2007

Library of Congress Cataloging-in-Publication Data

Slack, Teresa D., 1964-
  Evidence of grace / Theresa D. Slack. — 1st ed.
    p. cm. — (Series of Jenna's Creek novels ; 3rd)
  "Third in a series of Jenna's Creek novels."
  ISBN-13: 978-1-933853-48-2 (trade pbk. : alk. paper)
  ISBN-10: 1-933853-48-4 (trade pbk. : alk. paper)
  1. Witnesses—Fiction. I. Title.
  PS3619.L33E95 2007
  813'.6--dc22
                                         2007016191

This book is lovingly
dedicated to my parents,

Richard "Butch" Hooley and Naomi Glenn

Acknowledgments

S pecial thanks to Cathy Brewster of the Pike County Court of Common Pleas for her legal advice in writing this book. Any mistakes and inaccuracies are my own.

Thanks to my first reader, Bonnie Cooper for your time and honest evaluations of characters and plotting. Your input has helped bring the residents of Jenna's Creek alive.

Thanks to my readers at Rotary Forms Press, Inc. in Hillsboro, Ohio. What a thrill to hear your comments and questions about when the next book is coming out! Thanks to the prayer warriors at the Hillsboro Church of God who continually lift my books up in prayer. Thanks to all the readers in my hometown and those I've met at libraries and bookstores across the country. You are the reason I am able to pursue this dream of mine. Special thanks to my favorite readers: Karen Garrett, Gail Jackson, Robin Sorrels, Katrina Gibson, and Tammy Braniff. Your enthusiasm and faith in me means more than words can say.

As always, I would like to thank the folks at Tsaba House for their belief in me and this project. Thanks to Jodie Nazaroff, my wonderful editor who irons out my writing and catches grammatical errors an average fifth grader shouldn't make. Thanks to Pam Schwagerl, president of Tsaba House, for keeping me involved in every step of the publishing process. Thanks to Annie Lundgren and Corrie Schwagerl for your tireless efforts in letting the world know about the books.

A special thank you to my family, especially my husband, Ralph. I would never have made it this far without your love and support and constant encouragement. There have been highs and lows along the way, but you've always been in the wings, cheering me on. This roller coaster ride wouldn't be any fun without you in the seat next to me.

"Moreover the law entered, that the offense might abound. But where sin abounded, grace did much more abound..."

—Romans 5:20 KJV

Chapter One

S he awoke in a cold sweat, the remnants of the familiar dream fresh in her mind. Instinctively, she rubbed her hand against her nose to remove the moisture she felt as keenly as her hand on her face, knowing all the while her nose would be dry. Nevertheless, she rubbed until her nose was sore and the dream had faded to a tolerable level. She sat up in the narrow bed, removed her hand from her face and stared at it in the persistent gray light outside the bars of her cell. At times such as this, she almost appreciated the light's glaring presence.

In the nearly three years she'd been here, she had gotten used to doing without many of the things she had taken for granted in her former life. Among those was the simple act of going to sleep in comfortable darkness. At ten o'clock every night, somewhere in the vast recesses of the prison, someone pulled a loud audible lever, punctuated by a dull clang, and cells up and down the block went dark. She would close her eyes and will herself to believe she was back home in the bed of her childhood home with Mama and Daddy in the room next to hers. She thought of those long ago nights when she was lulled to sleep by their comfortable murmurings of things she didn't understand. She tried to convince herself the stiff, narrow mattress beneath her was the down filled one from her old room. Sometimes she even convinced herself she would awaken to the smell of hot coffee and frying bacon wafting upstairs to her room. But no matter how tightly she squeezed her eyes shut, she couldn't block out the gray light that illuminated the hallway outside her cell. Even after she put her arm across her face it was ever present, shattering the dream world of her little bedroom with the peeling wallpaper and water stained ceiling and Mama and Daddy next door.

Now, examining her hand in the pale light, she could see it was clean and dry as her rational mind knew it would be. Any blood that had once tarnished her face had been long washed away. Long gone.

She took a few deep breaths to silence the wild beating of her heart. Years ago, the dream had haunted her nearly every night. She dreaded going to bed, knowing what was waiting. The next morning, she would drink an extra pot of coffee and powder her face so no one at work would see the dark circles under her eyes or notice her dragging feet and absent-mindedness caused by sleep deprivation. No one suspected the secret hidden in her heart. Over time, she learned to push the memories and images farther and farther down inside her until her rest went undisturbed—most of the time.

Even then she had known her secret wouldn't remain hidden forever. Her sins would find her out. But knowing hadn't prepared her for the price she had to pay.

She reached over and took the windup alarm clock off the bookcase beside her bed. She was a petite woman, only three inches over five feet tall, but lying flat on her back on the cot, she was able to reach the bookcase beside her, the wall above her head, and if she scrunched down on the bed, she could even touch the cool metal bars with her toes. The toilet in the corner was two paces from where she now lay. She had trained her body to relieve itself as seldom as possible while confined to her cell, yet the stench still clung to her clothes and her hair; another thing she couldn't escape through her imagination.

According to the alarm clock her brother Sidney had sent a few months ago, it was five-fifteen in the morning. This was her fourth alarm clock in less than three years. Every time she turned her back, the alarm clocks, and everything else that wasn't nailed down, disappeared, even though the cells were allegedly monitored and off limits when prisoners weren't in them. Privacy or personal property did not exist here. Millions of dollars were spent to keep prisoners adequately confined within the prison walls to protect society from them, but nothing was done to protect the prisoners from each other.

In one hour and forty-five minutes, another buzzer and metallic clang would signal the turning on of lights and the beginning of another day. Knowing the likelihood of going back to sleep was highly improbable thanks to the dream that had awakened her, she swung her legs over the side of the bed and reached for her Bible on the bookcase. It was too dark to read, but the weight of the Bible in her hands brought her comfort. She smoothed her fingers over the imitation leather cover and the new smell drifted up to her nostrils. The Bible was new too, the former one having disappeared last month. She closed her eyes in a silent plea as she stroked the cover, but the dream's residue refused to fade.

The tension in her arms and legs that had woken her in the first place, remained. She felt as if she had just run a mile. She stood up and moved to the edge of the cell and pressed her head against the bars. To her left, someone cursed and rolled over in bed. Voices mumbled in their sleep from every direction. Boots thumped across the floor a flight below her. In the far distance, she heard a deep, throaty, masculine laugh. Even in the early morning hours, this place was never silent.

She turned back to face the cell and clutched the Bible to her chest, wishing for all she was worth she could erase the memories that had caused her dream. Without the memories, there would be no dream. She could sleep the unencumbered sleep of youth. Without the memories, she would finally be at peace.

Instead, the memories remained as crisp and crystal clear as though they'd occurred yesterday.

Standing on the cold concrete floor with the metal prison bars pressing into her back—a hundred miles and thirty years removed—she could still almost feel her body catapulting through the air as if in slow motion. Every moment of her flight across the room unfolded before her like an old movie reel, the images jerky and erratic in her mind. The impact of her body against the other woman's did nothing to slow her progress. The two became one as they fell, spiraling, cascading downward. In the agonizing unreality of a sleep state, it seemed to her that the fall went on indefinitely. The other woman slammed into the back of the couch. An exhalation of pain and surprise sounded in her ear, alarmingly loud—much louder than it had actually been. Still they spiraled downward, until finally, mercifully, the floor stopped their descent.

Sometimes the abrupt ceasing of the downward motion was enough to startle her out of sleep. She would awaken breathless and frightened, but thankful it had ended.

Other nights—most nights—the dream continued. She would hear the sickening crunch of the other woman's head as it banged against the antique boot scraper, the sound again magnified by the dream. She would see the pool of blood appearing under the thick mane of dark hair and she would feel its thick warmth on the end of her nose. Her nostrils would fill with the pungent aroma.

Just like that fateful night, her first thought was that she had bloodied her nose in the fall and that the blood she saw and smelled was her own. Her nose and chin smarted from a phantom pain where they jarred against the floor. But then she would put her hands on either side of the other woman's shoulders, raise herself off the floor, and watch in morbid fascination as a drop of blood fell slowly from the end of her nose and landed with a silent splash in the widening pool beneath her. At that moment, she would realize the blood was not coming from her own nose but from the wound on the back of the other woman's head. She would untangle her limbs from those of the woman and scramble to her feet. She would gaze down into those familiar exotic brown eyes and realize the woman was dead. In one foolish act of frustration and rage, she had snuffed out the light in those beautiful eyes.

The terror, the realization of that moment, almost always jerked her into wakefulness.

Noreen shuddered in the tiny cell and pulled the Bible closer to her chest.

Other nights she dreamed of the sounds of Sally Blake's lifeless body being dragged through Aunt Paula's immaculate house, and out the back door to her car; of the weight in her arms and the tiredness in her legs as she pulled and tugged and maneuvered the body into the trunk. The scent of blood, death, and disinfectant had filled her nostrils as she scrubbed away the evidence of their fight—the blood on the metal boot scraper where Sally had banged her head and the congealing pool on the aged wood floors. It wasn't until she heaved the body out of the car and into the hole in the ground where it would remain for more than twenty-five years that she would awake in a cold sweat; her arms and legs trembling with fatigue and with the sound of Sally's body skidding and thumping against the walls of the old well still ringing in her ears.

Three hours later, Noreen Trimble shuffled along in a line of women to which there seemed no beginning or end, to the area of the prison that housed the infirmary. As prison assignments went, hers was one of the most sought after in the system. In the outside world she had been a pharmacist's assistant in a drugstore. With her knowledge and skills, coupled with a nonviolent offender status in spite of the fact she was entering the third year of a murder sentence, she was put to work in the prison pharmacy. Any job was better than sitting in her cell counting the cracks in the walls, or worse, being shuffled outside to the yard where she sat on a wooden bench and tried to dissuade the approach of other inmates. Her first eight months at the women's correctional facility in Marysville, Ohio, a little town west of Columbus she had never heard of until three years ago, she had done exactly that until someone in an office somewhere noticed a position had opened for which she had the skills to fill.

Getting the job in the infirmary had been an answer to urgent prayer sent up on Noreen's behalf by the congregation of the Nazarene Church where her father had been the pastor for many years. Not only was she out of her cell for six hours, five days a week, she was doing something she enjoyed and was good at.

The inmates with whom she worked were like her, skilled, moderately educated, and less dangerous than most every other woman at Marysville. Unlike the guards who walked among the general populace, the guards in the infirmary and pharmacy treated the women like coworkers rather than prisoners. They sometimes asked for, and received, free medical advice for themselves or little ones at home. In return, one or another would occasionally bring in cookies or sodas or old magazines from the outside for them to enjoy. Every fall, one of the guards brought a bushel basket of golden and red delicious apples from his orchard at home that the girls munched on all week. One Christmas, another guard gave them slippers she had knitted during her breaks.

At times like that, Noreen could almost pretend she was a regular working girl with girlfriends, smiling bosses, and orders to fill—that is, if she didn't look too closely at the bars on the windows, the identical uniforms, or the sullen expressions worn by the patients.

Except for a doctor and another prisoner who swept floors and emptied trashcans, she was the oldest woman working in the infirmary. For obvious reasons, the median age wasn't high among her fellow inmates. Most women committing crimes worthy of Marysville were decidedly younger than she was. Those serving life sentences were either paroled or died within the walls sooner than they would have on the outside. A woman in her forties often appeared to be in her upper fifties or sixties if she'd been in the system any length of time.

Noreen believed it was more than simply her age that made the younger women and guards consider her as anything but a threat. The oldest of five children, her brothers and sisters had never been threatened by her status. On the few occasions their parents left her in charge, they returned home to utter chaos and mayhem, to find Noreen upstairs in her room in tears. She accepted early in life she was not leadership material. While in the outside world, a quiet and gentle nature could be seen as a virtue, within these walls it could get a person killed.

While Noreen's passive disposition didn't exactly command respect, she did possess a quality that drew people to her, even among Marysville's most hardened criminals. She had a truly compassionate spirit, something many inmates had never encountered. Within minutes of meeting her, women were comfortable enough, and even eager to bear their souls. Oh, the things Noreen heard. Things she never imagined one human being was capable of doing to another. Most often, she heard tales of injustices and vicious crimes committed against these women by the men in their lives. But many admitted things they had done; things no other living person knew of or ever would. It wasn't only the inmates who opened up to her. The guards sought her advice concerning spouses and children, even though everyone knew she had never married and didn't have children of her own. She figured, more often than not, most of them simply wanted a listening, non-condemning ear rather than actual advice.

This was nothing new to her. As far back as she could remember she was the one other girls told their secrets to. She had no doubt it was what drew Sally Blake to her.

By all outward appearances, two more different creatures had never been created. Where Sally was beautiful and vivacious, Noreen was plain. Her limp brown hair hung straight around her shoulders, her lips too thin, and her ears too big for her head. Sally reveled in her position as center of attention while Noreen strove to blend into the background. Sally had an opinion for everything and was not shy about making it known. Noreen's teachers were always reminding her to speak up.

Noreen Trimble met Sally Blake when she was assigned to Mrs. Hiestand's homeroom in the sixth grade. Both girls had grown up in Jenna's Creek, Ohio but had never crossed paths. Noreen's father was a preacher. Sally's dad owned a real estate agency in town. Noreen's family lived on the west side of town in one of the small tract houses that had been built after the First World War. Sally's family lived on the east side of town where the large houses sat on huge corner lots and well dressed families walked to the Episcopal church down the street when the weather was nice.

None of the girls in Mrs. Hiestand's class cared for Sally Blake, though they secretly admired her and openly emulated her. She was the tallest girl in the sixth grade, and she wore a brassiere long before the others had need of one. While their mothers insisted on braiding their hair or pulling it back into functional ponytails with childish ribbons, Sally had her hair cut at the salon in town. Her mother bought her clothes somewhere other than the tiny, outdated department stores of Auburn County. With her long flowing tresses and full lips, Sally reminded them of Vivian Leigh. That alone was reason enough to hate her. But then she added insult to injury by rubbing their noses in the irrefutable fact that every boy in school was in love with her.

Two girls from Sally's side of town, Patty and Peggy Something-or-other, followed her around and hung on her every word. They weren't sisters, but they might as well have been. They wore their dark hair in the same pageboy style, dressed however Sally dictated, laughed at her jokes, and basked in her shadow. The girls who weren't Patty and Peggy sometimes wished they were, but still hated them with more fervor than they hated Sally.

Then there was Noreen. No one ever compared her to Vivian Leigh. She had a secret crush on Charlie Kendall, the smartest boy in Mrs. Hiestand's class. Charlie was short and wore black-framed glasses. He didn't care that the other boys teased him when he was picked last for dodge ball or because he understood the equations Mrs. Hiestand wrote on the blackboard. He wasn't handsome like Doug Hastings or rich like Will Jansen or popular like Bobby Wilson, but Noreen thought he was cute. He was smart and funny, and he understood her when no one else did.

Noreen was sure he liked one of the smarter, prettier girls in class, of which there were plenty to choose from, even though he seemed to ignore them and talked to her whenever the teacher's back was turned. So she enjoyed the moments Charlie gave her and tried not to hope he might like her as much as she liked him.

But Sally noticed.

Sally didn't have much use for smart boys who weren't handsome, rich or popular, but she suddenly developed a use for Charlie. When it came time for the only sixth grade dance, Sally boldly asked Charlie to go. Noreen was crushed. She didn't blame Sally. After all, she had never told Sally she liked Charlie. She had never told anyone. And as soon as the dance was over, Sally never spoke to Charlie again. She made mean jokes about him behind his back to Peggy and Patty and the other girls in class. She told them how Charlie's mother had to pull her old car over before they got to the dance and put oil in it, how his dad didn't live with them, and his little brothers always wore the same clothes to school.

Noreen hated the look on Charlie's face when he came up behind them at recess and heard Sally talking. She especially hated that she had been laughing at Sally's impression of Charlie's mother at the time. But Sally said Charlie would do good to develop a sense of humor. If you couldn't laugh at yourself, you were bound for a hard time down the road, Sally assured her. Noreen still felt sorry for Charlie, and she hated that he stopped talking to her when Mrs. Hiestand wasn't paying attention. She told herself it didn't matter. His family moved away that summer, and she never saw him again. Meanwhile, her friendship with Sally continued to blossom.

The diminutive girl ignored all through elementary school suddenly became somebody. She was Sally Blake's friend.

Noreen was so thrilled to finally have a bosom friend, someone with whom she could share her deepest thoughts and desires with no fear of ridicule, she often overlooked the way Sally treated other people. She rationalized the way Sally teased the other girls and threw her weight around and flirted shamelessly with a boy one day only to publicly humiliate him the next, as a way to fulfill some need for attention she wasn't getting at home.

Noreen's family was close knit, sometimes to the point of suffocating, while Sally's parents were distant and sometimes too busy for their only daughter. Sally told Noreen how lucky she was that her mom was home waiting for her after school at the end of the day. She would give anything to have sisters and brothers. Noreen doubted it since Sally was used to answering to no one, but she didn't tell her that. Only children always dreamed of being part of a big family.

Over the years, their friendship grew. Sally was good to her. She listened when Noreen talked. She defended her against the other girls' teasing. She taught her how to wear makeup and fix her hair. She encouraged her to enroll in college after high school. With Sally Blake as her best friend, the whole world was within reach.

It never occurred to her that Sally might have been using her the way she used everyone else. Noreen wasn't totally naïve or stupid. She knew Sally wasn't a kind person. She saw how she took advantage of people. She knew she used her brains and beauty to get whatever she wanted. She had even heard rumors concerning Sally and older men, married men. When she asked her about it a few times, Sally would laugh and give her a playful slap.

"Nory, you know how people talk. Some girls hate me and make up miserable lies. That just proves how jealous they are. Besides, I can't help it that older men find me attractive."

Such intimations made Noreen uncomfortable so she pushed them out of her mind and focused on other things. Like the man she loved, Tim Shelton.

Noreen shook her head to clear it of those memories. They were too painful. She didn't want to think about Sally. She didn't want to think about the events that had led up to the moment behind her nightmares, the moment that changed so many lives. She especially didn't want to think about Tim.

"Noreen? Are you all right?"

Noreen looked across the battered, metal desk to the young woman she worked with every day. Cindy Burke was barely in her twenties, but her face bore the scars of a long, hard life. She had already served five years of a twenty-five-year sentence for robbing a liquor store with her boyfriend. The boyfriend vanished when the sirens filled the night air, leaving Cindy in a car they had stolen from Michigan with a handful of bills from the liquor store—the boyfriend had made off with the real cache—and several guns stolen from a man in the last town whose head had been bashed in by the boyfriend. Cindy believed the boyfriend when he told her he would take care of everything, and she wouldn't spend one minute in jail. She had waited through the trial, refusing to give him up, expecting to see him come through the door any minute and straighten out the whole mess. He didn't show, leaving Cindy to go down alone.

Noreen had learned not to believe most of the hard luck stories inmates told her. But if even a fraction of what Cindy said was true, her growing up years in the home of an alcoholic mother and more uncles than she could count who liked to take what they wanted from her after her mother passed out, had taken their toll on the girl. Even though her life hadn't turned out the way she'd hoped thirty years ago, Noreen thanked God every night she had been born to a mother who held her when she cried, and a father who sacrificed of himself to provide for his family and taught his children of a Savior who had given his own life on a cross for them.

She gave Cindy a tired smile. "I didn't sleep well last night." There was no need in telling her about the dream. She had never told anyone.

"Who could sleep good in this place?" Cindy said with a wry smirk. "We got another busy day. Have you looked at the roster?"

Noreen shook her head and took the clipboard off the wall near her chair. She groaned audibly. The list was already sixty names long. Sixty prisoners coming for relief of some type of ailment; one third would require medication. The state was stingy about doling out medication to prisoners. The patient would have to prove they were in dire straits before Uncle Sam spent a nickel on curing them. But it was Cindy and Noreen's job—under the supervision of Officer Wayne Oglethorpe—to keep the records of who got what, and for what condition.

Within fifteen minutes the infirmary became a riot of activity. Doors slammed, inmates cursed and complained, guards barked orders, and nurses called out names. Noreen and Cindy worked with barely an upward glance. They seldom saw inmates in their inner office, and they both preferred it that way. Anytime the door opened, it was usually another inmate office worker returning a patient's records or orders from a doctor to see someone else's.

When the noise level outside the office door rose to a feverish pitch, Noreen didn't miss a stroke on her typewriter.

It wasn't until the door burst open and Cindy shrieked and leaped out of her chair that Noreen looked up. Two women in blue prison issue coveralls ran into the room. One went straight to the locked medicine cabinet behind Officer Oglethorpe's desk. Officer Oglethorpe knew how to handle such situations. He leaped out of his chair and intercepted the inmate with one arm and reached for his walkie-talkie with the other. The second woman was busy at the door fighting off two other guards while the hallway quickly filled with more guards and prisoners wanting to see the excitement.

With one deftly laid blow to the head by Officer Oglethorpe, the first inmate dropped at his feet like a sack of potatoes. He returned his nightstick to his holster and spoke quickly into the walkie-talkie. Meanwhile, Cindy grabbed a paralyzed Noreen by the shoulder and pulled her against the far wall.

Noreen watched the fight by the door in fascination. The second inmate showed fierce tenacity. She obviously desperately wanted the drugs in the office. Noreen winced as a blow caught the inmate on the shoulder, and the sound of cracking bone reverberated through the room. The wound only enraged the woman further. She turned to the offending officer and bit down on the man's wrist. He cried out in pain and drew back to land another blow. A third inmate appeared out of nowhere and leaped onto the man's back.

Suddenly it was as if someone had opened the floodgates. Inmates and guards alike spilled into the office, jumping, biting, pulling, and cursing. Noreen couldn't tell who was doing what to whom. Officer Oglethorpe stepped around his desk and headed into the melee as if it were a minor inconvenience. He wasn't aware that the inmate at his feet had regained consciousness. As he stepped over her, she jabbed a long sharp object into his ankle. His leg gave out from under him as he spun around. He tried to keep from falling while he fumbled in his holster for a can of mace. The inmate jerked the weapon out of his ankle and drew back for another blow. He tried to kick out with his good leg, but his wounded ankle couldn't hold him up. As he fell on top of the inmate, the blow glanced off his shin. Blood darkened the pant leg of his uniform.

Cindy grabbed Noreen's shoulders and shoved her under the desk they shared. As she was going down, Noreen heard shouts, running feet, and women in the hallway shrieking in pain. Under the legs of the desk Noreen saw the inmate at the cabinet pull herself out from under Officer Oglethorpe and crawl toward the locked medicine cabinets. Officer Oglethorpe got onto his knees and pinned the woman's arms behind her back. Her homemade weapon skittered across the floor. It came to a stop a few inches from Noreen. She stared at what looked like a sharpened spoon, still glistening with Officer Oglethorpe's blood.

Her hand tensed. She could reach out and take it and no one would be the wiser. She could give it to the guards after everything was over. In plain sight, it was an open invitation to another inmate who wouldn't hesitate to turn the tables in their favor. Before she could decide what to do, Cindy's hand closed around Noreen's wrist. *Stay out of it*, her wide-eyed gaze warned. Noreen pulled her arm back to her side. She didn't have to be told twice.

Suddenly the sound above them intensified and several bodies were thrown against the desk. A typewriter and several reams of paperwork crashed to the floor as the desk was pushed back. Cindy's head hit the underside of the desk. She cried out and toppled over onto her back. Noreen stared in horror at the blood spouting out from her hairline. Then she realized she was exposed. Two inmates and two guards fell on top of her. Noreen tried to move, but she was pinned to the cold tile floor. Noise and shouting rang in her ears. She tried to cry out, but she couldn't draw a breath. Someone's fist closed around the shank still lying in the middle of the floor. A size twelve boot slammed down on the fist. The fist opened and another boot kicked the shank in Noreen's direction. Noreen felt herself growing lightheaded with fear and lack of oxygen. She should get the weapon while she had the chance. She didn't want to get involved. They would blame the whole incident on her if they found it on her. But she couldn't just lie there and let someone else use it on one of the guards or Cindy or herself.

If it was at all possible, the noise level increased. More officers had crowded into the small room. A sharp kick caught her soundly on the temple. Her head swam, and she fought hard to remain conscious. When she jerked back to avoid another kick, her head bounced off the floor. This time she knew she was going to black out. Then suddenly, the weight on top of her shifted. With a strength she didn't know she had, she scurried out from under the wriggling mass atop of her. She could make out the corner of the desk and Cindy's feet sticking out from under it.

Cindy was hurt. She could be bleeding to death. Noreen rose onto her elbows and started across the floor toward the desk. She saw a flash of movement out of the corner of her eye, and rolled in barely enough time to miss a kick aimed at the side of her head. She rolled onto her back and found herself staring at the fluorescent lighting overhead. She took a deep breath and prepared to roll back onto her stomach to crawl away from the mass behind her. She felt rather than saw an inmate trip over her legs and fall on top of her.

For one paralyzing moment, she saw the other woman's face inches from her, contorted with rage. Noreen started to put her hands on the woman's shoulders to push her away, but suddenly she became aware of a hot ball of pain emanating from her lower belly. It felt as if someone had plunged a hot poker under her ribcage and was now twisting it deeper and deeper. The woman's eyes widened in alarm and then she rolled off of Noreen. Her head was spinning. Someone had hold of her legs. She couldn't move. She tried to look for Cindy. Cindy would help her. If only she could get to the desk. Black dots circled before her eyes. She reached down to her stomach to take out the poker. She pulled her hand back and brought it to her face. Just like in her dream, her hand was covered with blood.

This time the blood wasn't Sally's. She swirled into blackness.

Chapter Two

A harsh banging jarred Christy Blackwood from a fitful night's sleep. The electronic alarm clock beside her bed blinked 8:20. A crack of sunshine filtering in between the curtains confirmed the time. She couldn't decide if she should be ashamed at getting caught sleeping so late on a weekday, or wish the party on the other side of the door had left her to sleep the rest of the day away.

She threw the covers back and reached for her terry cloth bathrobe. "Just a minute," she called out as she knotted the belt around her waist and hurried through the tiny apartment. Then she remembered she shouldn't have called out. She could almost bet money the person on the other side of the door was someone she didn't want to see. Such as the building manager after the rent, her boss—make that ex-boss, or Sean.

Sean. Her heart skipped a beat in spite of herself. Where was he? Had he realized the mess he'd gotten her into and was back to make things right?

She chided herself at the ridiculousness of the thought. Of course he knew what he'd done. He had used her and then walked away without a thought about the repercussions his deeds would bring crashing down around her head. He wasn't coming back to save her. Not now. Not ever.

She stopped at the door and straightened the front of her robe, insuring the knot was still holding the thing together, and smoothed her hands through her sleep-tousled hair. She rubbed her index finger across her front teeth and exhaled into her cupped hand. Ugh. Don't let it be Sean, she thought as she turned the knob.

It wasn't.

Mrs. Bailey stood in the hallway dressed in one of her multi-colored, cotton muumuus and a pair of worn house slippers. In the five years she'd lived here, Christy had never seen the building manager wearing anything that required a belt. Mrs. Bailey was a petite lady of indeterminate age and weight. On many occasions she and Christy talked and enjoyed coffee or tea together. Mrs. Bailey had been like a grandmother to her. Christy knew all about her three husbands: the first one killed in the war; number two, a traveling kitchen utensils salesman who never returned from a trip to Minneapolis in 1953; and dear Walter, the last and most beloved, who Mrs. Bailey finally had the privilege of putting in the ground in the Catholic cemetery in Westerville, even though she wasn't Catholic. Walter's mother, the original Mrs. Bailey, didn't like her and threw away the flowers she left at his marker. She knew this to be fact since the time she sneaked back to her car and waited for over an hour before the senior Mrs. Bailey came to the cemetery and plucked the roses out of the urn next to his marker and crumpled them in her bony little fist.

Christy had been appropriately shocked upon hearing the story, but later laughed as she imagined the two old ladies fighting over dear sweet Walter's memory.

Her close relationship with Mrs. Bailey made this moment doubly painful. Mrs. Bailey's hands were clasped in front of her like Christy knew they would be, her round open face, a mask of concern and contrition.

"Good morning, Mrs. Bailey," Christy said through a tight smile.

Mrs. Bailey tucked a lock of fire engine red hair that could only have come from a box sold at the five and dime behind her ear and looked down at her fuzzy clad feet. By the time she brought her gaze up to meet Christy's, she was wringing her hands and forcing a smile of her own.

"Good morning, Christy, dear," she began falteringly. Her eyes flitted over and around Christy's face in an effort to avoid eye contact. "You know I would do anything to keep from coming to you this way…"

Christy groaned inwardly. She was a crumb. If Mrs. Bailey only knew how much she hated that the situation had come to this. Or rather, how much she hated Sean for putting her in this predicament. "I know, Mrs. Bailey. Would you like to come inside?" She took a step back to allow the older woman entry, but Mrs. Bailey held up her hand.

"No, dear, I don't think that would be a good idea."

It was the first time she had refused an offer to come inside. Christy's self loathing grew with each passing moment.

"I hope you realize I would do anything for you if I could," Mrs. Bailey continued. "But it isn't me. I just manage the building. If I don't do my job, I'm out on the streets. It wouldn't be so tough being unemployed if I was a younger woman, but I need to keep a roof over my head. Poor Walter's pension doesn't go as far as it used to, so I have to do what's required of me, regardless of my personal feelings. You know I think the world of you, Christy, but it wouldn't be fair to the other tenants if I let you slide. It's already been six weeks. I got a call from Mr. Dillon last week. He said if you don't pay everything you owe immediately, I have to get rid of you. I already gave you an extra week." She smiled conspiratorially. "I told him I couldn't catch you at home."

Christy's heart sank even further. Her careless actions and poor choices in men had forced people who cared for her to lie to protect her. "Oh, Mrs. Bailey, you didn't have to do that. I never meant to cause you any trouble—"

Mrs. Bailey held up her hand again. "It's just been so long, honey. Is there anyway you can get the rent to me by the end of the week. I know you've hit a rough patch, but that's nothing to be ashamed of. It happens to all of us at one time or another. Maybe you could call your family."

Christy shook her head in agitation. "No, I couldn't do that."

Mrs. Bailey ducked her head and twisted her arthritic hands together. "Oh, dearie, I'm so sorry to hear that. I'm afraid I can't wait any longer than the end of the week. Mr. Dillon will surely call the sheriff to post a letter on your door if I tell him again I couldn't get hold of you."

Christy was humiliated. How had she let things get this bad?

"I know, Mrs. Bailey. I'm sorry I put you in this situation in the first place."

Mrs. Bailey glanced around the empty hallway and then leaned toward Christy. "Have you heard anything from your young man? I'm sure he would help out if he knew what a bind you were in."

Christy shook her head again, even more emphatically than she had when Mrs. Bailey suggested she go to her family for help. As long as there was breath in her body, she would never admit she had made such a foolish error in judgment by falling in love with Sean Hatcher.

"That's out of the question, Mrs. Bailey. I'll be gone by tomorrow." Even as the words left her mouth, she realized she had nowhere to go. She didn't know if she even had enough money to fill up her gas tank to make a dignified getaway. "I apologize for falling behind in the rent," she said. "There's no excuse for letting it happen."

The relief on Mrs. Bailey's face saddened her further. "I'm so sorry it had to come to this, Christy. You've been a wonderful tenant these past five years. If I could do anything for you, you know I would."

Christy fought the urge to burst into tears. As badly as she felt for causing the dear old woman worry, she could barely acknowledge it in her realization that within hours she would be homeless. What would she do then?

Mrs. Bailey reached out and took her hand. "I'll be praying for you, sweetheart. I know everything will work out. You're a darling girl. When you get back on your feet, please come and see me. I hate to think you'll move out of here, and I'll never see you again."

Christy cleared her throat, but her voice still cracked when she spoke. She squeezed Mrs. Bailey's hand. "I'll come see you, don't you worry about that. After I find another job, maybe I'll even get my apartment back."

Mrs. Bailey smiled, genuinely relieved that Christy was taking her eviction so well. "I'll do everything I can to make that happen."

"Thanks a lot, Mrs. Bailey. I really appreciate everything you've done for me." She thought about pulling the older woman into her arms, but she would most certainly lose what little control she had left.

Mrs. Bailey's smile widened. "Stop in and see me before you leave, dear. We can have a cup of tea and toast our friendship."

Christy nodded wordlessly as she stepped back into her apartment and closed the door. That wasn't going to happen. She was going to slink out of here like the dog she was with her tail between her legs and never look back. How could she look Mrs. Bailey or any of her neighbors in the face again? She slid the bolt latch closed and turned to lean her back against the door.

She sank onto the worn hardwood floor. She put her elbows on her knees and buried her face in her hands. Where could she go? She had been fired from her job; a job she loved more than anything and had worked so hard to get. Not only had she broken the trust of one of the most respected law firms in the state, she had ensured no other firm would give her a chance to prove herself after such a stupid and careless mistake.

You'll never work in this town again.

She smiled in spite of herself. Her boss, Mr. Banociac, hadn't used that exact phrase, but he may as well have. Her career was over.

Christy had loved her job at the law firm. She loved the dream of becoming a lawyer herself someday. It would happen; or at least she once thought it would a few months ago. She was a paralegal, the only female one at her firm. All the other women were under appreciated and underpaid secretaries and receptionists. In parts of America, the feminist movement was in full swing, but in her world in Central Ohio, it was often hard to see any progress.

Christy rubbed her hands over her face and looked over the tiny well kept apartment that had been her home since she graduated from college and went to work at the bottom of the ladder at Bennis, Banociac, and Weiss. Landing the coveted job had been the greatest moment of her life. Her parents were so proud of her. Dad always said she'd earn a law degree. At the time she wasn't sure she wanted one. When she was in school, women weren't taking pre-law. They went into nursing, education, or the arts. Not law. She let herself buy into that mindset. It was easier than setting her sights on a goal she might not achieve. But after going to work at BBW, she knew she wanted to be more than a paralegal her whole life. She loved the work, the excitement, the fact that she had broken the Good Old Boys' Club rule. She wanted more, just like Dad had predicted.

Her heart ached for her dad. Seven months ago she had gotten the call. She would never forget the night as long as she lived. She had just stepped out of the shower and into her bathrobe. She planned to watch a little television to unwind before going to bed. As soon as she heard the voice of her brother-in-law on the other end of the line, she knew it was bad news.

"Christy, it's your dad," Roger said without preamble. "He was in a car accident tonight on his way home from work. He's at the county hospital. Can you come home right away?"

It wasn't really a question. Christy left a message with the law firm's answering service that she had a family emergency and would let them know as soon as she did when she would be back to work. Then she broke every speed limit between Columbus and Jenna's Creek. By the time she arrived at the hospital, it was apparent Dad's condition was dire. He passed away before morning. She missed him so much. Sometimes it seemed like he'd been gone her whole life, at others, she had to remind herself he wasn't at home with Mom and Eric where he belonged.

He would be so proud to see how far she'd come in five years… and so ashamed.

She stood up and brought herself face to face with her image in the mirror across the room. *Oh, Daddy, I'm sorry. I can't believe I let myself get into this mess. I should've known better.*

Her reflection hardened, and she looked away. If Dad were still at home, she wouldn't be trying to figure out where to go now. She would know where to find sanctuary. She might still be without a job and a career. She might still be ashamed of what she'd let happen because she was so blindly in love with Sean. But at least she'd have somewhere to go. She would know that in the loving arms of her family, she would find solace.

It wasn't like that anymore. Home wasn't home. Not since she found out what her mother had done.

Her mother wasn't who she had pretended to be for the last twenty years. She had committed a despicable act for which Christy would never forgive her. The rest of the family may have thrown up their hands and let bygones be bygones, but not her. Her father never deserved what his wife did to him. As far as Christy was concerned, she didn't care if she ever saw her mother again.

But at this moment, what choice did she have? Where could she go if she didn't go home? The only friends she had were in this apartment building or associated with the firm.

She headed to her bedroom to get dressed. Whatever she decided to do and wherever she decided to go, she needed to pack her stuff and get out of the apartment. Boxes; she needed boxes. There were always plenty behind the grocery stores every morning. She would have to hurry before someone came and took them away.

Abigail Blackwood set her coffee cup on the table in front of her and lowered herself into a kitchen chair. She cocked her head and listened as the clock over the stove ticked away the morning. She didn't think she'd ever heard a lonelier sound. She should know. She'd been listening to the moments of her life ticking away for seven months. Since Eric, her youngest, had left last month for his last year at Ohio University, the ticks had grown louder—almost deafening.

She doubted she would ever get used to waking up in an empty house or fixing dinner for one. But the worst part by far was all the free time she suddenly had on her hands.

She and Jack used to talk about what they'd do after Eric went away to school and they were free to make some decisions without the worry of fitting four children into their plans. Occasionally Jack would talk about retiring from his job at the factory. Abby would laugh and tell him he wasn't allowed to retire without a written outline—approved by her—detailing how he would spend his time so he wasn't puttering around the house under her feet. When she made her careless comments, she never dreamed she would one day long to have him puttering around the house and getting in her way.

Jack's old truck had been broadsided one evening last April on his way home from work. He had died early the next morning at the hospital. That was seven months ago. Seven months of listening to the seconds tick away on the kitchen clock.

Dear, sweet Jack.

He deserved so much better than her. For those first few months after his death, she had walked around like a zombie; worse than a zombie. She had wished for all she was worth, she was the one killed in the accident instead of Jack. Jack was the good parent, the honorable one. He would never have put his own needs and desires before that of the family the way she had.

He loved her in spite of her flaws, even from the very beginning.

He had looked so dashing in his dress uniform, waiting at the end of the aisle when she stepped out of the vestibule on her father's arm. The first notes of the wedding march resounded throughout the tiny church, and she and her father started down the aisle toward him. Their eyes met, and she had been startled by the adoration she saw on his face. Unable to maintain eye contact, she blinked away tears and scanned the crowd of family and friends. Though she cared deeply for Jack, she didn't love him.

The man who had her heart was nowhere in sight.

She remembered her father's boss sitting stiffly in the back of the church next to his wife. Uncle Chamblin had caught her eye and smiled broadly to alleviate the apparent fear and anxiety on her face. Further up the aisle sat her grandmother Frasier, whose expression remained the same whether attending a wedding or a wake. Next to her was her mother's Aunt Doris, who had practically raised her after her own mother passed away when she was a girl. She pivoted her head and looked at all those pale, ruddy-haired Blackwoods on the other side of the church. How they must have thought her the perfect image of a blushing, bashful bride.

What did they think of her now? She could only imagine since she hadn't been able to face them after revealing her twenty-two year old secret two months ago.

By the time Abby graduated from high school, America had entered the war. Like many of her female counterparts, she got a job at a factory down the river in Ironton. A bus picked them up in front of Wyatt's Drugstore in town and dropped them off again every evening. Because of gas rationing, Abby rode her bike into town to wait for the bus. Noel Wyatt was considerably older than her, yet somehow they always found something to talk about. Abby sensed in him a loneliness that mirrored her own.

She had only been vaguely aware of his presence when she was a kid, and she and her friends stopped in the drugstore after school for malteds at the lunch counter. He was just the man in the white coat behind the pharmacy counter who had recently taken the place of his father. But suddenly the two of them were chatting and laughing like old friends. She began arriving a half an hour before the bus was due to prolong their time together. Their growing friendship lasted her through each dreary day at the plant.

She couldn't remember the exact moment she realized she felt more than friendship for Noel Wyatt. He was so much older than she was for one thing. Twelve and a half years to be exact, which seemed like eons to her nineteen-year-old mind. He was educated and came from one of the more prosperous families in the area. Her family had migrated from West Virginia a generation earlier with barely a penny to their names after the mines gave out.

To complicate things, she had a boyfriend overseas. He was more a friend of the family than a boyfriend, but her parents thought a lot of him, and it was assumed they would marry as soon as he got home.

Abby didn't particularly want to marry anyone. Though she hated the assembly line work at the factory, she liked the idea of earning her own money, even if she did hand most of it over to her parents after cashing her check. She liked having lunch with her girlfriends in the cafeteria. She dreamed of buying her own car, and she dreamed of going to college; something a Frasier had never done.

She didn't share any of these thoughts with anyone—except Noel. It would hurt her father to think she wanted more than the humble lifestyle he provided for her. Even though she could barely explain her dreams to herself, they all made sense after discussing them with Noel in the drugstore every morning.

For months, she told herself it wasn't Noel that she loved, but the independence her friendship with him represented.

Slowly it became clear that he was more than just a friend. She was confident he felt the same way about her. Even though she was naïve, she didn't miss the way his eyes lit up when she came into the store or the way he spoke her name as if it tasted good in his mouth.

Then she got word Jack was coming home from Italy. Her mother told her she could finally quit work at the factory and marry Jack. Abby felt like she had been punched in the chest. She didn't want to quit her job. She most certainly didn't want to marry a man she barely knew and didn't love. But how could she explain that to her family?

She rushed to the drugstore to tell Noel. All the way into town she imagined how he would beg her not to do it. He would give her the courage to stand up to her family and tell them what she wanted, for once. He would touch her cheek and take her hand and tell her she couldn't marry Jack Blackwood. If she did, it would break his heart. He loved her. He might even get down on one knee right there in the store...

None of Abby's girlhood fantasies came to life that day. When she told Noel that Jack would probably ask her to marry him, he didn't beg her to say no. He didn't tell her he felt about her the same way she felt about him. Instead, he wished her all the happiness in the world and disappeared behind the pharmacy counter.

Three months later, Abby had quit her job at the factory and stood at the front of the church next to Jack like her family expected her to. She said "I do" when the preacher told her to. She kissed Jack and then her mother and all the out of town relatives who hugged her and told her how lucky she was. She smiled and nodded through her tears. Tears of joy, she heard Aunt Doris say.

She cried often those first few days of her marriage. Dear Jack was so gentle and patient and understanding. After all, didn't all girls cry when they left their homes for the first time, and it sunk in how their lives had changed, and they were suddenly dependent on this man who was practically a stranger?

Slowly, Abby realized all the tears in the world weren't going to change a thing. She wasn't being fair to Jack. She needed to stop feeling sorry for herself and love her husband. Happiness was a choice. So was misery.

She forced herself to stop thinking about Noel Wyatt and how her life might have been different had he proposed instead of hiding behind the pharmacy counter. All childish illusions of romance would have to end. She was Jack Blackwood's wife. It was high time she started acting like it.

She threw herself into being the best wife she knew how to be. What she didn't know, she learned. She became an excellent cook. She finally sat still long enough for Aunt Doris to teach her to knit. She sewed darling little vests and rompers. She gave Jack a daughter who looked just like him, and then two more within a few years. Every morning when she arose, she reminded herself she was Mrs. Jack Blackwood. Most times it was easy. Jack was loving and attentive. She had three beautiful babies and a household to run. There was no time for wishing for things that would never be.

But occasionally she would forget. Sometimes during a trip to her mother's or the grocery store, she would turn the car into Noel's neighborhood. She'd drive past his house, and her heart would quicken in her chest. Of course she always drove by in the middle of the day when she knew he wasn't home. Regardless, she searched the windows, hoping for a glimpse of him inside his ivory tower. Then Christy would start to fuss in the back seat or Karen would take Elaine's toy, and Abby would remember who she was, and she'd push the accelerator and go back to her life.

Noel never married. She refused to believe it had anything to do with her. Instead, she became convinced he was too tight with a dollar to let another woman latch onto him. It was common knowledge that his first wife had taken him to the cleaners. That was all there was to it. She was better off without him.

Jack was wonderful. He was devoted to her and the children. Over the years, their financial strain lessened, and he did as much as he was able to give her a good life. He tried so hard to please her. She tried equally hard to please him, but they both knew something was missing from their union.

Then one Friday when all three girls were finally in school and Abby found herself with a few hours of peace and quiet in the mornings, she went to Linda's Cut and Curl for her weekly appointment; her only extravagance. The beauty parlor was abuzz with the news; Noel Wyatt had had a heart attack over the weekend.

Abby had gasped aloud in shock and pain, but Sandra Maxwell was shampooing her hair and didn't hear over the rush of water. She had barely been able to sit still long enough for Sandra to finish her cut, before rushing out of the beauty parlor and across town to Noel's house.

She let herself in the back door, knowing she shouldn't be here but beyond caring. It didn't matter how hard it would be to explain if anyone found her here. She had to know for herself that Noel was all right. At the sight of him in the living room in his bathrobe, her heart crumpled inside her. Any doubt she had about her feelings for him flew out the window. She loved him as much as she had that last day in the drugstore; probably more. The ten years she had spent trying to forget him had been to no avail.

She thought of Jack and the girls and told herself to turn around and go.

She rushed to him and sank to her knees instead. "I was so worried," she said through her tears. "I came over as soon as I heard."

After assuring her he had indeed survived and would more than likely live another forty years despite his best efforts not to, she unloaded on him with both barrels. All the years of suppressing her feelings for this man came rushing out in a torrent.

She hated him, she shrieked. He ruined her life. She loved him and had wanted nothing more than for him to love her in return. Now it was too late. Before she knew what was happening, she had stopped screaming and was in his arms, clinging desperately to him.

Noel did the worst thing he ever could have done. He told her he loved her back. He said if he had known how she felt back then, he would've acted, but he thought she wanted Jack. He couldn't take a girl from a returning war hero when he had spent the war years safe at home.

Then he kissed her.

"Get out of here," a voice screamed in her head. *"Leave and never come back."*

Abby returned his kiss.

"What about Jack? Think about your little girls—your family."

She pulled away. She couldn't do this. She hadn't been raised this way. She knew better, but she was weak. And she loved him so much. Didn't God know her heart? Surely he knew how desperately she loved Noel Wyatt.

For two months, the two lovers stole away to be together at every opportunity. While in Noel's arms, Abby felt safe, loved, and beautiful. But every time she headed back to town, the self-loathing set in. She was wicked, dirty, and evil. She would burn in hell for all eternity. She sat rigidly at church every Sunday next to her daughters and husband and hated herself even more. She couldn't go back to Noel's. She knew he was on the opposite end of town in his own church, battling the same demons that tormented her. They suffered equally, but neither was strong enough to do anything about it.

At home, she was cranky and distant to everyone, especially Jack. Though he deserved it the least, she found herself taking her frustration toward herself out on him. They grew apart. She didn't want him to touch her. Jack assumed it was female trouble. He didn't press when she claimed to have a headache. She suffered from allergies, and he was used to ushering the girls to the other end of the house and keeping them quiet and the shades drawn while Abby nursed her headaches. He worried about her. He tried to get her to see a doctor. She snapped at him and told him to leave her alone.

Then she missed her cycle. She held her breath and counted backwards on the calendar. A few weeks went by. She continued to see Noel two or three times a week. After their meetings, she would leave his arms almost wishing her car would crash on the way home and this terrible mess would end. She wanted him so desperately, but she loved her children. Sometimes she thought if it weren't for the girls she would keep driving, away from Jenna's Creek and the horrible, wanton woman she had become.

She didn't blame Noel. She didn't blame Jack. She didn't blame circumstances. The fault lay with her. She had fallen into sin and was now paying the price.

"Come back to me, Daughter. You haven't fallen so far that I've lost sight of you."

Abby ignored the still small voice in her spirit. She couldn't seek forgiveness. God couldn't forgive her when she wasn't sorry for what she'd done. At least she wasn't sorry when in Noel's arms.

She waited and she prayed yet her cycle didn't come. Part of her wanted to rejoice. She was carrying Noel's child. She would put her hand over her stomach when no one was looking and imagine what it would be like to wake up in Noel's arms the next morning. He would rub her feet and make her comfortable and laugh as her belly grew rounder and rounder. Then she would catch sight of herself in the mirror and know the Lord would never smile on their union. They had sinned, and now an innocent child would be punished for what they'd done.

"I am waiting for you, Daughter", the voice in her spirit nudged. *"I am here. I care about your pain."*

Not only had she betrayed her marriage vows, she had sinned against God. She knew she was wrong. Finally one Sunday, when her sin had become too great to ignore, she went to the altar and repented. No one in the congregation knew why quiet, respected Abigail Blackwood was sobbing at the altar and ignoring everyone around her. But she knew. And the next day, Noel Wyatt knew too. She ended their relationship and told him their child would be raised as Jack's. She was going to be the wife and mother her family deserved.

The night of the accident, Jack told her he knew their only son didn't belong to him. He told her he loved Eric, and he loved her. Then he told her he forgave her. Abby hated herself anew for hurting such a wonderful man. But finally the day came when she realized she was still a child of the King, washed in the blood of the Lamb. Her sins had been forgiven, by Jack and by her Heavenly Father.

Unfortunately, that realization didn't make telling Eric and her daughters about Noel Wyatt any easier.

Abby took a sip of coffee and gazed around the kitchen. She and Jack had remodeled it six years ago. At the time, she thought she had died and gone to heaven—her dream kitchen. They knocked out a wall to make room for a large dining table and added another bank of cabinets. They laid new flooring, painted the ceiling, hung wallpaper and put a new light fixture over the mahogany dining table. The wallpaper would need to be replaced soon. It was faded, and she had grown tired of the pattern. Who would help with the job, she wondered? Now the money spent on the large airy kitchen seemed like a waste with her family no longer here to share it.

She wasn't completely alone. Karen and Roger brought the kids over at least once a week. Eric came home every third or fourth weekend from school. But how much longer would that go on? He was getting married. What if he took his bride out of Jenna's Creek? Abby needed to face facts; the house on Mulberry Street where she'd raised four children was too big for one woman. What would she do with all the space?

What would she do with herself?

A significant portion of her life stretched out ahead of her. Before Jack's death, she hadn't given much thought to her latter years. She always figured she would do whatever Jack wanted. He was the one who had worked and paid and sacrificed for the kids. If he wanted to travel, she would travel. If he wanted to sell the house and move out to the country where they'd raise beans and chickens, she'd do that, too. Jack had been good to her. It was the least she could do in return.

But now he was gone. Besides the fact that she had little to fill the time on her hands, she had to think about her financial future. The house and vehicles were paid for. Her needs were minimal. She was subsisting carefully on savings and Jack's insurance policies. He had made sure she was taken care of. But what if she lived another thirty years? What if she needed medical care as she aged?

What about monthly expenses that came regardless of how much money she had in the bank?

She had begun reading the want ads in the bi-weekly Jenna's Creek paper; something she'd never done in her life. She couldn't believe she was thinking of getting a job. Not just thinking, planning and worrying.

She shuddered every time she thought about entering the work force. She would be the oldest woman in the typing pool. The only things she was qualified to do were cook, clean, wipe runny noses, and answer the telephone. In Jenna's Creek, people did those jobs themselves; they sure didn't hire them done.

Still she perused the want ads and considered her situation. She hadn't built up her courage to answer an ad or write a resume yet. She hadn't told her children the way her mind was leaning. No use getting them worried about her financial situation when they couldn't do anything about it.

She rinsed out her empty coffee cup in the sink and headed into the living room to watch Merv Griffin. She wondered if there were jobs out there for middle-aged housewives who liked to watch television.

Chapter Three

More and more evenings, like tonight, Noel Wyatt stayed at the drugstore until the lights went off at eight even though he closed the pharmacy counter at six. Most of the other pharmacists in town closed their counters at four. Unlike him, they had reasons to go home—wives, kids, ball practice… Time consuming errands that made men dream of the day they'd send their youngsters off to college. Noel had none of those. He never had. He'd spent most of his adult life in the large Federalist style house on Bryton Avenue. For an embarrassingly brief amount of time in the late thirties, he shared it with his wife. But Myra Curtsinger did not belong in Jenna's Creek any more than he belonged at peewee football practice.

All evidence of Myra Curtsinger-Wyatt, along with most of the memories of those days, had long abandoned the house on Bryton Avenue that Noel had bought with her in mind. Over the years, news of Myra would reach him, most generally through his college alumni newsletter. She didn't languish on the vine long after divorcing him and moving back to her parents' home in Lexington, Kentucky. Within months she was involved with a young engineering student from one of the right families. Then suddenly, she was keeping company with a young prosecutor, the engineering student—like Noel—a steppingstone to something better. The young prosecutor ended up State Auditor, and Myra's picture was often seen in society pages across the South.

She wouldn't have made any society pages in Auburn County married to the town pharmacist. There would be no place to wear the off-the-shoulder gowns and diamond broaches Noel had seen her sporting on the two occasions her picture appeared in national newspapers alongside her powerful and well respected husband who many said was destined for Washington. He hoped Myra got what she was looking for out of life but hadn't found with him. He only wished her happiness. Everyone else in Jenna's Creek hated her, simply because they didn't understand her. Noel couldn't hold their failed marriage against her. He chose to forget the two years of strife and remember instead the pretty young woman on campus who had turned his head with her ready smile and enormous brown eyes.

The house on Bryton Avenue was now his and his alone. Sometimes he thought it was a shame such a huge beautiful house would go to waste on an old man like him. He didn't need five bedrooms and three and a half baths. His sisters never visited. He hadn't seen his nieces and nephews in thirty years. He was the last descendant of the original Wyatt clan who settled Jenna's Creek. He supposed that was part of the reason it was so important to him to keep the house. It was a tangible link between him and the land his ancestors tamed. After all these years, he couldn't imagine himself anywhere else. It was where he kept his stuff. It was a never ending source of handyman projects that broke up the monotony of his weekends. It was home—as much of a home as a crusty, sixty-two year old man could have.

Things in this house could have been so much different.

Noel shook his head as he moved through the house, turning on lights as he went. He didn't play the "if only" game. His life already had too many regrets to torture himself over on nights when sleep wouldn't come.

It had been nearly two months since Jenna's Creek found out about his love affair with Abigail Blackwood. Noel received his share of stares and phone calls behind the pharmacy counter from busybodies who didn't have anything to do but remind him of his indiscretions; as if that was necessary. He was chewed out, threatened that business would be taken elsewhere—where people had respect for others and understood the principles in the Bible, and given regular dressings down. But Noel was not thin skinned. The only thing that bothered him was knowing that Abby and Eric were receiving much of the same treatment.

Eric.

Noel looked in the mirror above the fireplace and touched his jaw. He saw Eric's youthful face staring back at him underneath the wrinkles and gray hair. Eric was twenty-two years old. He was marrying Jamie Steele, one of Noel's employees, in a few months. Would the young couple someday bring their children here to meet him? Would this house finally know the sound of children's laughter, running footsteps, and the refrigerator door opening and closing as it increased Noel's electric bill.

He smiled to himself. How he wished that might someday become a concern.

Eric had also worked at the drugstore. Jamie Steele had helped him get the job. Of course, neither of them had known at the time what Eric was to Noel. Noel had hoped Eric would never find out, if only for Abby's sake. But in a small town, secrets didn't stay secret for long. It had been a miracle that no one figured out Eric's paternity years ago. Every time Noel looked at Eric, he was amazed all over again that no one in Jenna's Creek had noticed the resemblance between them.

He hadn't been surprised when Eric didn't show up for work after finding out Noel was his real father, nor was he surprised three nights later when his doorbell rang at nearly nine-thirty. He was getting ready for bed and not expecting company. As he suspected, it was Eric standing on the other side of the door when he swung it open. The young man had stared at him for a half a breath, his eyes wide and almost panicked, and then hauled off and punched Noel in the jaw. Had Eric not caught him off guard, he could've dodged the punch. As it was, Eric was so angry, he almost missed altogether. Noel reeled back a step and clutched the side of his face with his hand, marveling at how much worse a poorly laid punch could hurt now that his jaw was past sixty. Neither man spoke. After a few tense moments of standing on either side of the threshold, each man sizing the other up, Eric turned and walked back to his car. Noel hadn't seen him since. He knew Eric was back on campus at Ohio University in Athens for his last year, but he kept his ear tuned for the doorbell nonetheless. The boy would be back. He just hoped the next visit wouldn't involve getting punched. Eric's aim would certainly have improved, and Noel didn't know if his old bones would pop back into place as effortlessly.

In the family room he had converted into a den for himself when he realized no family would ever reside in the big house, Noel dropped what mail interested him on his desk while the rest of it went into the wicker trash basket on the floor. He turned on the lamp next to his chair and leaned forward to switch on the television set for noise the way he always did before heading upstairs to change. The unexpected sound of the telephone jarred the silence before he reached the television. Noel didn't get many calls at home. When he did, it was more often than not one of his employees telling him they couldn't work the next day.

"Hello, Noel? This is Sid Trimble," the voice on the other end said when Noel picked up. At Noel's hesitation, the man clarified. "Noreen's brother."

Noel was instantly on guard. Noreen Trimble, his former assistant behind the pharmacy counter and dear friend, was now serving time in Marysville for the murder of Sally Blake. Against her friends' and family's advice, Noreen had pled guilty and accepted the judge's ruling without a jury trial. She insisted there was no reason to waste the State's time or taxpayer dollars to try her when God already knew she was guilty.

Her brother, Sid lived in Piqua, Ohio, a small city north of Dayton. Noel had only met the man a handful of times and couldn't imagine why he was contacting him now. Whatever it was couldn't be good. Noreen's widowed father, two sisters, and other brother all lived locally. If Noreen had asked someone to contact Noel, it would have been one of them rather than Sid.

"Hello, Sid. What can I do for you?"

"Noel, I really hate to come to you about this," Sid said after a long, painful pause. "If there was any other way, I'd do it. I'd prefer to speak to you face to face, but I can't get away from work until the weekend and it could be too late by then. This is urgent."

"Sid, what's the matter?" Noel broke in.

"It's Noreen. But I guess you figured that."

Noel heard a deep inhalation of breath on the other end of the line. He imagined Sid composing himself before continuing. Then he realized he was holding his own breath. Something had happened to Noreen.

"Noreen was involved in some kind of altercation at the prison this morning," Sid said, confirming Noel's suspicions. "Apparently there was a fight in the infirmary, and she somehow got in the middle. She was stabbed. She's alive, but they transferred her to the county hospital up there."

Noel shoved his hand through a lock of graying hair and exhaled through clenched teeth. "Oh, no. How's she doing?"

"She's in serious condition. The knife punctured a bowel and they had to operate, but the doctors are expecting a full recovery. Anyway, the reason I'm calling you, Noel, is because something needs to be done to get my sister out of prison."

"Listen, Sid, whatever I can—"

Sid kept talking, cutting off Noel's offer. "I've been on the phone all day with the family. Dad's in a bad way. We don't want to get him involved. He knows about Noreen's injury, but we downplayed the whole situation. He's retired from his pastoral duties now. I don't know if you knew that or not. He's up in his eighties, and this affair with Noreen has been the last straw for him. You know how protective of her he's always been. The whole mess is eating him alive. Jean, Jackie, Bill, and me," he said, rattling off his siblings' names, "have got to figure out something to do with Noreen. We've talked to her for the past three years, but you know how she can be. Once she gets something in her head, there's no getting it out. She says she killed that Blake girl, end of story. She won't listen to anything about extenuating circumstances or what have you.

"That's when I thought of you, Noel. If anyone can talk sense into her, it's you. She respects you as a man of integrity. We've got to get her out of that place. Someone's going to end up killing her." Sid's voice quaked. "She doesn't belong there, and we all know it," he ended in a whisper.

Noel's heart wrenched at the desperation in his voice. "Sid, you know I love Noreen like a sister. But I don't know what else I can do. I've talked to her before about her plea. I sat in on the consultations with her attorneys. We all did everything we could to talk her out of making that plea, but she wouldn't listen to anybody."

"She has to listen to us now. She has to see how dangerous this situation is. She never should have made a plea with the judge. If she had taken her chances with a jury trial I believe she would be home right now, where she belongs."

Noel empathized with the man's pain, but he wondered if the whole family wasn't getting their hopes up for nothing. Noreen had pled guilty to murder. What did they think Noel could possibly do to undo her confession?

"Sid, I'm more than willing to talk to Noreen again. But I don't know if it'll do any good." He didn't add that it could well be too late.

If Sid heard the doubt in Noel's voice, he ignored it. "My sister isn't a murderer, Noel. I don't know exactly what happened that night, and I don't care to know. But I do know Noreen wouldn't willfully hurt a fly. I don't want to see her hurt up there because of some misguided sense of responsibility she has for the Blake girl's death."

Now was not the time to remind Sid that Sally Blake was dead, and Noreen had pled guilty to killing her. "Give me the hospital's number and I'll call tonight," Noel said instead. "As soon as she can have visitors, I'll drive up and talk to her."

"Thanks, Noel. You don't know how much that means to all of us. You can call tonight if you want, but I think it will be the weekend or better before she's able to see anyone besides immediate family. Jean and Jackie are driving up in the morning. Bill and his wife are going to stay home with Dad. They don't want him getting any ideas as to the seriousness of the situation just yet.

"Anyway, listen…" Sid's voice cracked again. "You've got to help my sister. We've got to get her out of there."

"I agree, Sid. I'll do everything I can."

Sid thanked him again and then gave him the number to the hospital where Noreen had been sent.

Noel jotted it down on the back of an envelope and hung up. He sank heavily into his leather recliner. Yes, Sally Blake was dead, allegedly at Noreen's hand. But like Sid, Noel believed there was more to the story than anyone knew. He did not believe Noreen deserved a twenty-year prison sentence anymore than Sid did. Something needed to be done, but what? There was only one thing he knew would help the situation at this point. Before calling the hospital to check on Noreen's condition, he dialed the number of Frank and Margene Keaton, the leaders of the prayer chain at his church, and told them what was going on. Then he called his mother and filled her in. Noreen was going to need all the prayer she could get.

Chapter Four

C hristy Blackwood spent the day packing and forming a course of action. Neither pursuit proved as simple as it should have been. She didn't want to leave her little apartment. It wasn't much. It wasn't located in the best neighborhood in town, but it represented all her dreams of independence and an exciting career. She had started pre-law classes at the campus not far from her apartment last winter. She knew it would take a long time and a lot of work since she was working full time while taking classes, but she was willing to make the sacrifices.

Now, of course, none of that mattered.

Her law career was pretty much shot in these parts, thanks to her foolish decision to put Sean ahead of common sense. But it was a big world out there. She doubted the arm of Bennis, Banociac, and Weiss reached from sea to shining sea, regardless of what they liked their clients to think. She would find work somewhere, even if it meant starting at the bottom again. She would work herself up to a salary that would afford her the ability to start her courses again. There were even scholarships out there, once she had the time and fortitude to hunt them down.

The only problem was she currently had forty-six dollars in her pocket. That, along with the change in the ashtray of her car, wouldn't go very far toward starting a new life.

What to do in the meantime? She wasn't too proud to wait tables while passing her resumes around another city. Of course her work history consisted entirely of BBW. If she didn't tell her prospective employers about them, how would she explain where she'd been since graduating from college five years ago?

It was a quandary to which she didn't have an answer.

What direction to go after leaving Columbus was another question to which she couldn't settle upon an answer. It would be easy enough to get lost in a city like Cleveland or Detroit or maybe somewhere in Pennsylvania. But something inside her said to go south. She could start her new life, while remaining close to home. She didn't want to consider that she may have to swallow her pride and turn to her mother for help after their last encounter, but she couldn't ignore the fact that she could have to do exactly that.

It took the rest of the day to pack her belongings and decide what to leave behind. Everything she owned wouldn't fit into her hatchback, but she couldn't come back for another trip. Maybe Mrs. Bailey could sell what she left behind to pay part of her debt to the landlord. Christy fell into an exhausted sleep across her bare mattress at dusk that night.

Before sunup, she tiptoed back and forth, up and down the stairs, loading the accumulated boxes of her life into her car. By five-fifty, she had loaded the last box and left the apartment door unlocked for Mrs. Bailey. She wouldn't let herself think about what had happened to get her into this predicament as she hurried down the flight of stairs from her second floor apartment. She heard the usual morning sounds of early risers coming from several of the apartments as she passed by. She prayed none of the doors would open and someone step out for the paper or to head for work. Mrs. Bailey was probably putting on her first pot of coffee inside her little apartment. More than anything, Christy wanted to say good-bye, but she kept going. The last thing she wanted was to break down at the first sign of kindness or sympathy from her old friend.

Fortunately she made it out the front door, down the stoop, and to her car without encountering a soul. She exhaled with relief as she slid behind the wheel and started the engine. She pulled away from the curb and started driving without so much as a backward glance.

The Rand McNally road atlas was on the seat beside her, flipped open to the southern half of Ohio.

"You don't have to stay in Ohio," she said aloud. Her voice in the confines of the car startled her ears. She swallowed back a lump of self-pity. There was no time for this. It was too late anyway.

She turned on the radio already programmed to a morning talk station. "It's a big country out there," she said to the windshield. "You can go anywhere you want."

Her bravado didn't bring much comfort.

Noel woke with a start at the very first ring of the telephone. His first thought was the alarm, which was odd since he usually woke on his own right before it went off. Forty years of self-employment had made him stringent about not oversleeping. He raised his head and saw the florescent numbers of his electric alarm clock glowing 5:50. The alarm was set for six. When the ringing sounded again, he realized it was the telephone and not the alarm. His heart slammed in his chest.

Nothing good ever came from a telephone call at 5:50 in the morning. Mother, he thought in horror. She still lived alone in the big house where Noel was raised. Her housekeeper spent most days with her, but at night she was alone. Then he remembered the phone call last night from Sid Trimble. Noreen. *Please let both of them be all right,* he prayed as he lunged for the phone.

"Yeah?" he said after clearing his throat.

"This Noel Wyatt?" asked a gruff voice.

The voice didn't belong to Sid or Noreen's father or any of his employees. He imagined a doctor in an emergency room somewhere delivering bad news. He sat up in bed, pulling the blanket along with him. "Yes, speaking."

"I got some information for you," the caller said. "Do with it what you will."

"Is this about my mother?" he asked, trying to quiet the beating in his chest.

There was silence on the other end.

"Hello?" he practically shrieked. "Are you still there?"

"This has nothing to do with your mother," the man said.

Noel exhaled with relief. Now that he knew his mother was safe and sound at home in her bed, he focused on what the caller might want. It sounded as if the man was trying to disguise his voice. He wanted to remind him he had things to do this morning and didn't have time for riddles. But something about the man's tone let him know this was more than a kid making prank calls. "I'm listening."

"Noreen Trimble didn't kill Sally Blake."

Noel nearly dropped the phone. Could this be the answer to the prayers sent heavenward on Noreen's behalf all last night? "What? Who is this?"

"Listen to what I'm telling you. She didn't kill Sally. Not intentionally."

Noel strained his ears. Something about the man's voice sounded familiar. He was sure they had spoken before, but he couldn't nail down any specifics. "You've got to give me something more than 'she didn't do it'. How do I know you're not some crackpot?" He also wanted to keep the man on the phone so he could figure out where he'd heard his voice before. "How do you know anything? Noreen contends she and Sally were alone that night."

There was a long pause on the other end of the line. Noel was afraid his caller was about to hang up. He needed to tread lightly. It was imperative he get all the information the man had before the connection was broken.

When the man spoke, his voice was low and husky, as if he was growling into the phone. He was definitely trying to disguise his voice. Was he afraid Noel could recognize him? "What if I told you I know somebody who was there that night?" he said. "Somebody who saw everything."

Noel's pulse quickened. It couldn't be possible. If someone out there had seen what happened between Sally and Noreen, why hadn't he come forward thirty years ago?

"Then I need to talk to that person. If he saw anything, he's duty bound to come forward. There's a woman in prison because this friend of yours didn't do the right thing sooner?"

"Isn't going to happen," the man said flatly. "He won't come forward, and if the authorities force him to, he'll say he didn't see anything."

The caller had forgotten to keep up the act of disguising his voice. Noel was more convinced than ever he had heard the voice before.

He took a deep breath to slow his heart rate. He had to make the man see reason before he hung up. "Look, I can see why a man wouldn't want to cause trouble for himself. It was a long time ago, and I know it might look bad for this person that he didn't come forward when Sally first disappeared. But if someone knows Noreen was only defending herself, they have to tell the truth. She was almost killed in prison yesterday."

"That's why I'm calling you. My friend doesn't want to see Noreen get hurt."

Noel was pretty sure the caller was talking about himself and not a mysterious friend, but he wasn't about to point it out and scare the man into hanging up. "Then make him tell what he knows."

"It's out of the question. He can't do that. But now you know what I know, so you can figure out something that might save Noreen's life."

The phone clicked in Noel's ear.

"Hello? Hello? Are you still there?" He pulled the phone away from his ear and stared at it. Then he slammed it into the cradle. He swung his legs over the side of the bed and gazed unseeingly at the wall.

What could he do? His gut told him the caller was on the up and up. It wasn't a joke. Someone out there—probably the caller himself—had seen the fight between Noreen and Sally. Nothing short of an eyewitness would convince a judge to give Noreen a new trial after all this time. But it didn't matter if a hundred people had seen her kill Sally in self defense, if none of them were willing to come forward.

The alarm came to life, jarring Noel's heartbeat into overdrive. He slammed his hand down on the button and the bedroom descended into silence save the sound of his own rapid breathing. He leaned farther past the clock and switched on the lamp. He pulled a notepad and pen out of the drawer of the nightstand and wrote down everything he could remember about the phone call. As he wrote, he searched his memory for where he'd heard the voice before. In his breathless, muddled state, he came up empty. Within minutes, he feared the voice he heard so clearly in his head would be gone.

At the last moment, Christy Blackwood decided to take the bypass around Cincinnati and continue south into Kentucky. Somewhere in her psyche she had a romantic notion of southern hospitality she couldn't shake. Was it possible men in the South still cherished their women and wouldn't dream of taking advantage of them? Over and over as she drove the I-75 corridor, she told herself she was being silly. Still she continued southward.

She set her sights on Louisville. If the women's movement was only just catching up in central Ohio, she imagined it was sorely lacking in Kentucky. She smiled to herself. Maybe she'd be the first paralegal in the city. Wouldn't it be wonderful to play a key role in spurring Louisville into the twentieth century?

More importantly, she had used up most of the money she had budgeted for gas, and Louisville was about as far as she could afford to go.

She tried not to be disappointed when she stopped for coffee and to stretch her legs at a café near Campbellsburg and no one spoke with a southern accent or extended any form of cordiality to a woman traveling alone. She reminded herself the view of the south that had sustained her all morning was only a figment of her imagination. Probably as far off the mark as her notion that the equal rights movement needed any help from her.

When every other song on the radio reminded her of Sean, she finally turned it off with an angry twist of the dial. Then the oppressive silence inside the car reminded her of how lonely she was. She missed Sean. She even missed her family. For a few miles, she entertained the thought of turning around and heading for Jenna's Creek. But she didn't.

She would love to see her sister, brother, and niece and nephews. But she had painted herself into a corner during her last visit home. Christy was proud; too proud for her own good. Dad always said she was a typical redhead.

"You've got a temper, little missy," he'd say playfully, tousling her stubbornly curly, carrot red locks. "Just like your Irish grandmother."

"Don't trivialize her behavior, Jack," Mom would admonish. "She has to learn to control her outbursts. Red hair and Irish blood don't excuse the things that come out of her mouth."

Maybe Mom was right, but Dad was always more fun to be around. He was also just a shade on the money. Christy held a tighter bond with her paternal grandmother than any of the woman's other grandchildren. As she grew older and more opinionated—although those who knew her in elementary school would say that was unlikely—she began to see the similarities for herself.

Laura Blackwood had a rapier wit and sharp tongue, which she wielded with abandon. She had a way of telling someone exactly what she thought while making it sound funny. Even the injured party had a difficult time staying angry at her. On the other hand, she could hold a grudge like nobody's business. She went to church every week and paid her tithes regularly, but she was almost proud of her ability to recount a perceived slight from the last decade.

Christy loved and respected her grandmother like nearly no one else alive, and was delighted every time someone compared the two. If she had to take after someone, she preferred it be her strong-willed grandmother who was decades before her time, than someone like her mother who had lived a lie her entire adult life.

Every time Christy thought about her mother's indiscretion with another man, she got riled up all over again. Even though two months had gone by since she found out the truth, and the realization had sunk in that her kid brother didn't belong to their father, she still couldn't understand how Abby let such a thing happen. Nor was she particularly interested in understanding. She didn't want details or explanations. She just wanted to punish her mother the way Abby had punished Jack for over twenty years.

If Dad hadn't known what happened between Mom and Noel Wyatt, the whole sordid affair might have been easier for Christy to bear. But the fact that Jack went to his grave with the knowledge weighing on his heart that his son didn't belong to him was too much for her to forgive. Mom assured her Dad had forgiven her years ago, but that wasn't good enough for Christy. Dad was weak, apparently. He never could stand up to Mom.

She remembered the last time she talked to her sister in Jenna's Creek. Even though she had sworn to anyone who would listen she would never darken her mother's doorstep again, she missed the rest of her family and had called Karen to touch base.

All she got for her efforts was a lecture.

"You need to get off your high horse and come home, Chris," Karen had said. "We're all upset over what's happened, but turning your back on the whole family isn't doing anyone any good."

Christy could not believe Karen's attitude. She wasn't the one at fault here.

"Excuse me, but I haven't turned my back on my entire family. That's why I'm calling you. Mom is the only one I don't want to see. I miss the rest of you. I would love for you to come up here for a visit."

"Thanks for the invitation. I appreciate it. But it's too hard to travel with kids. It would be so much easier for you to come here to see us. You wouldn't even have to go to Mom's if you didn't want. You could spend the weekend with me and Roger."

"I don't buy it, Karen. You'll tell Mom I'm coming, and she'll coincidentally show up the same time I do. It would be too uncomfortable."

"It doesn't have to be. I wish you would just talk to her. She is still our mother, regardless of the past. We all make mistakes."

"I'm sick of hearing that, Karen. It sounds like a nice way of excusing every rotten thing a person's ever done."

Karen didn't speak right away. Christy knew she was considering her next words so she wouldn't say more than she intended. Karen and Elaine were like Dad in that respect; careful, thoughtful, always measuring their words so they wouldn't offend. Just once Christy wished they would let down their guard and say what was on their minds.

"I'm not excusing anything, Chris," Karen said finally. "But what Mom did has nothing to do with us. It's between her, Dad, and Eric. If Eric has come to terms with it the best way he knows how, then the rest of us need to move forward. She loves us, and she'll do whatever it takes to make everything right again between you and her."

"And I suppose she's told you all this."

"She doesn't have to. Don't you think she's spent the last twenty years punishing herself for what happened? Can you imagine what she must have gone through?"

"No," Christy snapped. "I can't imagine, and I don't feel sorry for her. If she's hurting now, it's about time. All I can think about is what Daddy went through all those years, knowing what she did. I don't feel sorry for her, Karen, and I don't want anything to do with her."

Karen had exhaled in resignation. "Then I guess we'll see you when we see you."

"Yes, I guess you will."

"Bye, Christy. I love you. We all do."

"Yeah, bye."

Christy hadn't called since. Let Karen close her eyes to the whole situation, but she wouldn't. She couldn't just pretend what Abby did was a mistake in her youth that should be swept under the rug. Pretending it didn't happen was no way to honor their father's memory.

After she was fired, and she realized she was broke and going to lose her apartment, she briefly considered turning to Karen for help. Then she decided against it. Karen would definitely take her in, but she wouldn't know how to stay out of Christy's life. She would do whatever was necessary to put Christy and Abby together so they could work on a resolution.

When she realized she couldn't stay with Karen and risk being treated like one of Karen's kids, her thoughts turned to her dad's parents. Grandma and Grandpa Blackwood would welcome her with open arms. But then she would have to explain what had happened to her job and her apartment. Laura Blackwood would not accept some flimsy excuse about lay-offs, cutbacks, or Christy's own desire to move home. She would demand to know the whole story and wouldn't quit until she got it.

No, it was better that Christy stay away from home and Jenna's Creek altogether. She would have to make do somehow on her own. She just hoped her forty-six dollars held out.

The lack of funds weighed heavily on her mind. She had eaten a paltry breakfast of the last of the corn flakes and powdered milk in her apartment before setting off on her adventure. She splurged on a pack of M&M's to eat along with her black coffee at the café in Campbellsburg. Now she feared she would become physically sick if she didn't give her stomach something more substantial.

She already had a headache from driving into the setting sun for the last two hours. She had taken the outer belt around

Louisville simply because it was rush hour and there was no sense in going downtown this late in the day. Any place that might consider hiring her would have closed its doors by now. She needed a hot meal—preferably a home cooked one—a shower and a bed, before she could even think of venturing into the city in search of employment.

Halfway around the outer belt, she flipped on her turn signal and changed lanes at an exit promising food and lodging. She waited through four red lights before she was able to turn left off the exit ramp onto a minor highway. Apparently she would have been better off waiting for the next exit. But the heavy traffic was a good sign. At least she hadn't found herself in the middle of nowhere with no quick way back onto the freeway.   Once she got through the intersection, she made a quick right into a service station and pulled up to a gas pump. The height of the oil embargo seemed to have passed and she didn't have to wait in a long line to fill up her tank. She winced inwardly as she handed six precious dollars over to the harried attendant who pumped her gas. Then she went inside the station to borrow the key for the restroom facilities outside the building. She filled her lungs with air and held her breath before opening the green door. Fortunately the restroom wasn't as repulsive as some she'd been subjected to on the open road. She washed up and ran her finger across her teeth. She wished she'd brought her toothbrush in with her, but didn't want to go back out to the car and root around in her suitcases until she found it. Back inside the service station, she relinquished the key, and squandered another fifty cents on a small glass bottle of orange juice. On her way out, she noticed a sign in the window of a smiling cowboy on horseback: *Marlboro cigarettes—forty-five cents a pack.*

At least that was one expensive habit she didn't have to satisfy.

She moved her car away from the gas pumps to make room for the drivers on their way home from work and parked in front of the free air pump. She got out and leaned against the front fender to drink her orange juice. She watched the passing cars for a moment and then focused her attention on a man in his thirties who had pulled up to a pump in a dark green Grand Prix. While an attendant pumped his gas, the man exited the car and headed inside the station. He wore tan trousers and a white button down shirt. A green and brown plaid tie hung loose around his neck. He walked with the confident swagger of a man accustomed to getting his way. He reminded Christy of all the men who roamed the halls at Bennis, Banociac, and Weiss. A lump formed in her throat. With difficulty, she swallowed the mouthful of orange juice.

Her half-baked plan to start over someplace new wasn't going to be as easy as she anticipated. Her independent bravado was a farce. She missed her family. She even missed Sean. But more than anything, she was heartbroken that she had been forced out of her firm.

She squeezed the juice bottle, wishing for the thousandth time, her hands were around Sean's neck. Then she realized her anger was misplaced. She couldn't spend the rest of her life angry with a man, who in all likelihood, she would never see again. This whole mess could have been avoided if she had listened to her gut. She should have recognized Sean for the lying, manipulating snake that he was. She couldn't blame anyone but herself.

She swallowed the last of the orange juice and screwed the lid back on. She was going to have to learn to put all her baggage behind her—her job, her fiasco of a relationship with Sean, her family. She was tough. She could do it.

"Excuse me," a voice came from the other side of her car.

Christy forgot how tough she was as she gasped and whirled around.

A young man held his hands up in front of him. "Hey. Sorry. I didn't mean to startle you."

Christy exhaled with relief, feeling ridiculous. "That's okay. No big deal."

The young man took another step forward until he was standing against the opposite side of her car. He was few years younger than her. He wore the dark gray coveralls of the service station attendants. The name stitched over his breast pocket read: Stanley. He smiled, revealing a set of badly aligned teeth stained from too many cigarettes. But his smile was warm and friendly.

"You having car trouble? You've been standing here awhile. We do service, or we can give you a tow if you need to take it somewhere else."

Christy was shaking her head before he stopped talking. "No, no, the car's fine. I was just standing here thinking how hungry I am and wondering if there's anywhere around here that serves a good dinner. Hopefully cheap," she added with a smile. Stanley seemed like the sort who'd understand that consideration.

He did. His crooked smile widened. "Sure. There's Imogene's down the road about a half mile on your left. Today's Wednesday, the special's meatloaf. Across the road from her is McDougal's. They do fish and chips. It costs a little more, but you get a lot for your money."

Over Stanley's shoulder, Christy watched the man in the tan trousers climb back into his car and drive away. She thought wistfully of a white house in a subdivision where a wife, two-point-four kids, and a spaniel would greet him at the door and listen attentively as he told them about his day. She could almost guarantee he wouldn't be having Imogene's meatloaf or greasy fish and chips.

She ignored the ache in her chest and brought her attention back to Stanley. "That sounds good."

"What part of Ohio are you from?" Stanley asked.

Her brows went together to form a tiny v.

He pointed to the front end of the car. "Your plates," he hastened to explain.

"Oh." Of course he would notice the out of state tags. "Columbus," she replied, and then wondered if she should be so quick to give out personal information. But she wasn't in Columbus anymore. What did it matter if some kid at a service station knew where she was from? It wasn't like he would track down her old apartment and tell Mrs. Bailey he had seen her in Louisville hiding out from paying what she owed in back rent.

"I've got family in Beavercreek," Stanley offered. "Ever been there?"

Christy wondered if he was stalling to keep from going back to work. She didn't really blame him. The attendants hadn't stopped buzzing around the parking lot since she'd pulled in. They earned most of their meager pay from tips, so she figured Stanley must not be too ambitious if he was wasting prime business time talking to her.

"I don't think I have," she said, "but I know where it is."

"Um." He nodded and looked reluctantly at the island of pumps. He was definitely stalling. "I recommend McDougal's myself. You have to go through the tavern to get to the restaurant, but the service is pretty good, and the food's hot."

"Okay, thanks. Sounds good."

"I can take that for you." Stanley held out a hand that looked like the nails hadn't been cleaned under since he started pumping gas.

It took Christy a moment to realize he was referring to the juice bottle in her hand. "Sure. Thanks."

She handed it across the hood of the car. Stanley smiled again. She smiled back. Maybe chivalry wasn't dead after all; just severely neglected.

Christy wasn't a huge fan of meatloaf so she heeded Stanley's advice about McDougal's. At precisely a half mile down the road, she turned right into the parking lot under a sign offering the best fish and chips in the tri-state area. She had lived in Ohio her entire life and never heard of any reputation, good or bad, for batter-dipped fish and French fries. But who was she to judge? When in Rome, she thought as she locked the car and headed inside.

It turned out Stanley knew his fish and chips. Not only did she receive a basket of fish and chips bigger than her appetite, it came with a bottomless glass of Coke that the waitress refilled three times. As an added bonus, she saw a clean, relatively modern looking motel behind the restaurant with a sign that advertised rooms for thirteen-ninety-five. The waitress assured her it was reputably maintained and safe enough for a girl traveling alone.

She smiled to herself when the waitress referred to her as a girl. Her pleasure was short lived. After some quick mental calculations, she realized that even while dining at all-you-can-eat establishments and paying rock bottom prices for a roof over her head, she could only afford about two more nights of life on the road. She was going to have to do some quick job hunting. She considered asking the waitress if they needed any help, but knew her tips at McDougal's wouldn't be enough to keep her under the red roof behind the restaurant. She'd have to get up early tomorrow, drive back into the city and start knocking on doors.

She wouldn't stop until someone hired her. She couldn't afford to take no for an answer.

Somewhere in the fuzzy region between sleep and wakefulness, Christy became aware of a knock at the door. Her first thought was Mrs. Bailey after the rent until she remembered where she was. Surely it wasn't worth tracking her all the way to Kentucky to collect the relatively small amount she owed. She forced her eyes open and blinked several times before she could make out the numbers on the clock by her bed. It was just after midnight, but she'd already been asleep for over three hours.

She stumbled out of bed and looked around in the darkness for her robe. "Who is it?" she barked, annoyed at the interruption, but not overly concerned. Someone had the wrong room; that was all.

"My car won't start," a male voice called back. "Can I use your phone?"

In her grogginess, she didn't even think to tell him to go to the manager's office before opening the door to peer past the security chain. She'd lived alone in a city long enough to know better, she berated herself later.

A booted foot kicked the other side of the door and the chain and wooden doorframe slammed inward on Christy. She stumbled backwards, pain emanating from her shoulder where the door crashed into her. Two men rushed in and slammed the door into its busted frame behind them. She barely had a chance to think about screaming before the larger of the two pulled her into a rough embrace and clamped a huge hand over her mouth.

Christy's heart hammered in her chest. She couldn't catch her breath from the hairy hand covering her mouth. She willed herself not to gag. She didn't want to choke on her own bile. Keeping his hand over her mouth, the man pushed her away from the door. She backpedaled until the backs of her knees hit the bed where she sat down hard on the mattress. The man came down on top of her. A muffled sob escaped her throat.

"Shut up, you hear me," he growled with a curse.

She nodded as tears flowed down her cheeks. She was going to die in this little forgotten motel. No one knew where she was. Her family would never know what happened to her. *Oh, God*, she prayed, *don't let me die here. The waitress said this place was safe.*

As if that fact would motivate God to spare her life.

"Don't hurt her," an oddly familiar voice came from near the door.

The second man parted the curtains a crack to peer outside. In the light, she recognized his slight build. Stanley.

The man on top of her tightened his hand on her mouth. Her bladder loosened in fear. What would he do if she wet her pants? Would it make him angry enough to kill her? The possibility was almost favorable to all the other images whirling around in her head.

"You're not going to holler, are you?" he said, his face barely inches from hers. His hand covered her mouth and nose, but she could still smell his foul breath.

She shook her head as much as she was able.

He mashed his hand down even harder. She tasted blood between her teeth. Her stomach clenched in an effort to purge itself. *Stay calm. Stay calm*, she repeated over and over to herself.

"You better not," he warned. His yellow eyes glared into hers for a moment before she felt a slight lessening of pressure on her mouth. She sucked in a bit of air between her lips. The urge to vomit lessened slightly.

"She ain't gonna yell," Stanley said from behind the man. "Are you, Ohio?"

He moved to the bed and grinned amiably down at her over the other man's shoulder. He looked as harmless as he had when asking if she had car trouble.

She shook her head again while keeping her eyes on Stanley. Her eyes pleaded with him. Surely he wasn't here to harm her. He couldn't. He absolutely was not the type.

The big man continued to stare into her face before he finally removed his paw from her mouth. She moved her tongue over her teeth and gums, thankful for the moment that nothing seemed out of place. Keeping his eyes on her in case she decided to bolt, the big man lifted himself off the bed and stood up. Whether from relief that he hadn't killed her or the lessening of pressure on her body, warm moisture soaked her panties and trickled between her legs onto the mattress. Christy resisted the urge to straighten her cotton nightgown and thin robe around her legs. She didn't move a muscle.

The big man still loomed over her, daring her to make a sound. Stanley moved to the tiny sofa built for two where her suitcase lay open. "So, where's your cash, Ohio?" he asked as he rummaged through her clothes. He slid his hand down into an inside pocket and withdrew it. He turned to glare at her. "Your money?" he snapped. "Hand it over, or we'll take something even better."

She didn't have to ask what he was talking about. The big man towered over her as if eager to carry out Stanley's threats. "I...I only have about thirty bucks," she choked out. "I'm broke."

He took a menacing step toward the bed. The friendly gas station attendant was gone. "Yeah, right; that fancy car out in the parking lot, your fancy big city attitude. You got plenty of money. Now hand it over."

"It's in my purse," she said, pointing a shaking finger at the nightstand. "But it's only a few bucks. I got fired a couple months ago. I got kicked out of my apartment. I...I came here because I don't...I don't have anywhere else to go."

The big man's shoulders sank. He turned and leveled a disappointed gaze at Stanley. "You said she was loaded, man."

Stanley raised his shoulders apologetically. "I thought she was."

Christy imagined them a couple of schoolboy would-be criminals who couldn't even pick an easy mark to rob. But her aching face told her there was still plenty they could do to her if they took a notion.

Please, please, please, she chanted over and over in her head. *Make them go away.*

Stanley looked around the room, mulling over his options, and then overturned her purse. Her car keys and wallet hit the nightstand with a rattle and thud. He scooped up the wallet and tore it open. He jerked the money out and held it up for the other man to see. He swore loudly. "She ain't lying. This is all there is."

"Now what?"

They truly seemed stumped. Could this be their first robbery? Didn't she have all the luck? Christy sat motionless on the bed and held her breath, willing them to go away.

Then Stanley's face lit up. He grinned exposing every one of his oversized, crooked teeth. Christy's blood rushed like ice water through her veins. Stanley scooped up the car keys. "This should be worth some money."

Christy didn't know if she should cry with relief or dread.

The other man left her and went to the suitcase. He overturned it. The contents spilled out onto the sofa and slid onto the floor. "Let's see if there's anything else worth taking."

She knew there wasn't. Would they become angry and take out their frustration on her? She eyed the door hanging crookedly in its frame, but decided against making a break for it. She knew she would never make it past the two of them. Even if she did, they could snap her neck before the first person heard her thwarted cries for help.

Stanley went through every pocket of her purse and suitcase. He took every dime he found. The other man continued to rifle through her clothes, digging into pockets and ripping the seams out of some of her blouses. She cringed as she watched him, unable to look away. Every moment his hands were on her belongings, it was as if he were physically violating her.

Finally Stanley threw the wallet on the stand and approached the bed. She shrank back into the mattress. The smell of urine wafted up around them. Stanley didn't seem to notice. He reached out and wrapped his skinny hand around her throat and lifted her neck until she was barely sitting on the bed. She gasped for air while at the same time was afraid to breathe.

"You're not going to tell anyone we were here, are you, Ohio?"

"N…no," she gasped, her eyes wide with terror.

His fingers tightened around her windpipe. "This is a small neighborhood. We know everybody. We'll know if you try to leave this room." Another squeeze. "So don't. Just sit tight until morning, and then you can call your mommy or whoever is waiting for you back in Columbus and tell them to come get you. Got it?"

She nodded against his hand.

He released her, and she fell back onto the wet mattress. "Good." He nodded over his shoulder at his accomplice. The man pocketed a few inconsequential items from her suitcase and went to stand by the door.

Stanley straightened up, but didn't move away from the bed. He looked down at her bare knees and smiled thoughtfully. Christy resisted the urge to pull her nightgown farther over her legs. The smile on his face widened.

"D'you leave our little princess a dry pair of panties?" he asked the man at the door. "I think she had a little accident." They both roared with laughter.

For the first time, anger welled up inside Christy. She enjoyed a brief vision of leaping off the bed and propelling herself into Stanley's thin, insignificant body and scratching his eyes out. She knew if not for the other man, he would never have the nerve to try this on his own.

When their laughter was spent, Stanley looked back at her and put a finger to his lips. "Now remember, not a peep out of you until morning. You don't know anything about the guy who works the night counter in this hotel, do you? He could be a cousin of mine."

He looked over his shoulder at the other man and roared with laughter again. Christy entertained an image of the two of them burning on a stake in the town square.

Then they backed toward the door and were gone. Christy listened to the engine in her car roar to life. Gravel spun as they flew out of the parking lot. Her legs felt like rubber as she got to her feet and stumbled to the window. Sure enough, her parking space was empty. No lights glowed anywhere through the motel complex save the one in the manager's office.

Stanley's words rang in her ears. What if he was telling the truth? It wasn't likely, but it would explain how they got into her room in the first place; a night manager who conveniently looked the other way when crimes were perpetrated against travelers. If she called the police and repeated her story, would they discover the night manager was related to the gap toothed lay about who pumped gas at the service station down the road?

Whether he had been telling the truth or not, she was too terrified to think about leaving the room. She slinked back to the urine-soaked bed and flipped on the light. She glanced over her shoulder at the window in case someone was actually watching her room like Stanley said. She rummaged in the drawer for a telephone book. It took almost two full minutes of fumbling with

shaking fingers before she found the number she wanted and figured out how to dial an outside line. When the police dispatcher
picked up the phone on the other end of the line, her fragile resolve
collapsed. She burst into hysterical sobs.

Abby Blackwood sat up in bed, disoriented by the distant
sound of the telephone. She still didn't have a telephone in her
bedroom. At least there was one in the hallway. She had been the
one to convince Jack to install a phone upstairs. He had balked
at the trouble of running cords through the ceiling downstairs to
install it.

"You're just making it easier for those girls to tie up the phone
lines," he had complained good-naturedly. "Don't they spend
enough time on the phone?"

But in the end, he had done it—anything to make her happy.

She was wide awake now and concerned over what could be
so important to warrant a phone call at this ungodly hour. It had
to be Elaine in Germany. It was already morning over there. She
was pregnant with her first child. She and her husband Leo had
been disappointed more times than not with miscarriages and false
alarms. She was six months along now. Too late for a miscarriage,
but still plenty could go wrong. Why else would she call when she
knew it was the middle of the night in the States?

Abby flipped on the lamp by her bed and checked the clock
as she hurried across her room and into the hall. At the top of the
stairs was a small table where a black rotary phone screamed into
the still night.

She murmured a prayer of safety for her unborn grandchild as
she picked up the handset. "Hello?"

"Mom!"

She didn't recognize the hysterical voice on the other end.

"Mom, it's me. Christy."

Her heart stood still. "Christy?" she croaked disbelievingly.
"Where are you? What's the matter?"

By now Christy, her put-together no-nonsense daughter was crying uncontrollably. "Mom, I'm in Louisville. Can you come get me?"

Surely she hadn't heard correctly. Christy should be safe in her bed in her apartment in Columbus, getting a good night's sleep for work tomorrow. "Louisville? You mean Kentucky? What are you doing there? What's happened?"

"I'm in a police station, Mom," Christy wailed. "You have to come get me. I was robbed."

"Oh, dear God! Christy, baby, are you all right? What happened?" She couldn't make herself stop asking the same question.

"Please, Mom, hurry."

A detached sounding police deputy came on the line and gave Abby the address of the sheriff's department where Christy would be waiting. Abby begged the officer to tell Christy she would be there in about five hours. She never got the chance to ask how her daughter ended up in a police station in Louisville, Kentucky.

Chapter Five

Sid was right. Noel wasn't allowed to go to the hospital to see Noreen until the following Monday. He cleared his schedule and was out of the drugstore by noon. He told no one where he was going or when he'd be back.

In Ross County, he turned his Cadillac onto Highway 35 and headed north to Columbus. After she pled guilty to the murder of Sally Blake, Judge Herman Rudduck, Auburn County's common pleas court judge and one of Noel's golfing buddies, had sentenced Noreen to twenty years at Marysville. He confided in Noel it had been the hardest sentence he had ever handed down. He was of the mindset that Noreen could have walked out of the courthouse a free woman if only she'd agreed to a jury trial.

"I'm guilty," she said over and over to Noel and the attorneys he hired for her. "I killed my best friend. I shouldn't have gotten away with it for as long as I did."

Before his mysterious late night phone call, Noel didn't have the heart to tell Sid that anything he could think to say to Noreen to change her plea wouldn't change things as far as the courts were concerned. She had pled guilty to murder, and nothing short of a miracle would get her sentence overturned—that, or an eyewitness.

Noel didn't think it would be as difficult getting in to see Noreen in the county hospital as it was when he visited the prison.

He was wrong. Upon telling the smiling hospital volunteer whom he was here to see, her demeanor changed instantly. She gave him terse directions to a separate wing on the hospital's third floor. There he was further interrogated, asked for identification, and commanded to sit on a bench along a long cold hallway with a motley crew of relatives and friends waiting to see other inmates.

Noel perched himself on the wooden, unforgiving bench, clasped his hands in his lap and stared straight ahead. He couldn't help but wonder if any of the loved ones of those waiting in the hallway with him today had been involved in the altercation that nearly killed Noreen. He studied each visitor in turn out of the corner of his eye. Many of the bodies were unwashed, the eyes vacant or preoccupied, and their demeanors distressed.

He glanced at the stooped woman next to him who probably wasn't his age but looked twice as old. Had her daughter or sister been the one to plunge the knife into Noreen's body? The woman clutched a frayed purse in her lap and coughed repeatedly, seldom bothering to cover her mouth. In other circumstances, he would have offered his handkerchief. Not here. Don't get involved. Don't draw attention to yourself, he had learned. He wouldn't do anything to upset the fine balance the guard at the end of the hallway had stricken and possibly affect his chances of seeing Noreen.

He glanced casually in the direction of a very pregnant, young girl at the end of the room. She looked like she should be worrying about whether the boy she liked would ask her to the homecoming dance instead of sitting in this hallway waiting for the guard to call her name. It was no small wonder she was in her present condition if the only advice she got from her mother was during visiting hours at Marysville.

Noel's heart broke inside him. If not for the grace of God, he could have been born into much different circumstances, thus affecting the way his life turned out. In a rush of self-awareness, he realized the inconvenience of being the current object of gossip among Jenna's Creek busybodies over his love affair with Abigail Blackwood was trivial and insignificant compared to the burden this young woman carried every day. He looked at her one last time, committing her face to memory, and reminding himself to lift her up in prayer, along with the unborn child she carried.

Regardless of guilt or association with the person or persons who had injured Noreen, these people needed prayer, not his condemnation.

Finally his name was called. He went to stand in front of the guard where he emptied his pockets into a plastic tub. The young man gave him a perfunctory pat-down and then opened a door leading to an ordinary hospital hallway and motioned Noel through. The door closed behind him. Another guard, about twice as old as the first, nodded wordlessly and walked him to the nurse's station. Noel asked for Noreen's room number and was followed down the hallway to the room number the nurse gave him. Outside Noreen's room, the guard patted him down more thoroughly before opening the door. The invasion didn't offend Noel, but he hoped the guard wouldn't be as suspicious of the young girl waiting in the hallway when her turn came.

Satisfied he wasn't carrying a weapon or some kind of contraband, the guard stepped back so Noel could enter the room first. Noel sensed rather than heard the guard follow him inside. Apparently his entire visit with Noreen would be supervised.

He advanced to the bed. He hadn't seen Noreen in several months, but she had changed a lot. She looked small and vulnerable lying there in the bed. At least she wasn't handcuffed. He glanced over his shoulder to the guard at the door. The man was looking in his direction, but seemed to stare straight through him. Noel figured he could say anything to Noreen, and the man wouldn't blink an eye as long as no laws were broken.

He reached out and touched Noreen's hand. Her eyes flickered. The first emotion he saw when she opened her eyes was fear.

Then she recognized him and a pained smile spread across her face. "Noel," she rasped.

He patted her hand and leaned over her. "How are you doing, old girl? It looks like you got yourself into a little scrape."

Her smile widened, then she winced in pain. "I bobbed when I should have weaved."

Noel chuckled. "You need to find yourself a better class of friends."

She nodded and her lips curved upward in an attempt at a smile. "How did you find out?" she asked, breathing heavily.

"Sid called me."

Noreen shook her head apologetically for any inconvenience Sid's call might have caused.

Noel patted her arm again. "He did the right thing. He's worried about you. Everybody is. We want you back in Jenna's Creek where we can keep an eye on you. We're afraid you're going to corrupt all these young things up here."

Noreen smiled, but her eyes grew moist. "I'm sorry I'm such a bother."

This time tears stung Noel's eyes. He cleared his throat. "None of that, Noreen, you have nothing to be sorry for."

Keeping his eyes on hers, he pulled a chair to the side of the bed and lowered himself into it. They watched each other for a few moments before either spoke.

"You don't belong here, Noreen," Noel said gently.

Noreen turned her eyes toward the window even though she couldn't see anything beyond the overcast sky.

"When you're released," he said, referring to the hospital, "I'm going to have your lawyer come up here and discuss changing your plea."

She shook her head. "A waste of time," she said, still looking toward the window.

He tightened his hold on her hand. "I need you back, Noreen. Angie and I are overworked, and there's not another decent applicant in the county. The drugstore's falling apart without you."

She smiled slightly at his attempt at levity and brought her eyes around to look at him. "I told the judge I was guilty. Nothing's changed. I appreciate everything you've done for me, but I put myself into this situation. I deserve what I'm getting."

"No, you don't. You were young. You made a mistake. You were only protecting yourself. Besides, something has changed."

Noreen's eyes narrowed in confusion. Noel couldn't help but notice how much she'd aged in the past two years.

"What do you mean?" she asked.

Noel cast an anxious look at the electronic screen over her right shoulder that monitored her pulse and heart rate. He hadn't come here to upset her.

He stroked her hand. "Noreen, is there any chance someone might have come back to the house the night of the party and witnessed the fight between you and Sally?"

"What? No. Of course not." She broke eye contact again, focusing her gaze on his Adam's apple. "It was just Sally and me."

"Maybe neither of you heard him. Maybe he came back to get something he forgot. Maybe it was someone who knew your aunt and uncle were out of town and he was up to no good. He didn't expect you or Sally to be there."

She frowned and shook her head in confusion. "Noel, you aren't making any sense."

"Noreen, I need you to think really hard. Do you remember hearing anything outside your aunt and uncle's house before Sally arrived or while she was there? Was anything out of place when you went outside to your car? Could there have been someone hiding somewhere?"

She considered his words for a moment and then shook her head. "No, I don't think so. I don't remember. I never even thought about it. All I could think of was...Sally lying there..."

A single tear slid down the side of her face and into her hairline. The numbers on the monitor began to rise. Noel leaned forward and brushed her hair away from her face.

"It's all right, Noreen. Please don't get upset. If the nurses see this monitor, they'll kick me out of here. Okay? Are you all right? I really need to talk to you."

"I'm all right. Please don't leave yet." She sniffed and motioned with her eyes at a box of tissues on the nightstand. Noel removed one and held it against her nose. She blew into it.

Noel watched the monitor. Her heart rate was leveling out, but her blood pressure was too high. Maybe talking to her right now wasn't such a good idea.

"I know you're trying to help, Noel," she said, after he wadded the tissue and discarded it in the trashcan. "And I appreciate everyone's faith in me. But nothing's changed. I committed a crime. If I had nothing to hide, why didn't I come forward when it first happened? Why did I let twenty-five years go by before I told the truth? Any prosecutor is going to want to hear my answer to that. If I didn't do anything wrong, I would have been honest from the beginning."

"Why don't you let a jury decide that?"

Noreen pulled her hand away from his. "Someone died because of me, Noel. I can't just put on a pretty dress and stand in front of a jury and tell them I made a mistake. If that's all it took, the prisons would be empty in a matter of minutes."

Noel turned his eyes to the window she had been studying earlier. *Give me the words to say, Lord. I want to help her.*

"Noreen, I believe you when you say you were only protecting yourself. That isn't a crime. What if there was someone out there to corroborate your story?"

"Trust me, Noel, there isn't. No one saw anything other than what really happened. Sally and I got into a fight and…I killed her."

Noel swallowed his frustration. He didn't want her to see the desperation in his face. He knew it would only make her worry about him or her family.

"Time's up," said the guard at the door.

Noel cast the man a glance over his shoulder and then stood up. He leaned over and kissed Noreen's cheek. "Let the jury decide if you acted premeditative or out of self-defense. That's what they do. Our justice system might surprise you, Noreen."

"Thanks for coming, Noel," she said through a sheen of tears. "I'm sorry Sid bothered you."

"It was no bother, Noreen. I love you. We all love you."

She nodded and turned her eyes back to the window.

The deputy escorted Noel back to the corridor. He trudged outside to find his car and began the long drive home.

Noreen had fixed her gaze on the window as she listened to Noel's footsteps recede. The door swung shut softly behind him. The sound of the nurses' murmured conversations in the hallway reached her ears. Someone laughed. Her heart constricted inside her chest. How she envied their freedom and camaraderie. She wondered if they appreciated it. It wasn't likely. She hadn't appreciated her freedom until it was gone.

She heard the door open and close in the room next to hers, followed by hushed conversation. She didn't know anything about anyone else in the rooms around her, and she wouldn't ask. She had learned in the last twenty-six months at Marysville to stay to herself and not get involved in anyone else's problems.

Her thoughts returned to Noel's words. He was right; she never meant to hurt Sally. She loved her like a sister. The whole thing had been a mistake; a huge, terrible mistake. The last thing she wanted to do that night was fight.

What were all those questions about a prowler or someone returning for something they'd forgotten? Nothing like that had happened. If someone had seen the fight between her and Sally, they would've told the police the next day. Everyone at the party had to go to the sheriff's office and fill out a report. If anyone saw anything, they would have spoken up then.

"Wait a minute, Officer. I saw something last night. I forgot my pocketbook in the hallway closet so I went back to get it. Somehow the closet door shut on me and while I was in there, Noreen and Sally got into this huge fight. When I peeked out, I saw Noreen Trimble drag

Sally out of the house and dump her body in the trunk of her car. I didn't do anything to stop Noreen, Officer, because I was afraid I'd be next."

Sally and her date, James Steele, had been the only sore spot of a perfect evening. Tim Shelton had publicly announced his and Noreen's engagement. She had stood there next to him in the center of the living room and gazed into his face while their friends applauded the news, even though they knew it was coming—everyone except Sally. She hadn't applauded. She had crossed her arms over her chest and glared at them before turning her attention back to James.

It wasn't long after the announcement that Sally and James got into a fight and knocked over a table. Noreen never knew exactly what started the fight. At the time she thought Sally was upset that James had not proposed to her, even though that didn't seem likely. The last thing Sally wanted was a husband, especially one with as few prospects as James Steele. Someone told her later Sally had been hanging all over another friend and James became jealous. Everyone knew what a temper James had. Especially Sally. She had confided once in Noreen that sometimes he got so mad, she was actually afraid of him. Noreen had the sneaking suspicion his temper was what Sally liked about him most. She liked dangerous men. There was nothing more appealing to her than volatility and a wild side.

It was the main reason Noreen didn't believe her when Sally said she loved Tim and Tim loved her back. Tim Shelton was as different from James Steele as anyone could get. He was quiet and reserved and charmingly predictable. For Noreen, he was perfect. But for someone like Sally, he was painfully inadequate.

For years after the altercation that led to Sally's death, Noreen had tried to make sense of the whole episode. For starters, she didn't think Tim would cheat on her with her best friend. Not only did she believe Tim loved her, she couldn't picture him behaving with the abandon necessary to perpetuate an affair. He wasn't that way. And if had happened the way Sally said, why would she pursue boring, predictable Tim Shelton when she could have nearly any man she chose?

Sally's whole story had been lies. Noreen was sure of it.

Despite her belief in Tim, the years had bred doubt. What would Sally have gained by making up her wild story? Why would she say Tim loved her if he didn't? Why tell Noreen their engagement was a farce because Tim was too weak to tell her the truth?

What about the baby? Had Sally been carrying Tim's baby like she said? Had Noreen taken two lives that night?

The years only added questions instead of answering them. Shortly after Sally's disappearance, Tim went to work for Mr. Blake at the family's real estate agency. Noreen hadn't understood that move at all. As long as she had known Tim, he had talked about working on the dairy farm with his father. He even talked about building a little house for them on the other side of the property after they were married.

"It won't be much at first, Nory," he'd said. "But after a few years when we've saved some money, we can add on. That's the way Mom and Dad did it. We'll have to, of course, after the babies come."

He had pulled her into his arms and snuggled his face into her hair. Noreen had held tight to him, breathing in the scent of him and basking in their mutual love.

Why had he left the family farm to go to work for Sally's father?

Within days of Sally's disappearance, Tim started to pull away from her. Or possibly she was the one pulling away from him. She wasn't sure anymore. All she knew was that something had happened to the Tim she loved. Sally had succeeded in planting doubt about their relationship in her mind. Did Tim really love her? Had he had an affair with Sally? Every time he looked at Noreen, was it Sally he saw?

In no time at all, they were breaking dates and making excuses not to see each other. Almost by mutual decision, Noreen gave Tim back his ring. She finished her schooling and hid behind the pharmacy counter at the drugstore. She started noticing For Sale signs in the front yards of houses represented by Tim Shelton. Every sign she saw was like a knife in her chest.

When she saw the announcement in the paper that he was marrying Joyce Davenport, she was too numb to cry. How had he gotten over her so quickly? Or was it the loss of Sally from which he'd recovered?

With one hand attached to the IV, she reached down with her other and touched the thick bandage that encased her ribcage. According to the doctor, an inch either way and the sharpened spoon would have punctured her abdominal artery. One inch had spared her from death. As it was, after a few weeks of bed rest, she would be fit enough to return to general population. She wasn't sure the inch had been worth it.

Chapter Six

A bby quickly refolded the newspaper and smoothed out the wrinkles when she heard Christy's feet on the stairs. She didn't want her daughter to see her reading the want ads. She wasn't sure what she was afraid of. Surely it had crossed someone's mind besides her own that her next logical step would be to find a job. But she didn't want people to feel embarrassed for her when they realized how unqualified she was to hold down any type of position. Nor did she want her children thinking Jack had left her destitute and desperate.

She put her hands on the folded newspaper as Christy's soft footfalls grew closer. Just last week she had been thinking how quiet and lonely the house was with her family gone. Now she had her youngest daughter back; the one who vowed never to forgive Abby when she had found out what happened between her and Noel Wyatt. While the tension between them was palpable, Christy was going out of her way to be polite. Abby knew it was only because Christy felt she owed her as much for picking her up in Louisville the other night and not peppering her with questions on the ride home.

The drive to Louisville to get Christy had been agonizing for Abby. Although the deputy had assured her that Christy was fine and had not been seriously injured, Abby had a hard time keeping the evil images that clouded her thoughts from taking root. All the way there, she wished she had gone ahead and called someone from church to go with her. Even the minister's wife, who was in her thirties and a little flighty and chatty for Abby's taste, would have been better than being alone inside the car with only her thoughts for company. She hadn't called Karen and Roger since Roger had to work in the morning, and Karen would have driven her crazy working out worst-case scenarios the whole way. While she dressed and gathered her wits that night, she mentally crossed women from her church off her list. Since finding out about her past with Noel Wyatt, even her fellow congregation members were holding her at arms' length. Now was one of those times when a girlfriend would come in handy, but she never had many of those. With the secrets she carried, she never felt worthy of getting close to anyone else. What kind of a confidante could she be when she couldn't divulge her deepest sin?

In the end, she drove to Kentucky alone, alternately praying and crying the whole way, not knowing what to expect.

When she arrived, a sheriff's deputy filled her in on the details of the robbery. She would have to get the rest from Christy.

In the car on the way home, Abby made a few bumbling attempts to ask the questions she was terrified to have answered.

Finally Christy cut in to reassure her; "No, Mom, they didn't touch me except to keep me quiet. I'm all right," she finished quietly.

Besides those moments of strained conversation, Christy said little the rest of the way to Jenna's Creek. She sat stiffly in the seat next to Abby and stared unseeing out the window while she clutched her arms around her middle.

Abby cast nervous glances at her as the sun climbed higher in the sky ahead of them. Her heart broke inside her that her little girl was hurting and there was nothing she could do to take the hurt away. Even if she could, she didn't think Christy wanted any comforting from her.

"Good morning, dear," Abby said with a gentle smile when Christy entered the kitchen. "Do you feel like breakfast?"

Christy shook her head and went to the coffee pot. Abby noticed a slight tremor in her hand as she reached into the cabinet above her head for a mug. The girl looked terrible. She'd lost at least ten pounds since she'd seen her last; too much to be attributed to the attack the other night. Her auburn curls hung loose and untamed around her shoulders. She didn't look like she'd had a decent haircut in months. The old tee-shirt of Eric's she wore over a pair of his jeans contributed to her waif like appearance, but Abby knew something more was going on than being burglarized in a motel room three nights ago.

"The Oldham County sheriff's office called this morning," she said. "They found your car."

Christy didn't turn around or acknowledge her words.

"It's a total loss I'm afraid," she continued. She watched Christy's posture for any reaction. There was none. "It seems Stanley and his cousin took it for a joy ride and crashed it in a cornfield. Then, being the rocket scientists that they were, set it on fire figuring no one could tie them to the crime."

Christy finished filling her mug and turned toward the refrigerator.

"The milk's already out," Abby said, motioning to the carton on the table.

Without a word, Christy topped off her mug with a dollop of milk and sank into a kitchen chair. She still hadn't looked at her mother.

"They couldn't salvage anything, honey." Abby reached across the table and covered Christy's hand with her own. "Even the boxes and suitcases in the trunk were destroyed. I'm so sorry. But your insurance should cover it."

Wordlessly, Christy slid her hand out from under her mother's.

"The sheriff's deputy said Stanley's mother posted bail for both of them. He'll call you when they set a court date."

Christy lifted one shoulder in a disinterested shrug. "They don't need to keep me up to date. I don't care what they do with them."

Abby's brow furrowed. What was going on? "Honey, you have to go back to testify. You know that."

Christy looked at her for the first time. "I'm never going back there, Mom. Stanley and his stupid cousin are not my problem."

"They'll subpoena you, Christy. You don't have a choice. And your insurance company might not be willing to pay for your losses if you don't prosecute."

Christy exhaled wearily. "There's no insurance, Mom. I didn't call them the day we got back like you told me to because they won't care. I haven't paid a premium in over a month. I'm not covered."

Abby's mouth dropped open. This could not be her daughter. Responsible, mature Christy Blackwood would never let her insurance lapse. She wouldn't put all her belongings in the back of her car and drive to Kentucky either.

"What do you mean you don't have insurance? You can't be serious."

"I wouldn't joke about something like this."

"Christy, what's going on? I can't help you if you won't talk to me."

"I don't need your help, Mom. I just need a place to stay for a few weeks until I figure out what I'm going to do. But I'll tell you one thing, I'm not going back to Oldham County or anywhere else to see justice served. They'll have to do their jobs without me." She got up from the table, took her coffee cup, and headed up the stairs she'd just come down. With her free hand, she reached behind her and hitched up the jeans that were slipping off her narrow hips.

Abby watched her go in utter amazement.

God, what's going on with my daughter? she pleaded. *I don't know how to help her if I don't know what's happening. Help me understand.*

By the time Christy got to the top of the stairs, she was shaking so badly some of the coffee sloshed over the top of her cup and splashed onto the borrowed tee-shirt she wore. She didn't care if the Oldham County sheriff showed up himself to drive her back. Nothing would make her return to Kentucky. At this moment, she feared if she saw Stanley or his accomplice—a dimwitted cousin named Rudy Fielding—she'd strangle them both with her bare hands. She felt so out of control. She hated them with a vengeance for what they'd done to her; for what they'd forced her to become.

She jumped at every sound. While many Jenna's Creek residents still went to bed in the summertime with the inner door wide open and only the screen door latched, more in an attempt to keep out critters than to deter intruders, Christy couldn't sleep until she checked and rechecked the locks on the front and back doors a half dozen times. She didn't want to be alone. If she couldn't hear her mother moving around somewhere in the house, her palms got sweaty and her breathing quickened. She had never been a nervous Nellie. She didn't even recognize herself.

While waiting for the police to arrive at the motel the morning of the attack, Christy had agonized over whom to call to come get her. She couldn't bother Karen at one o'clock in the morning. She and Roger would break their necks to get down there, but it wasn't fair with Roger's work schedule and three kids to deal with. Grandma Frasier didn't drive and Grandpa had severe night blindness, though he was the only one in the world who didn't know it. Grandpa Blackwood would have come in an instant, but Grandma Laura would have insisted on coming along. Christy could imagine her marching into the grimy police station and demanding the head of her granddaughter's assailant on a stick.

She wouldn't have honored Christy's desire not to talk about it either. She would have lectured Christy all the way back to Jenna's Creek for opening her door to a strange man who claimed his car had broken down. "What happened to your good sense, girl?" she would have demanded, fixing her with a disapproving stare.

"That's the oldest trick in the book. You know better than to fall for that."

She would have badgered and nagged until Christy finally snapped and confessed as to what she was doing in Kentucky at a motel in the first place. No one could stand up under Laura Blackwood's interrogation. She'd missed her calling when she didn't go to work for the KGB.

With no other options, Christy had swallowed her pride—what little remained of it—and called her mother. As soon as she heard her voice on the other end, she forgot the anger, bitterness, and disappointment over what Abby had done, and the scared little girl inside her came bursting forth. She had cried like a baby and didn't stop until Abby came through the door several hours later.

To her mom's credit, Abby didn't ask more than the most necessary questions. She respected Christy's desire for quietness. They didn't stop for food or fuel until they were back in Ohio. When a smiling attendant approached the car to pump their gas, Christy had locked her door, wrapped her arms around herself, and stared straight ahead. She didn't realize she was shaking uncontrollably until Abby pulled the car back onto the highway and asked if she wanted her to turn the heat on.

As soon as they got home, Christy practically ran upstairs, found a flannel shirt hanging in Eric's closet, grabbed a pair of sweat pants from a drawer, and headed to the bathroom. She stripped out of the clothes she had put on while waiting at the motel for the police, rolled them into a tight ball, and stuffed them into the wastebasket. All she could think of was Stanley's cousin's hands all over them. She couldn't get out of them fast enough.

Christy Blackwood had never been weak. She despised weakness in people. It was why she was so angry with herself for falling into Sean's trap. If she'd been smarter, paid closer attention, allowed herself to see him for what he was, it never would have happened. Now two other men had violated her, and there was nothing she could do about it. She couldn't decide if she was angrier at them for doing what they did to her, or at herself for allowing their actions to rule her life.

She wrapped both hands around the heavy mug and went into her old bedroom. The room hadn't changed since she left it nine years ago for a college dorm.

For sixteen years, she shared this room with Elaine. The sisters fought over the only desk drawer, space in the closet, whose pillow was the softest, even what posters to hang on the wall. Karen and Eric had their own rooms, for obvious reasons. Christy didn't appreciate the fact that she would always be low man on the totem pole and never get first dibs on anything. Even Elaine was above her on the food chain. Then her prayers were answered when Karen married Roger and moved away from home. Elaine had her stuff moved into Karen's old room before the ink on the marriage license was dry.

Christy was never so happy as that first night when she moved her pillow to the center of the double bed she shared with her blanket stealing sister and snuggled in. She had stared at the ceiling wide awake for what seemed like hours. Sleep wouldn't come. She was so disgusted with herself. Here she was, sixteen-years-old, and she missed Elaine's snoring, kicking, and drooling.

Each night got easier. She tore Elaine's Peter, Paul, and Mary posters off the wall, repainted, and hung up a nearly life size poster of the Rolling Stones. Her father helped her remove the closet door and hang beads in its place. She tried to talk her mother into letting her get a lava lamp. Abby said it was a fire hazard, but Christy figured she was afraid watching the lava bubble up and down would turn her into a dope head.

She eventually tired of the beads over the closet door, which had a way of snagging her hair every time she backed out of the closet with her outfit of the day. Mick and the Stones were long gone, leaving a slightly cleaner spot on the wall to mark their place. But the bed wore the same bedspread while the same scarred desk where she'd written reports and love letters still sat under the window.

She sat down on the straight back student's chair and ran her index finger over the indentations of years of homework and journal entries. Tears sprang unexpectedly to her eyes. This wasn't what her life was supposed to be. What happened to her dreams, her plans? She couldn't wait to get out of this house and out on her own. She had been so excited when she got the job at the law firm right out of college. Her friends were green with envy. Now here she sat at the same desk, broke, without a car, and no clothes or personal belongings to her name.

She had left everything in the car when she checked into the motel except for one suitcase and her makeup and toiletry bags. She couldn't bear to bring anything from the suitcase into the house after Stanley's cousin had defiled it. Her mother had taken it down to the curb with the trash. All she had left was a hair dryer, brush, comb, toothbrush, and a few cosmetics.

What an accumulation for a woman who dreamed of her own corner office in one of the most prestigious law firms in this part of the country.

She had been stupid to let her insurance lapse. She had been stupid, period; stupid for letting a rat like Sean into her life. She even imagined marrying him, for about two minutes. It never occurred to her he was nothing more than a common thief waiting for the opportunity to clean her out.

By the time everything came out on the evening news, it was too late. She had already been asked to leave Bennis, Banociac, and Weiss and not come back. That very day she had stood in Marvin Banociac's office like a naughty child chastised by the principal. Mr. Banociac had come around his oversized desk to where she stood, weak-kneed and trembling. He had extended his hand and held something out to her. She looked down, knowing already what it was. Sure enough, her office keys dangled from his hand.

"I suppose you know where we found these this morning," he said in his practiced gravelly voice. "Hanging from the lock to the file room," he went on before she had a chance to reply. It was just as well. She wouldn't have been able to speak had she tried. "Your friend was kind enough to leave them behind."

Christy didn't know if he expected her to take the keys from him or not. She didn't. She was unable to move.

"The security cameras captured everything," he continued. "Mr. Hatcher let himself into the office with these keys and then took what he needed from the file room; how convenient for him that you work here."

Christy recognized the implications. "Mr. Banociac, I—"

"Don't worry, Christy. We have no evidence to prove that this young man didn't hit you over the head and take these keys by force. And we wouldn't want to do anymore harm to the firm's reputation than what's already been done, now would we?" He wrapped his fist around the keys and dropped them into his pants pocket. "You may clear out your desk. Your services are no longer required here."

"Y...yes, sir." With great effort she kept her bottom lip from trembling as she turned to the door.

"And Ms. Blackwood?"

She stopped halfway across the carpeted floor and turned back to face her former boss.

"I wouldn't bother sending resumes to any other firms in the city. You prove yourself untrustworthy to one of us, and you are undesirable to all."

"Yes, sir," she said in a whisper that barely reached her own ears. No one spoke to her as she exited the building.

Sean was long gone, not only with her paltry savings, but with enough money to have half the state's law enforcement looking for him.

He was the same as Stanley; a common criminal. No, even worse! At least Stanley had not developed an intimate relationship with her. Stanley hadn't whispered her name and told her she was beautiful...

She stood up quickly and went to stand in front of her old dresser. "What a fool you are," she said aloud to the woman glaring back at her in the mirror. "You let a professional crook take advantage of you, and then fall prey to a deadbeat thug like Stanley."

She ground her teeth together as she remembered the friendly smile on Stanley's face when he offered to throw away her juice bottle. After winning her confidence, he had turned it around to use against her. She never would've suspected he was capable of committing such a crime, just like she had never doubted a word out of Sean's mouth. How could he be lying when he looked so good doing it?

She had learned one thing in the past few months. She was a lousy judge of character. She never would have succeeded in the law profession with that flaw. If nothing else, Sean and Stanley had saved her a fortune in tuition fees.

Chapter Seven

I t was a four-hour drive from his law office in Portsmouth to the Women's State Penitentiary in Marysville, Ohio. Jarrod Bruckner had made the drive only a handful of times in the past four years since becoming a defense attorney. But the money was good in these cases; worth losing a day doing something else. His father, Harrison Bruckner, who was the senior partner at Bruckner, McManus where Jarrod was a lowly associate, had gone to school with Noel Wyatt in the 1930's. Harry and Noel had been fast friends, a friendship that neither man forgot as they grew older.

When Noreen Trimble had confessed to the murder of Sally Blake, Noel had immediately dialed Bruckner, McManus. Harrison did all he could to convince Noreen it was not in her best interest to plead guilty and avoid a jury trial. Noreen wouldn't listen to the old man's advice. Harrison would have withdrawn himself as council altogether had it not been for his friendship with Noel Wyatt. As it was, he assigned the case to Jarrod who had passed the bar that spring. Noreen was Jarrod's first client. The old man couldn't have found a more challenging and frustrating case on which Jarrod could cut his teeth.

The drive to Marysville gave Jarrod plenty of time to think. He loved every facet in the judicial process; even the assignation of the lowliest cases didn't bother him. If he didn't work in his father's firm, he could imagine himself working his way up through the ranks and being perfectly satisfied as a small town attorney. The election to prosecutor in a smaller town appealed to him even more.

But for now his future was at Bruckner, McManus. His brother Jeff, or J. Harrison Bruckner as the letterhead identified him, had done very well at Bruckner, McManus. He was twelve years older than Jarrod. He was now a partner and lived in a nice neighborhood with his wife and three daughters. Jarrod had grown up in Jeff's shadow, incapable of doing anything, great or small, that Jeff hadn't already done. When he got in trouble, Jeff had a more fantastic tale of the same infraction. When he came home with a perfect report card, Jeff had earned perfect marks that entire grade. Jarrod tried not to compare himself to Jeff. Jeff would always be first. He could never outdo him, not that he really wanted to. All he wanted was outside of Jeff's long reaching shadow.

By the time Jarrod took over Noreen Trimble's case, she had already made her plea to the judge and was awaiting extradition to Marysville. There was little he could do for her at that point besides assure her he was always available should she require his services. He had been right in assessing she would never ask.

He had never met a client more deserving of an acquittal. Like his old man said when he first took the case, he doubted the woman would've seen jail time if she hadn't entered a guilty plea to the judge. She was a sweet, diminutive lady; every defense attorney's dream. No jury could have convicted her after sitting through her tearful testimony. She looked absolutely incapable of lying. And Jarrod, who'd been lied to by the best, didn't think she was.

Today was going to be the turning point in her case. He would return home tonight to tell his father he had Noreen Trimble's full cooperation. In no time—maybe even today—she would help them figure out the identity of the anonymous caller who had witnessed the crime at Will Trimble's farm nearly thirty years ago. Jarrod was determined to convince her to fight for herself, something his father had been unable to do.

Noreen had been discharged from the hospital on Wednesday and was recuperating in the prison infirmary. She sat on the edge of her bed and stared out the window at the opposite end of the ward. The best thing about the infirmary was the windows. The ward had huge ones at each end of the room, and most of the doctors' offices and waiting rooms were equipped with them as well. She wondered if it was partly the reason so many inmates reported to sick call every morning, besides the break in routine. She was however, anxious to get back to her cell and her job. She missed Cindy. Cindy had come to visit her this morning when she arrived from the hospital. The nurses and two of the doctors had been by to express their concern. She could almost convince herself she had a normal job and was being welcomed back to it by her colleagues.

Prison was probably easier for her than most inmates. Noreen had been imprisoned her entire adult life by the secret she carried. She was twenty-years-old the night Sally was killed. She began living a lie that very moment. She guarded every word out of her mouth to protect the secret. She lived with a cloud over her head, knowing that at any moment anything could change and she would be found out. She could never forget what she'd done, nor ignore the nagging doubt in the back of her mind that Sally was telling the truth about her and Tim.

There was little difference in prison and the life she led back home in Jenna's Creek. By the time she was thirty, she had saved enough money to make a substantial down payment on her little house. Sadly, it was the Theodore Blake Realty Company that handled the sale. At least Tim was not her agent. She managed to avoid running into him during every visit to the office. She wondered if maybe he was avoiding her as well.

She loved her little house. She dug up flowerbeds and over the years, became the mother of several cats who mysteriously appeared on her doorstep during the night. She made improvements to the house, painted walls relatively often, and searched estate sales for pictures and furniture. On the outside, she seemed perfectly content with her life. Every October on Beggar's Night, as her family called it, her windows were usually soaped and she often had to hose the remains of pumpkins off her front walk where neighborhood kids would smash them. She was never insulted. It wasn't their fault they found her a little odd. She was odd. It wasn't only kids who thought so.

"Trimble," an orderly boomed from the end of the hallway. "You got a visitor."

Noreen's sisters, Jean and Jackie, had been to see her last week. Bill, Sid, and Sid's wife came over the weekend. Noel hadn't been back since last Monday. She knew he wouldn't be here two Mondays in a row unless the sky had fallen over Jenna's Creek or something equally tragic.

The orderly pointed her out to a guard who approached her bed. The guard was a female officer named Morales who always treated her decently. Officer Morales was short, nearly as short as Noreen, and round as an apple. She always had a ready smile for inmates who gave her no trouble. It wasn't difficult to get on Officer Morales's good side. Follow the rules. Do what was expected of you. Don't ask a bunch of insipid questions. And keep your mouth shut when the occasion required. Doing those things came naturally to Noreen.

It was equally as easy to get on the officer's bad side. For a little woman, she had a big attitude when crossed. Noreen had once seen her knock an inmate senseless for walking too closely on the heels of another guard. Officer Morales took guff from no one.

"Your attorney's here, Trimble," Officer Morales said, her dark eyes brimming with concern. "You up to a visit?"

Noreen tensed and her palms grew damp. She had forgotten all about Noel telling her he was going to send her attorney up here to talk to her about changing her plea as soon as she was released from the hospital. She wished everyone in Jenna's Creek would stop worrying about her and leave her alone. They were wasting their time. The prison system did not release murderers into society. Not as a general rule.

While she had no desire to see her lawyer, she felt bad that he had made the long drive here to see her. He was a nice enough young man who probably had better things to do with his time, and she so hated to be an inconvenience.

She nodded to Officer Morales. "Yes, I can handle a consultation." The officer turned away, and Noreen sat back in the bed and pulled the sheet over her legs. She gingerly touched the bandage at her side. She drew as deep a breath as her wounds allowed and grimaced at the pain. The bandage that encased her ribcage wasn't as bulky as it had been three days ago. She averted her eyes every morning when the doctor came to check the wound and the nurses rewrapped it. She was squeamish at the sight of blood, especially her own.

"Ms. Trimble?"

She stared at the outstretched hand of the young man who approached the bed, and then up the long arm to his face. Again, she was sorry he had made this trip for her. He was too handsome for a place like this. She could already hear the catcalls and lewd remarks that would travel up and down the cellblock when he made his exit. She held onto his hand for a brief moment, her eyes averted. Color crept into her cheeks, embarrassed for him.

"Jarrod Bruckner of Bruckner, McManus," he said. "We've met before." He pulled a chair over to the side of her bed, sat down, and rested his briefcase on his knees.

"Yes, I remember, Mr. Bruckner," she said, giving him a timid smile. He reminded her of a little boy dressed in his father's suit. "I'm sorry you had to drive all the way up here."

"No, I'm sorry, Ms. Trimble."

Noreen could not get used to the new title the women's liberation movement had given unmarried women. She was too old to be a Miss and since she had never married, the world suddenly decided to address her as Ms. She didn't know who to tell she never had a problem with Miss. But no one had asked what she preferred to be called. No one asked her opinion on much of anything.

"I got a call from Mr. Wyatt last week concerning your unfortunate accident."

She wanted to remind him it wasn't an accident. Someone had stabbed her very much on purpose, but he was so nice, she didn't want to be unnecessarily rude.

"I'm glad you're out of the hospital. Are you healing all right?"

She nodded. "Yes, thank you," she said, without going into any details about her injuries. She figured he had only asked to be polite.

"Mr. Wyatt and your family are very concerned about you," he went on, "as is our firm. I'm here to go over your options about petitioning the court for a new trial. Anytime new evidence surfaces, that's our general course of action."

"What new evidence? I told you everything that happened that night. There's no point in me trying to convince people I was forced into it, crazy at the time, or any other excuse. Sally Blake is gone and I'm still here. I know the prosecutor in Auburn County. He's very good at his job. He'll have no problem convincing a jury I am right where I should be."

Jarrod flipped open his briefcase and pulled out a thin file. "I have your statement to our firm right here, Ms. Trimble. You said Sally Blake attacked you. You only retaliated when you felt your own safety was in danger. A new development has come to light that may help me convince a jury you're telling the truth."

Why had he come? Didn't he know the president was urging drivers to conserve fuel? She didn't want to think about the night Sally died. She had spent the last thirty years trying to forget it. The last thing she wanted to do was convince the world she had killed her best friend in self-defense.

"I appreciate all of you worrying so much about me, Mr. Bruckner, and I appreciate you driving all the way up here to tell me my options, but I'm not going to get my hopes up about new evidence and a new trial."

"The morning after your attack, Noel Wyatt received a very disturbing phone call. The caller said he knew someone who knew you had only been defending yourself against Sally; exactly as you said in your statement."

"How can that be? No one else was there."

"The man never identified himself, but Mr. Wyatt noted that he kept calling you Noreen, not Ms. Trimble. That indicates the caller knows you personally."

Noreen twisted the corner of the sheet into a tight roll. "But I don't understand. There was no one else there…That's what Noel was trying to tell me last week when he came here, wasn't it? He asked me to think back to that night and consider the possibility that someone might have been lurking outside. He said maybe there was a prowler."

"That was his theory when he spoke to me. That would explain the caller's reluctance to give his name or the name of the friend he referred to. That's why I need your help, Ms. Trimble. I need you to make a list of any and every person who might have been in the area that night. Was it possible someone from the party came back? Was there anyone who may have wanted to speak to you alone? You need to consider the possibility that someone intended to do you harm."

"Oh, no," she gasped, twisting the crisp white fabric tighter and tighter. "They were our friends. None of them would have…" She shuddered and looked down at her hands.

"We must consider all the possibilities, Ms. Trimble. There is someone out there who claims you were only protecting yourself. If this person is simply interested in making up a story, why not come forward and report it to a local news broadcaster rather than call Noel Wyatt and refuse to identify himself? How would this person even know enough about the story to make something up unless he was actually there? This person saw at least part of what happened. The only problem is we don't know who he is. Without solid evidence to take to the judge, there is no way you will be granted a jury trial."

"But—but—I don't see how any of this will do any good." Noreen realized with a start what she had been doing to the sheet and forced her hands to be still. "Even if this person, or whoever it was, did see something, it doesn't change what happened. I hid my crime for twenty-five years. Why didn't I tell the truth if I had nothing to hide? Why did I let Sally's poor mother suffer all those years?"

Jarrod waited a moment for propriety's sake before speaking. "It sounds like something a frightened young woman would do in a highly stressful situation. If you petition the court for a new trial, Ms. Trimble, you will be tried in Auburn County where you'll be among friends and family. Everyone knows you there. They know you aren't capable of a heinous act. You must realize everyone will be sympathetic to your case, even the prosecuting attorney."

"Everyone except Mr. and Mrs. Blake. They won't be sympathetic. They lost their daughter." She sniffed and wiped the back of her hand across her nose.

Jarrod removed a handkerchief from the inside of his jacket and handed it to her. Noreen pressed it carefully to her nose so not to soil it too badly. She inhaled men's cologne and fabric softener, two things she hadn't smelled in a long time. She imagined the young man's mother washing a pile of identical, monogrammed handkerchiefs and folding them into neat little squares and putting them into rows in a drawer in his room. At his age, it was unlikely he lived with his mother, but she sort of liked the picture in her mind. He seemed like a young man who would have a good relationship with his mother. In another life, she may have had a son much like him.

"I don't want people feeling sorry for me," she said firmly, more to herself than the young attorney. "They should feel sorry for Sally. She was my best friend and I loved her. I knew she had a temper. I should have found some other way to deal with her when she was mad. I'd seen her like that a hundred times before. I knew better."

Jarrod patted her hand. "Please, Ms. Trimble. Keeping you in here won't do Sally's memory any good. If you had as close a relationship as you say you did, don't you think she bore some responsibility to keep things from getting out of hand the way they did? If she were here, don't you think she would admit she pushed you farther than she meant to. Neither of you were to blame."

Noreen liked this young man. More than she liked his father, who had tried to bully her into doing things his way.

"I suppose," she said weakly. She dried her eyes and carefully refolded the handkerchief. "I'm sorry," she apologized, holding it out to him.

He smiled and tucked it back into the inside pocket of his jacket. "No problem, Ms. Trimble. Now if you would go over this report you wrote out for my father three years ago. Maybe by reading it aloud with me, it would spark some memories you don't even realize you have. We can make a list as we go of possible people who may have come back to the house. Even though the caller referred to his friend in the masculine sense, we have to consider the possibility he was referring to a woman. Anyone who was a friend, enemy, acquaintance, whether they were at the party or not; that's who we're interested in."

Noreen hated to waste the young man's day, but it wasn't the worst way to spend hers. "I really don't know if I can help you, Mr. Bruckner. I'm positive no one came back that night. And I certainly don't know of anyone who might have wanted to hurt me."

"They might not have come back to see you. They may have followed Sally from wherever she came from. It could be someone who was interested in seeing her, and they didn't know why she was going to your aunt and uncle's house."

Noreen watched the young man take a few more forms and a legal pad out of his briefcase and lay them out on the bed. She could think of plenty of people who may have been interested in seeing Sally again. Sally had a way of leaving an impression on people, whether negatively or positively.

She shuddered and took her Bible off her lap and cradled it against her chest. If they hadn't got into their fight over Tim, would someone have broken in to hurt them? Were they in danger that night from an outside force and neither she nor Sally knew it?

Gently and methodically, Jarrod walked Noreen through the report and explained what might happen over the next several months.

Two hours later, Jarrod Bruckner headed back to his office in Portsmouth with a list of twenty-eight names in his briefcase. It had been slow going at first. Ms. Trimble had been hesitant to name anyone, reluctant to get someone in trouble or remind her old friends of her crime.

The more they talked, the more names she recalled. The most interesting tidbit to strike Jarrod was the rumor that Sally had been dating a married man. Noreen had never met this man, nor could she get Sally to confirm his existence, but the story had been repeated from several different sources.

"Everyone whispered about it," Noreen told him, her eyes modestly downcast. "Whether it was true or just one of those stories you hear from a friend of a friend, it may be worth looking into."

Jarrod agreed a married man would have plenty to hide and a good reason to avoid coming forward, even if over twenty-eight years had gone by since that night.

Chapter Eight

S he hadn't been out of the house since the day her mother picked her up at the sheriff's station in Oldham County. Between a few changes of clothes Karen sent over and frequent visits to Abby's closet, Christy now had a few things to wear besides Eric's castoffs. The only problem was that every woman in her family was at least fifteen pounds heavier than her. Karen's blouses continuously slipped off her shoulders and Abby's cotton slacks slid down her hips every time she stood up. Safety pins alleviated the problem, but there was always the possibility they would open suddenly and impale her. Besides, wearing someone else's clothes was uncomfortable and wearisome.

Angry all over again that fear of two good old boys breaking into her room had made her a prisoner in her mother's home, Christy was fed up. She dressed in a pair of Eric's jeans—his clothes fit best—and a blouse Karen had outgrown somewhere between her second and third child. She borrowed sixty dollars and the family car from her mother and headed to the small department stores of Jenna's Creek.

She hated it that she had to borrow money from her mother. In her mind, it made her even more beholden to her. She hadn't even begun to forgive her for the affair with Noel Wyatt, but she would never find a job looking like she did now. She needed clothes. Sixty dollars wouldn't go far, but between clearance rack bargains and what she borrowed or begged off women in the family, she should be able to find some type of employment and work her way back to independence.

She didn't know all the details of her mother's financial situation, but it couldn't be much brighter than her own. Mom and Dad were always good about putting back some sort of nest egg, but with Dad's factory job, how impressive could it be? The life insurance policies Abby had collected—one personal and another provided by his company to help cover burial expenses—surely wasn't enough to support Abby comfortably until she was old enough to draw on Jack's social security account. Christy knew Abby would never toss her out on the street or make her aware of what her presence was doing to the household budget, regardless of how dire the situation, but she couldn't afford to take in every deadbeat relative who found themselves in bad circumstances either. Christy was determined to earn enough to get out of this town and back to her life; preferably before anyone pestered her too much about what brought on this financial disaster.

Too soon, her sixty dollars were spent. But at least she had enough pieces to build a decent work wardrobe around. She drove through Jenna's Creek's business district and studied storefronts, pondering which ones might prove promising in her search for employment. Auburn County boasted a grand total of twelve law offices, several of which were one or two man operations. She imagined most did their own paralegal work due to lack of qualified applicants to do it for them, or lack of funds to hire one.

She pursed her lips and wondered if she dare apply. Would they expect a resume and work history, or could she bluff her way in on her qualifications alone? It was highly likely she knew the law as well or better than most of the practicing attorneys in town. But what if they expected references? She couldn't very well make up a fictitious law firm who was distraught over her decision to support her widowed mother back home. She certainly couldn't give them the name of Bennis, Banociac, and Weiss. A year ago, Marvin Banociac himself would have handwritten a glowing recommendation for her. Not today. Today he would probably have her brought up on ethics charges for even approaching another firm after the breach of confidence she had committed.

She sighed and turned onto Jenna's Creek's main street. She may as well forget working at another law firm. She could forget law school as well. She needed to face reality and resign herself to some low paying, menial job and living under Abigail Blackwood's roof the rest of her days.

She pulled to a stop for a red light at the main intersection. Her eyes wandered to her right where Wyatt's Drugstore stood on the corner. In the turmoil of the last week, she had nearly forgotten Noel Wyatt and what he had done to her family. She tightened her grip on the steering wheel.

Christy had never spent much time concerning herself with the needs of others. Unlike her sisters, she didn't dream of the day she'd hold a child of her own in her arms. She preferred an education and a good job over motherhood and succumbing to the wants of a man. Her dreams focused on Christy and what would make Christy happy.

It never crossed her mind that her mother, of all people, might have needs and desires that couldn't be met within her family.

Was it possible? Had Abby once dreamed of doing something with her life that didn't involve Jack, Karen, Elaine, Christy, or Eric? When she was a girl, did she imagine living and dying in the same little town where she'd been born? Or had her dreams included exotic locales and swarthy men and passionate embraces on windswept beaches? Christy grimaced. Even at twenty-seven, it wasn't something she wanted to consider. In her mind, Abby would always be her mother, a good Christian woman. The fact that she was flesh and blood, and full of the same lustful desires as every other person on the planet, was too much for Christy to contemplate.

She had planned to go straight home and return Abby's car. Suddenly she found herself wondering about the man who owned the drugstore on the corner and the hold he once had on her mother. For all she knew, his hold was as strong as ever. The way she understood it, Abby hadn't forgotten her love for Noel Wyatt, even after she married Jack and gave him three daughters. That love had driven her into his arms and produced Eric.

The light turned green, and Christy sounded the horn when the slowpoke in front of her took too long to get moving. Instead of going straight through the intersection, she swerved into the left hand lane, ignoring the chorus of indignant car horns behind her, and turned east.

After a few wrong turns, she found herself on Bryton Avenue in the better end of town. She wasn't sure which house she was looking for, but she figured she'd know it when she saw it.

She didn't want to think about the passion between Abby and Noel that led them to risk everything for the sake of an extramarital affair. While still taboo today, they were absolutely scandalous in the 1950's. Had they been discovered, Jack would've had all rights to a divorce, with everyone in town cheering him on. Abby would have lost custody of her daughters and the respect of everyone she knew. Noel would have fared better, chiefly because he was a man and had money to boot. Men in his situation could do anything and come out smelling like a rose. Christy imagined his standing in the community would have suffered a much graver consequence than it did today.

Why had they done it? Who was this man, and why would her mother risk everything to be with him, if even for a few moments? Christy decided she wasn't going home until she found out.

She knew Noel drove a 1976 black Cadillac with a white vinyl top. She had driven past the drugstore over the Labor Day weekend the day after her mother told her about Eric. It was just after one o'clock, and she had seen Noel turn his Coup de Ville into the alley next to the store. She had circled the block and turned up the alley on the backside of the street. Noel was just walking around the corner of the building toward the store's side entrance when she pulled up behind his car. She had entertained the notion of smashing in the car's windows or scratching it with her keys. Before committing any misdemeanors, she decided she was a bigger person than that. Her next thought was going into the store and confronting him in front of everyone. Unfortunately she wasn't as nervy as she liked to think. So she'd done nothing.

This time she wasn't leaving until she talked to him.

She drove slowly, studying each property as she moved along Bryton Avenue. The small, neat lawns were well tended, possibly even professionally maintained. Past lacy, gauze curtains over a picture window, Christy saw an overstuffed, floral patterned sofa and brocaded wall coverings that screamed a woman's presence. A basketball hoop over the garage discounted the next house. In the side yard of another, sat a swing set. A yippy, long-haired little dog sniffed the bushes near a white privacy fence. She imagined Noel Wyatt was the German Shepherd or Golden Retriever type, if he was into dogs at all.

Just when she was beginning to think she missed it, she saw what she was looking for. A large brick, two-story Federalist stood sentry among the elms and maples halfway down the block. Even before she spotted the black Caddy in the driveway, she knew Noel Wyatt lived inside. She was instantly intimidated. Even the house looked powerful. It looked like a place where Marvin Banociac would feel at home. Not her. How had her mother, with her own humble beginnings, ever been comfortable here? The house seemed so cold and distant, as if it didn't belong on a street with swing sets and expensive dogs. She imagined the man inside was the same; didn't a house represent its occupants?

She pulled over in front of the house across from the Federalist and watched the front door. What was he doing home already? She glanced at the clock on the dashboard. It was barely five o'clock. She'd heard Noel was a workhorse. Her former bosses never left the office before five. It wasn't uncommon to see them bent over their desks at nine o'clock and back to work when she entered at eight the next morning.

Was it any wonder most of them had mistresses and couldn't remember their children's birthdays?

Christy looked upward to the second story where three tall imposing windows faced the street. Which room had he used to seduce her mother? Had Abby ever left Noel's arms to stand at one of those windows and gaze out over the impressive neighborhood below her, and wish she didn't have to go back to her dreary existence on Mulberry Street?

Without thinking long enough to talk herself out of what she was about to do, Christy swung the car in a wide arc and into the driveway. She came to a stop behind the Cadillac.

She turned off the ignition and got out of the car. She looked up at the side of the house and listened for signs of life. She didn't hear a sound except for the birds in the trees. No TV, no radio, no sounds of dinner preparations. Then again, houses like this were constructed for privacy. You could strangle someone in the dining room—or cheat with another man's wife—and the neighbors wouldn't hear a thing.

She pivoted her head toward the front of the house and then reconsidered. Guests used the front door. People with business on their minds went around back.

She hitched up Eric's ill-fitting jeans and strode around the side of the house, up three concrete steps, and along a narrow walkway lined with carefully mulched flowerbeds. Fall mums in masculine shades of gold and burnt orange bloomed in precise clumps. The sidewalk ended at a lovely brick patio, which wrapped around a raised back porch. She stepped up on the porch and passed a set of wrought iron patio furniture with cushions done in dark blue brocade. A potted topiary in need of a drink and some time in the sun stood next to the back door. She stepped around the plant and onto a half circle brick step in front of a raised panel door. The whole area exuded sedated taste and money. Anywhere else, she would have paused to admire her surroundings and imagine herself someday possessing something similar.

But at the back door of Noel Wyatt's house, she found everything pretentious. Someone had gone to a lot of trouble to make the house look pleasant and inviting. Only one of the cushions on a wrought iron chair looked like it had ever been sat in. There were no muddy boots beside the back door. No watering can or garden hose near the flowerbeds. No worn path of grass through the backyard. It was as if she was looking at a house in a magazine. It alluded to a family inside, but no one actually lived there.

She ignored the bell and rapped heavily on the polished panel door. If Noel was in there, she wanted to make sure he heard her.

She stopped pounding after a shadow passed over the etched glass panel in the center of the door. Then a handsomely rugged face, an oddly familiar face, trimmed in thick dark subtly graying hair appeared.

When the door swung inward, the familiarity of the face above her hit her like a ton of bricks. Eric. Every question, every accusation she had wanted to hurl at the man should they ever meet face to face, flew out of her head. She couldn't even remember what she had hoped to accomplish with this trip across town. She stood on the step eight inches below the man who had once loved her mother, awestruck by the resemblance between him and her kid brother.

Noel gazed wordlessly back at her. Finally he took a step back and made a sweeping motion with his free hand.

"Do you want to come in?"

She couldn't even manage a nod. In mute assent, she crossed the threshold.

Noel had never seen any of Abby's daughters up close, but as soon as he saw her through the window, he knew she was one of them, presumably the youngest. When Abby came here at the end of August to let him know she was going to tell her family about their relationship, she said her middle daughter lived in Germany with her Army husband. The oldest daughter had three kids of her own. This one didn't look old enough for that.

He also knew why she was here. He was mildly surprised this sort of confrontation hadn't occurred sooner.

"Ms. Blackwood?"

"Yes. I'm Christy. Or did you know that already?"

He stepped away from the door. "I assumed."

She stepped into the foyer between the den and the kitchen and looked around quickly. The back stairwell was directly in front of her. She took in the dark paneled stairway, the newly remodeled kitchen that had run over the estimate by more than Noel cared to admit, and the river rock fireplace visible through the doorway in the den before turning back to him.

"I thought my mother might have shown you pictures or talked about us."

Noel resented the implication. "I haven't seen your mother in over twenty years, except for a brief visit nearly two months ago."

She snorted. "Yeah, I'll bet."

"Listen, the truth's out now. I have no reason to lie to you." He immediately checked his ire and decided she had a right to feel the way she did. Then he realized he wasn't out of line. She could be as angry as she wanted to be, but this was his house, and he had a right to explain himself.

"My father knew about you," she said quickly.

He glanced down at the floor and then back to her. "I'm sorry for that."

The sincerity in his reply seemed to throw her off balance. Had she expected some sort of ogre who carried no remorse for the havoc his reckless actions had perpetrated on her family? While they stood in his entryway, looking at everything but each other, he took in her haphazard appearance. She was tiny, barely over five feet tall he figured, even smaller than her mother, and didn't look like she weighed a hundred pounds. She wore a pair of men's jeans that were too big for her and a blouse with the sleeves rolled up around her wrists. He wondered what her story was since she looked like the confident type who knew how to dress for success. She reminded him of a little girl, trying to get up the nerve to stand up to a schoolyard bully.

"Would you like to sit down, Ms. Blackwood?" He motioned toward the den.

Again she clearly didn't know how to respond. She looked from his face to the direction he pointed, an inner war going on inside her. She didn't move away from the door. Finally she brought her eyes back to his. "I guess I wanted to know why my mother loved you all these years instead of my father. I wanted to see for myself. I thought maybe I'd figure it out as soon as I saw you."

"Did you?"

She shrugged her thin shoulders. "I used to think it was for your money. But if that were the case, she'd be living here today, wouldn't she?"

"It was never about money," Noel said gently.

"Then what was it? What could you give my mother she couldn't find at home?"

This time, Noel was the one at a loss for words. He hated knowing the pain in the young woman's voice was his fault. But he didn't have an answer to her question either.

"Don't blame your mother," he said after a few moments of heavy silence. "I take all the responsibility. She was very young when we started spending time together. I was older. I should have known better."

"I don't believe in that," she said looking past him into the kitchen over his left shoulder. "You're responsible for your own actions. You don't blame them on someone else."

Her face took on a faraway expression. He wondered if they were still talking about the same thing.

"Listen, Ms. Blackwood," he began awkwardly, "I'm sorry for what happened. I'm sorry for what you're going through now. I won't insult you by thinking an apology from me will make one whit of difference. But you have to know what happened between your mother and I had nothing to do with you, Eric, or even your father. I don't know if that's a comfort to you or if it makes you hate me that much more. But it's the truth. This whole situation was caused by two irresponsible people following their flesh and not caring about who might get hurt in the process. Just try to be patient and understand your mother's side of things."

Christy turned her eyes back to him. "It may not have been about me, my sisters or my dad, but we're the ones paying the price."

"You're right. That's the problem with sin. The innocent victims who never asked to be put in the middle of the situation are the ones to suffer the most."

"I suppose you think by admitting your sin you've eradicated any guilt on your part."

"I've never believed that."

Abruptly Christy turned and put her hand on the doorknob.

"Ms. Blackwood," he said, his voice stopping her, "for what it's worth, I am sorry."

Keeping her hand on the knob, she turned her head to look at him over her shoulder. "I believe you really are, Mr. Wyatt. But that doesn't change anything. I guess it's not for me to know why my mother loved you. Who can explain why they ever love anyone?"

She pulled the door open and stepped out. The sound of a car's engine shutting off in the driveway reached both their ears. What now? Noel thought. He wasn't ready to defend himself against another Blackwood. He followed her onto the porch. He could see the front end of a Chrysler behind her car. Then the attorney he had talked to this morning appeared around the corner of the house. Harrison Bruckner had turned Noreen's case over to his son when he realized Noreen wasn't going to do anything to help herself. Noel preferred dealing with his old friend, but he guessed the son would have to do.

The Blackwood woman's step faltered when the young Bruckner—Noel couldn't remember his first name—came into view. Then she tossed back her auburn mane and continued walking. So much like her mother, he observed, a tempest in a teapot. Then he remembered it wasn't his place to make comparisons.

He'd already done enough damage to this family. They probably all hated him, Abby included.

He felt a tightening in his chest. After all these years, he still couldn't think about Abigail Blackwood without the familiar ache of sadness and regret. Thirty years of wanting something he couldn't have. He should know better by now.

When Ms. Blackwood and young Bruckner drew side by side, she gave the young man a withering look and stomped past without breaking stride. Bruckner tilted his head to watch her go past, then turned back to Noel with a slight smile that belied confusion, humor, and interest, in that order.

Noel watched Ms. Blackwood climb into her car and maneuver around the Chrysler. He wished he could have said something to make her feel better. But after all the damage he'd done, there wasn't anything left to say.

He turned his attention to Noreen's lawyer.

"A friend of yours?" the young man asked when he reached the covered patio.

"Not exactly."

"She looked happy."

Noel shrugged. He could see the gears turning in the young man's head. Young Bruckner would do himself well by forgetting about tangling with that one. He kept his advice to himself. "How was Marysville?"

Young Bruckner nodded, forgetting the redhead backing out of the driveway. He gestured with his briefcase. "We made progress. I guess that's all we can hope for at this point."

He followed Noel into the den where he discussed at length everything he had learned from Noreen Trimble.

Christy drove several blocks toward her side of town before pulling the car into an alley behind a Laundromat. She killed the ignition and put her hands on the steering wheel. She took a deep shuddering breath and stared at the gray block wall in front of her.

A small part of her wanted to cry, but the rest was too confused for tears. Her mind was a jumbled mess. She hadn't gone to Noel Wyatt's house for an apology. She wanted him to accept some responsibility for the boy he'd helped bring into the world. She'd wanted him to understand the situation her mother was in now that her husband was gone. She wanted...

She combed a hand through her hair. Maybe she wanted to take out her frustration toward Sean, Stanley, and every other man on the planet who took advantage of women every single day on him. To slap his face; to call him every dirty name she knew; to make him understand how much her family was hurting.

Instead of hating Noel the way she wanted to, she almost felt sorry for him. He was much older than she realized. Though well maintained for his age, he had to be at least sixty. She had always imagined a handsome, broad-shouldered, wife-stealing snake-in-the-grass that turned her mother's head with his smooth words. Noel Wyatt didn't seem conniving, manipulative, or wretched. All she could think when she remembered his fancy house in his overpriced neighborhood was that it seemed so lonely. Had Noel lived a lonely, miserable life knowing the woman he loved was on the other side of town going to bed every night in the arms of another man?

Christy clenched the steering wheel. She didn't want to empathize with his pain. She didn't want to understand that he and Abby may have never set out to hurt anybody, but were victims of circumstance, youth, and poor choices. She didn't want to think they were honest, caring people who did a stupid thing.

They were wrong—wrong and evil and selfish. They hurt Jack. They hurt Eric. Jack knew all along Eric wasn't his son, but he loved him and treated him as if he were. They stole Jack's only son from him. They stole Christy's brother. She wouldn't forgive Abby for that. She wouldn't forgive Noel Wyatt. Neither of them deserved her understanding or her compassion.

Chapter Nine

Things weren't working out the way Paige Trotter had imagined. She had been biding her time with the bombshell she had on Noel Wyatt for nearly two years. Years ago, she had figured out what every other thick headed yokel in this town was too dense to see. Her upstanding, goody two-shoes boss had messed around with another man's wife and produced a son. She sat on her discovery, waiting to see how the information would best serve her down the line.

After considerable time contemplating, she figured out what she wanted and how to get it. Her nephew Calvin, the only son of her husband's brother—a clever enough boy if he'd stay focused on something long enough to make a go of it—had enrolled in pharmaceutical school, after much prodding from her, of course. Someone had to get the boy moving. He was drifting along with no idea of what to do with his future, and his parents were about as useless as he was. So Paige put the bug in his ear. Once she mentioned pharmaceutical school and told him of the fine opportunities awaiting a young man like him now that Noel Wyatt's old assistant was in prison for murder, he agreed to take the classes.

He managed to finish the two-year course in a little less than three years and was ready to seek gainful employment. Angie, Noel's current assistant, would be out of the way soon. Calvin was ready to step into her place.

Paige felt absolutely no remorse for holding the dirt she had on Noel over his head to benefit herself. She had dedicated the last thirty-four years of her life to the man, slaving away behind the counter in his drugstore. He owed her something for all her years of loyalty.

She started working at Wyatt's Pharmacy the year her husband Edgar Ramsey went off to war. Edgar wasn't her first choice in a husband, the same way she knew she wasn't his first pick. Johnny Wooten, the man of her dreams, had been stolen by a little strumpet by the name of Claudette Waterhouse, at the Sweetheart Dance in 1941. Paige never forgave Claudette and didn't shed a tear when the two of them moved off to Wheelersburg, West Virginia to start a dry cleaning business which soon went bankrupt because everybody knew Johnny Wooten had no concept of money management and would plunk down every penny he had on any ridiculous get-rich-quick scheme that came down the pike.

When Pearl Harbor was bombed in December and all the county's young fellows clamored to join the fighting, her new husband, Edgar, whom she had married to punish Johnny Wooten, was rejected for having flat feet, though Paige always figured it was because of his flat head. As the war wore on, Uncle Sam lowered his standards and decided Edgar could serve his country at a postal company in Virginia. So Edgar went to do his part for his country and Paige went to work at the drugstore. She wasn't cut out for working with people since she hated every one of them, but she managed to keep from killing any of the store's regular customers by ignoring them whenever possible.

Edgar didn't write regularly. She didn't appreciate it since he worked for a postal outfit, but he wasn't a romantic sort, and she didn't particularly cotton to all the mushy stuff anyway. God help her, she tried to overlook his shortcomings.

Paige found out about Germany's surrender in Europe over the radio like most of Auburn County. She remembered how people had run out of their places of business that morning and were whooping and hollering in the middle of Main Street. George Templeton, the county treasurer, brought out the shotgun he kept under the counter in his office in case anyone ever got out of line after seeing their name in the paper when they were arrears on their taxes, and fired it into the air. That got Fred Simpson all riled up. He and his dimwitted brother-in-law, Clem Dugan, started shooting off every firearm Fred kept in his pickup truck, which was quite a few in those days. Clem—who couldn't shoot straight stone sober and was even worse when half lit; who had only bagged a deer once, purely by accident, when he fired at the back end of Cecil Wagonner's Ford, and the deer happened to be grazing nearby—was still hung over from the night before when the Associated Press made its announcement. Somehow Clem managed to hit the water tower, which most people thought was out of gun range until that day. The bullet ricocheted and broke out a window in the old elementary school building and lodged in the blackboard of Mrs. Arnetta Hartley's second-story classroom, scaring the socks off a roomful of eight-year-olds who were currently mastering long division.

Arnetta and the third graders didn't take kindly to being shot at. Upon hearing the ruckus outside on the street, followed by gunfire, they assumed Auburn County was under attack. When the sound of breaking glass and screams from the third graders reached the ears of the rest of the student body, panic broke out in the elementary school. Students and faculty alike stormed out of the building. Many of the youngsters ran all the way home in terror before the people outside could make them understand the town wasn't under attack, and peace in Europe had in fact been declared.

Most of Jenna's Creek sympathized with Clem for getting caught up in the moment since they knew he was a few bricks shy of a load, and forgave his foolish stunt. Everyone that is, except for Arnetta Hartley's husband Eugene. He drove out to Clem's shack on Redbird Knob that evening where he was sleeping it off, dragged him out into the yard, and beat the living daylights out of him. Soon after, Clem got religion and never touched another drop of the rotgut he loved so well, though he never did learn to shoot straight. There was no way of knowing for certain, but folks wondered if it wasn't the Holy Spirit so much that led Clem to repentance, but the two black eyes and cracked ribs administered by Eugene Hartley.

Paige watched the melee that day in 1945 from behind the drugstore's plate glass window. She didn't join in the revelry, even after the fear of gunfire was over. All she could think was her days as a working woman were over. Edgar was coming home, and she could quit her job of smiling and catering to people who annoyed her out of her skull. Since Edgar was stateside, it wouldn't be long before he'd come marching home with the rest of Jenna's Creek's brave young men. She briefly entertained the notion of beginning a family. She wasn't particularly fond of children, but it seemed like the right thing to do when a man returned from war. Even if the only action that particular man saw was from behind a desk in Newport News, Virginia.

But Edgar didn't come home. Paige didn't hear from him for two years. Everyone knew Edgar hadn't left the States so she couldn't lie and say he had been killed or taken prisoner like some more fortunate wives she knew. The Army claimed to have no records of him after relieving him of his duties on July 8th, 1945. It took some detective work on her part, but she finally tracked him down in Richmond, Virginia, where he was living in sin with a floozy who had frequented the NCO dances during the war.

With no love lost on her part, Paige quickly gave Edgar the divorce he asked for and started concocting the story she would tell everyone back in Jenna's Creek. Edgar had been wounded by friendly fire at a weapons qualifying trial in the last days of the war. His wounds were so grievous, he could never burden his wife with a husband who was now less than a man. She could see in their eyes that most people doubted her story, but she didn't care. The only thing that bothered her was she was now stuck working at Wyatt's Drugstore until she died.

Four years later, the spring before she turned thirty, Paige met Howard Trotter. Howard had actually seen combat during the war, which earned him status far above Edgar Ramsey. It didn't matter to her that Howard was fifteen years older than she or that he had already buried two wives. One died along with an infant son during childbirth, the other got scalded from a pan of water while canning tomatoes outside one summer. She and Howard tried to treat the burns themselves. The burns became infected. Howard was sure she was strong enough to fight off the infection. He was wrong. She died with more tomatoes still hanging on the vine.

Paige had nothing to fear. She had no intention of producing an heir for a skinflint like Howard, nor was she dumb enough to pour a washtub of scalding water on herself while canning tomatoes.

Holy matrimony wasn't all it was cracked up to be. Especially to an independent thirty-year-old woman who soon began to think of her husband as a doddering old fool. Fortunately for Paige, Howard contracted tuberculosis that first winter. His first wives weren't the only people to suffer because he was too cheap to pay for doctoring. He didn't make it through February.

Low and behold, old Howard had some money socked away. Not much, but enough for Paige to throw him a funeral, the likes of which the town hadn't seen in some time, and still have a little nest egg left over. As angry as she was at him for keeping his financial position a secret, Paige needed to regain face in the community for the way Edgar Ramsey had left her.

By that time, she was relegated to the fact she wasn't suited for the chains of marriage. She even enjoyed working in the drugstore. She got used to her boss's quiet presence and the idiosyncrasies of the townspeople and their inane questions.

The first time Eric Blackwood came into the store to apply for a job, Paige was suspicious. No one else seemed to notice the resemblance between Eric and Noel Wyatt. But that didn't keep Paige, who liked to see the worst in people, from nursing her suspicions. She kept a close eye on the young man, measuring every habit and mannerism alongside those of her boss.

What cinched it was an article she came across in a newspaper when she was cleaning out a closet. It turned out she had picked up a few habits from Howard during their brief marriage. He was a packrat. He refused to throw out anything, including newspapers since he might find a use for them someday, like plugging up rat holes or starting fires on the gas range. While she hated it in Howard, she found herself keeping sometimes a year's worth of papers before throwing them away, figuring she had almost another year's worth saved to take their place should a need arise.

Before throwing out the old papers she went through each edition to make sure she hadn't missed an obituary that had given her particular pleasure, a recipe she might try someday, or a tidbit of gardening or canning hints. She was still fascinated with canning tomatoes and couldn't imagine why someone would want to do it when they knew it was a potentially deadly job.

On page two of a two-year-old paper, she found an article on Noel Wyatt presenting the annual Benjamin F. Wyatt Memorial Scholarship for Science, a lucrative award he had founded a few years earlier in honor of his late father.

Paige almost skipped the article out of spite. The Wyatts were always finding some vaguely concealed way to make it into the paper; either donating money to some charitable cause or funding an expansion at the school or library or some other foolishness rich people used to hide their wealth from the IRS.

Just as Paige was ready to toss the paper into the stack she had already gone through, she took a second look at the picture accompanying the article. There was Noel, all dressed up and grinning like an idiot, his mother, the school superintendent who was just as fond of seeing his ugly mug in black and white as the Wyatts, and a young man Paige didn't immediately recognize. When she looked closer, she realized it was Eric Blackwood, Noel's recently hired stock boy. Then something else caught Paige's attention. She hurried into the kitchen to retrieve the magnifying glass she kept there for reading recipes. It irritated her to no end that cookbook publishers insisted on printing recipes so small that no one could read them without the use of a magnifying glass.

It was then she realized why Eric Blackwood had been awarded the scholarship and why he was now working in the drugstore's stockroom. It was as plain as the big nose on Noel's face—and Eric's.

Paige clipped the article and tucked it away in the drawer of her bureau for future use. Oh, and it would come into use.

She knew she couldn't approach Noel right away. Not until she had some leverage. What could she gain from this tidbit of information she had figured out, while the rest of Jenna's Creek remained blissfully ignorant? Then her nephew Calvin was fired from his job. The poor boy was college educated and didn't have the sense God gave a fencepost. Lights went on in Paige's head. It was a perfect solution. Calvin needed direction in life. Noel needed a new pharmacist's assistant, what with his last one languishing in prison and all.

She put the bug in her brother and sister's-in-law ears that Calvin might benefit from finding a new career path. Malcolm and Eudora were only too willing to finance another few years of tuition if it meant they might someday be free of the boy. Now Calvin had finished his schooling, and Paige had the ammunition with which to get him the cushiest position in Auburn County.

Somehow her plans had gone awry. At the first of September while waiting in the checkout lane at the only grocery store in town, she heard Sylvia McAllister telling Marge O'Brien that Jack Blackwood's widow had an affair with none other than Noel Wyatt. Paige was livid. Not only had her plan for securing a job for Calvin been derailed, she couldn't believe the nerve of that busybody Sylvia McAllister, blabbing other people's business all over town.

Now what was she to do with Calvin? He had moved in with her after finishing his schooling so Paige could mold him into the perfect applicant to satisfy Noel's idea of an assistant. Calvin got on her nerves a hundred ways from Sunday, but he was kin. The only descendant she had, thanks to two husbands too lazy to procreate.

She went to the bottom of the stairs and yelled. "Hurry up, Calvin. Your breakfast is getting cold. I didn't wake up early to fix you a decent breakfast just to have it grow cold on the stove."

"Coming, Aunt Paige," Calvin called downstairs.

Paige ground her teeth at the sound of his voice. There was nothing she despised more than a man's voice in the morning. As a matter of fact, there wasn't a thing about the creatures that didn't get on her nerves. They spat, scratched parts of their body that a good cleaning would keep from itching, and emitted rude noises for no earthly reason. She couldn't for the life of her imagine what a sane woman would see in needing one.

At least she'd never had brothers to deal with, and her two marriages had only resulted in sharing her bed for a combined total of nineteen months. Looking back, she couldn't remember why she held it against Edgar for never coming back from the war. One of these days, she'd try to get in touch with the little floozy from Newport News and thank her for sparing her years of grief and aggravation.

She headed back to the kitchen. She had enough time for one last cup of coffee before heading off to the drugstore. Calvin's thundering feet on the stairs grated further on her nerves. She gripped her coffee cup and some of the hot liquid splashed out onto her hand. She put her hand to her mouth and sucked off the coffee, then blew on the burned spot. He was twenty-four-years old, for crying out loud. Didn't his addle-brained parents teach the boy any good habits? Even dragging his feet—another habit she couldn't tolerate in men—would be preferable over the flat-footed stomping he always did.

"Morning, Auntie," he sang out merrily as he entered the kitchen.

Paige was still sucking on the fleshy pad of her hand. She turned from the coffee pot and glared at him. His thin brown hair was still wet from the shower. He wore it parted on the side and combed across his dome of a forehead. The thick lenses in his outdated black glasses made his eyes look perpetually out of focus. The poor thing looked just like his dork of a father. If Paige couldn't help him get that job in the drugstore, he didn't have a prayer for success.

"What's the matter? Did you hurt yourself?"

No thanks to you, she thought. "What are you doing today?" she demanded in way of a reply. "You're not going to sit around here accomplishing nothing again, are you?"

Calvin's smile grew wider. She hated it that he was always so blasted chipper even when she lambasted him about something. "No, Auntie. I am going to the library to do a little job research. You don't mind, do you?"

Paige couldn't see what he still had to research since he had already finished his schooling, but she didn't want to point out her ignorance on the subject by asking. For all she knew, Noel would expect him to take some kind of aptitude exam. Might not be a bad idea since Calvin hadn't exactly graduated at the top of his class. "Of course, I don't mind. Why would I mind?"

"I thought if you needed me to do something else, I would." He flopped down at the kitchen table and punctured the soft yoke of his egg. He swabbed the yoke with a piece of toast that had grown cold and limp. "Anything you need, Auntie," he said around a mouthful of toast, "I am at your service."

Paige wrinkled her nose in distaste and turned away. She couldn't stand to watch a man eat. "Just don't leave your dishes sitting on the table after your finished. The last thing I want to come home to tonight is hard, crusty egg yoke on my plates that I can't get off with a sander."

"No problem, Auntie. Your wish is my command." He gave her a mock salute.

She glared at him as she reached for her purse on the counter. "Don't forget. You're here to get in good graces with Noel Wyatt. Now that the whole town knows about his dalliance, I don't have any pull in getting you into the drugstore. You're going to have to get the job on your own merit."

He pushed his thick black glasses up on his nose. "That's what I planned to do from the beginning," he answered piously.

"Well, that had better be good enough," she scolded. "Neither your parents or I want to be supporting your sorry backside for the rest of our days."

"Oh, Aunt Paige, when you talk like that, I almost think you don't want me around."

"Good grief," she mumbled under her breath. That boy was going to be the death of her.

As soon as the front door slammed behind her, the insipid grin dropped from Calvin's face. He grimaced and dropped the soggy toast into the wastebasket and scraped the contents of his plate in after. He went to the cabinet in search of some dry cereal or oatmeal. He didn't know how much longer he could keep living here with his dried up old aunt. She was the most negative, mean spirited woman he'd ever met. His mother had warned him, but he was too desperate to be picky. He could put up with anything until he got what he wanted. Besides, he sort of enjoyed getting under the old bat's skin.

Despite everything he'd heard about his cantankerous Uncle Howard, Calvin couldn't imagine what the old man had seen in Paige Ramsey. Maybe he was looking for another wife to bury and figured it wouldn't hurt so much if the wife was as mean as Paige. Not that he thought for a minute Uncle Howard felt much remorse after losing either of his first two wives.

Much in the same way he felt no remorse for cheating Calvin's dad out of his share of the family inheritance.

Calvin had heard the story so many times over the years, sometimes it seemed the memories were actually his own.

His grandpa, Jeremiah Trotter, was as tightfisted and mean spirited as Howard, according to Malcolm. He never had a kind word to say to either of his sons, but if it was possible for his cold heart to feel affinity to one, it was toward Howard.

The boys' mother died when Howard was twenty and Malcolm was fifteen. Not long afterwards, Jeremiah bought a piece of property on the side of a hill in Auburn County and built a little shack on it. He moved out of the house Aunt Paige now occupied and pretty much left his sons to their own devices.

No one understood what Jeremiah wanted with that hillside for a number of years. The Trotter brothers got on with their lives as best they could. Howard bought a truck and some equipment for a pittance off a man who had lost nearly everything when the banks collapsed, and started a lumber business. Malcolm was too busy finishing high school and trying to figure out what to do with himself to keep much of an eye on his brother or his surly father, who didn't seem to want anything to do with anybody.

After Malcolm graduated from high school, he got a job at the bank, took some business management classes, and started working his way up the ladder. When Howard announced he was getting married and Malcolm would have to find somewhere else to live, he didn't think much of it. Yes, half of the house rightly belonged to him, but he understood Howard's desire to begin a family. At the time, it didn't occur to Malcolm how hard it would be to get your share of a piece of property when a family member still occupied it.

A few more years went by. Malcolm didn't keep in close contact with Howard, but he could see as well as anyone in Jenna's Creek his lumber business was thriving. Or so it appeared.

Malcolm made the trek out to Jeremiah's property every couple of months out of obligation and a grim fascination that the old man might fall over and die up there in his shack and no one would find him until the buzzards had picked his bones clean. He didn't want to see that happen. The old coot was his father, after all. One autumn afternoon after leaving the bank, he drove his Studebaker up the rut-covered road toward the shack. He couldn't believe what he saw on either side of the road. Some major development had been going on since his last visit. Unbeknownst to anyone but Jeremiah, the hillside had been a prime location for a new highway through Auburn County.

Jeremiah had sold a king's ransom worth of standing timber to Howard for a fraction of its worth, and then the hillside to the government.

Before long, dozers eradicated the hill from memory to make room for the highway, and Jeremiah moved back to Jenna's Creek with an undisclosed sum of federal money. He bought a tiny house in one of the cheaper neighborhoods and sat on his fortune. How much money, Malcolm never could find out.

Jeremiah Trotter had a thirst for bootleg whiskey. The years were flowing by, and he was becoming more senile and belligerent. Malcolm couldn't do anything with him, even though he tried desperately. Malcolm was married by now and wanted to start a family of his own. Dealing with his father was more than he could take. Eudora, his wife, grew increasingly enraged that Howard lived in the family house with the memory of two wives who had conveniently died on him, while she and Malcolm were barely holding their heads above water. Malcolm was still only a clerk at the bank, and there was a baby on the way.

Malcolm confronted Howard about selling the house and splitting the proceeds down the middle, which was only fair.

"No need for that, little brother," Howard assured him. "As soon as the old man's gone, neither of us will have to work again. Be patient."

Malcolm wasn't sure what he meant by that statement, but it made sense. While still not knowing the sum, he knew the old man had fallen headfirst into money with his deal with the government. He took his big brother's advice and waited.

Meanwhile, the affects of long-term alcohol abuse continued their work on Jeremiah's brain.

He took to sitting on his front porch with a shotgun across his lap. The police were called to his tiny house, located within shooting range of the A.M.E. church, every time the old man threatened neighborhood children who he claimed were stealing rocks out of his driveway. The man was a menace, Jenna's Creek claimed, and needed to be put away. But in those days, holding a gun across your lap wasn't a crime. One police officer would settle him down whenever they went to the house while another slipped in the back door and poured his whiskey down the sink. His temper usually settled down for a few weeks after that.

During those years, Jeremiah got it into his head that Malcolm was trying to kill him. Whenever Malcolm or Eudora would call the house to check on him, he would curse and threaten them until they hung up the phone. Visits to the house came to an abrupt halt after he met Eudora and little Calvin in the driveway with the shotgun leveled at the windshield.

"Get off my property, woman," he hollered through the windows. "I'll not have your thieving devil spawn coming for my money before I'm even dead."

Eudora didn't hang around to try and make sense of the old man's ramblings. But later she and Malcolm tried to decipher what he was talking about. They smelled a rat; a rat that resembled Howard.

Jeremiah became convinced Malcolm, Eudora, and even little Calvin were out to get him. He told anyone who would listen they had tried to burn Howard's house down one night to get their share of the insurance money. When Howard's car slid off the road one blustery day the following January, taking out a fence post and suffering minor damage, he told people Malcolm had been the one to run Howard off the road.

At first Malcolm and Eudora thought it was all Jeremiah's wild imaginings brought on by the booze. But then an old friend of Jeremiah's, Dawber Olaker, who was as old as the hills and never seen without an enormous chaw of tobacco stuffed inside his cheek, ran into Malcolm at the bank when he was there to cash his government assistance check.

He pumped Malcolm's hand and laughed with glee. "I hear your ole pappy's out to git you, boy," he said.

It took a moment for Malcolm to realize what Dawber was talking about. He worked in the bank's loan department by now and knew everyone in town. People were always trying to get on his good side by stopping to chat with him anytime he left the sanctity of his desk. It was the main reason he stopped leaving the bank for lunch, and he timed his restroom breaks for when there was no one lurking outside his cubicle.

"What do you mean, Dawber?" he asked, returning the old man's handshake. He knew Dawber wasn't looking for a loan or a favor. He didn't own anything except two pairs of faded overalls and the bottle of rum in his hip pocket.

"Your pappy," Dawber said, wiping away the thin line of tobacco juice dribbling down his chin with the back of his hand. "Ain't you heard, boy? He's tellin' everybody in town you're out to git 'im, but he's gonna git you first."

"Get me first? I don't understand."

Dawber was still smiling and chewing on the wad of tobacco tucked inside his jaw. "Jeremiah's sure as shootin' you're after him, boy. Me and 'im was havin' us a little taste of shine the other night when Howard dropped by. He waited till your pappy was pretty liquored up, then he told 'im again how you wanted his money. Howard said if Jeremiah didn't die soon, you might come over and take care of 'im yourself."

Over Dawber's shoulder, Malcolm could see Hazel Justice and Lula Anne Easter perched inside their teller booths, holding their breath and straining to hear the rest of the exchange. When they saw him looking, they hastily went back to counting out their drawers, but he could tell they were still listening.

He took Dawber's greasy elbow and steered him into the enclosed glass foyer at the front of the bank. The glass door slid closed, trapping them between the two sets of doors. Malcolm hoped to have the whole story out of Dawber before someone entering or exiting the bank would overhear them.

"What do you mean by *again*?" he asked. "Howard had been telling my father I'm going to come over to his house and take care of him myself?"

Dawber snorted with laughter. "Yup. That's what he tells 'im. Purt' near every time I'm over there leastways."

"Dawber, that can't be right."

Dawber nodded again. He shifted the wad of tobacco inside his mouth with his tongue. Malcolm managed not to gag.

"Sure enough. I heard him with my own ears," Dawber said. "Howard's always nice and proper-like in the beginnin'. Ain't no time at all though before he starts tellin' your pappy that you're after his money. Gits Jeremiah all tore up ever' time. Tell you the truth, I git sick of the whole biz'ness myself. Sometimes it's all I can do to keep Jeremiah from gittin' in that old car of his and drivin' out to your house."

Malcolm couldn't believe what he was hearing. His own brother! Did he want their father's money so much, he was willing to make up such ridiculous accusations against Malcolm to get it? It answered so many questions. It explained Jeremiah's belief that he and Eudora had tried to burn down Howard's house. It was why he believed they had run Howard off the road last winter. It wasn't the wanderings of an old man. He was simply repeating what Howard told him.

At that moment, a man came in the front door and Malcolm and Dawber had to step aside to let him through the second set of doors that led into the bank. Outside, another man was headed for the bank, followed by a woman and two children. Malcolm needed to get back to his desk. There was always a line waiting for him.

"Um, it was good talking to you, Dawber," he said, distracted.

Dawber reached out and caught hold of his suit coat. "Don't worry young fella. I don't believe none of what your brother says you're doin'. And I don't think your pappy does neither, least not when he's sober."

Malcolm wasn't comforted. He nodded in agreement anyway and headed back into the bank.

When he repeated Dawber's claims to Howard, Howard insisted Dawber was as big a lush as their old man. While that couldn't be denied, Malcolm believed Dawber. But there was nothing he could do. Jeremiah's mind had already been poisoned against him.

For the next year and a half, Malcolm redoubled his efforts to get close to his father. Now that he knew what Howard was capable of, he was almost afraid Howard might hurt the old man. But when Jeremiah was found dead in his easy chair with a spilled whiskey bottle in his hand, no one expected foul play, not even Malcolm. He and Eudora were not surprised when the Will was read. Howard got everything.

When Howard died a few years later, he left no Will behind. Everything went to his widow of eleven months, who gave a few token articles to Malcolm and Eudora to appease them. By then they were too tired of the whole affair to be disappointed.

Calvin grew up hearing how Uncle Howard had cheated him out of his share of his family inheritance. As a child, Calvin didn't understand or care anything about inheritances. He was clean, healthy, and well fed; he had no need of anything more. But as he grew older, he realized he had been cheated the same as Malcolm.

While it was too late to get anything out of Uncle Howard, there had to be something left of Jeremiah's estate. For reasons only God and Paige knew, she hadn't spent a dime of the money Howard left behind. If she had, there was no evidence of a luxurious lifestyle around the old house.

Paige Ramsey certainly didn't deserve more than she already had for putting up with the old miser for eleven months. The law might be on her side, but Calvin planned to get a piece of what was rightfully his.

Chapter Ten

Noel didn't have a moment all day to go over his copy of the list of names Noreen had written out for young Bruckner. He planned to as soon as he had the chance, so he could let the young man—Jarrod or Jeremy, he thought—know which ones he could talk to himself. Bruckner agreed with Noel that most of the people in town would be more apt to talk to him about Sally Blake's death than a lawyer they'd never met.

Ever since receiving the early morning phone call last week, the caller's identity had been driving Noel crazy. He was sure he knew the voice on the other end. If he could only hear the man again, he was certain he could identify him. He wanted to go over the list and see if there was anyone he knew personally. His caller might very well be on that list. Seeing the name in print might be enough to jog his memory about whom the voice belonged to. If nothing else, it should eliminate a few.

He had spoken with the county sheriff a few days ago, and told him what had happened with Noreen in Marysville. He told him about the phone call and said he might need his professional assistance in the near future. Sheriff Patterson reminded him that David Davis, a retired judge, had been the county prosecutor at the time of Sally Blake's disappearance in November of 1947. Like the rest of Auburn County, the then young prosecutor was certain the responsible party was Sally's current boyfriend, James Steele.

After months of investigation, Sally's body was never located. The absence of a body in those days made it impossible to convict someone of murder. Even though they couldn't pin the crime on Steele, everyone in town thought the young man had gotten away with murder.

Twenty-five years later, following his funeral, his daughter Jamie became determined to find out what really happened to Sally Blake. She also turned to the retired judge for help. The two of them uncovered enough new evidence that coupled with the discovery of Sally Blake's remains on Will Trimble's property, authorities were able to finally put the decades old mystery to rest.

Judge Davis met Noel Wyatt at his house a little after eight that evening. When Noel called him during his lunch hour, he jumped at the chance to see the list of people Noreen thought might know something about the case. No one was excluded. While a woman had not been the late night caller, she could certainly be the friend the caller referred to.

According to Noreen, Sally had returned to the sight of the party after everyone else had gone home and provoked Noreen into a fight. In the ensuing scuffle, Sally hit her head on an antique boot scraper and was killed.

The people who knew and loved Noreen believed her story of self-defense, but even they wondered what made her dispose of the body and then keep the crime a secret for over twenty-five years.

Noel poured iced tea for both of them and led Judge Davis into the dining room where he had the list of names waiting on the table along with several steno pads of paper and a few ink pens. He was ready to brainstorm all night if necessary.

"How's Bernice getting along these days?" he asked as he settled into the high backed walnut chair at the head of the table. Judge Davis took the one on Noel's right.

Bernice Davis had been diagnosed with multiple sclerosis five years ago, and her condition had forced Judge Davis into an early retirement. While she still had more good days than bad, the judge administered her medication and physical therapy and wanted to be home with her as much as possible.

"She's doing fine, thank the Lord," he replied. "Last winter was a long one. It's the worst I'd ever seen her. Her doctors seem to think those days will get closer together as time progresses, but Bernice is a fighter. She won't take anything lying down."

"That's the spirit," Noel said with a chuckle. "Let her know we're all praying for her."

"She's always glad to hear that. As am I."

Neither man spoke for a moment. Noel rested his elbows on the table and made a steeple with his fingers. He eyed the judge. "I've been thinking of something I remember from those days."

David was watching him, giving his full attention.

"I don't know if you knew this, but Sally used to work for me at the drugstore back then. She was always on the rebellious side. She liked to have her fun. And she was a flirt. She even tried flirting with me a time or two. I knew she was only doing it to raise a few eyebrows, but I played dumb, and she lost interest soon enough. Anyway, she had lots of male admirers, that much was fact. But there were rumors floating around she was dating a married man. I never heard any names or saw anything that backed up the rumors, but they were out there."

David nodded thoughtfully. "A married man; what better reason to keep your mouth shut if you witnessed something?"

Noel slid the list across the table. "That's what I'm thinking."

"Do you know if any of the people on here were married at the time?"

Noel shook his head. "Most of them were college kids or locals. I didn't see any names that looked like they didn't belong there." Nor did he recognize any of the names as belonging to his possible caller, but he didn't tell the judge that.

"Did Noreen mention anything about Sally seeing a married man?" David asked.

"No. Unless she knew something to be fact, she wouldn't pay attention to rumors. She knew how Sally was, but she only saw the best in people. She'd hate to believe Sally could date another woman's husband."

He swallowed his discomfort. He was sure no one thought Abby Blackwood was the type of woman who would have an affair either, nor he the man she would have it with. But it had happened nonetheless. He wondered what Noreen would think when she found out about Eric. Even though he was over sixty years old, Noel still hated to give a person a reason to think poorly of him. He had been a Christian most of his life, and it bothered him that his past behavior had tainted his witness. Of course he and the Lord had had a long talk years ago about his relationship with Abby, and all had been forgiven in the eyes of the Almighty.

The only problem with that was that most people he ran into weren't as forgiving and willing to cast a transgression into the sea of forgetfulness. They would use his past sins to mock his present Christianity. Thankfully, Noreen wasn't that type. She wouldn't judge him, regardless of his shortcomings. Noreen was a good woman; Noel only hoped he could be as supportive of her as she would be of him if the shoe were on the other foot.

"Hmm. Tim Shelton," David said, reading aloud the first name on the list. "Has Noreen told you about him and Sally?"

Noel's eyes widened, distracted from his personal concerns. "Tim and Sally? I wasn't aware there was anything to tell."

The judge picked up the list and studied it. "Noreen doesn't remind me of one for airing other folks' dirty linen."

Noel nodded in solemn agreement, although he couldn't help but be a little curious about what dirty laundry the judge was referring to.

"Seems Tim and Sally were something of an item for awhile. They even went to Sally's parents and told them they were getting married."

Noel didn't see that coming. "You're kidding me. Noreen's boyfriend was fooling around with her best friend?"

"That's what Donna Blake told me not long after Sally's remains were found. She said Sally was carrying Tim's baby. She was sure James Steele had killed Sally out of jealousy. After she told me that, I remember thinking maybe our old buddy Tim had a motive for killing Sally himself. If he truly loved Noreen, he might not have been exactly thrilled to hear about a baby."

"Well, if that don't beat all." Noel chewed on the end of a ballpoint pen for a moment. "But we know Tim didn't do anything to Sally since Noreen confessed to the whole thing."

"No, but what better person to come forward after all this time and say he witnessed what really happened? He would have a reason to be at the house that night after everyone left."

"But why wouldn't Noreen have told us he was there? And what motive would he have for keeping quiet all these years if he saw what happened?"

David shrugged. "Who knows?" He studied his hands for a moment in contemplation. "Listen, you know Noreen better than probably anybody. You don't suppose she would be taking the blame for something Tim did?"

Noel considered the possibility and then shook his head. "No way. I don't think she's capable of an outright lie. That's the reason she wouldn't go to trial. She said she killed Sally and deserved to be punished."

"Unless she was afraid if the investigation was reopened, the authorities might find something to implicate Tim and she didn't want to take that chance."

Noel stared hard at a spot on the polished walnut table top, concentrating on this new information. "But that would still mean she had to lie for Tim. I seriously don't believe she could do that."

The judge still looked skeptical, but he said; "Like I said, you know her better than I do."

"Did she know about Tim and Sally?" Noel asked.

"I assumed that's what she and Sally got into the fight over that night, but I don't know. Donna Blake acted almost insulted when I even mentioned Noreen. In her opinion, Tim was devoted to Sally, and Noreen was an inconvenience. We could always see if Sheriff

Patterson would let us have a look at Noreen's arrest statement. She might've mentioned what caused the argument."

"I'm sorry, but I can't imagine Noreen lying for Tim or anyone else. She was devastated about this whole thing. I truly believe she took the blame for her own sin. At least I did believe it."

"How about I go see Vernon tomorrow and see if he'll let me borrow a copy of her report. And one of us can talk to Mr. Shelton."

"That sounds good. He might be more apt to talk to us than Noreen's attorney who is most definitely going to want to talk to him after he hears Tim had a motive for getting rid of Sally."

"And Noreen had a motive for covering up for him."

Noel snorted. "The things we do for love."

Judge Davis smiled ruefully.

The other names on the list did not arouse particular suspicion in Noel and Judge Davis, but they weren't discounting anyone. Some of the names they located in the local phone book. Others they knew they could find easily enough. Only three of the names listed weren't familiar to either man. And neither Noel nor Judge Davis had heard anything about the remaining two on the list in years. It wasn't likely they were still living in the area.

The one both men wanted to talk to was Tim Shelton. Besides the married man, who no one could say for certain ever existed, Tim was the most likely candidate to come back to the house after everyone else left.

The end of the month was a typically slow time for Noel; as slow as times ever got at one of the few pharmacies in Auburn County. Early the following afternoon when Angie had everything well in hand, he headed down the street to the Theodore Blake Real Estate office. There were several agencies in Auburn County, but Blake's was the largest and most prestigious by far. The agency had a cadre of eighteen agents and three field offices throughout the county. Though well into his seventies, Ted Blake still oversaw the day-to-day operations. He had operated the company since before the Depression when he was the only agent. Things had grown amazingly well and even now, no one in Auburn County could foresee a time when Ted Blake wasn't a major player in the real estate game.

Noel had called Tim that morning to ask if he could have a little of his time this afternoon. Tim checked his calendar and said he could open up some time around three. Noel smiled at Tim's congeniality over the phone. The man probably thought Noel was about to become a client and would willingly jump through hoops to make that happen.

Noel didn't feel the least bit guilty of the subterfuge when he walked into the agency and was greeted by Tim himself. The commission off the sale of Noel's Federalist would make any real-tor stop what he was doing and clear time on his calendar. The receptionist smiled broadly even though her services weren't required. The three agents behind spacious desks around the large open reception area looked up with open envy on their faces as Tim stepped forward and pumped Noel's hand.

It was no secret that Noel was a man of means in Auburn County. Most people, regardless of their line of business, catered to him. He was so accustomed to receiving preferential treatment wherever he went, that he barely noticed anymore when it happened. His hand was shaken anytime he met his butcher on the street, or the local undertaker, florist, plumber, excavator, or the man who operated the septic cleanout truck. It was impossible to tell when Noel Wyatt may require the services they offered, so they strove to make a good impression at every opportunity. He recognized that look on Tim's face.

"Noel, great to see you. Gorgeous weather out there isn't it?" Tim said grandly as he turned and led Noel toward his private office at the rear of the reception area.

Tim was the senior man in the office after Mr. Blake himself. He had been working here since the late forties. His hiring had almost coincided with Sally's disappearance, Noel noticed. He wondered if it had anything to do with Tim and Sally telling her parents they were going to have a baby.

"Good to see you too, Tim," Noel said as he followed Tim into the office where he was motioned into a leather chair. "I appreciate you freeing up some time to see me."

Tim closed the door and circled around to his side of the desk. The casters squeaked as he sat down and leaned forward to rest his elbows on the table. "Not a problem at all, Noel. Always a pleasure. Now what can I do for you?"

Noel hadn't seen much of Tim in years. Most men in their early fifties didn't have much need of a pharmacist. Medical complaints were often ignored since they were hesitant to see a doctor who would prescribe blood pressure medicine, heart pills, or worse, suggest he lay off the fried foods and get a little exercise. Noel could tell by looking, he would begin to see more and more of Tim as the years passed. From the added girth Tim had acquired over the last twenty years, the flushed face, and the potentially high stress position he held at the agency, he was a ticking time bomb. Noel's own heart attack twenty-three years ago had taught him a lesson he wouldn't forget, and made him loathe to see other men repeat his mistakes.

He didn't offer medical advice. He was here for a reason other than Tim's physical health, and he wanted to get to it. "I'm not here for what you might think. I'm perfectly happy on Bryton Avenue. The reason I'm here is Noreen Trimble. I don't know if you've heard, but she was attacked in prison the week before last. She was nearly killed."

Tim's florid face went white all the way up to his artificially tinted locks. He sat back in his chair and let out a gasp. "Noreen?" For a brief instant Noel thought he spotted a young man still grieving his first love underneath all that pomp and affluence.

"Yes, I'm sorry to be the one to tell you."

Tim recovered by degrees. The color returned to his face, and he sat forward again in his chair. "I appreciate you coming here to tell me in person. What happened to her?"

"She got caught in the middle of a knife fight between some inmates. She took a pretty good shot in the stomach. They had to do an emergency bowel resection. She was transferred back to the prison infirmary a few days ago. She's expected to recover nicely, though she won't be competing in any marathons."

"No, I guess not. Poor Noreen, I worry about her up there. I wish there was something I could do."

Noel was glad the conversation was going in the direction he hoped, and Tim wasn't ticked that he wouldn't be getting a listing out of the meeting.

"Actually there is something you could help me with, Tim." He watched Tim's face closely for any reaction. "The day after her attack, I got a phone call from someone who claimed to know someone who witnessed the fight between Noreen and Sally Blake." Noel paused. Tim's face seemed to have been cast in stone. "According to the witness, Noreen killed Sally in self defense, and she doesn't deserve to be in prison. Do you know anything about that?"

Tim's head began to move side to side as if in slow motion. "No, this is the first I've heard of a witness."

"Do you have any idea who this caller may have been? He did not identify himself, but I had the distinct impression I've met the man before." Noel added the last bit intentionally, hoping to scare Tim into confessing if he was indeed the caller, although his voice wasn't ringing any bells in Noel's head.

Tim didn't bite. "I remember being questioned by the police when Sally disappeared. All of us got together later and compared stories. No one mentioned anything about a witness. None of us knew anything, or at least I didn't think any of us did."

He was clearly thinking of Noreen. Noel didn't say anything more for a moment. He wanted to give Tim time to decide to give up any evidence he might have. Finally he asked, "Noreen has said from the beginning the crime was committed in self-defense. She said Sally came to her that night telling her all kinds of hurtful things. Only after Sally pushed her, did Noreen push back. That's how Sally fell and hit her head. Do you have any ideas what Sally might have come back to tell Noreen? What would they have to fight about? They'd been best friends for years."

Tim sat back in his chair and pulled open the narrow middle drawer of his desk. He removed a roll of breath mints and held it out to Noel. Noel shook his head. Tim hooked a mint with a trimmed thumbnail and popped it into his mouth. "Sorry. I quit smoking this week—again. Joyce's been on me for years. She quit after the kids were born and now she's turned into a real Nazi about it. Trust me, the mints don't help."

Noel nodded knowingly. "Tell me about it. I quit after twenty years. I still wake up some mornings craving a smoke."

"Vile things. But, man, what I wouldn't give for one right now."

I'll bet, Noel thought ruefully.

Tim crunched down on the mint and swallowed before speaking. "I never knew Sally went back to the house that night. I always thought she disappeared with James Steele, and then he did Lord only knows what to her. I couldn't believe it when I heard Noreen had been the one to…" His hands shook slightly as he tore back the foil on the roll and popped another mint. "Sorry, Noel. I just never… I still can't imagine that Noreen did that. She was so…"

Noel almost thought Tim was close to telling him he loved her.

"She was the gentlest person I ever met," Tim went on, "nothing like Sally. I guess it goes to show you never know about people."

"I don't necessarily agree with you there, Tim, at least not about Noreen. I do know her. I believe the caller who said she acted in self-defense. The only problem is, unless this caller comes forward with what he knows or what his so-called friend knows, Noreen is going to die in prison. I think the caller might have been under the impression that all he had to do was say he knew of a witness, and it would be enough for a judge to order a new trial. Well, that isn't all there is to it. There has to be new evidence or proof Noreen was misrepresented—something. She almost died the other day. I can't sit here on my hands and wait for that to happen."

Before Tim could respond, the intercom on his desk buzzed and the receptionist's voice filled the small room. "Tim, you have a call on line one."

Tim pressed down on a button. "Take a number for me, will you, Linda?"

"I'm sorry, Tim, its Mr. Blake."

Tim sighed apologetically at Noel.

Noel doubted anyone ever kept Ted Blake waiting. He stood up. So did Tim. Both men stuck out their hands. "Tim, if you have any idea who that caller may have been, we've got to go to the authorities and get Noreen a new trial. We both know she doesn't belong in Marysville." Noel grabbed a business card out of his shirt pocket and thrust it into Tim's hand. "If you think of anything or remember something that might be helpful, please give me a call."

"Sure thing." Tim picked up the receiver as Noel opened the office door and said in a loud voice for the benefit of his boss and everyone in the reception area; "Good talking with you, Noel. If I can be of any further assistance, don't hesitate to call."

Noel closed the door behind him and left the agency without looking back. He knew there was plenty more Tim wasn't telling him. If only he could've had a few more minutes with him; enough to ask if he thought Noreen might be covering up for someone. He liked to think he could tell by looking into Tim's eyes if he was lying or not.

After a brief discussion with his boss about the upcoming auction of a large dairy farm in the northern part of the county, Tim opened the bottom drawer of his desk and took out a pack of cigarettes he kept hidden there for moments like these. He shook one into his palm and exited the building through the back door. The building had no policy against smoking; nearly every agent and client alike smoked anytime the mood struck them. A blue cloud hung over the desks in the reception area during all business hours. Tim only noticed the cloud during those awful weeks when he was trying to give up the habit.

Outside, he took a few steps away from the building to the graveled area where the agents parked their cars. He leaned against Harvey Turner's shiny new LaBaron and lit up. The agents' parking lot resembled a car dealership. All of them drove newer model cars, even the ones recently hired. Most agents signed on new cars before they ever made their first commission.

Image was Ted Blake's mantra. "Our job is trust and prestige, and that begins with image."

The old man must have been doing something right. He hadn't started the company from the ground up and turned it into the most successful agency in the tri-county area by not knowing what he was talking about.

Tim cast a look toward the building and inhaled deeply on the cigarette. He almost didn't care if his daughter Leslie, one of the newly hired agents, came out and found him with the evidence still on his breath. Let her go running home to Mama. Then again, if he didn't care, he wouldn't be hiding in the parking lot where no one would see, he reminded himself.

Leslie was just like her mother. Strong, confident, determined. Everything Tim was not. Her drive often intimidated him. She had already proven she had more business savvy than her younger brothers would ever have. She had drive and ambition that Tim and her siblings lacked.

At twenty-four, she was the youngest person at the agency. She had known from the beginning what she wanted to do and how to make it happen. She spent four years at the University of Cincinnati earning a business degree, taking all the right courses to make herself the most qualified person at the agency. She was determined to show Mr. Blake what a great asset she was.

Tim cast another anxious glance at the door to make sure Leslie hadn't followed him outside before leaning back and blowing a cloud of smoke into the sky. He hadn't given any real thought to Noreen Trimble in years. Regret was not something he liked to dwell on, and Joyce could always spot it on his face no matter how hard he tried to disguise it.

Tim Shelton knew the exact moment Sally Blake began to pursue him. Guys always talked about girls who wanted them. Usually it was nothing more than wishful thinking. But Tim knew he wasn't simply flattering himself about Sally's intentions. He also knew he wasn't worthy of a girl like her. He was a poor, undereducated farmer's son, destined for a life like the one his parents had lived—sore back, scarred hands, stooped shoulders; all the reward of scratching out a living on the family farm. Oh, he didn't think he was above farming. It was good honest work, like his old man was fond of saying. But Tim couldn't work up much enthusiasm about his future. He didn't want to be a farmer. He dreamed of moving to town, joining civic organizations. He didn't necessarily desire wealth. Money was fine, but his father had managed to keep his family warm and fed while earning little money. Tim had learned a lot from the old man; enough to know his father was more of a man than he'd ever be.

At the same time, Tim would sit upstairs in the room he shared with two brothers and stare out across the pasture, wondering what it would've been like to be born to someone else—anyone else. Shame at those thoughts made him duck his head at the sound of his father's voice asking the blessing over the dinner table that night. Who did he think he was, wishing he could have been born in a different place, to different circumstances?

His parents were good people; loving, caring, God-fearing people. He didn't want to be ashamed of them, but he was. He never admitted his thoughts to anyone, never wrote them down on paper. He wanted nothing more than to make his parents proud of him, but in the privacy of his own thoughts he was a prince's son, a businessman's son, an educator's son; anyone but the third in a family of six of poor white farming folk.

When the prettiest, richest girl in Jenna's Creek started making cow eyes at him, Tim thought he was overreacting like he heard his friends do all the time when a girl so much as asked if they got the math assignment. Tim wasn't vain enough to think Sally Blake would give him the time of day, nor did he particularly care if she did. He was already smitten with Noreen Trimble.

Noreen was pretty, shy and sweet-tempered. Every time he looked at her, he thought of the song his old man sang; *I want a girl just like the girl, who married dear old dad.* Noreen was all of that in a nutshell. She had a level head, a ready smile, her own opinions, a face that wasn't hard on the eyes, and it wouldn't hurt if she could fry a decent chicken; just what he'd been waiting for.

He was going to marry Noreen. Once in a while, after Sally laid her hand on his arm and laughed that deep, throaty laugh of hers over something he said, or she'd watch him speak with rapt attention in her eyes, he would daydream about how easy his life would be if he chose her instead. No more farm work. No more four a.m. wake-up calls regardless of the weather. No more listening to farm reports on the radio and calculating if there would be Christmas that year. Everything would be so much easier.

That would also mean he'd have to wake up next to Sally every morning, or at least until she tired of him and found someone else to chase. He knew how her game was played. The chase intrigued her more than the capture. As soon as she caught Tim, she would lose interest. He had no interest in being another notch on her belt, or however girls measured those things, if they even did.

She was funny, witty, and charming—not to mention beautiful. More importantly, she was Noreen's best friend. So if it suited Noreen to spend nearly every evening hanging out with him with Sally in tow, it suited him, too. Whatever it would take to keep Noreen happy.

So Tim ignored Sally's advances and tried to convince himself her flirting was harmless. Noreen didn't seem intimidated by it. He wondered if she was even aware of it. She was so sweet and naïve, maybe she couldn't see it. She would never dream of doing something that might hurt Sally. Consequently she couldn't fathom Sally doing the same thing to her.

The more time Tim spent in the company of the two friends, the more he fell in love with Noreen and realized Sally took much more out of the relationship than she put in. He tried to gently point out the obvious to Noreen a few times to spare her any hurt feelings down the line.

"Oh, Tim," Noreen said, putting her hand against his face after he brought it up one night. "That's just Sally. She has to be the center of attention. She doesn't mean anything by it. And besides, I'm used to it. Anyone who spends more than five minutes with her knows that she's going to outshine them. I don't mind. I've never been much of a shiner myself."

"That's not true, Nory," he'd said. "You are ten times the woman Sally Blake'll ever be."

Noreen blushed and gave him a playful slap on the arm. "Oh, Tim, how sweet of you to say that."

"I'm not just saying it, Noreen. You're beautiful...and I love you."

He hadn't intended to tell her so flippantly what had been pressing on his heart for weeks. He had meant to make his first proclamation of love an occasion; something she could tell their grandchildren about when they sat side by side in their rocking chairs, Noreen's face soft with age and her hair streaked with gray. He didn't want to blurt it out while comparing her to another woman.

It hadn't mattered. Noreen's eyes filled with tears, and she buried her face in his shirt and told him she loved him, too. Not long after that night he proposed, and Sally's fascination with him intensified.

For years afterward, he wondered if Sally ever had any feelings for him at all or if pursuing him was just another game to her. She loved to take things that didn't belong to her. She didn't care who she hurt in the process, even someone who adored her as much as Noreen did.

Tim ground out the cigarette on the gravel parking lot. How would he live with himself if Noreen had been killed in that prison? It was his fault she was in Marysville in the first place. If he had been able to withstand Sally's advances, Noreen wouldn't have had any reason to defend herself against the hurtful things Sally must surely have thrown at her that night.

He could almost picture the look on Sally's face as she delivered her news. It would have been with smug satisfaction and faked contrition as she explained how she and Tim had given into the lust of the flesh.

Tim gritted his teeth in anger and reached into his shirt pocket. The cigarettes weren't there. They were hidden in the bottom drawer of his desk. Joyce was going to have a fit when she smelled the smoke on his breath tonight. He wondered if the mints he was always sucking on would kill the smell. He doubted it was enough to fool Joyce.

He wondered what would happen if Noel's witness actually came forward to tell what he saw. Tim's part in the drama would surely come out. He would be called to testify to back up the caller's testimony. Did the caller know of Tim's role in what happened? The thought made his forehead glisten with sweat.

How could he take the stand and say how his boss's daughter loved to manipulate and destroy people; that it was a game to her? Ted Blake had been good to the Shelton family. Without him, Tim would still be on the farm living in a little farmer's shack, coming home from work every night covered in silt and grease from the tractors that were always breaking down.

He doubted he ever would have snagged Joyce had he not gone to work for Mr. Blake. After they married, she made no secret of how much she dreaded going to the farm to visit his parents. She always complained about a pair of shoes she ruined or how she caught cold after spending time in the drafty old farmhouse where Tim was raised. She didn't like it that it took an entire morning of soaking the kids' clothes in bleach to get the dirt stains out.

Joyce seemed to forget her own humble beginnings. She wasn't raised with a silver spoon in her mouth. Her father owned the local feed and grain, and he was barely better off than Tim's family. She should have been accustomed to dust, grime, and hard work. But she didn't want to remember that. She would have made a terrible farmer's wife.

She would be destroyed if he rocked the boat by bringing shame to the Blake family name—and what of Leslie? The girl was bent on making a name for herself in the business world. She liked being one of only three female real estate agents in Auburn County. She liked plowing the road. She wouldn't appreciate it if Tim did anything to draw negative attention to himself, which might possibly stain her own budding career.

Tim needed to find out the identity of Noel's witness before anyone else did. He hated to think of what might happen to Noreen, but that wasn't his main concern. He had to think of what was best for his family. The news that Sally Blake was a user, a liar, and one who would stop at nothing to get what she wanted, wouldn't benefit the Shelton family in any way.

Chapter Eleven

L eslie Shelton watched out of the corner of her eye as Noel Wyatt exited the agency with barely a backward glance. She smiled to herself. She'd been secretly delighted when she found out about him and Abigail Blackwood. The old man wasn't as uptight as he let the town think all these years. Everyone in town had believed he never remarried because of a bad first marriage. Now they knew the truth. Leslie's smile widened. Oh, she didn't blame him. If she were a man and could get away with half the stuff they did, she'd push the envelope, too. She sniffed and lowered her head back to her ledger.

Men got all the breaks. They had the opportunities to make the real money. They had their fun at another's expense. If they happened to get some poor girl in trouble they could walk away and never look back, just like what happened to that stupid Blackwood woman. She faced her unwanted pregnancy alone. She was the one who had to figure out a way to trick her husband into believing the baby belonged to him. Had the plan backfired in her face, it would've been her problem and hers alone. And then there were the financial considerations; while she and her husband tightened their belts to make room in their family for another baby, Noel Wyatt went back to his job, his church, and his country club without a care in the world.

Where was the justice in that? At twenty-four years old, Leslie
had seen enough to know she would never let a man use her that
way. If anyone would do any using, it would be her.

She knew she was attractive. Although not in contention to
win any beauty contests, as if she wanted to, she could hold her
own. She wore her pale blonde hair in a short sassy style that
looked businesslike and elegant, while at the same time was femi-
nine enough to attract attention from the opposite sex—not that
she ever had trouble doing that. She ditched the glasses that hid
her violet blue eyes as soon as she went to college and learned
of the existence of contact lenses. They were uncomfortable and
irritating, and her parents said she would ruin her vision, but she
got used to them. At five feet, three inches tall, she was naturally
petite, which she believed put men off guard around her. They automatically wanted to protect her and couldn't see her as a threat of
any kind. She wanted to be taken seriously in the business world,
but at the same time, she didn't want her appearance to intimidate
the men she dealt with on a daily basis.

Intimidation might get her what she wanted in New York or
Chicago, but not in Jenna's Creek. The men here still thought of
women as princesses, not half as smart or business savvy as they.
It galled Leslie to think they still controlled the way the game was
played, but if she wanted to win, she had to play by their rules.

She had been surprised when Noel walked into the office this
afternoon. Her heart had skipped a beat as she wondered how she
could get to him first without trampling one of the other agents.
Was he in the market to sell or buy? Either way, the commission
off such a sale would be a coup for whichever agent closed the deal.
She was forced to hide the smile as she thought of how good it
would make her look to Mr. Blake if she was the one to get Noel
Wyatt's account. She would smile and convince the old geezer to
spend more money than he intended. She could make a good impression with her sweet, girl-next-door demeanor, and possibly get
more business from his friends. A client like Noel Wyatt would
make her career.

She had watched Turner at his desk out of the corner of her eye and knew he was salivating over the prospect as badly as she was. She had scowled and wondered how she could get Noel's attention without throwing Turner to the floor and stepping over his bloated carcass. He had been here for fifteen years and still didn't have a private office. He was useless as an agent; useless as a human being for that matter.

But then her father appeared out of nowhere to welcome Noel inside. Leslie's heart sank. What a waste. Tim wouldn't even appreciate a client like Noel. She had stewed the entire time the two men were in her father's office, getting nothing done with her paperwork. When the phone rang and Linda announced Mr. Blake was on the line, Noel had exited the office. That puzzled her. It probably meant he hadn't come into the agency on business, or he was still at the thinking it over stage. Either way, she wasn't going to get anything done the rest of the day until she knew what was going on.

She worked at looking busy for a few more minutes to avoid suspicion from Turner and Mildred Hapner who occupied the desk facing hers, and then got up and went to her dad's office door. She tapped lightly before letting herself in. The leather chair behind the desk was empty and turned toward the office's separate entrance. She grinned knowingly. Dad was out back sneaking a smoke. She considered going out to catch him in the act, just to enjoy the panic on his face when he realized she'd go home and tell Mother. Then she decided against it. What did she care if Dad smoked? Everyone did. It was just another of her Mother's many hang-ups.

Instead she walked around the desk and lowered herself into the expansive leather chair that had acquired the curves of her father's body. She rolled the chair forward and settled herself in front of the desk. She leaned forward and rested her elbows on the ink blotter. She imagined a young couple sitting across from her, their future in her hands. She smiled benignly at the imaginary pair. She liked them and would do what she could to find them something that suited their needs. Her commission wouldn't make much of an impact on her checkbook, but that was only the immediate reward.

Leslie liked to look down the road. Soon she would have this office as her own, and someday, she would occupy Mr. Blake's. The old man couldn't live forever. He had no heirs to take over the business. Everyone assumed someday he would make Tim his business partner and change the sign out front to read, *Blake-Shelton*.

The sign would read *Blake-Shelton* someday, that was for sure, but not because Tim had taken the reins. He was a hard worker and a capable manager of a small town operation, but he lacked the leadership qualities Ted Blake would look for when he finally realized he needed to step down. Leslie would reveal those qualities at the opportune time.

She was still smiling at the image of herself ruling over Blake Enterprises when the back door of the office opened and her father stepped inside, reeking of cigarette smoke. She dug her toes into the carpet and spun the chair around to face him.

"Daddy, where have you been?" she sang out in mock concern.

Tim's surprise at seeing her was immediately replaced with a smile. "Trying out the old man's chair again, huh, darling?"

Leslie stood up and rose up on her toes to kiss his cheek. "Just keeping it warm for you." She perched on the corner of the desk as Tim lowered himself into the chair.

She crossed one leg over the other and pretended to admire her new designer shoes swinging in a steady rhythm as Tim fumbled through the drawer for breath mints. "Don't tell me Noel Wyatt's putting his property up for sale," she said casually. "I'm sure he knows how soft the market is right now."

She didn't miss the dilation of her father's pupils even though she didn't turn her head away from the direction of her shoes.

Tim crunched down on the mint and chewed madly. It was apparent he wanted another cigarette. "No, no, I doubt he'll ever sell that house."

"Oh." She stopped bouncing her foot, uncrossed her legs and put both hands on either side of her. She leaned slightly forward and dropped her head as if she had all day and was simply killing time talking to her father. "So what was he doing here, then?"

Tim lifted one shoulder. "Just to see how things are going. We haven't seen each other in years."

Leslie hated being in the dark. Noel Wyatt and her father had never been friends. Neither man had enough free time to clear his schedule in order to pass the time with someone he barely knew. Something was going on, but she didn't have the foggiest notion as to what. Still, she couldn't bully her father into telling her.

"You should have invited him over to the house for dinner," she said as she slid off the desk. She pressed her hands down over the front of her skirt to smooth out the wrinkles. It was bad enough Mr. Blake insisted his female agents wear skirts to work like it was still the dark ages and not 1976, but then she had to go to extra lengths to look neat and pressed, too. She painstakingly ironed her wardrobe every morning, only to lament the wrinkles that appeared before she even got to the office. They could put a man on the moon, but they couldn't develop a fabric that didn't wrinkle across the bend in her legs the first time she sat down.

"I will the next time I talk to him," Tim said absently.

Leslie moved around the desk to the door. She glanced at her watch. "Well, I have an appointment in fifteen minutes. I'd better get going." She put her hand on the doorknob and looked back at him over her shoulder. "Daddy..."

"Hmm," he said, fumbling for another mint.

"If you ever want to tell me what Mr. Wyatt was really doing here, you know where to find me." She smiled at the look of alarm on his face as she spun out of the office.

From her position behind the first cash register, Paige Trotter watched Noel Wyatt reenter the drugstore. He'd walked out the front door at ten minutes past three without a word to anyone.

That was thirty minutes ago. Paige had tried to see where he was going, but the line of customers waiting to pay for their purchases were blocking the plate glass window so she couldn't see which direction he went.

She'd been biding her time since it became apparent everyone in Jenna's Creek knew about his business with the Blackwood woman. She was dismayed and shocked the news hadn't caused a bigger stir. Barely a ripple really. People were talking about it all right. They were shocked and horrified, but not enough to take their business elsewhere as Paige had hoped. That was the only way to get the attention of people like Noel Wyatt; in the pocketbook.

When she first figured out the truth, she was sure Noel would do anything to keep his secret. He would have agreed with her to give Calvin the job recently vacated by the moderately competent Noreen Trimble. But now Paige wasn't so sure. He might have simply laughed and told her to go ahead and do her worst; he didn't care what people thought of him.

Paige slammed the cash register drawer shut in consternation and looked up to glare at the next customer. How could people be so tolerant? If anything, it seemed the drugstore was more crowded than ever. Oh, she saw the cautious way they studied Noel, like they were wondering what else he was capable of, but they still kept coming in and spending their money—stupid sheep.

As much as she disliked her bigger than life boss and the senseless minions who paid him homage, she would rather be here at work than at home with Calvin. She didn't know how much longer she could put up with him. His insufferable cheerfulness was about to drive her out of her mind. Half the time she suspected he was putting on an act to get under her skin, but she couldn't for the life of her figure out why. She wished he'd go back home to his parents. Now that she couldn't use her leverage with Noel to get him the job behind the pharmacy counter, there was no sense in him staying under her roof.

Calvin wasn't her responsibility. Nonetheless, she couldn't help feeling a little guilty whenever she thought of how Howard had turned his old man against Malcolm and Eudora, thus cheating them out of their share of his money. She had heard the stories long before she married Howard. She wasn't the type of woman to put much stock in small town gossip, but after living with Howard Trotter for eleven long months, she knew firsthand no underhanded trick was beneath him when there was money to be gained.

Of course none of this was her fault. Howard and his lying treachery toward his own brother had transpired long before she entered the picture. She didn't owe Malcolm or that simpering Eudora one thing. Neither of them ever approved of her and made no secret about it. Why, they even insulted her at her own wedding. Told her flat out she was only after Howard's money. And then at the funeral the very next March, three weeks shy of her first anniversary, Malcolm and Eudora had refused to sit in the front row beside her that had been reserved for immediate family. They stuck their big noses in the air and sat in the row behind her. Neither of them shed a tear throughout the entire service. She knew because she kept turning around to check.

So she had to sit in the front row all alone and bear the scrutiny of the small-minded busybodies of Jenna's Creek, sitting behind her and whispering. Even the funeral director—after all the money she had paid him—looked down his hawk-like beak at her.
She didn't have any family of her own to occupy the pew beside her. Her own father had passed away several years before, and her mother was living in an old folk's home out on Highway 16 by then. She wasn't lucid half the time, and cursed and argued with Paige every time she visited, calling her by her sister Florence's name and accusing her of accosting the doctors and orderlies in the broom closet. Then there was Florence who never had any kind of relationship with her and thought she was so much better than Paige for marrying well.

So she had endured her husband's funeral alone and gone back to the house after the service, unable to attend the wake at

Malcolm and Eudora's. They would spend the whole day rehashing how Howard had cheated Malcolm out of his share of the inheritance. Paige had heard enough verses of that song to last her a lifetime. Besides, they hadn't invited her.

What the Trotters didn't know was that Howard hadn't left that much behind. Besides the stash of money Paige found in Howard's bedroom closet she used to pay for his funeral and the house they lived in, only a few insignificant bank accounts and a couple of nearly worthless properties scattered about the county were all that remained of Jeremiah Trotter's estate. She didn't know if Jeremiah drank up his fortune before his death or if he didn't have that much to begin with. Either way, Howard died leaving her barely able to keep the taxes paid on the properties she hadn't sold as soon as he was gone.

Had she known there was no more money than what she found in the closet, she wouldn't have buried him in such grand fashion.

She did feel a little responsibility and compassion toward Calvin. Whether she wanted to think about it or not, she wasn't going to live forever and Calvin was Howard Trotter's only heir. She needed to do right by the boy. Possibly undo some of the harm Howard had done to Malcolm by turning the old man against him. All that money, if there ever was any, sure hadn't done Howard any good. He had continued out his life in abject poverty, afraid to loosen his clutches on one thin dime. Meanwhile, Malcolm and Eudora lived a pretty decent life after Malcolm got himself situated at the bank. They appeared to love each other and seemed happy. Of course, they had Calvin, but that was another story.

She had already decided to let Calvin have the house after she was gone. It wasn't in very good shape anymore—the floors sloped, the roof leaked, and the neighborhood had gone to the dogs—but it was better than anyone ever handed her free and clear. It wouldn't hurt Calvin to learn beggars couldn't be choosers.

She glared in the direction of the pharmacy counter. Just a few months ago she thought she had everything figured out, but her good intentions to do right by Calvin had blown up in her face.

It just went to show you couldn't do a good deed anymore. Since Noel's secret life had come to light and no one in Jenna's Creek cared enough to take their business elsewhere or at least face Noel down and tell him what a no-account, lily livered, wife-stealing, veteran disrespecting rat he was, she had no leverage left to get what she wanted for Calvin. She would have to depend on Noel's sense of decency and loyalty, to reward her for the tireless years of service she had given him.

Blast it all, she could grow old waiting for Noel Wyatt to do the right thing.

Chapter Twelve

C hristy Blackwood dropped the car keys into her front pocket. She put her hand on the doorknob and hesitated. She turned her head and looked over her shoulder up the staircase. The house was quiet. It was almost always quiet. She should go upstairs and remind her mother she was leaving. She was on her way to her sister's house. Karen and Jamie Steele, Eric's fiancé, were already there going through bridal catalogs and discussing the wedding. Karen had called this morning to invite Christy and Abby over. Abby had a headache and didn't feel like getting out of bed. She assured Christy she could take the car and drive over herself.

Eric was home for the weekend, too, but he had no desire to watch his future bride and sisters pour through bridal magazines. He had left early in the morning to play ball with some friends he hadn't seen since his last weekend home.

Christy was just as happy that Abby wasn't going. She and her mother had struck a fragile existence inside the house, both making strides to keep out of the other's way. It wasn't exactly Ozzie and Harriet, but it satisfied Christy.

Now she wondered if she should at least go upstairs and tell her mother good-bye. It seemed like something civilized people would do, and she liked to think she was a big enough person to treat her mother civilly without overlooking her transgression with

Noel Wyatt like the rest of the family had done. She could hear the gentle whir of the electric fan Abby used to block out noise from the street when her head was bothering her. Christy had told her she was leaving around ten, so it wasn't really necessary to go upstairs to remind her. If she had dozed off from the pain medication she took this morning, Christy would only end up disturbing her.

Her decision made, Christy hurried outside and slid behind the wheel of her mother's car. She stared at the back of Jack's truck as she turned the key in the ignition. Eric drove it some when he was home from school to keep the engine and gears lubricated, but for the most part, it sat in the driveway, a grim reminder that Jack Blackwood wasn't coming home.

The worst part for Christy about being home was missing Dad. At least when she was still in Columbus, she could almost convince herself everything was fine back in Jenna's Creek. She didn't have to think every single day about the void in her family caused by Jack's absence. Now, every time she walked past his bedroom or looked at the couch and saw the collapsed cushion where he always sat, the wound inside her broke open all over again.

She needed him; more now than she ever had. He had always been her anchor, the one to diffuse the battles between mother and daughter. If he were here, he could tell her how to get along with her mother. Even if he didn't agree with her, he would understand her inability to let go of her anger and bitterness. Instead of trying to talk her into forgiving Abby, he would listen while she raged and vented, and then offer his plainspoken advice and compassion.

He would be the one to whom she could confess what happened between her and Sean. Though she would have to face the consequences brought on by her actions, he would've been right there beside her, offering his solid support.

Why, God? Why did you take him? I need him. Then she reminded herself she didn't pray anymore. She hadn't prayed in years. She didn't even know if she believed in God, though she never would have admitted as much to her father. His faith had been an important part of who he was. While Christy respected him for it, she didn't share his passion. What was the point in believing? What was the point in praying? People died whether you prayed for them or not. Tragedies and wars took place everyday. Wives cheated on their husbands. Boyfriends used their girlfriends.

Why bother praying for things when God, if he existed at all, was going to let people do what they wanted anyway?

She sighed at the futility of her thoughts. She knew what was wrong with her. She hadn't gone this long without working since high school. She didn't know what to do with herself. She needed a job. She hated sitting around doing nothing. It gave her too much time to think, and thinking was the last thing she wanted to do. When she did, she ended up thinking about Sean, and then she inevitably ended up missing him. As if that wasn't the craziest thing!

How could she possibly miss the rotten jerk after all the lies he told her?

He told her he was originally from Denver, but saying it didn't make it true. Most of what he told her had little or no truth behind it. His parents hadn't died when he was young, leaving him a substantial inheritance, which he used to go to college. He didn't grow up in Delaware, Ohio with his grandmother and countless cousins who pointed out what a burden he was on the old woman. Christy realized after it was too late that Sean Hatcher said whatever it took to make her feel sorry for him, lower her guard, and put her trust in him.

When the news of his cousin's arrest hit the airways, she learned his parents were alive and well and living in Wooster—not fifty miles from Columbus. When she saw the close-up of their house in a quiet, upscale neighborhood, she had sunk into the couch cushions and cried. She imagined his mother on the other side of those brick walls experiencing the same betrayal.

In the nine years she'd been in Columbus, including the four years she spent earning her degree, Christy had fooled herself into believing she knew enough about men to spot the ones out to exploit or use her. She had been working in a man's world too long to fall for any old line. Somehow Sean slipped in under her radar.

Not somehow. She knew how. She became vulnerable. She was twenty-seven years old and she had started to wonder if she would ever have what her sisters and girlfriends took for granted. She had put so much effort into her career, she neglected her personal life. She didn't even have one. She realized the pursuit of what she viewed as success had cost her something else. The women's magazines were fond of reinforcing her beliefs that she could have it all. They were just lousy at explaining how.

Was it even possible?

Sean had recognized that vulnerability.

She remembered the first time she ever saw him. It was in a restaurant down the street from her office building where she sometimes went for lunch. Most days she packed a peanut butter sandwich and an apple in a paper bag and worked through lunch. But there were days when she felt the walls closing in around her, and she had to get out. She would either eat her lunch on a park bench or go to the café.

That particular day was overcast. Rain clouds threatened, but the air was heady with the smell of apple blossoms. Nothing could have kept her inside. She didn't have much time so she grabbed a pita sandwich to go and headed back out of the restaurant. At that moment, a tall figure came rushing in. They crashed into each other, and Christy's lunch sack flew out of her hand and skated out the open door and onto the sidewalk. Another patron on the heels of the man she crashed into, stepped square onto her bag, squashing everything inside.

She had groaned aloud, barely aware of the man holding onto her elbow. "That's my lunch," she wailed, looking accusingly at the balding man in the trench coat who had barely slowed down.

"Sorry," he said dismissively as he ducked past her and into the restaurant. His coat was spattered with raindrops. The sky had turned ominously dark. The storm had arrived.

"I'm so sorry," said the man at her elbow. "It was my fault."

She looked up to assure him he was not to blame but stopped short. She was looking into the deepest charcoal gray eyes she had ever seen. She was aware of her mouth hanging agape. She only hoped she wasn't drooling.

The charcoal eyes, which seemed to darken with amusement at her loss of intelligent response, were fringed with long black lashes, neatly arched eyebrows, and a thick mane of almost black hair, through which she envisioned running her hands.

Only when he released his grip on her elbow, did she realize he had been holding onto her. She felt the heat of his hand long after he took it away. He bent over and picked up the flattened bag that held what once was her lunch.

He straightened up and held out the bag for her to see. "I'm afraid this is unsalvageable. Could I buy you another? I feel terrible."

It took a moment for her to realize he was asking a question. She was too busy staring at the large, tanned hand gripping her bag and the finely muscled wrist and forearm that disappeared into a Madres shirt.

"Oh, um, uh..." she stammered when she noticed him staring at her. She snapped to attention and looked at her watch. She jerked her head around to look at the café's interior. The line at the counter was nine people deep. "I...um...I don't have time to wait in line again." She attempted a bright smile she hoped would make up for an apparent inability to communicate. "I'll just grab something from the vending machine back at the office."

"Oh, no, I hate to think you'll have to do that, all because I wasn't watching where I was going."

Christy tried to listen to what he was saying and not focus on the nice way his mouth moved when he talked. "No, no, it was my own fault. That's what I get for hurrying."

A woman in dangerously high heels, holding a newspaper over her head, dashed past them to get inside the building. The rain had increased. They moved out onto the sidewalk. They were forced to stand close to stay under the tiny awning. Christy stepped aside to open her umbrella. "At least let me walk you back to wherever you work," he offered. He held up a black umbrella. "Mine's bigger. We can share."

Christy considered his offer for a brief instant. He didn't look like a lunatic. There was only half a block between them and her building, and the sidewalk was full of lunch hour foot traffic. How dangerous could the situation be? She'd keep her umbrella in her hand in case she had to turn it into a weapon to defend herself against unwanted advances. Somehow she couldn't imagine this gorgeous creature behaving improperly without a written invitation. She imagined he received plenty.

"Okay, sure."

He dropped her ruined lunch in a trashcan, opened his umbrella, and stepped out from under the awning. Not only was Sean Hatcher nice to look at, he was attentive, charming, funny, and sensitive; an amazing combination in Christy's workaday world. Men like Sean didn't exist—did they?

Sean showed up at her office building two days later. He was in the lobby when she got off the elevator, reading the directory of businesses in the building. When Christy walked up to him, he actually blushed and admitted he was there looking for her. "You didn't say which company you worked for," he said. "I guess I planned to hang around and see if you came out."

It crossed her mind to be suspicious, but he looked so cute standing there, almost digging his toe into the carpet like a naughty child, she couldn't be anything but flattered. After all, how many other good-looking, considerate men in the city were waiting for her to get out of the elevator? She let him take her out to dinner. Three nights later, it was dinner and dancing at a club. From then on, Sean Hatcher didn't leave her mind.

Sean was an investment broker, though he was vague about which firm he worked for. He claimed he did a lot of consulting for various firms in the area, sometimes going out of town to Cleveland and Indianapolis. He was currently investigating a contracting company that had been awarded a bid from the highway department to build a bridge on a rural two-lane highway in Logan County. The investors Sean represented were interested in learning more about the company, owned by a local small business owner named Peter Scowden, who happened to be a client of Christy's firm.

Sean looked the part, acted the part, dressed the part, and walked the part; he never gave her a reason to doubt a word out of his mouth.

On their very first date she opened up to him about her father's death and the difficult time she was having dealing with it. She told him of her concerns for her mother who was leaning too much on her kid brother for support. She confided that she and her sisters feared Abby was trying to get Eric to take their dad's place.

When she found herself choking back tears, Sean took her hand and brushed a stray wisp of hair away from her face. After dinner and two hours talking in a nearly deserted coffee shop where much to her horror and chagrin, she monopolized the conversation, Sean did not kiss her goodnight. Instead he unlocked her door for her, squeezed her hand, and backed down the hallway to the stairs, grinning and giving her a little wave the whole way.

Christy floated into her apartment, absolutely smitten.

Each subsequent date had more of the same effect on her.

When Sean asked a few covert questions about Mr. Scowden's construction company, Christy had blithely answered without worrying about compromising any attorney-client privilege. His questions never pertained to anything classified or inappropriate.

One Friday afternoon, Sean was waiting in the lobby of her building when she exited the elevator. He had been out of town on business the entire week, and she didn't realize until that moment how much she missed him. It was all she could do not to drop her briefcase and run into his arms. That evening he spent the night at her apartment. Christy pushed the guilt aside by telling herself they were consenting adults and could do whatever they pleased. Besides, she was pretty sure she was in love with him.

Saturday afternoon, he promised he would call the next day. She followed him out of the apartment and leaned over the banister to watch him leave. He kept his eyes on her as he bounced down the stairs, smiling and waving the whole time. She couldn't remember ever seeing him so happy and content. She liked to think she was the one to put that new light in his eyes. In a way, she had.

Sunday came and went without a phone call. "You shouldn't have let him spend the night," she scolded herself aloud whenever she found herself listening for the phone. "That's why he isn't calling."

Then she reminded herself how old fashioned she sounded. Things had changed in the last twenty years. Sleeping with a man before you married him was no longer taboo but a practical choice. How would they know if they were right for each other if they didn't explore every aspect of their relationship? She needed to get over her uptight, middleclass upbringing and enjoy the freedom of being a modern woman.

It sounded good to her ears, but it didn't stop her from tossing and turning in her bed late into the night.

Christy was absolutely bowled over the next morning when she turned on the news and saw the face of Peter Scowden looking back at her. He and his contracting company were under investigation. It seemed the bridge Mr. Scowden was paid to build in Logan County hadn't even been started. For nearly a year he'd collected money for material and labor for the project. An investigation of the job site by the highway department revealed Mr. Scowden had not turned over the first spade of dirt.

Mr. Scowden had been found in the Bahamas and taken into custody, though the three hundred thousand dollars of taxpayers' money was missing. Mr. Scowden was making no comment except to say he had no idea what had happened to the money.

"In a related story," the smiling morning anchor continued, "the law offices of Bennis, Banociac, and Weiss were broken into

Saturday night, though it is unclear what the perpetrator was after."

Christy's throat closed as a picture of the downtown office building came onto the screen.

"Bennis, Banociac, and Weiss represents Mr. Scowden's contracting company," the anchor went on to explain. "The perpetrator left behind a pair of keys allegedly used to enter the sixth floor offices. Security cameras captured images of the man entering and exiting the building. If anyone knows anything that may lead to the arrest and conviction of..."

Christy stared at a fuzzy security camera image of a tall man in dark clothes getting off the same elevator she used every day. Elapsed time footage showed someone, who looked to be the same man, reenter the elevator a few minutes later. He was careful to keep his shoulders hunched and a dark ball cap pulled low over his face. Something about the way the man carried himself seemed vaguely familiar. Looking down on the man before the elevator doors slid shut struck a chord in Christy. In a flash, she saw Sean loping down her apartment stairs Saturday afternoon after spending the night in her arms.

Then she remembered something else. He had been particularly interested in Peter Scowden. Had he ever represented a team of investors interested in Mr. Scowden's company?

She raced to the bedroom and overturned her purse onto the bed. The key ring that held her car and apartment keys rattled against a compact and her wallet. She stared at the jumbled pile on the bed, the missing item glaringly apparent.

She kept her keys to the firm's file room on a separate key ring in her pocket while she was at work. The room was locked at all times unless someone from the firm was in there. When anyone entered or exited the room, they locked the room behind them. Christy kept her purse locked in her desk drawer, and it was inconvenient to carry a heavy key ring around all day in a skirt pocket.

As if on automatic pilot, she finished getting dressed. All the way to work, she tried to convince herself she had left the keys laying somewhere in the office Friday. Losing keys was a major offense, but it didn't compare to letting her boyfriend take them out of her purse and use them to break into the file room.

As soon as she stepped off the elevator, she knew she had not left her keys in the office on Friday.

June at the front desk said Mr. Banociac wanted to see her immediately. She knew she might as well clean out her desk.

After she was fired, she spent the rest of the week in her bathrobe in front of the television waiting for the news. Her worst fears had been realized. It took several days, but the whole story finally came out.

Sean had lied about everything, even his name. In truth he was David Scowden; Peter Scowden was his father's cousin. Sean, or David, never worked for an investment broker… He was a small time crook who discovered his cousin had worked out what looked to be the perfect scam.

The only problem for Peter was disappearing after committing his crime so he could collect the accumulated three hundred thousand dollars. That was easier said than done, especially since he had family and ties to the community.

Sean had none of those hindrances weighing him down. All he needed was a way into Peter's accounts. That's where Christy came in. He emptied the accounts as Peter was being indicted and disappeared, leaving his cousin to take the fall.

It was not a coincidence he ran into Christy outside the restaurant that day.

How could she have been so blind? To add insult to injury, after being relieved of her duties by Mr. Banociac, Christy went home to discover her own savings and checking accounts had been wiped out. Apparently three hundred thousand dollars wasn't enough to satisfy the likes of Sean Hatcher.

⚖

"Ooh, look at this one, Jamie. What do you think?" Karen Swayne pushed the magazine under Jamie Steele's nose.

Jamie pushed her dark hair behind one ear and looked away from the magazine she had been studying to see the one Karen indicated. Her hair was at an awkward length, and she couldn't do anything with it. She wanted to let it grow out for the wedding—an event for which a date had not been set—but she didn't know if she'd have the patience to wait that long. She'd cut most of her length off three years ago, and had even adopted a Dorothy Hamill wedge when they were all the rage last winter. Short hair was much more practical for a young woman with a busy lifestyle, but part of her enjoyed the romantic notion of pulling her long dark hair into some sort of flowing hairstyle for her wedding.

She had returned home from college Thursday evening after her last class of the week and was looking forward to a three-day weekend with her family. She was in her third year of college, and her groom-to-be, in his last year. There was so much to do with planning a wedding and considering life as Eric's wife, she had a hard time concentrating on her studies. It was hard enough at college where she didn't have to field questions from her family. Now that she was back in Jenna's Creek, all she could think about was the wedding.

"Oh, Karen, I love it," she said breathlessly. "But look at the price. I'll never be able to talk Grandma Cory and Uncle Justin into spending that much for a dress."

Jamie's grandparents lived on disability insurance and a small income from a farm outside of town. They couldn't afford a big fancy wedding even if her Uncle Justin pitched in and paid for most of it like he promised he would.

Karen slapped the bottom of the page, covering the price with her hand. "The prices don't mean anything. We're just looking in these catalogs for ideas and styles you like. Then we'll go to the city to one of those discount outlets and get the same dress for a fraction of the price."

Jamie grimaced. "Even a fraction is more money than we have."

"It's only money," Karen reminded her. "This will be your only wedding. The last thing you want to do is look back on pictures of you wearing a dress you settled for."

Easy for you to say, Jamie thought. She knew without asking what Grandma Cory would say about spending so much money on a dress she would wear once. Even if her grandmother told her money was no object, her own practical nature balked at paying the price of a good used car for a wedding gown.

She moaned and pushed the magazine away from her. "This is getting too complicated. Maybe we'll just elope."

"If you do, I'll never forgive you," Christy exclaimed from her side of the table. "I want to see my baby brother get married."

"Me, too." Karen patted Jamie's hand. "It's complicated but worth it. Don't let the cost and all the work rob you of enjoying your moment in the sun. You're the bride, Jamie. For a brief instant, the whole world will revolve around you. Believe me, it won't last, and it will never happen again. Relax and enjoy it."

Jamie wasn't exactly comforted. All she could think of was how much it was all going to cost, and how her family did not have that kind of money to spend.

Christy turned the magazine around to face her and flipped a few pages. "We need to start taking notes. There are so many more details besides what you'll wear. You need a date, or at least a season. Do you want an off the shoulder summer number or long sleeves and a train? What kind of flowers do you like? If you're thinking of Christmas, you could go with poinsettias, holly, and ivy. The church would be gorgeous. Your bridesmaids could wear alternating red and green. Or in the spring, you could change the color scheme to blues, greens, and yellow. If you wait until the summer after Eric graduates, you'll have more time to plan and save money..."

Jamie dropped her face into her hands. She exhaled between her fingers before she looked back up. "This is too much. I don't like complicated. I want something simple." She turned to Karen. "I know you think I'll regret it if I don't make a big production of this, but all this planning is robbing me of the fun of it. I imagine myself in a garden under a rose arbor in a simple white dress, holding a simple bouquet of white roses, with just a small crowd of family and some friends. Then afterwards, we could move over to the yard where there will be a few round tables and white folding chairs and a simple rose centerpiece on each table. We'll eat some food, unwrap a few gifts, send everybody home, and get on with the honeymoon."

Christy slapped the table. "Sounds like a plan. See how easy that was."

Karen nodded. "A garden with a rose arbor means June."

Jamie wrinkled her nose. "June. That's so far away."

"But that'll give you eight months to save money and get all those annoying little details worked out. And Mom'll be happy if it's after graduation. So will your grandma."

"I guess it is the most practical choice," she said without conviction.

"You just can't keep your hands off my little brother." Christy winked.

Jamie turned pink.

"Christy!" Karen shrieked.

"Oh, give me a break. We're adults here." Reading their shocked expressions, she changed the subject. "Back to the money issue. Jamie, I agree with Karen. Now is not the time to pinch pennies. You should have the wedding of your dreams."

"But I have to be practical," Jamie defended herself. "I have no choice."

Christy cocked an eyebrow. "Not necessarily. You have all the money you need at your disposal if you'll ask for it."

Jamie knit her brows together in confusion. She turned to Karen who looked as if she had already figured out what Christy was getting at.

"Well, why not?" Christy snapped at her sister. "Don't you think he owes it to them? He never paid a dime of child support. We know he can afford it."

"Christy, no!" Karen exclaimed, her face going red.

"He owes Eric," Christy declared. "He owes all of us. Let him open that wallet and pay for what he's done."

Karen pushed away from the table and stood up. "No, it's wrong. I don't want any of his money. We'll look like gold diggers. Everybody's already talking about Mom. Do you want them to say she's trying to benefit financially from the situation?"

"Oh, get over it, Karen. Who cares what people say. They're going to say whatever they want anyway. And this isn't about us or Mom. Eric and Jamie shouldn't have to scrimp on their wedding when he can afford to pay for whatever they want."

Slowly, realization of what the two sisters were arguing about dawned on Jamie. She held both hands up in front of her. "Wait one minute. If you're talking about what I think you're talking about, I'm putting an end to it right now. No way am I letting Noel Wyatt pay for my wedding. The bride's family pays. Anything else would be charity. I do have some pride, you know. Besides, he's not even…family," she finished weakly.

Christy was too confident that she was right to consider the other woman's feelings. "*Traditionally,* the bride's family pays. But those old fashioned notions are being pushed aside, Jamie. Plenty of couples pay for their own weddings fifty-fifty without any input from either partner's relatives. Believe me keeping up with tradition can be nothing but a big hassle. I say if one side can afford it, let them pay. In this case, we have someone who can pay and then some. You shouldn't let your pride keep you from having your dream wedding. Maybe he even wants to help out, but doesn't know how to approach you or Eric. And whether or not any of us want to admit it, Noel is family to Eric. He's got off scot-free long enough, if you ask me."

"Nobody asked you, did they?" Karen exclaimed.

Christy started to say something to Karen, but Jamie jumped to her feet. Hot tears stung the back of her eyelids. She gathered the bridal magazines to her side of the table and started turning them right side up and stacking them on top of each other. She swallowed hard and forced herself to look at Christy. She hated confrontation, especially with a future sister-in-law she barely knew, but Christy was way out of line.

"Christy, I won't let you use my wedding to settle some vendetta you have with Noel."

Christy gasped. "That's not what I'm doing."

Jamie went on as if she hadn't spoken. "He's my boss and a friend, that's all. What's between he and Eric doesn't concern me, at least not yet. And it doesn't concern you either." She picked the magazines up off the table and held them to her chest. Tears still threatened, but she held them in check. She took a deep breath and continued. "It would break my grandmother's and my uncle's hearts if I told them what they could afford wasn't good enough for me. I've economized and made do my entire life, and I never thought my wedding would be any different. It doesn't matter who can afford what. All that matters is my family, we stand by tradition. You're right; this wedding is about Eric and me. We'll do things our way, or they won't get done. I appreciate your help, but we're not taking money from Noel Wyatt or anyone else."

She turned to Karen. "Thanks for going over this stuff with me and pointing out some things about the date. I'll keep it in mind."

She turned on her heel and left.

Karen turned to Christy and glared at her.

"What?"

"From now on, if we want any opinions out of you, we'll ask for them."

Chapter Thirteen

C hristy wasn't wrong. Everyone else was letting their stubborn pride make their decisions for them. If Jamie and her family would only hear her out and think about what she was saying, they would see that her way was not only reasonable, but practical as well. Noel Wyatt was Eric's father; the fact was undisputed. He hadn't paid a cent in raising Eric in twenty-two years, unless Abby had more secrets in her closet that she hadn't yet disclosed. If Jamie and Eric wanted a big wedding but couldn't afford one, what would be so wrong in letting Noel toss in a couple thousand bucks? She knew he had a soft spot for Jamie, and he *owed* it to Eric.

She hadn't meant to hurt Jamie's feelings, nor had she suggested Noel pay for the wedding so she could extract her pound of flesh for what he had done to her family. Yes, she was angry. The man was a big hypocrite for letting the world think he was some sort of wonderful philanthropist when all the while he had gotten another man's wife pregnant.

Her feelings toward him and the situation were irrelevant when it came to asking him to help pay for Jamie and Eric's wedding. He owed it to them. He could afford a big wedding, Jamie's family could not—plain and simple.

She got back into Abby's car and headed across town. By the time she reached the intersection at the center of town, she knew she was doing the right thing. Noel needed to be brought up to speed. He probably hadn't even thought about how Eric and Jamie would pay for their wedding. Men didn't think about things like that. She doubted he knew what wedding dresses and reception halls were going for these days. If the situation were presented to him in a reasonable manner, he would realize it was his duty, even if the rest of the family was too timid to point it out to him.

She saw an empty parking space close to the side entrance of the store and pulled her car into it. She turned off the ignition and stared at the glass door, willing him to come out. Her nerve faltered. Maybe this wasn't any of her business. How Jamie and Eric paid for their wedding was no concern of hers. Why should she stick her neck out to make a request of a man she didn't know when they didn't want to accept his money? Why did she care so much if Noel did the right thing or not?

Stop being a baby, Christy, she scolded herself. *If you don't ask, no one else will.*

Any other father would pay for his son's wedding if the bride's family couldn't afford to. It was common courtesy. She was sick to death of old fashioned notions. The next thing Jamie would suggest would be that her family present the Blackwoods with a pig, two goats, and a chicken for a dowry. What was she, a piece of property to be bartered over?

This was ridiculous. Christy slapped the steering wheel and pulled her keys out of the ignition. She wasn't doing anything wrong. The least she could do was bring Noel abreast of the situation and then let him decide for himself what, if anything, he should do about it. She got out of the car and tucked her keys into her front pocket. She strode purposefully to the side entrance before she could lose her nerve.

"Aunt Paige, I don't have anything to say to the man."

Paige Trotter gritted her teeth in frustration. One more minute with Calvin under her roof and she would go stark raving mad.

She had been pressuring Calvin for the last week to go to the drugstore and talk to Noel about a job. It was all over the drugstore that Angie's husband had been transferred to his company's Oak Ridge, Tennessee plant, and she would be leaving at the end of the year. Now was the time for Calvin to go to Noel and apply for the assistant's position. Before she left, Angie could train him to take her place. By then he would be ready to step into her position.

As usual, Calvin was stonewalling her. He seemed perfectly satisfied to spend the rest of his life sitting on her couch watching television.

"You're going to get off your lazy backside and go down to that drugstore and demand that Noel give you a job."

"And why would he do that?" Calvin whined in a voice that reminded Paige of Howard.

"Because I've seen the applicants who've been in there. Not a one of them have your qualifications. You could make something of yourself, Calvin, if you just had a little gumption."

Calvin straightened his shoulders and looked up at her. "I don't want to spend my life in this town, drying up in that wretched drugstore," he said, sounding surer of himself than she thought he was able. "I'm a song writer, Aunt Paige. I'm going to go to Nashville and become famous."

It took a moment for her to recover. She had never heard anything so preposterous in her life—and from Calvin of all people. Unfortunately she didn't have all day to point out the holes in his half-baked plan. "Nashville? What do they need with another out of work songwriter? They already have enough waiters and bathroom attendants."

"What makes you so sure I'd be out of work?"

She gave her head a slow shake. "In the first place," she said slowly in case he had trouble wrapping his brain around her words, "the only successful songwriters are also singers. We all know you couldn't carry a tune if it had a handle. And in the second place, why for the love of Mike, did you take all those classes if you weren't going to become a pharmacist?"

"Because Mom, Dad, and you have been hassling me as long as I can remember to do what you want. The only way Dad would pay for my schooling was if I took the classes he wanted me to take. He doesn't know I also took some drama and creative writing courses on his nickel. Besides, who says I can't sing."

Paige crossed her arms over her chest and gazed down at him. "Well, if that caterwauling you've been doing around here the last few months is any indication of your talent, I say it. You'd best put your head on straight and get downtown and apply for that job. Don't worry, if anybody from Nashville shows up looking for you, I'll tell them where they can find you." She cackled at her own joke.

She didn't notice the disgust in Calvin's face as he stood up and pushed past her on his way upstairs to change into his only suit and tie. He would show her. He would show all of them. He had no intention of going to work behind a pharmacy counter. But if going along with whatever his aunt said kept him here a little longer, so be it. He had things to take care of before he made his grand exit.

Christy was so intent on her mission to confront Noel Wyatt, regardless of what her family thought, she didn't notice the man in the suit barreling down the sidewalk, headed for the same entrance as she. She saw a flash of dark clothing a moment before his body crashed into hers.

She cried out and jumped backward, stumbling over an uneven piece of concrete sidewalk. The man grabbed her arm to steady her. Christy regained her balance and jerked herself free.

"Don't touch me," she shrieked. "Get away from me."

The man held his hands up in front of him and backed up a step. "All right. I'm sorry. I didn't see you there."

Christy felt like her heart was pounding a thousand beats per minute. Even though she knew she had overreacted, she was having a hard time catching her breath. Her head was spinning. She needed to sit down. She put her hand over her heart and exhaled slowly to steady herself. "Okay, I'm fine," she said aloud, though more to herself than the man in front of her. To him, she said, "Just...just leave me alone." She turned toward her mother's car and again lost her balance. She wondered if people knew what was about to happen the moment before they blacked out.

"Excuse me, miss. Are you all right?" the man said.

A hand grabbed her shoulder. She ducked out from under it and spun around to face him, her head spinning like a top. "I said, don't touch me." She backed away, keeping her eyes on him until her legs came into contact with the bumper of the car. The man looked familiar, though she couldn't remember if she'd actually seen him before or if her mind was playing tricks on her.

Confusion darkened his handsome features. It was apparent by the look on his face he had no idea what he'd done to elicit such a response.

"Okay, okay, I'm sorry." He took a step farther back. "I didn't mean to upset you."

Christy's pulse began to slow to its normal rhythm. She put her hand to the side of her head. Her face was on fire. A natural redhead with fair skin and freckles, her face always betrayed her emotions. Anytime she laughed too hard, became anxious, scared, embarrassed, and especially when she became angry, her cheeks turned scarlet red. It made her the brunt of teasing all through school. The more the boys teased her about it, the redder she got, until she either burst into tears or lashed out at one of them. That always made the situation worse.

She could imagine what she looked like now, standing in front of a complete stranger, flushed and sweaty and screaming like a madwoman. He probably thought she was some kind of freak, possibly a dangerous one. People bumped into her all the time on the sidewalks in the city. It never bothered her before. Why was she suddenly so paranoid?

She took a shuddering breath as she fumbled inside her purse for the keys to her mother's car. "You didn't upset me," she said, though visibly upset.

"If you're sure you're all right..." he asked cautiously.

"I said I'm fine," she said testily to cover her embarrassment. It was evident he had never posed any real threat. What was happening to her? She was falling apart.

"Wait a minute," the man said, holding up a hand again. His brown eyes narrowed. "Have we met? Don't I know you from somewhere?"

So she wasn't wrong. She had seen him before. It was comforting to know she hadn't completely lost her mind.

Suddenly he snapped his fingers. His handsome face split into a smile. "Now, I remember. You were at Noel Wyatt's house last week. I didn't get a chance to introduce myself then, either."

She stopped fumbling with the car keys and gave him her full attention. Now she remembered him, too. He was the young man who pulled into Noel's driveway as she was leaving. She had barely looked at him then, in too big of a hurry to leave, but it was definitely the same man. She couldn't help noticing that he had nice eyes, piercing and gentle at the same time. His mouth was nicely shaped under a straight nose and almond shaped brown eyes. She disliked him instantly. He was probably like every other good-looking guy on the planet; used to getting his way with women.

She forced herself to take another deep breath. She clasped her hands around the car keys, hoping he wouldn't notice how badly they were shaking. "Yes, I seem to remember we almost ran into each other that day, too." Her lips twitched in an effort to smile.

He smiled back apparently relieved she wasn't going to mace him or yell for the police. "My apologies." He stuck out his hand and took a hesitant step toward her. "Jarrod Bruckner."

Christy stared at his outstretched hand for a moment before realizing she was supposed to shake it. She winced inwardly at the spectacle she had made of herself. After all her years of living alone, she was pretty good at determining the difference between a real threat and an imagined one. Apparently her encounter with Stanley had thrown off her judgment. She transferred the keys to her left hand, made a quick swipe down the side of her pants with her right palm to dry off any perspiration and took his.

"Christy Blackwood."

"Nice to meet you, Christy."

"Um, I'm really sorry about…that." She made a motion with her hand. "I'm not usually so jumpy."

"No, it was clearly my fault," he said generously. "I should have been watching where I was going. I didn't hurt you or anything, did I?"

"Oh, no, it isn't that." She couldn't very well explain that she had imagined him knocking her down and stealing what little dignity she had left. She needed to say something, but any intelligible explanation eluded her. Then again, what did she care what he thought? She would never see him again, and he was probably a jerk anyway. She stepped off the curb between her mother's car and the one beside it. "I should really be going…"

She definitely couldn't go into the drugstore and face Noel now.

"Okay, sure," Jarrod said. "Um, Christy, the least I can do is buy you a cup of coffee to make amends for startling you."

"Oh, no, that's not necessary," she said, too quickly, and then checked her voice. There was no need to be rude. "I—uh, have an appointment I need to get to."

"Okay, another time then."

"Sure," she said, not meaning it.

She could see on his face he knew she was giving him the brush-off. "Thanks anyway, Jarrod," she said, managing some sincerity this time. "Some other time," she added, not meaning *this* part.

"Sure," he said. "Nice meeting you, Christy."

"You, too." She opened the car door and ducked inside before he had a chance to say anything else. It took several attempts for her shaking fingers to slide the key into the ignition. She sensed him watching her. After she started the engine, she looked up, but he was gone.

A trickle of perspiration ran down her back. Her hands were still shaking. Tears threatened to erupt any minute. She needed to get home before she had a total breakdown. She was a basket case; all because two psychos had broken into her motel room and stolen everything she had. When would she get past this? It had only been a couple of weeks, but she didn't like feeling this way. She was used to being in control. Truth be told, she hadn't been in control of anything since Sean Hatcher entered her life.

While Calvin waited at the main intersection in his old Pontiac, he saw a well-dressed man collide with a pretty redhead on the sidewalk in front of the pharmacy's side entrance. It looked like an innocent incident to him, but the woman appeared shook up. He thought about pulling into the empty parking space three slots down and offering his assistance, but by then the situation had defused itself. He would only make a fool of himself anyway. Guys like the one on the sidewalk never needed help explaining their intentions to women. Only short, chubby men who looked like Calvin, with his coke-bottle glasses and overbite ever had to explain what he was doing, attempting to talk to someone like the redhead.

No, Calvin's talents were better served on the printed page. He could be a ladies man, a wounded cowboy, or anyone he chose. He never had to see the disappointment, or worse, the disgust on a pretty girl's face when he tapped her on the shoulder and she turned around to see *him* standing there. That was how he liked it.

He hadn't pointed it out to Aunt Paige, but he happened to have quite an accomplished singing voice. He was always a favorite among his music and choir teachers. He remembered a teachers' conference when he was in the second or third grade at which a teacher told his parents he had real musical talent. She strongly suggested they enroll him in some kind of music classes, either voice or piano lessons. His father had snorted derisively, and his mother had tittered behind her hand. They told the teacher in no uncertain terms that money wouldn't be wasted on a trivial pursuit like learning the piano, especially for a boy, when it was virtually impossible to make a living at it.

From that moment on, Calvin kept his musical aspirations hidden. His family would never understand his need to express himself through the arts. Quietly he studied what he loved and played around with the songs in his head. Before admitting as much to Aunt Paige, no one knew he dreamed of making a living with his music.

He shouldn't have opened his big mouth. Now he'd never hear the end of it. She'd tell his mother who would in turn tell Dad, and the ribbing and cajoling would start all over again. He had to get out of this backwater town.

He stole a glance at the bank clock as he turned the corner. 10:35. Aunt Paige didn't have to be at work until noon. That gave him a little over an hour to kill before he could go back to the house and what occupied his time when she was out—finding her money. His aunt trusted no one, including the banks. That would be her downfall. He had found her savings and checking passbooks last week. She only had four hundred dollars in checking and a little over two thousand in savings. Even if she invested some—which he seriously doubted—a large portion of her money had to be hidden somewhere in that house.

He had already sold a few poems and submitted a couple of songs to a publishing company in Nashville. Aunt Paige was right; it would take a lot more than a few songs sold to some big name artists to get rich. He needed a nice little nest egg so he wouldn't have to wait tables and scrub toilets, as she had so eloquently put it, until he had made a name for himself. He knew where that nest egg could be found. He didn't plan to take the whole stash. Just enough to get by until the songs started paying off and he could land himself a singing gig or two. Aunt Paige didn't need the money. She'd end up sitting on it until she died the way Uncle

Howard had done. Then her own worthless relatives, who never had anything to do with her as far as he could tell, would swoop in and pick her bones clean; might as well put some of it to good use now.

Calvin wasn't blowing smoke when he said he had no intention of gathering dust in that drugstore the rest of his life. The Lord helps those who help themselves his mother was fond of saying. Well, he'd help himself to some of Aunt Paige's money and hope the Lord understood his motives.

Chapter Fourteen

J arrod had spoken to nearly everyone on the list of names Noreen Trimble gave him, yet he was no closer to figuring out who called Noel Wyatt's house the morning after her attack. There was still the possibility the call was a hoax. There was no witness to the fight that led to Sally Blake's death, and the people he had questioned truly knew nothing about it.

No one had been able to substantiate the rumor that Sally was seeing a married man, although several sources believed she was. Jarrod was beginning to believe that rumor was true. A married man made perfect sense.

Still, after all his questions and investigation, he felt like he was hitting his head against a brick wall.

If Noel's caller was a married man, he had the most logical reason not to come forward with what he saw. Even nearly thirty years after the fact, a man with a wife and family, and possibly a standing in the community, would not want to admit he had been wooing a twenty-year-old girl. No matter how much time had passed, it would be uncomfortable trying to explain to a wife that he had witnessed the death of the girl he was seeing.

Jarrod couldn't shake the notion that the man who called Noel was none other than Tim Shelton. Tim worked for the dead girl's father and might be rue to admit to the world and his boss that

Sally Blake had instigated the fight that led to her death, or worse, he was guilty of killing her.

Upon hearing Noel's version of his visit with Tim last week, doubts had been planted in Jarrod's head that Noreen was the one to commit the crime. Every time Tim's name came up in Noreen's presence, Jarrod sensed strong emotion on her part. She was still in love with the man. What about Tim? Had he allowed Noreen to take the blame for Sally's death in order to protect him? Had he come back that night, possibly to defend himself against Sally's allegations, and ended up killing her? Maybe he and Noreen were in on it together.

Jarrod couldn't bring himself to believe Noreen was involved in any sort of conspiracy, but stranger things had happened in the name of love. What if the two of them killed Sally together and came up with a way to cover the crime?

After Sally's remains were found, Noreen was still so madly in love with Tim, she decided to take the blame herself. Tim had more to lose than she, and she cared too much for him to bring him down with her. But why would the caller tell Noel Noreen had killed Sally in self-defense? And if Jarrod's suspicions were close to the truth and Tim was the real killer, why would he call Noel and raise all these questions that would point to him? As long as Noreen was behind bars, he was off the hook. The same was true if the caller had been an anonymous prowler. No would-be burglar would come forward after thirty years to say that while in the process of breaking into a house, he had witnessed a murder.

The more Jarrod thought about it, the more uncertain he became. He was almost ready to tell his father to forget it; there was no point in trying to get Noreen Trimble out of prison if she was happy taking the blame for a crime she didn't commit. Let her stay there. But deep down, he knew Noreen didn't belong in prison. Whether she was covering for someone else or had killed Sally in self-defense, she was innocent of the murder charge she pled guilty to. He had to do something to get her out of there; if not for her own sake, for the sake of her family and friends.

After going over Noreen's list for the fortieth time, he realized he'd save himself a lot of grief by going to Tim Shelton himself. He called Blake Realty, identified himself to Mr. Shelton allowing him to draw his own conclusions, and made an appointment to see him. Tim had a client in another part of the county and said he could meet Jarrod for lunch in Blanton instead of Jenna's Creek.

Jarrod readily agreed and cleared his day's schedule. He would do almost anything to make sure Tim Shelton had no excuse to back out of the meeting. He was more than a little anxious to meet the man. During his forty minute ride to Auburn County from Portsmouth, he couldn't help but wonder if there was a reason Tim didn't want to be seen anywhere near Jenna's Creek with him. Was he less than anxious to be seen with the lawyer representing Noreen Trimble? What did he have to hide?

Jarrod had used his unexpected free morning to touch base with Noel Wyatt, or at least that had been his intention. After practically running over Christy Blackwood in front of the store, he found it hard to concentrate on anything useful Noel might tell him about Tim before their meeting.

He was supposed to be thinking of Noreen Trimble and what she might be covering up in Sally Blake's murder. That's what Dad was paying him for. Instead, he couldn't get Christy out of his head. At first he had been annoyed and confused that she went ballistic on him for bumping into her on the street. It had been as much her fault as it was his. But as he watched her fumble with her car keys after she got into her car, he couldn't help wondering what her story was. The first time he encountered her at Noel's she was brusque and preoccupied there, too. Something was up with her, and he couldn't stop himself from wondering what it was. He almost asked Noel about her when he went to the drugstore, but decided Noel would think him definitely too young and immature to be handling Noreen's case. He'd already gotten the impression that was exactly what Noel thought.

Still, as he drove through Auburn County, he wondered about Christy. It was more than just her looks; he came across attractive women everyday. He wanted to get to know her in spite of—or possibly because of—the vibe she gave off that she wasn't interested. It wasn't often he didn't get at least a once over upon meeting a woman. He had received enough positive affirmation since the onset of puberty to know the opposite sex found him mildly attractive.

He told himself to stop wasting his time thinking about her and focus on Noreen's case. A woman did not fit into his plans right now, especially one as jumpy as a scared rabbit, who he couldn't even talk into joining him for coffee. He didn't have time in his life for added complications.

Tim Shelton was waiting when Jarrod pulled into the parking lot of the Highway 68 Diner just outside the Blanton city limits. Tim climbed out of a newer model Grand Marquis and absently patted his shirt pocket, then dropped his arm back to his side. Jarrod pulled into the vacant spot next to him and turned off the engine. Always the salesman, Tim came around the car with his arm extended. "Mr. Bruckner, I presume."

Jarrod hurriedly slammed the door of his car, which was considerably smaller and older than Tim's, and shook his offered hand. "Yes, nice to meet you, Mr. Shelton."

"You, too." Tim released his hand and stepped back. "Are you hungry? They cook a mean hot shot here."

Jarrod cocked an eyebrow.

Tim laughed and explained. "Its roast beef on white bread cut down the middle, with a pile of mashed potatoes between the two halves, and the whole thing's smothered in brown gravy."

"Where I come from, those are called short-orders."

"Anyway you slice it." Tim put a hand on Jarrod's back and steered him toward the door.

Jarrod immediately sensed Tim was trying to gain control of the situation. Underneath Tim's bravado was a fear that Jarrod would ask questions he had spent thirty years trying to avoid.

Inside the restaurant, Tim waved at a waitress and motioned to a table. The waitress nodded in response, and he steered Jarrod in that direction. "Let's go ahead and order," Tim said without looking at a menu. "Sometimes the service is slow."

"I can see why," Jarrod said, looking around diner's small interior. Every stool at the counter and nearly every table were occupied. He plucked a menu from its position between the napkin holder and the wall.

A different waitress set two glasses of water in front of them and took her pencil from behind her ear. "Are you up for the hot shot?" Tim asked Jarrod.

Jarrod closed the menu and shook his head. "I'll have a fish sandwich, a side salad, and iced tea."

Tim looked apologetically at the waitress and ordered a hot shot for himself. After she moved away from the table, Jarrod spoke first. "I don't want to waste a lot of your time, Mr. Shelton."

Tim held up one hand. "Tim. Please."

Jarrod clenched his teeth against his impatience. He had not come hear to make a friend. "Okay. Tim," he started over. "We're both busy men with plenty of better things to do than sit in a restaurant and make small talk. I believe, along with everyone in my firm, that Noreen Trimble does not belong in prison. If she killed Sally Blake, it was in self-defense as she contends." He leaned forward and fixed his gaze on Tim. "Or possibly she did not cause Ms. Blake's death, and she's covering up for the person who did."

Just as he suspected, Tim Shelton averted his eyes. When he looked back at Jarrod, he attempted a smile. "If she's covering up for someone that would involve lying—Noreen doesn't lie."

"You're not the first person who's told me that."

Tim took a sip of the iced water, allowing a chip of crushed ice between his teeth. He chewed it with relish. After swallowing, he said. "Everyone loves Noreen. She's a good person."

"So good someone would take advantage of her?"

Tim jiggled his water glass, his eyes riveted on the ice cubes inside. "I don't know who would do something like that to her."

"I don't know either, Mr. Shelton." Jarrod wasn't comfortable calling Tim by his first name. He didn't trust the guy. "As you probably know, Noel Wyatt is a very good friend of Ms. Trimble's. He is determined to see her acquitted. He told me about his meeting with you last week."

Tim took another sip of water. Jarrod doubted he was a very good salesman. He couldn't cover his own anxiety. A mediocre defense attorney would tear him to shreds on the witness stand. Jarrod would love to have a crack at him.

"All I know about the case is what Noreen wrote in her report to the police," Tim said.

"I'm sure Mr. Wyatt told you about a phone call he got the morning after Noreen was stabbed in prison. The one where someone claimed to know of a witness to the events that led to Ms. Blake's death."

Tim was having a hard time meeting his eyes again. "Yes, he told me about that."

Jarrod leaned forward and rested his elbows on the table, forcing Tim to look him in the eye. "We must find out the identity of this witness. It is imperative we talk to him or her. His testimony is Noreen's only shot at a new trial. And we at my law firm are confident that as soon as that happens, she will be acquitted."

"Like I told Noel, I don't know anything about a witness."

Jarrod opened his mouth to ask another question. He had learned the longer he kept a witness dodging questions and running in circles to defend himself, the sooner he talked himself into a corner. But over Tim's shoulder, he saw the waitress approaching the table. He closed his mouth and waited. After she put the food down and moved away, he allowed Tim a few minutes to get into his lunch and lower his guard. They talked a while about things other than the case.

Then casually, Jarrod asked, "Had you heard anything about Sally Blake being involved with a married man?"

If it was possible to choke on mashed potatoes, Tim Shelton nearly did so. "That wasn't true," he said after forcing down a mouthful of food. He took a careful sip of his iced tea, and the color slowly returned to his round cheeks. "That was a rumor a lot of jealous people made up about Sally."

Jarrod nodded thoughtfully. "What reason did they have to be jealous of her?"

Tim lifted one shoulder. "You know how people are," he said vaguely, and then filled his mouth again. Jarrod didn't respond. After a moment, Tim expounded. "Sally was a beautiful woman and she knew it. She wasn't exactly as..." he twisted his mouth as he searched for a word "...sweet as Noreen. Lots of people didn't like her, especially other women. I think Noreen was her only girl-friend. Of course, Noreen saw the good in everybody."

"What about you, Mr. Shelton? Did you see the good in her?"

Tim's face hardened. "I don't know what you're getting at."

"I have it under good authority you had an affair with Sally Blake."

Tim pushed his plate back and glared across the table at Jarrod. "Who told you that?"

"Does it matter?"

Tim continued to glare at Jarrod, and then his expression softened. "That was a mistake I made in my youth. I loved Noreen, but Sally was... persuasive. No, I'm sorry. I won't put the blame on her, but it was a mistake I would appreciate you not going out of your way to make public. I have a wife and family that I don't want to see hurt."

"Surely they wouldn't hold something like that against you. It was over long before you married Mrs. Shelton. Right?"

Tim patted his shirt pocket again before dropping his hand back to the table. "Of course, but that doesn't matter. I should've known better. I'm ashamed of myself that I didn't."

Jarrod could see the meeting was about over. He still didn't know what he came here for. He pushed his plate toward the center of the table and leaned forward onto his elbows. "Look, Mr. Shelton, the only two people I can see who would have a reason to fear coming forward to help Noreen Trimble are this married man who may or may not exist, and you. If you came back the night of the party to maybe confess your sins to Noreen or tell Sally she was a mistake you'd rather forget, and you saw something that might get Noreen another trial, you've got to put it on the table. I know you don't want to cause any trouble with the missus by bringing up this ugly matter after all these years, but if you care about Noreen at all, you'll want to see she gets a new trial. And if you know anything about another man Sally may have been seeing, you need to let me know that too. Maybe this man is like you and doesn't want to hurt the people in his life. He's probably as ashamed as you are. He might have a lot more to lose if his affair with a young girl were to become public. But you've got to think of Noreen. She doesn't deserve to die in that prison."

Jarrod had been so enraptured in his plea to get Tim Shelton to do the right thing he hadn't seen the waitress approach the table. "Could I get either of you some dessert?" she asked in a voice that belied the fact she'd overheard at least part of his words. "The lemon meringue is delicious."

"No, thank you," Jarrod said, shaking his head. Tim stared glumly at the center of the table and didn't respond.

"Okay," she said, casting a questioning look to the top of Tim's head. He was usually one of her more talkative customers. She tore their receipt off her pad and placed it facedown on the table. "You two have a nice day."

Both men waited until she moved out of earshot. Jarrod palmed the receipt with one hand and extracted a business card from his shirt pocket with the other. "If you think of anything, Mr. Shelton, that could help Noreen, or if someone comes to mind who may know something, we would all appreciate it if you give us a call."

Tim patted his shirt pocket again and then hissed an oath under his breath. "Sorry about that. I'm trying to quit smoking and not having much luck." He gave Jarrod a weak smile. "Yeah, sure, if I think of anything, I'll call you. I do care about Noreen, Mr.

Bruckner. After Sally disappeared, I knew something was wrong. I guess I was afraid to find out what. I kind of figured Sally told her about us, and I was afraid to get close to her. I've never been good at confrontation." Then he clamped his mouth shut as if he couldn't believe he'd confided so much to a defense attorney.

"I understand, Mr. Shelton." Jarrod slid to the edge of the booth and stood up. "Thanks for meeting me. I hope we talk again," he added, his voice pregnant with meaning.

Tim had his hand halfway to his empty shirt pocket again before he stopped himself and stretched it out toward Jarrod instead.

Jarrod shook it and then went to the counter to pay for their lunch. He didn't know anything more than he had when he sat down. All he knew for sure was that he was more convinced than ever Tim Shelton was hiding something.

"Tim, is that you?"

Tim dropped his car keys into the crystal dish on the entryway table and draped his suit jacket over the banister. The October afternoon had warmed up to the high seventies, and his shirt was soaked through with perspiration. He could almost kill somebody for a cigarette. Then he checked himself. Not a good thought so soon after meeting with Noreen's attorney.

Joyce appeared in the doorway between the kitchen and formal dining room. She wore a lime green dress with large white polka dots all over it. On her feet was a pair of green pumps with a white stripe and cutaway toes Tim had never seen before. Her hair was twisted into a neat French knot. She was either expecting guests or had just finished entertaining. He searched his mind to remember her schedule. On Friday afternoons, she had her bridge club over. He glanced at his watch. It was after two. They had probably already come and gone. He hoped he would be so lucky.

"What are you doing home so early?" she asked.

"I had a free calendar. Thought I might come home and spend some time with you."

She looked skeptical. "All right. I was straightening up the patio. I have some finger sandwiches left over from my bridge game. Are you hungry?"

The hot shot sat on his stomach like a ball of lead. "No, thanks, I'm fine."

Joyce smoothed her hands down the front of her dress. He never ceased to be amazed at her ability to keep a trim waistline after twenty-five years of marriage while he continued to soften and widen. She was secretly proud of the fact she still wore a size eight after five children and nearly fifty years of living. Of course it didn't hurt that she sneaked off to a fat farm in Virginia every few years where she ate bean sprouts and lemon wedges, took mud bathes, let attendants beat her with reeds, and occasionally had something nipped or tucked. She never admitted that part, even to Tim, as if he couldn't tell the difference.

Sometimes Tim wished she would relax and let nature take its course on her body as it inevitably would. He never said as much. She liked to think Virginia was only a formality, and her own sheer will kept her young and beautiful. Who was he to burst her bubble? The mirror would do that soon enough.

"Are you feeling all right, dear?" she said, sounding almost concerned. "You look a little out of sorts."

"Yes, I'm fine, just hot. It really warmed up out there today."

She set her mouth in a thin line. "If you'd lose a few pounds like the doctor said, you wouldn't get overheated so easily."

Tim wasn't in the mood for a lecture. "I quit the cigarettes, didn't I? It'd serve you right if I ballooned up fifty pounds."

She crossed her thin arms over her flat stomach. "Don't blame your thirty year smoking habit on me. Excuse me for wanting you around long enough to see your grandchildren."

Tim loosened his tie and unbuttoned the top button on his shirt. He rubbed the back of his neck. "I'm sorry, honey." He took a step toward her. "I'm just hot and cranky. I want a cigarette, and the last thing I need pointed out is my weight." He smiled conciliatorily and reached out to take hold of her arm.

Joyce spun around on her pretty green pumps and moved out of reach. "Go upstairs and take a shower. You've got time for a nap."

"Time?" he asked her retreating back.

"We've got dinner with the Blakes and the Hamiltons tonight at the club. Remember?" she said over her shoulder as she moved off toward the back of the house.

Tim groaned audibly although he was the only one left in the room to hear it. The last thing he wanted to do tonight was to listen to a lot of blustering and backbiting from his oldest and dearest friends and colleagues. He got enough of that at work. But he'd have better luck explaining to Joyce she was aging regardless of how much money and plastic she put into her body than tell her he would rather stay home. He took his jacket off the banister and trudged up the stairs to his bedroom.

"You didn't say two words to the Blakes tonight," Joyce admonished as she unzipped her dress and let it slip off her shoulders. She stepped out of it without letting it touch the floor and moved to the closet to retrieve a hanger. She would send it to the dry cleaner's tomorrow. Tim had told her over the years it wasn't necessary to launder a dress every time she took it off; dry cleaning wasn't free and it wore out the clothes, not to mention she didn't exactly get dirty sitting at the club sipping martinis. As usual, his input went in one ear and out the other. She accused him of being cheap at suggesting she wear soiled clothes. Finally he stopped voicing his opinions about pretty much anything.

"I told you earlier I was tired."

He heard a muffled snort from the closet. "Well, Donna Blake thought you were rude," she said when she stepped out of the closet. "I could see it all over her face."

Tim sat down on the bed to unlace his shoes. "I'll apologize the next time I see her," he said, a little out of breath from leaning over his stomach.

"No, that will only make matters worse. Just make an effort to be civil next time. It isn't anyone's fault you're tired. If you'd take better care of yourself…" Her statement trailed off, the remainder of the sentiment unnecessary.

He was relieved. He didn't want to hear another litany about his poor physical state. Joyce slid her slip down over her hips and tossed it into the hamper. When she disappeared back into the closet for her nightgown and robe, Tim stood up and went to the mirror over her dressing table. He leaned forward and stared at his reflection. His cheeks were red and puffy. He smoothed his hand over the top of his head, feeling more scalp than he had this time last year. He was falling apart while Joyce remained youthful and vibrant. He wondered what kept her around. She stepped out of the closet with a designer gown and robe over one arm.

Question asked and answered.

"What are you doing?" she asked on her way past him to the adjoining bathroom. "It's not time to color your hair already if that's what you're thinking."

Tim straightened up and watched her retreating back. When she was totally out of sight, he said, "Noel Wyatt came to see me in my office last week."

Joyce instantly appeared in the bathroom doorway, her eyes glittering with excitement. "Oh, really." Carefully, she brought her emotions under control. "How's he doing?" she asked casually.

"It's not what you think," he said, delighting in bursting her bubble. "He wanted to talk about Noreen Trimble."

Her eyes dimmed. She turned and headed back to the bathroom. "Why would he want to talk to you about her?"

Tim raised his voice to be heard over the rush of running water. "Noreen was stabbed in prison a couple weeks ago. She almost died."

Joyce turned off the tap and straightened up. She fumbled blindly for a hand towel and put it to her face. She patted it dry and then lowered the towel. "That's too bad," she said noncommittally. "But I don't see why Noel Wyatt thought he needed to bother you at work about it. You could have read it in the paper."

"I was engaged to Noreen when Sally Blake disappeared."

She glared at him. "I know that."

"He's trying to find evidence that'll get Noreen a new trial. He says she killed Sally Blake in self-defense, but needs to go in front of a jury to convince them."

"You don't kill someone in self-defense and hide the body for twenty-five years. No new evidence is going to convince a jury that a person capable of that should be let out of prison."

Tim leaned over and retrieved his shoes from the floor so she wouldn't see the pain in his face. He moved to the closet to put them away. "If there was an eye witness who saw what happened, she'd get a new trial."

Joyce stepped out of the bathroom and put one hand on her hip. She could model sleepwear on a runway in New York looking the way she did. "What eye witness?" she demanded. "Don't tell me Noreen is saying someone else was there when she murdered Sally. That doesn't make any sense."

Tim took an extra moment in shelving his shoes to let the ire at his wife's thoughtless remark fade away. When he came out of the closet, he said, "Noreen's not saying anything. Noel is the one doing all the legwork." He didn't mention the early morning caller.

"Well, the whole thing's ridiculous. And I don't appreciate Noel trying to involve you."

"If the case goes back to trial, I could be called to testify."

Joyce's face turned a ghostly pallor. "You? Why? What could you possibly have to contribute to the case?"

"No one understood the relationship between Sally and Noreen better than me, except of course the two women themselves. Noreen's attorney is under the impression I might know what caused the two of them to fight in the first place."

Suspicion marred Joyce's pretty features. "When did you talk to her attorney?"

Tim gulped. Nothing got past his darling wife. "Today. We met for lunch."

"And what did you tell him?"

Tim turned away, uncomfortable under her steely gaze. He hadn't said anything to the young lawyer, but Joyce made him feel like he had just sold his own children down the river. "I didn't tell him anything, but I could see how his brain is working. He figures I know more than I'm saying."

Joyce advanced and grabbed his arm, pulling him around to face her. "And do you?"

"I told you, I knew Sally and Noreen better than anyone. I knew what Sally was really like. I knew how she treated Noreen—how she treated everyone. I imagine the defense is thinking I'd make a pretty good witness when they try to prove Noreen was provoked into killing her."

"Oh, no, you would not. You are not getting on the stand and saying one bad thing about Sally Blake. Do I need to remind you how wonderful Ted and Donna have been to us through the years? You wouldn't be anything if they hadn't set you up in business after Sally's disappearance. You'd have nothing. You'd *be* nothing."

"I realize that, Joyce."

"You owe everything to them, Tim. This house." She made an expansive gesture with her arms. "Your country club friends who mean so much to you."

Their country club friends meant something to her, but now wasn't the time to point that out.

You have five children depending on you," she continued.

"I said I know," he enunciated.

She dropped her hand from his arm, apparently mollified. "Well, I hope you told that parasite and Noel Wyatt you won't be any help to their case."

Tim braced himself. "Honey, I agree with them that Noreen doesn't belong in prison. If she said she killed Sally in self-defense, I believe her. She never should've pled guilty to murder in the first place. If she'd had a jury trial three years ago, she'd probably still be working at that drugstore."

"Well, that's her problem, isn't it? It doesn't concern us. She committed a crime, and then she pled guilty to it. Just because she's reconsidered, doesn't mean you should risk your career—and the career of your daughter, I might add—to ride to her rescue."

As mad as Joyce was at his suggestion that he help Noreen, he knew Leslie would take it harder. The girl had big dreams. She knew her old man had gone about as high as ambition and position allowed in the realty company, but she wasn't going to let that stop her from marching right over Ted Blake's head. Ted had groomed Tim for years to take over, but anyone with the slightest hint of business sense could see he was no Ted Blake. The company would falter and stagnate under his leadership.

Not so with Leslie. Being a woman would not keep her from getting what she wanted. Somehow she would make it work for her. She was headed for the top, and she had the guts to walk over anyone she had to to get there, including her own father.

"Doesn't it bother you that Noreen almost got killed?" he asked Joyce. "She's in prison with real criminals; animals that would just as soon kill you as look at you. She's not one of them."

Joyce stepped up next to him, her toenails gouging the side of his foot. "She killed somebody, Tim. Don't you get that? Just because she's sorry, or she's getting tormented in prison, doesn't change what she did. She's a murderer. And I'll not stand by and let you ruin everything we've worked so hard to achieve because of some youthful notion that you can save her."

Tim felt the fight go out of him. Joyce had a point about what would happen if he spoke up against Sally. He would be out of Blake Realty before Ted could rip his nameplate off his office door and throw it in his face. But shouldn't he say something? Wasn't he obligated as a human being to tell what he knew, and then let a jury decide if Noreen should be acquitted or not? He didn't have the heart to remind Joyce that if the identity of Noel's witness were to become known, he would be subpoenaed, and he would have to tell the truth and worry about any financial repercussions later.

He finished undressing and hung his sports jacket and slacks back in the closet. He could tell by Joyce's manner she considered the argument settled. She was right and he was a doddering idiot, as always. He took four aspirin and went to bed early. He wasn't aware of when his wife came to bed.

Chapter Fifteen

The front door slammed downstairs announcing Eric had returned home from his date with Jamie. Christy glanced at the clock beside her bed. 9:50. A pretty early evening considering Eric was marrying this girl. Christy had realized years ago her kid brother had some pretty chaste ideas concerning dating. The only times he and Jamie were alone together was when he was picking her up or taking her home. Their dates were restricted to public places, the homes of friends, or church. She only hoped neither of them woke up one morning after ten or fifteen years of marriage to realize they resented the other for not allowing them to find out if the grass was any greener in someone else's backyard.

But then again, she had never known what it was like to be held in such high regard by a young man that he was willing to jump through hoops to preserve her integrity. The few times a man convinced her he placed any value on her, it was only to further the physical aspect of the relationship.

Sean, it seemed, had two motivations for making her feel highly regarded.

She couldn't get over the sick feeling in her stomach that had plagued her for hours after her encounter with Jarrod Bruckner outside Noel's store.

If anyone had told her a simple robbery in a motel room would have such an effect on her two weeks after the fact, she would have laughed and reminded them she wasn't as fragile as she looked. After all, the men hadn't hurt her. The police photographer had taken a picture of a handprint shaped bruise under her chin on her neck where Stanley's cousin had grabbed her. Her abdomen had hurt for several days every time she took a deep breath or bent over without thinking where his knee pinned her to the bed, but she would recover.

Other than the humiliation of wetting her panties and allowing the thieves into the motel in the first place, she was none the worse for wear. She heard of break-ins and robberies every day in Columbus. Unless someone was raped, beaten, or killed, the story didn't even make the nightly news.

All afternoon and evening, she had sat in her room listening to her mother move around the house doing whatever it was she did all day, and told herself she needed to get a grip on herself. This was no way to live. She couldn't go around screaming at every man who bumped up against her in a crowd. What would she do when she got a job? How would she react to male clients? What if she had to be alone in a room with one? She couldn't freak out every time a man loosened his tie or stood up unexpectedly and scraped his chair across the floor.

Now that her shakes had settled down, she was humiliated. What was happening to her? Was her reaction to Jarrod Bruckner a residual effect of her experience in the motel room, or was she going to spend the rest of her life distrustful of all men, thanks to Sean?

Sean. That was one thing she didn't want to think about.

She left the room and padded downstairs in her bare feet. She found Eric in the kitchen, the top half of his body swallowed up by the massive Kenmore. Some things never changed.

"Hey, baby brother, you're home early."

Eric backed out of the refrigerator and turned to face her. He had a dill pickle clamped between his teeth like a cigar and in his hands were the fixings for a sandwich.

"Hungry?" he mumbled around the pickle.

She shook her head. "I'm surprised you are. Didn't you take Jamie out to eat?"

"That was hours ago."

"Worked up an appetite, did you?" She lifted her eyebrows.

Eric's eyes darkened, her insinuation not appreciated. Christy instantly felt like a heel. Even if she personally saw no need for all the limitations Eric put on his relationship with Jamie, she had no right to tease him about them. She approached the table and pulled out a chair. "I'm sorry. Jamie seems like a sweet girl."

"She is sweet," he said after taking a bite of the pickle and depositing the rest of it, along with the lunchmeat and cheese, on the table. "And she's going to be your sister-in-law. I'd appreciate you treating her with respect."

She wondered if he was referring to their conversation at Karen's house over the wedding magazines. He probably felt the same as Jamie about approaching Noel for money for the wedding. She held her hands up in front of her. "Okay, okay. I apologize for that. I was just trying to be funny."

He studied her for a moment before heading to the breadbox apparently satisfied. "I'm sorry if I'm being touchy. I just never know anymore…" His sentence went unfinished when he held up a loaf of Wonder Bread. "Sure you don't want a sandwich? I'm buying."

Christy was tempted. She couldn't remember the last sandwich she'd eaten on white bread. There was nothing like a bologna, tomato, and mayonnaise sandwich. But she didn't eat like that anymore, especially this time of night.

"No, thanks."

She watched Eric load his bread with three slices of ham, two slices of American cheese, tomato, and dill pickle. Small town America; no wonder they all dropped dead of heart attacks.

He saw her watching him and smiled. She smiled back. He put the top on his sandwich and bit into it as he lowered himself into the chair across from her.

"What were you going to say a minute ago?" she asked.

He frowned with a mouthful of sandwich. "Hmm?"

"You said you never know anymore. Then you stopped. What don't you know?"

He took another huge bite out of the sandwich. Only two bites and the large sandwich was nearly gone. Christy waited while he chewed enough to swallow. Then he returned to the refrigerator and poured himself a glass of tea. He took a long drink and grimaced. "Yuck. Too strong." He went to the sink and dumped the remains of the pitcher down the drain, but kept the glass he poured.

"Eric? What were you saying?"

"Give me a minute. I was starving." He wiped his mouth with the back of his hand and returned to the table. He took a human sized bite out of the remainder of the sandwich and chewed thoughtfully before finally addressing her question. "I was going to say I don't know how to take you anymore."

Christy furrowed her brow. "What do you mean?"

"Sometimes you make these little comments disguised as jokes, but underneath I know they're put-downs."

"What are you talking about? I don't do that."

Eric tore a piece of crust off what was left of his sandwich and stuck it in his mouth. He nodded while he chewed. "Yes, you do. You've been doing it for years," he said after swallowing, "and you're getting worse. Since you moved away from home, you treat the rest of us like a bunch of hicks. The bigger you got at your job, the smaller we got."

Christy opened her mouth to protest, but he hurried on. "It's especially bad when I talk about Jamie. Any time I say something about our relationship, you look at me with this look on your face like I don't have a clue about the real world."

"Eric, I never meant—"

"I know in your world it's probably no big deal to sleep with somebody before you get married. You probably think I should sow my wild oats before I tie myself down to one woman for the rest of my life."

Christy felt color rush to her cheeks. That was exactly what she had been thinking only moments ago when she heard his car in the driveway. "Eric, I—"

"Maybe you don't mean it, but that's exactly what you do. I decided years ago I wasn't going to spend my time pursuing the opposite sex. I wanted my life to be about more than how many cheerleaders I slept with. I entered into this decision with a lot of prayer. I do have natural male urges, you know. I'm not a eunuch or anything. I knew I couldn't live up to my convictions on my own. After Jamie and I started dating, I was more tempted than ever. But Jesus is the Lord of my life—every aspect of my life. And if you can't respect me for that, well then, I'd rather you keep your opinions to yourself. This lifestyle is hard enough to maintain without members of my own family ridiculing me for it."

It was the second time today she'd been asked to keep her opinions to herself. Christy had always been one to speak first and think later, but she didn't think she ever intentionally hurt the people she loved most. Apparently she was wrong. She looked down at her hands and then at her brother. "Oh, Eric, I'm so sorry. I never meant to make fun of you. I guess I have become a bit of a jerk the last few years. I don't think I'm better than anyone here in Jenna's Creek. If I act that way, I'm truly sorry. Will you forgive me?"

Instead of answering, he fixed his gaze on her. "Christy, when's the last time you've been to church?"

She laughed nervously and picked an imaginary piece of lint off her shirt. "You didn't answer my question. And it's impolite to ask people about religion or politics."

"Not when one of those people is your sister."

She stopped fidgeting and looked him square in the eye. "Okay, fine. Not counting when Daddy...well, besides the funeral, I haven't been to church since last Christmas when I went with all of you."

Eric examined his fingernails for a moment. Christy couldn't understand why she was uncomfortable with the conversation. She was twenty-seven years old. She didn't have to explain her spirituality to anyone, least of all her baby brother. "In fact, I haven't been to church on my own in a couple of years. Just because you don't go to church, doesn't mean you're an evil person."

Eric looked up at her, and a slow smile covered his face. "I didn't say it did, Chris. You can have church anywhere or anytime. But anything you do is easier when you surround yourself with people who are doing the same thing. It's a lot easier to fall away from the Lord when you isolate yourself from His family."

"You're not going to start preaching at me, are you?" she asked, giving his arm a playful slap.

"Not today. I'd rather you explain what's going on with you. We all understand what happened to you in Louisville had to be very traumatizing. We're not trying to trivialize that, but..." He gave her a long hard look. "It's more than two guys breaking into your room and stealing your car. Like why were you there in the first place? Why aren't you still working at your firm? We can't help you, Christy, until we know what's going on."

"I don't need any help."

"Okay, see there. That's what I'm talking about. You can square your shoulders and put on this tough guy act if you want, but I'm not buying it. We all need something, Chris. None of us like to admit it, but it's true. I think that's why Christianity, the church, and all that is getting a bad rap these days. We want to think we can do everything on our own. Make our own rules. Solve our own problems. The only problem with that is the emptiness on the inside while we're smiling on the outside. When you don't find what you're looking for in a church or within the pages of the Bible, you'll look for it in the world; inner peace, fulfillment, whatever you want to call it. Let me be the first to tell you, until you turn around and let Jesus back into your heart, you're going to wear yourself out looking."

Tears pricked the back of Christy's eyelids. She wrinkled her nose at her brother to cover up her discomfort. "I knew you'd start preaching at me."

Eric reached across the table and took her hand. "Because I love you, Sis. I know you're hurting. If things were fine, you wouldn't be here. You'd still be in your apartment in Columbus instead of sitting here with me on a Friday night, wearing my old clothes."

Christy pulled self-consciously at the neck of the t-shirt she wore.

"What were you doing in Louisville?"

"Christy?" he persisted when she didn't answer. "Why aren't you working? Are you ever going home?"

His questions managed to tie Christy's stomach in a tight knot. It should be easy to blurt out the truth. She didn't need his approval. Surely she wasn't the first woman to fall for a man who turned out to be bad news. So she didn't have a job. She didn't even have a home to go back to. She wasn't expecting a big insurance check for her stolen car and all her belongings. She'd messed up royally, big deal. Who'd never made a mistake; or a half dozen for that matter?

Unfortunately a cavalier attitude toward her circumstances was not something she could muster at the present time. Everything still hurt too much. Her overreaction to running into Jarrod Bruckner this morning came rushing back to her. She knew there was more going on in her head than getting held up at a motel. She didn't need her little brother to tell her that. She had taken a few psych courses in college. But the last thing she wanted to do right now was analyze her life and the rotten turn it had taken.

Eric was staring at her. "You are going back to work, aren't you? Christy, what's going on?"

"I don't have a job," she said abruptly, unable to meet his gaze. "I was fired."

The shock Christy dreaded seeing on everyone's faces when they heard the truth was now on Eric's. "Fired? Why?"

She wanted to shrug and say, "I don't want to talk about it." For all she was worth, she wanted to pretend it was no big deal. But it was a big deal and she would have to talk about it sooner or later.

"It concerned a man."

Eric's eyebrows shot up, but he didn't comment.

"I know. I know. I should have known better. I let him get close to me, but it turns out he was only interested in getting some information from my firm."

This time Eric's eyebrows went down into a frown. He clearly didn't understand.

"We dated for awhile. He borrowed," Christy made quotation marks in the air with her fingers, "my office keys one night and broke into the firm's file room. The security cameras captured the whole thing. It didn't take any great deductive reasoning to figure out whose keys he was using since everyone knew we were seeing each other. Just in case there was any doubt though, he left them hanging in the door when he left."

"That was big of him."

She nodded. "I thought so, too. Anyway, it was stupid and careless of me. That's what my boss said; breach of security, confidentiality, and all that jazz. So I got canned. I can't really blame them."

Eric reached across the table to pat her arm. "I'm so sorry for you, Chris. What was he looking for in the file room?"

"Some information on a client of ours who just happened to be his dad's cousin. Apparently he found it. He's gone, along with my reputation and a few hundred thousand dollars he stole from the state."

"You've got to be kidding! This sounds like a plot out of some bad romance novel."

"That sums up my life—a bad romance novel."

"Chris, I didn't mean to make light of it. I know it must've been horrible for you." He paused and chewed on his lip a moment before his next question. "Were you crazy about this guy?"

Christy smiled in spite of the fist tightening around her heart. This was definitely not a conversation she imagined having with her baby brother. "Oh, you know how it is, just one of those things."

Eric didn't look convinced. "So, that's what you were doing in Kentucky."

Christy nodded. "Yeah, running away from home. Did I mention the last time he was in my apartment, in fact it was the very night he broke into the law office, he stole my credit cards and every dime out of my purse? He used my credit card to buy himself a plane ticket to Chicago where he rented a car—also on my dime—and disappeared into the wind. The feds or no one else has been able to track him after Chicago. Fortunately for all of us, I didn't have a very big limit on my cards. Where he is now, is anyone's guess."

She stopped talking, blew out her breath, and lowered her chin into her hand. She actually felt better now that everything was off her chest. At least the weight of the world no longer seemed to be hanging around her neck.

Eric got up and came around the table to stand behind her. He leaned over and wrapped his arms around her neck. "That's the worst thing I've heard in my life. I'm so sorry."

Christy reached up and patted Eric's hands. "Thanks. I appreciate it. But really, I'm fine; except for losing my job, my dignity, my apartment, and all my worldly possessions in a little over a month." For the first time in a long time, she smiled. A chuckle worked its way up through her throat. Before she knew it, she was laughing.

Eric hugged her against him. "You're crazy, you know that?" he said, laughing with her.

When he released her, he moved around her and leaned against the table. He looked down at her, his face sober. "You don't have to be strong for our sake, Sis. Nor do you need to feel guilty or embarrassed. We're your family. We can help you through this."

Christy pulled herself to her feet and reached up to touch his cheek. Before finding out Eric was not a Blackwood, she had never wondered where he'd got his height, thick dark hair, or square jaw. Now their differences jumped out at her in glaring contrast every time she looked at him.

"You've been a big help to me already. I can't tell you the last time I had a good laugh. You know, sometimes it's healthy to laugh at yourself."

"So I've heard."

"I won't tell you the last few months haven't been rotten. First Dad, then this man comes into my life, and of course, all the stuff going on with you and Mom." She turned her back to the table and leaned her hips against it the way Eric was doing. She crossed her arms and leaned against him. "To tell you the truth, I'm more embarrassed than hurt. I'll probably never work again in the law profession because I let this jerk get close enough to me to steal my keys. Then I open my motel door to a crook who claims to have car trouble. How stupid is that?"

"Aw, Chris." Eric put his arm around her and pulled her close.

"No big deal. I'll survive. I'm none the worse for wear except I may have to live off Mom's charity until I find a job waiting tables or something. That's as much bother as I want to be right now."

He removed his arm from around her shoulders and looked down at her. "But Christy, that's what family is for. We're here anytime you make a fool of yourself."

"Gee, thanks."

Eric smiled, and she smiled back. "Anytime you need to talk, Chris, I promise not to judge you."

"Glad to hear it. You know you can talk to me about anything on your mind, too."

Eric hooked a chair leg with his foot and slid it away from the table so he could sit down. "You mean about Mom or Jamie?"

"Well, either one would be fine." Christy lowered herself back into her chair. "But I wasn't exactly thinking of them. I was thinking more about the man on the other side of town who looks an awful lot like you."

Eric got up and carried his watered down tea to the sink. He turned on the tap full force and poured the tea down the drain. After much longer than necessary to rinse out his glass, he shut off the faucet and turned to face Christy. He leaned his hips against the counter and crossed his arms over his chest.

"I don't have anything to say to him."

"Maybe not this minute, but you may in the future." Christy paused, giving Eric time to anticipate what she was going to say. "You are getting married soon. Did you ever think Noel might want to be involved in that?"

Eric stiffened. "Jamie told me what you said about asking him to pay for the wedding. That isn't going to happen, Chris. You shouldn't have even brought it up."

"I know," she said, "and I'm sorry I hurt Jamie's feelings. I still think I'm right, but it's none of my business."

"You're right, it isn't. We'll elope before we let anyone else pay for our wedding."

"Okay, okay. I'll mind my own business on that count from now on. But that wasn't what I was getting at. You quit your job at the drugstore after you found out about Noel and Mom. You've cut off all ties with him. But you need to think about the future. Have you thought about inviting him to the wedding?"

"You've got to be—"

"No, now wait a minute. Hear me out. He is your father, Eric. He's already missed so much of your life. What are you going to prove by keeping him away? Isn't he pretty close to Jamie? Maybe she wants to invite him, but can't because she knows you'll freak out if she mentions it."

Eric approached the table and sat down in the chair he had vacated. "You're being awfully charitable considering you're the one not talking to Mom."

"I know. I guess I don't have any room to talk." Christy put her elbows on the table and leaned toward him. "What I'm really thinking about is your epilepsy. It might run in his family. What's if that's where you got it? What if you and Jamie decide to have kids?"

Eric pushed his hand through the thick dark hair that fell haphazardly over his left eye. "Okay, I guess it's been on my mind a little bit lately, too," he said. "But we're not talking about my problems. We're talking about yours."

"I'd rather talk about you. I'm sorry I stuck my nose in about Noel paying for the wedding, and I apologize for all the times I've acted like a snob in the past."

"And I'm sorry you have lousy taste in men."

Christy wrinkled her nose. "Oh, you are a laugh riot." She leaned toward him with her arms extended as if to put her hands around his throat.

He caught her hands as she moved toward him. "We're quite a pair, you and me. We're both out of work, and it looks like we'll be sponging off Mom for the indeterminate future."

Christy pushed out her bottom lip. "Now I think I am going to cry."

Chapter Sixteen

"Dad, are you all right?"

Mark Eisinger looked up from the grill he had been staring into for the last five minutes into his daughter's concerned face. "Oh, sorry, dear." He touched her arm to reassure her, and then took his tongs and turned the hissing blackened steaks. "Almost let them get away from me, didn't I?"

He smiled, but Brenda didn't smile back. "Why don't you let Steve finish these? Steve," she called out across the yard.

"No, please," he said quickly. "I've got it." The last thing he wanted was to be treated like an invalid. It was the reason he had been tempted not to tell his two children and their spouses what he'd found out from the neurologist. He sat on the prognosis for a week, too numb to make decisions. He was fifty-nine-years old, too young to find out a tumor the size of a baseball was lodged in his cerebral cortex, but decades older than many of the patients he saw sitting around the neurologist's waiting room.

He gave Brenda another encouraging smile. She turned to shake her head at her husband, who had stopped defending the basket over the garage against his son and was headed toward them. Steve arched his eyebrows in question to make sure he wasn't needed, and at Brenda's signal, went back to his ballgame.

The grandkids didn't know anything beyond the fact that Granddad was sick and had gone to a hospital in Cincinnati for some tests. Tad was eleven and Julie was nine. Mark Junior's children were even younger; too young to know too much too early. They would know soon enough. The neurologist at University Hospital wasn't optimistic. A practicing surgeon himself, Mark had demanded the cold hard facts. Six months on the outside. Upon hearing that, he almost wished the doctor had been kind enough to sugarcoat the truth. The prognosis had been delivered last month. He figured if the high priced specialist was on the mark, he might last until Valentine's Day.

For now, Mark was trying to get as much normal living done as possible. He had given up performing surgery during the summer when he first detected the need for tests. Consequently, everyone in his office knew something was wrong. Then the hospital staff caught on. Before long, it seemed every medical professional and almost every non-professional knew of the tumor, which he had jokingly named Chuck after Chuck Berry, whose music had given him so many headaches during Brenda's growing up years.

Brenda did not appreciate his attempt at levity. She was too much like her mother, always serious. "You've got to laugh at yourself, sweetheart," he told her the first time she chastised him about it. "If you can't laugh, you'll fall apart crying."

"Maybe I want to fall apart. There's nothing funny about any of this."

He had pulled her into his arms. "Exactly. That's why we need to laugh. We can't let this thing steal what little time we have left."

He continued turning the steaks and pretending he didn't notice the pain etched on her face. Brenda had been mothering him since he finally told them the truth last month. Actually she'd been breathing down his neck since the family lost Betty in 1964. Since the diagnosis, she had gotten almost unbearable. He would have to say something to her if she didn't get a handle on her emotions. He knew she was worried. She hated it that he lived here alone. She wanted him to move in with her, Steve, and the kids. He had told her in no uncertain terms that was impossible, allowing her to think he would miss his independence too much. While that was true, he was much more concerned about the grandkids being there to watch his decline, which would become rapid and painful as time grew short.

Besides protecting the grandchildren, he feared he may welcome death more than his survivors would appreciate if he was forced to live with his smothering daughter fulltime.

Brenda stuck out a platter for him to put the steaks on. "I can finish this, Dad. You shouldn't be on your feet so long."

He sighed and started to tell her that manning the grill on a Sunday afternoon was not beyond his capabilities when he heard a car in the driveway. "There's your brother," he said, relieved at the interruption. "Go and sneak me a piece of Mona's key lime pie before the kids get it all."

She knew he was only trying to get rid of her, but she turned obediently and headed across the yard to intercept her sister-in-law.

Mark turned back to the grill and reloaded it with hamburgers and hotdogs. The cold meat hissed when it hit the hot grill. There was nothing he liked better than grilling outdoors on a late Indian summer afternoon. There wouldn't be many more of them this year. Most of the bright orange and red leaves that colored the hillsides were fading and falling rapidly with every breeze. In all likelihood, this would be his last outdoor barbecue, his last autumn, unless the Lord chose to perform some sort of last minute miracle on him.

He smiled ruefully. It wasn't likely. He had seen plenty of what could only be called miracles during his thirty years in the operating room, but if God handed out miracles based on merit, Mark was certainly farther down the list than most. He believed one got out of life what one put into it. For all the pain he had caused those who loved him most, the brain tumor was the least he had coming.

"Be sure and burn my hotdog, Dad," Mona said, coming up behind him. She put her hands on his shoulders, stood on her toes, and kissed his cheek.

He waved the tongs at her. "Already got yours charred."

She smiled and moved off toward the picnic table. He smiled appreciatively at her back. If only Brenda, who hovered over him constantly, could take some lessons from his daughter-in-law. Mona treated him the way she always had, since the first time Mark Junior brought her home from college. Nothing had changed with the news of his condition. She was always quietly respectful without babying him or looking at him like she might never see him up and walking around again.

He had a hard enough time not looking at himself in the mirror like that. He thought how much easier it was on people who didn't wake up knowing their days were numbered. In his opinion, the lucky ones were killed instantly in car crashes or died unexpectedly on operating tables. While devastating for those left behind, it had to be a better alternative than counting the months, mentally marking each day off the calendar with a big black X and dreading the look in his doctor's eyes every time another test result came back. Knowing this was his last barbeque, his last October, possibly the last time he'd see his grandson fake a lay-up shot over his father, was more than he cared to live with.

The minister from the church he had attended regularly with Betty heard about his condition and showed up at the house last week. He said Mark should be grateful God had given him a chance to prepare. Get his affairs in order. Mark told him his affairs had been in order for thirty years.

Though he didn't say as much to the minister, the last thing he felt was grateful. He was receiving a just punishment, but he would be lying if he said he appreciated it. Did a man on death row appreciate the electric chair even after confessing his crimes?

Mark's biggest regret was Betty. Not in marrying her, that was one of the few things he'd done right. What he regretted was all the things he hadn't done for her while he had the chance. Betty died unexpectedly of a brain aneurysm in 1964, the year Brenda married Steve, and Mark Junior graduated from high school. When he lost her, he decided God definitely blessed people based on merit. He had been a lousy husband so God punished him by taking the best thing that ever happened to him.

But in God's infinite wisdom, did he have to punish Betty as well, or their children?

He had planned to do so many things for her to make up for those first years when he was building up his practice, working long nights, and ignoring his husbandly duties. But God snatched her away from him before he had the chance. For years he blamed God for spoiling Betty's chance at happiness and his chance at redeeming himself in her eyes. Then he realized it was his fault. He learned you had to do things when you got the chance, not wait until better times to do what you really never got around to.

He was especially repentant for those mistakes early in their marriage when he strayed from their marriage bed. At the time, Mark told himself he was just blowing off steam from too much work and all the adult responsibilities staring him in the face. All married men did it. Deep down he knew his indiscretions weren't because of circumstance, youth, too much wine, or too much time at an out-of-town convention. Each time was a calculated decision. He could have walked away or given in to temptation. All too often, he gave in.

When Betty confronted him about the young secretary he was seeing in the early fifties, he knew he had to change things. He didn't want to lose his family. He finally realized after many years of wasted time that she was too good to lose. The secretary left town, and Mark got down to being a husband. He didn't come clean about the other affairs and close calls. He didn't tell her about the stewardess he met during a flight to Dallas for a convention or the pregnancy scare that resulted from that weekend. He had been scared straight for almost a year. But then along came the young college girl who made him lower his guard all over again.

She had proved impossible to resist. He had wanted Sally Blake more than any woman he'd ever met. He didn't mind that she was using him as much as he was using her. Their relationship was purely physical—a refreshing first. Most women wanted a commitment, even though they knew he had a wife, two children, and a budding medical practice, none of which he was willing to risk. But the last thing Sally wanted from him was a relationship.

Not long before she disappeared, Sally told him she didn't want to see him again. He had served his purpose. When she explained what that purpose was, Mark became furious. At the same time, he was willing to do whatever she asked to stay in her life. She laughed at his reluctance to walk away from her. Never rebuffed by a woman before, Mark became obsessed. He started following her in hopes of seeing for himself the man she wanted more than him. He called her at home a few times and sat in his parked car outside her friends' houses to see if she was there.

He remembered clearly the night she disappeared. He had watched her with James Steele from a distance, but knew it wasn't James she was looking to win. She already had him wrapped around her little finger. Mark suspected she was using James in the same way she had used him. After she disappeared, he didn't know if he should be alarmed or elated. While relieved such a loose cannon was out of his life, his life was suddenly empty without her. He had become addicted to the exhilaration she brought him. He doubted he was the first man who had.

Sally was only one of his many sins that Betty never found out about. After her death, he often wished he could bring her back for a day so he could admit his shortcomings and cleanse his soul. She had the right to know that he wasn't the husband she thought he was. But coming clean would be for his satisfaction, not hers. Reading off a long list of indiscretions would only break her heart all over again. She didn't deserve that.

He removed the hamburgers and hot dogs from the grill and set the platter in the center of the patio table. He looked around at his family; his son and daughter, their smiling spouses, and the four grandchildren Betty had never known.

Somehow he had earned God's favor in spite of the life he had led. If he was going to die, he owed it to Betty's memory to do the right thing. She would've insisted he tell what he knew.

"Dad, are you all right?" Brenda asked.

They were all seated around the table looking up at him, their eyes full of questions.

"Yeah, Dad," her husband, Steve said, smiling for the benefit of the children seated around the picnic table. "Sit down and join us."

Mark's smile encompassed them all. He lowered himself onto the bench seat. Brenda handed him a Styrofoam plate.

His last barbecue with his family, his last autumn; for the first time in his life, he had to do the right thing before it was eternally too late. He couldn't let an innocent woman spend one more day in prison for a crime he knew she didn't commit.

It wasn't simply because his mortal life was ending and he had nothing more to lose. He had to do something to make amends for the evil life he'd led.

Judge David Davis sat back in his leather recliner and scratched his head. There was work that needed to be done outside with the horses, but it would wait until later. After he and Bernice returned home from the evening church service, he had opened the gates between the pastures and the barn. He heard rather than saw the horses moving from the field to the barn for another feeding. Instead of waiting for them like he normally did he had turned and headed back to the house. He loved watching them moving through the meadow, smelling them as they moved past him and into the barn. He loved watching them and talking to them while they ate; everything about them was simple and graceful.

The horses were on their own tonight. Bernice was having a bad week. She had missed the church service this morning, and he had tried to get her to stay home that evening, but she wouldn't hear of it. She hated it that her disease had already robbed her of so much of her life. She hadn't imagined that she and David's golden years would be dictated by something neither of them could control. She had been the picture of health her entire life and didn't appreciate her body setting limitations for her. Multiple sclerosis was a bitter pill for an active woman like Bernice to swallow. In public she accepted it graciously, but David knew how deeply she resented it.

Immediately after church he helped her into the den he had converted into their bedroom when it became too much for her to climb the stairs. She had balked at the idea of moving downstairs. "I'm not so old and feeble that I can't climb stairs, David," she had scolded. But by that winter, they had moved all their furnishings and clothes downstairs. The den wasn't as roomy as the old bedroom, and he still hadn't gotten around to adding a master bath, but the couple was adjusting.

Now Bernice was asleep in the cozy, wood paneled bedroom she threatened to repaint every couple of weeks. She wouldn't let David do it for her or hire it done, but the pain and fatigue had kept her from doing it so far.

The judge tried not to worry about his wife's condition. They were both people of faith, who believed God was faithful and would see them through whatever the years ahead might bring, but he knew the disease was difficult on his wife's morale. For his own selfish reasons, he couldn't imagine life without Bernice. They had married while they were both sophomores in college, much to their parents chagrin. They spent their first five years in dorm housing, scrimping for every penny. Their first son was born while David was in law school, and Bernice was waiting tables at a college café and waiting for a teaching position to open up at a nearby elementary school. Neither of their parents had been generous with financial help, believing the young couple needed to learn the hard way the consequences of getting married before they had degrees and good paying jobs.

Bernice was truly David's best friend; the only woman he had ever loved. He prayed every night that God would strengthen her body and help both of them accept the changes the disease had brought. Most of all, he prayed for another year with her in his life.

It had been nearly five years since he had presided over a case. When it became apparent that Bernice's disease was rapidly accelerating, he retired to stay home with her. Leaving behind the Appellate Court bench with so many years of his career ahead of him was not something he entered into lightly. He had tossed around the notion of entering the political arena for most of his career. He always thought it was something he would enjoy when he got older. Looking back, he figured he should have done it as a young man and not put it off until it was no longer feasible. Giving up political aspirations, and even the bench, had been for Bernice. She had not chosen to develop multiple sclerosis. As her husband, she was his first priority. He was duty bound to stand beside her, even if it meant sacrificing his own wants and dreams.

When he was satisfied that Bernice was comfortable in their room, David settled into his recliner with the folder of police report copies he had made from Sheriff Patterson's original files. Taking care of Bernice and the farm consumed much of his day, but a part of him was ecstatic that he was in some way involved again in Noreen Trimble's case. He had not been happy with the way it ended three years ago. He was confident Noreen would receive nothing more than a manslaughter charge, or second degree murder, and walk away from prison after three to five years. He didn't believe she deserved the life sentence she was now serving.

As of yet, he and Noel Wyatt had gotten no new information from any of the people on Noreen's list who might have come back to the party the night Sally Blake disappeared; first and foremost, Tim Shelton. After talking to him and consulting with Noreen's attorney, Noel was convinced Tim was hiding something. He just couldn't figure out what. Tim had either seen something the night of Sally's death, or he was ashamed to admit he had gotten involved with her in the first place.

David had never spoken to Tim before and doubted the man would have anything to say to him if he tried. Wearily he picked up Noreen's police report for the hundredth time and leaned back in his chair.

Was it possible Noreen was covering up for Tim or someone else? Noel didn't seem to think so. Why would she not mention a witness to her crime if she had known about it? Had there ever been a baby like Sally and Tim told the Blakes? Did Noreen know about it?

Forty-five minutes later, he finished reading Noreen's version of that night. His experience, first as a prosecuting attorney and then his years on the bench, had made him a decent judge of people. In his professional opinion, Noreen Trimble wasn't lying, at least not in her own mind. She truly believed she was wholly responsible for the death of Sally Blake, even if she hadn't personally dealt the fatal blow that killed her.

The most likely scenario was that if there had actually been a witness to the crime, Noreen was totally unaware of his existence. Why would the witness not come forward with what he knew? What did he have to lose by coming forward? He could have cleared Noreen and put Sally Blake's family at rest as to her whereabouts. The taxpayers would have been spared the cost of an investigation, and James Steele would have been spared the pain of an entire county judging him for a crime he did not commit.

What kind of person would keep quiet and allow the Blakes, Noreen Trimble, and James Steele to suffer for twenty-five years?

David removed his reading glasses and pinched the top of his nose. He put Noreen's stapled report on the bottom of the stack and looked down at the next one in the pile. Something occurred to him. Something he hadn't thought of before.

He put his glasses back on and picked up the report. It belonged to a young woman named Constance Noble. She was a cousin of one of the invited guests. She had been visiting from out of town and had gone to the party with her cousin for lack of anything else to do. David, who was the prosecuting attorney on the case, along with the investigators at the time, had pieced Connie's story together through interviews with several other attendees.

Connie had been enjoying herself like everyone else until the moment Sally Blake arrived with James Steele. That's when

Connie recognized her. Three months earlier, Connie had found Sally in an ardent embrace with Connie's then boyfriend outside a nightclub near Connie's hometown, which was about fifty miles from Jenna's Creek. Connie had approached what looked like her boyfriend's car. Surely it wasn't since her boyfriend had called earlier in the day to break their date, claiming he would be out of town visiting relatives. When she realized it was indeed the boyfriend's car, and he was inside with a woman, Connie had seen red. She opened the passenger door and yanked the offending young woman backwards out of the car. The young woman had been caught off guard so it was easy enough for Connie to wrestle her to the ground. Unfortunately for her, the boyfriend was out of the car in a shot and pulled her off the young woman before she could do any real damage. When Connie noticed his shirt was not tucked neatly into his trousers, nor was the unknown woman's blouse buttoned all the way to the top, Connie turned her wrath on the boyfriend.

The friend who had brought her to the club, along with several other bystanders, finally managed to break up the fight, fearing Connie would kill both of them. No introductions were made that night, but Connie would never forget the smirking, cursing young woman she had pulled from her boyfriend's car.

To come face to face with her at an engagement party for two people she didn't even know was a dream come true.

She walked up to Sally at the party and tapped her on the shoulder. Sally turned slowly from the man she had showed up with and gazed disinterestedly down at Connie, clearly resenting the interruption.

Connie clenched her fists and prepared to swing. "Remember me?"

Sally cocked an eyebrow and wrinkled her nose. "Should I?"

Her cocky attitude further infuriated Connie. But before she could react, her cousin saw what was coming and jumped between the two women. Only after getting pushed outside and reasoned and pleaded with by the cousin and a few other girls, did Connie agree fighting with Sally Blake at the engagement party was not worth it. But Connie swore to all of them she would not forget what Sally had done, and Little Miss Hot Pants would live to regret the day she crawled into a car with Connie Noble's boyfriend.

The cousin and the girls who helped defuse the situation had written nearly the exact same things in their reports to the police. Connie did not deny a word of it. After questioning her at the time though, investigators found no reason to believe Connie had come back to the party and done Sally harm. Her cousin testified to driving Connie back to her house, where the two of them slept that night in the same room. The next morning, the cousin awoke to find Connie still asleep in the twin bed across the room and had no reason to believe she had ever left the house.

Now Judge Davis was having second thoughts. Connie Noble was one of the five people on Noreen Trimble's list who had not been contacted for one reason or another.

Had Connie come back to the house after her cousin went to sleep? Had she seen what happened between Noreen and Sally and had been so pleased to see Sally get her just desserts, she saw no reason in saying anything that might bring trouble onto Noreen?

Then he remembered something else about Connie Noble.

He scanned through her report until he found what he was looking for. He read the words Connie had written nearly thirty years earlier.

"I don't have any idea what happened to that girl, but it'd be a lie to imply I'll be staying awake nights worrying about her. I hated her. Maybe it's not smart for me to admit that, but I don't care. It's the truth, and I have no reason to lie. She hurt my family, and I'm not sorry she's gone. She probably just up and took off anyway, playing another of her games. I don't see what all the fuss is about."

David thought it odd that Connie had written 'family', and not 'me' or 'my relationship with my boyfriend'. What had she been talking about—or whom?

He stared into space and thought of the possible familial ties Connie might have to Jenna's Creek. At least one cousin in Auburn

County was close enough to Noreen Trimble or Tim Shelton to be invited to their engagement party. He reread the address at the top of the page. Connie was from Kingston, a small town west of Chillicothe. Chillicothe wasn't so far from Jenna's Creek that it was inconceivable that Sally may have offended someone from there who happened to be related to Connie.

Chillicothe and the surrounding area were too large to hunt down every Noble or relative of a Noble to ask if any of them had a negative run-in with a young woman from Jenna's Creek thirty years ago.

On impulse, David got up and hurried into the kitchen for the closest Auburn County phone book. He wasn't even sure what he hoped to accomplish as he flipped through the thin book to the N's and scanned down the listings for Noble. There were only three. Two of the names meant nothing to him, but he was familiar with Wilbur Noble. He was a retired fireman who had worked for the city for at least thirty years.

The judge had gone to school with one of Wilbur's daughters—Cathy or Carol, he thought. He couldn't remember what had happened to her. But the younger daughter, Betty, was the one he remembered best. She had married Mark Eisinger and the two of them became members of the country club David and Bernice still belonged to. Dr. Eisinger had built up an esteemed practice and reputation in Auburn County. He had taken out David's daughter's appendix when she was eleven. Betty passed away back in the sixties, but David and Bernice still had a passing acquaintance with the doctor at country club affairs. The doctor had never remarried. He had thrown himself into his practice after Betty's death and had become something of a social recluse.

The cousin who had taken Connie to the party that night had been named Lytle. You couldn't swing a cat by the tail in Auburn County without hitting a Lytle, so it would be much harder to find out if any of them knew how to get hold of Connie. He'd check with the Nobles first. He hated to bother anyone on a Sunday evening, but it might prove to be the best time to get hold of them.

On top of that, he doubted he'd get much sleep tonight until he did what he could to find Connie.

He held the phone book open with the index finger of his left hand, and dialed the number with the right.

Wilbur Noble answered on the second ring. David was thankful the man was still alive. After introducing himself and exchanging pleasantries, he got down to business.

"I'm trying to get in touch with Connie Noble from Kingston," he said, without mentioning why. He hoped it wouldn't be necessary. "She's probably in her fifties by now with a different last name, but I was wondering if she might be related to your group."

Wilbur chuckled. "You're right about that. Poor Connie's had at least three name changes since she was a Noble; maybe four. She's my brother, Allan's girl. But I'm afraid I can't tell you how to get in touch with her. I doubt even Allan would know that. Last I heard of her, she was living in Seattle, or somewhere thereabouts."

"Not Seattle," the judge heard an old woman call from the background. "Santa Fe."

"It don't matter," Wilbur called back, "she's probably not there now anyway. Sorry about that, Judge. Guess you heard where the wife stands on the matter. Though I could swear it was Seattle."

David smiled when the old woman's voice sounded again. Regardless of where she was living now, it was highly probable that the family Connie referred to in her statement were indeed Jenna's Creek residents. He chewed his bottom lip, unsure of how any of this would help him now.

Chapter Seventeen

Tim knew they were watching him before he looked up. He also knew what they were thinking; what they'd been talking about all weekend. Joyce and Leslie were almost carbon copies of each other. They had been from the moment Leslie started displaying a personality. When people said, "She's just like her mother", they weren't exaggerating.

Leslie was born with a sheer cap of strawberry blonde hair and fine porcelain skin that could freckle through a brick wall. From the beginning, she didn't like getting dirty or wearing clothes that weren't coordinated. She played with tea sets and baby dolls and loved dressing up in her mother's earrings and high heels and parading around the house. She was all girl.

It didn't help that she was followed into life by four noisy, rowdy brothers. She played and cuddled with each new baby that came along, totally enamored with her real live baby dolls. As each boy became old enough to move around and push past their big sister, for none of them liked to cuddle, Leslie dismissed them and eagerly looked forward to the next baby. When there were finally no new babies forthcoming, she went back to playing with her baby dolls, which were easier anyway since they played by her rules and did what she said.

She didn't care for going to the farm to play with Grandma and Grandpa Shelton and her cousins. She had no girl cousins, and all the stupid boys ever wanted to do was go down to the pond and catch frogs and squish their toes in the mud, things Leslie abhorred.

Leslie didn't care that she had no playmates. Even the other little girls in the neighborhood inevitably tired of playing the role of squire or court jester to Leslie's queen and would go home. Leslie became her own best friend. Of course she had Mom. Joyce doted on her. Leslie was every mother's dream. She was sweet-tempered and beautiful and loved to wear frilly outfits. She was spoiled by every old woman in the neighborhood, and she loved every minute of it. When she was old enough to shop, she and Joyce spent nearly every Saturday driving to the city for new clothes and girl things that Tim and the four boys had no interest in and were only vaguely aware existed.

It soon became apparent Joyce and Leslie even shared opinions. They had the same politics, admired the same women, and shared a liberal stance on most social issues.

Tim had never seen anything like it. When Leslie entered her teenage years, he warned Joyce of the changes to come. "Mothers and daughters fight," he told her. "You won't have the same relationship you once did."

But it never happened. While he thought two women under the same roof with such identical personalities and strengths would butt heads, it was never a problem, at least never as far as he could see.

Sometimes he felt left out of their conversations. He envied the bond they shared and wished he could have a similar experience with the boys. But as years passed, he began to think that his and the boys' relationship was the normal one, while the one between his wife and daughter was a little peculiar.

Leslie was twenty-four now. She had her own apartment. She had moved out after college when she went to work at the real estate office full time. But she and Joyce still maintained close telephone contact. While Tim loved it that his daughter had gone into his line of work, he didn't like having her in his office. Every thing he did; every casual comment, every joke, every business deal, was shared with Joyce before Tim ever made it home.

He loved his wife and daughter, but sometimes he resented them deeply.

The house had been a zoo all weekend. The two youngest boys were arguing over school clothes. Richard, or Butch as he was known since he first made his appearance into the world weighing in at over eleven pounds, was a sophomore in high school while Russ was a senior. Butch would be getting his driver's license before the school year ended and felt he was entitled to his own car. Russ knew another car and the added insurance on the family budget would negatively affect how much money he was allotted each week. Every time Butch came home with anything costing more than a penny, Russ complained that this was his senior year and any extra money should be spent on him.

At twenty-one, Kenny was the oldest among the boys. He was also the only one who worked regularly. Straight out of high school, he got a job driving an over the road, tractor-trailer. He loved the freedom of the highway and having a boss who was safe back in Cincinnati rather than breathing down his neck. But for the next two weeks, he was on vacation and at home, egging on his younger brothers who couldn't stop fighting over every little matter.

Ray, the second son, was a sophomore in college and home for a long weekend from Otterbein where he lived on campus. The most laid back of the four and the one Tim considered to be most like him, he was also the only one Tim didn't mind having around for more than five minutes at a stretch. Typically, he was also around the house the least.

Ray was currently sprawled across the recliner reading a college textbook, one leg thrown over the side and a long arm thrown up over the headrest. Conscientious about his studies, Ray actually brought books into the house to read when he wasn't attending classes, the only one of the four boys to ever consider such a practice.

Russ and Butch were wrapping up the latest in a long string of arguments. Tim didn't even know why they were at it this time. He couldn't keep up from one moment to the next. Kenny's head and shoulders were buried in the refrigerator, even though his mother had just loaded the dishwasher with the dinner dishes. Kenny was small like Joyce's family. Barely five feet, six inches tall and weighing around one hundred and thirty pounds, he ate more food than his younger brothers combined. The family food budget always doubled when he was home for any length of time. His parents warned him his eating habits would catch up with him someday, but he turned a deaf ear. Twenty-one year old men seldom paid attention to advice from the old and feeble minded.

But it was Leslie and Joyce's whisperings that captured Tim's attention. He knew as well as he was sitting here that Leslie was giving Joyce her two cents about what really brought Noel Wyatt into the agency last week. And Joyce had told her of Tim's concern about getting involved with the Noreen Trimble case. His and Noreen's relationship was no secret to Joyce. Anyone who had been around Jenna's Creek in the 1940's knew they had been engaged until the disappearance of Sally Blake brought their torrid affair to an abrupt halt.

Joyce never saw Noreen as a threat to her marital bliss. Who would? Poor Noreen worked behind the pharmacy counter and had no social life. She was small and diminutive, hardly worth noticing, much less capable of becoming a threat to someone like Joyce. Joyce fancied herself as everything Noreen was not, even though she herself had come from similar humble beginnings.

Now Leslie and Joyce both realized what could be lost if Tim were called to testify on Noreen Trimble's behalf, even if Tim did not.

Out of the corner of his eye, Tim looked up from the television he wasn't really watching to study his wife and daughter. Their faces were grave masks as they contemplated something of great importance to both of them. He knew it was him. How he wished he could hide in the sleeper of Kenny's big rig the next time he went out on the road. Somewhere out west, he would slip out of the truck without Kenny ever knowing he had been on board and leave his troubles and responsibilities back in Jenna's Creek. Maybe that would be easier on everyone.

Butch chose that moment to irritate his brother by bringing up, yet again, the subject of the new car. "Dad, it isn't fair that I have to share the same car as Russ. You bought him a car when he was old enough to drive. I should get my own, too."

Tim continued to stare at the TV as if he hadn't heard. Even though the question had been directed at him, Butch was only using the topic to incite his brother into another altercation.

"That's because Raymond needed his old car to drive back and forth to college and wasn't here to share it. Russ had to have his own car," Joyce explained for the twentieth time in a week. "If Russ goes away to school next year, we'll consider a car for you, but not until then."

"See, that's not fair," Butch reiterated.

For the first time since Butch was added to the Shelton family roster, Russ agreed with him. "This is my senior year," he said. "I shouldn't have to share my car with a child."

Butch jumped to his feet. He was several inches taller than Russ already and outweighed him by at least twenty pounds. "I'll show you how much of a baby I am." He balled up his fists.

"Oh, for heaven's sake, shut up, the both of you," Joyce snapped. "I've listened to about all I care to on this subject. Tim, will you please make them quiet down?"

Tim looked up from the TV to find his entire family staring down at him. He pulled his feet in and stood up. Russ and Butch had squared off in the center of the room, both looking for the slightest excuse to pummel the other. Joyce was standing over Tim's chair, her arms folded across her chest, clearly exasperated that he had let the situation escalate this far. Leslie had gotten out of her chair too, and stood close to her mother, equally condemning Tim with her eyes. Only Ray had not moved. He idly flipped a page in his textbook and jotted a note to himself in a wire bound notebook.

"Okay, you two," Tim said to his two youngest, in a voice lacking the fervor Joyce would have preferred. "Here's the deal, and I believe we've covered this before. Russ, you're sharing your car with your brother. I don't care how much that cramps your style. You'll continue driving him to school and picking him up from practices as needed. Butch, when you get your license, you and Russ will take turns driving back and forth to school, and you will alternate weekends as the car's owner. When it isn't your weekend, you can bum rides off your friends like you do now. When, and only when, Russ goes away to school next year or goes to work and needs exclusive use of the car every day, your mother and I will consider buying you one of your own."

He glared at each of them in turn. "Now, I don't want to hear another word on the subject until that day comes. If I do, you both will be taking the school bus everywhere you go. Is that clear?"

Russ scowled and stared at his feet. Butch thrust his hands in his pockets and moved his eyes around the room.

"I'm waiting," Tim said.

"Yeah, got it."

"Sure, whatever you say."

Tim clasped his hands together and smiled at everyone. "Good. Now could we go back to an attempt at a nice quiet Sunday evening?"

Russ pulled one corner of his mouth into a snarl and skulked out of the room in the direction of the stairway. Not wanting to mirror his brother, Butch made an equally disgusted look and marched outside through the patio door. Tim started to lower himself back into the recliner to enjoy what was left of the football game he had been watching. The look on Joyce's face froze him in place. Now that the boys had been dealt with, it was his turn.

She turned to Ray, still sprawled in the other recliner across the room. "Can you finish that upstairs, dear?"

Ray looked from one parent to the other and quickly accessed the situation. There was either an argument coming, or most likely his dad was about to get a lecture, neither of which he wanted to witness. He pulled his lanky frame together, closed up the recliner with a kick of his legs and stood up. With one last look at his sister, who seemed perfectly content sitting in on another round of humiliation for Tim, he left the room.

Tim watched him go; all the while wishing he was going back to Otterbein with him.

Joyce waited until Ray was gone before she settled back into her chair, facing Tim. With a resigned sigh, Tim shut off the ball game and sat down, bracing himself for what was coming.

"You haven't had much to say the last few days, dear," she began, pleasantly enough. "Have you spoken anymore to Noel Wyatt or that lawyer of his?"

He didn't need to answer. He knew as well as she did he couldn't make a move without her knowing it. "No," he said anyway. "I haven't seen either of them. Hopefully they've gotten the answers to their questions without needing anything from me."

Leslie and Joyce exchanged glances. Tim felt like a child about to be scolded.

Joyce folded her hands in her lap and leaned forward. "We're concerned about you, dear. We're afraid they might trick you into saying something you could regret later; something that might not look good to Ted."

"I wish you wouldn't worry about what I may or may not say to either of them." He looked pointedly at Joyce. "I like to think they couldn't trick me into saying more than I wanted to."

Leslie got out of her chair and crossed the room. She perched herself on the arm of his recliner and leaned against him. "Dad, you know my whole life is at that realty office. I plan on going all the way to the top, even Ted knows it. But if you go to court and say something negative about Sally, something like she got what was coming to her, Ted wouldn't forgive you. It isn't just your future I'm thinking about. It's mine, too."

Tim stiffened. "Well, I'm glad you're only worried about yourself."

She sat up and looked down at him. "Daddy, I didn't say that."

Tim stood up, and the chair became unbalanced so that she had to jump up, too. "I don't want to get involved with this mess with Noreen, but I can't get up in court and perjure myself either."

"What I don't understand is why this lawyer is wasting his time trying to get more evidence in Noreen's case anyway," Joyce said to no one in particular. "She's already admitted she was guilty. You would think the taxpayers in this county have better things to do with their money than retry a woman who has admitted her crimes."

"I don't know what he's doing either," Tim said. He had no intention of telling either of them what Jarrod Bruckner had discussed during their lunch together. "But he is looking. And with Noel Wyatt's help, it's hard to tell what they'll dig up. All I know is if they come up with something, I'm not sticking my head in the noose by lying."

"We're not asking you to lie, dear," Joyce assured him soothingly. "You just don't have to be so quick to tell everything you know."

"You mean like Nixon?"

Joyce's smile pulled into a frown. "That isn't funny, Tim. And that isn't what we're saying. All we want is for you to consider how getting involved is going to affect this family. You have a son in college and two more right behind him. You heard Russ and Butch. All those two do is think up ways to spend your money. You can't risk losing your job because you want to help out an old girlfriend."

Tim had listened to all he wanted to hear. "Whether Noreen Trimble is an old girlfriend or not, doesn't matter. She's in prison, and I don't think she should be. No, I don't want to get involved, but if it comes to that, I need to tell what I know."

Leslie set her fists on her narrow hips. "And just what is it you know, Dad? You are only going on conjecture and personal opinions about both women. You assume because Noreen was the nicer of the two, she's the one telling the truth. Well, what if you're wrong? What if she's lying and she killed Sally in cold blood? You can't go on your opinion or your gut instinct in a courtroom. They won't be interested. They will only listen to fact, and you can't give them that unless you were there that night. You weren't there, were you, Dad?"

Tim looked from one of them to the other. He noticed Kenny standing in the doorway with a soda can in his hand, hanging on every word. When he saw his father looking at him, he spun around and disappeared back into the kitchen. Tim dropped his hands to his sides, considered several different things he could say, but decided against all of it. He turned and left the room. For the first time in his married life, he left the women in his family speechless.

Joyce was sitting at her dressing table removing her makeup when he came into the bedroom several hours later. He had managed to avoid her and Leslie the rest of the evening, but he had to go to bed eventually. Joyce always stayed up later than him, reading or planning something.

He moved past her into the master bath where he began preparing for bed. He listened for sounds of her following him, but all was quiet in the bedroom. When he finished in the bathroom and went into the bedroom, she was under the sheet and duvet, propped up against the headboard with several pillows. An open magazine was across her legs. When she saw him, she smiled and closed the magazine and set it on the nightstand.

Tim slid cautiously between the sheets. He didn't want to argue with her tonight. Monday was typically a busy day in the office, and he needed his eight hours of sleep, particularly after listening to Butch and Russ fight all weekend. He leaned over to kiss her cheek before settling in. She surprised him by turning toward him and meeting him with her mouth.

"Good night, dear," she said sweetly. She switched off the lamp and snuggled into the covers.

"G'night," he mumbled, hoping it would convey how tired and hesitant he was to get into a conversation.

She lay quietly. He could almost hear the gears turning in her head. After twenty-five years of marriage he imagined he knew her better than she knew herself. He clutched the sheet over his chest and stared at the ceiling. He almost spoke first, just to get it over with.

After a few moments of listening for the sound of her voice or her breathing to deepen in sleep, she spoke. "Tim?"

He thought about faking sleep, but that never worked. She'd been known to shake him awake when she had something on her mind.

"Hmm."

"Do you love me?"

His eyes widened. What was she doing? They weren't the kind of couple who lay awake trying to figure out where their relationship was headed.

"Of course I love you, Joyce." He reached for her in the darkness and stroked her arm.

She rolled toward him in the darkness and propped herself up on one elbow. He turned on his side to face her. Over her shoulder, he could see the digits of the electric clock. It was nearly eleven o'clock. He liked to be asleep by ten on Sunday nights. He mentally calculated the hours before six a.m. He was not getting his eight hours tonight.

"I know I wasn't your first choice."

Even though he recognized her attempt to get him to lower his guard so she could attack him about the real issue at hand, he answered appropriately. "Joyce…"

Her bottom lip jutted out a fraction of an inch. "It doesn't matter. Neither of us got exactly what we expected out of this marriage."

Never comfortable with conversations that required he examine his inner feelings, Tim did not like the direction this one was taking. "Joyce, what are you getting at?"

"I want you to be completely honest with me."

He resisted the urge to look at the clock. Why couldn't she let him go to sleep already? "I always have been," he answered.

"What really happened the night Sally Blake was murdered?"

He groaned inwardly and swallowed his impatience. "You know what happened, Joyce. It was on the news."

"No, I mean what really happened. It's just you and me now. You can be honest. Do you know anything more than what the police reported? Why are they trying to get Noreen a new trial?"

He didn't want to tell her, knowing the floodgate of questions and accusations it would release, but he had never been good at keeping things from his wife. She could always see right through him. Any time he tried to keep something close to the vest for her own protection, she could make him spill his guts despite his determination not to.

Don't tell her. Don't tell her, he urged himself. *She doesn't need to know what you know. If it actually amounts to something, you can plead ignorance.*

"Someone called Noel Wyatt the other night and said Noreen wasn't guilty. They saw, or knew someone who saw, what happened that night. They said Noreen was only defending herself. I think Noel and his lawyer friend think it was me."

"You're the witness," she exclaimed.

"No, no, I meant they think I'm the one who called. But I didn't. I don't know anything about it."

"But why would they think it was you? Are you hiding something? You know more than you're telling me, don't you?"

"No, I don't," he said in response to her third question. He wouldn't tell her what he was hiding. Knowing wouldn't do her any good.

"But this doesn't make any sense. If you weren't there and don't know who was, why do they keep talking to you? Why would Noel think you made the phone call in the first place?"

Tim sighed and wiped his hand across his mouth. "Joyce, I'm telling you I don't know. All I can figure is since I was closest to Noreen and Sally they assume I know more about the situation than anyone else. Because of that, they figure I know what drove Noreen and Sally to come to blows. And if there is a witness out there, it stands to reason that it's me."

"Can't you convince them you don't know anything? I don't want them to keep harassing you about something you know nothing about. They're going to cause trouble between you and Ted. If he knows what they're trying to do, he'll blow a gasket."

"He needn't ever know."

"But how will he not know if this thing goes to trial? You can bet he'll be sitting there in the front row, using his influence to make sure Noreen stays behind bars where she belongs."

Tim lay quietly in the darkness, waiting for her to run out of steam.

"You should go see Noel Wyatt tomorrow, Tim. Convince him you don't know what may have led to Sally's death. Tell him if he doesn't stop bothering you, you're going to get your own attorney. There are laws to protect innocent people against slanderous accusations, you know."

"Then he'll think I'm hiding something. This will all blow over, believe me. If the alleged witness never comes forward, there are no grounds for a new trial. And if he does exist, and he comes forward with what he saw, they might not even need me."

"That's not what you said the other night. You said if it goes to trial, Noel and his lawyer will call you to the stand."

He patted her arm. "Honey, worrying about this isn't doing either of us any good. Now please go to sleep. I promise to keep you up to speed if anything changes, but I don't think that's likely. They can't go forward without new evidence."

She flopped onto her back and pulled the sheet up to her chin. "Well, it better not, that's all I have to say. Our entire livelihood hangs in the balance. I won't have that woman jeopardize everything we've worked so hard for."

Tim didn't need to ask which woman she was referring to. He knew she would rather see Noreen rot in prison than have her husband take the stand and say anything in her behalf, even if every word of it was true. Justice and truth meant nothing to Joyce as long as all was well in her little corner of the world. Tim rolled over and stared at the opposite wall and willed sleep to come.

Mark Eisinger never had trouble going to sleep in his life. Even in medical school with exams and pressure keeping his friends pacing the floor and buried in books, he had slept like a baby as soon as the lights went out. But since the pain had started and the nagging realization of what was going on inside his head, followed by the doctor's diagnosis, he found himself watching the electronic digits on his clock change from one to the next with a gentle click.

These days—or nights—he was awake long after Johnny Carson went off, even when he had to be in the office the next morning. For appearances sake, he refused to stop seeing patients in his office though he no longer performed surgery. The neurologist had suggested he retire and spend his last moments in the warmth of his family. Go to the beach and golf away the last few months. Out of the question; he could never relax long enough to enjoy one round of golf, and if he had to spend one moment in the warmth of his family, he would go stark raving mad.

He needed to work. He had to keep busy. If not, he would spend every waking minute watching the clock tick away what was left of his life—doing it after Carson went off was enough for him.

Lying awake as another morning broke across his front yard was what made him call Noel Wyatt two weeks ago. He had dialed the number three times, and then hung up each time before the phone had a chance to ring on the other end. Finally he forced himself to stay on the line. When Noel answered, he forgot what he planned to say. Then he thought of Betty. He couldn't take what he knew to his grave. He couldn't leave Noreen in prison where she could be killed without doing what he could to see justice served. His plan was to call and plant a seed in Noel's mind. Let him and Noreen's high priced attorney do the work. But at least they would know her act hadn't been premeditative. His conscience would be clear. He would have finally done right by Betty's memory.

After he hung up, he had fallen asleep like in the old days and slept soundly until nearly noon. But upon awakening, he knew right away a phone call wasn't enough. Telling Noel about a witness wouldn't get Noreen a new trial. She would still grow old in that prison and it would be his fault. He had to go all the way if he was going to atone for his sins and let Betty rest in peace.

"Dear Betty," he said aloud to the four walls. "I shouldn't have done that to you." He punched his pillow and rolled over. Sleep was a long time coming.

Chapter Eighteen

Calvin couldn't believe his luck. He had all but given up on finding anything that even alluded to Aunt Paige's fortune. He had begun to question the likelihood that a fortune ever existed. What if old Granddad Trotter hadn't made out as well as everyone thought he had on the land deal with the government? It was within the realm of possibility that he had drank up all the money or squandered it away before he died in the little house behind the A.M.E. church. Everyone in town whispered the money was buried in the back yard. What if it was true, and someone had dug it up one night when he was on one of his benders, and the old man was never the wiser?

Living with his Aunt Paige—he used the term 'aunt' loosely since she had only been married to Uncle Howard for eleven months before he croaked—this entire summer had made Calvin doubt there ever was a fortune. Everyone said she married the old rooster for his money and nothing else. To her credit, why else would anyone marry Uncle Howard? Wasn't she in for a rude awakening, they said, when she found out how desperately he clung to a nickel?

The whole town held its collective breath and waited for Paige to loosen her purse strings. Trotters from far and wide even dared hope she might take pity on their financial situations and throw a dime their way. Of course those were the ones who didn't know her very well. Even those familiar with her heartless disposition wondered if the sudden freedom from financial concerns would cure those quirks in her personality.

Years went by and nothing in Paige Trotter's life changed. If anything, she grew more cantankerous and ornery. But what about the money, where was it? Was it possible she had married Uncle Howard for his money, only to discover he didn't have any?

Calvin began to doubt his mission. What if he was wrong? He lay in his bed, mulling over what he knew, and dreading the possibility that he might actually have to go to work in the drugstore for Noel Wyatt after all. Yes, he had taken all the courses and passed the final exams on his third attempt. If he never learned another thing in his life, he knew he didn't want to spend the rest of his life as a pharmacists' assistant. He would rather be drawn and quartered. At least that would be a poetic end to a wasted life rather than working behind a counter in a white lab coat, growing paler and duller with each passing year. He had dreams, visions.

He would start out small like his hero, Hugh Nelson; writing beautiful lyrics that rocketed Nashville's most talented songbirds to the top of the charts. When the time was right, he would break out with a hit song he had been sitting on for years and make a name for himself. Just like Hugh had done, he would change his name from boring, forgettable Calvin Trotter to something like Willie or Waylon, and Jenna's Creek would be nothing more than a brief mention in his biography.

Three days ago, he had received affirmation that his dream was still alive and well. From the post office box he secretly rented, he had drawn a letter from a publishing company in Nashville; one of the many to whom he had been sending his songs for the past two years. He had already sold several, but the royalty checks he received thus far had barely been worth the stamp it cost to mail them.

This song was different. He knew he had a winner when the lyrics came to him one night as if out of the blue. He had fine-tuned it and then sent it off to his contact person at a company who had bought two previous songs. That was six months ago. He had written more songs and tried not to agonize over it, but he felt a part of him was out there in the world, withering on the vine because no one would give him a chance.

Then the letter came. Not only did they love the song, they had presented it to one of the top female recording artists in country music today, and she couldn't wait to get it into the studio. The fact that they were changing it into a woman's song didn't bother Calvin one bit. If the price was right, and it put him one step closer to realizing his dreams, they could train a seal to sing it for all he cared.

Until now, none of Calvin's songs had made it onto national radio. But with this artist crooning away, it would be heard all over the country, maybe all over the world. Calvin even let himself dream of attending the Country Music Awards next year when his song was nominated for song of the year. The artist might even perform it live on stage. Wouldn't that be something! He imagined the camera panning out into the crowd to find him in the audience, dressed in his black tux with a beautiful, statuesque model type hanging on his arm. Not too statuesque; it wouldn't do if she was taller than him. When the winner of the category was announced, he would be called onto the stage. He would leave the model in her seat as he made his way through the throngs of his peers all rising to their feet to honor him.

He imagined his parents, Aunt Paige, Noel Wyatt, and the rest of Jenna's Creek glued to their sets, watching in slack-jawed wonder as he moved forward to claim his award. He wouldn't mention any of them in his acceptance speech. What had they done to encourage him or help him out when he needed it? He would thank his producers and the singer for bringing his words to life, and a few more important people in the business, and then he would humbly take his seat.

When his parents called later to congratulate him, he wouldn't even take the call. He'd have the model take a message.

But none of that was going to happen if he didn't get to Nashville. He had to get there now and strike while the iron was hot. While this song was in production and a few doors were open a tiny crack for an obscure writer like him to slip through, he had to make his move. Sadly, he wasn't going anywhere without money.

He already knew Aunt Paige had very little money in her savings and checking accounts, and he couldn't very well go to the bank to draw it out. Every bank teller in town knew she would never give her passbook to a nephew to make a withdrawal for her.

He needed cash.

Just as he was beginning to think he might have to hitchhike to Nashville with the last sixteen dollars he had to his name, Mom and Dad of all people, came to his rescue.

Aunt Paige didn't attend church, and she had no friends, so she was downright giddy when they called to invite her to a dinner theater out of town. She would be gone the entire evening.

As soon as she left, Calvin hurried upstairs to widen his search of the house. He had already meticulously turned her bedroom upside down those afternoons she was at work. He had been through every drawer, cabinet, and closet downstairs. He had even tapped around the fireplace for loose bricks and the base boards for loose floorboards; inspiration from all the Hardy Boys Mysteries he read as a boy.

The house had no basement. That left the attic and crawlspace. He prayed the attic turned up something so he wouldn't have to face the crawlspace. He loathed cramped, damp spaces.

He wasn't thrilled to search the attic. He feared he would find nothing more than mice, spiders, and dust bunnies as big as a Plymouth. But his father had told him stories of the cans and mason jars of money Grandpa Jeremiah left setting in cabinets and drawers and boxes. Uncle Howard was rumored to be the same way. If he had left jars and boxes of moldy money hidden around the house, Paige either hadn't found them yet or wasn't going to start spending money until Malcolm was dead and buried and she no longer had to fear sharing Howard's wealth with anyone.

Calvin figured he had three hours at best to search the attic. He wanted to be finished and sitting downstairs in his robe and slippers looking like the absent-minded dolt the whole world thought he was by the time Aunt Paige returned home.

He stuck his head into the small, crowded space above the second floor hallway and shuddered. Stale air crowded around his head and shoulders. The ceiling was barely high enough for him to stand crouched over. He didn't know how much time up here he could take. How he prayed this search turned up something. He would be pleased with one can of crumpled bills, one rubber banded bundle, anything; he wasn't greedy. Okay, he was greedy. But his desperation to get to Nashville by the end of the week outweighed his greed at this point.

He panned the flashlight around the entrance of the attic to make sure the ceiling joists were strong enough to hold him before leaving the safety of the ladder. The house had been built around the first of the century. Very little had been done to maintain the structure since the contractors finished and walked away.

Starting with the boxes and trunks closest to the trapdoor, Calvin made his way into the recesses of the attic. Most of the boxes were quickly disregarded when he discovered they contained useless things like old clothes or Christmas decorations. He had a hard time imagining Uncle Howard or Aunt Paige celebrating the Savior's birth, or anything else for that matter. When he found a box of photo albums, his pulse quickened—the perfect place for Uncle Howard to hide his booty. Only a sentimental sot would be interested in old pictures, not someone after monetary gain. Leave it to Uncle Howard to reward the one looking at pictures of old Aunt Bessie while thumbing his nose at the gold digger.

Calvin pulled the photo albums out of the box and set them on the floor beside him. He leafed through them quickly, aware of the rapidly passing time. Some of the pictures' edges had curled away from the album pages. He carefully peeled away a few with his fingernail to peek behind. Hiding a property deed or stock certificate behind the photograph of a sour faced relative sounded right up Uncle Howard's alley. By the time he closed the last page on the last photo album, Calvin was ready to hurl the archive of Trotters through the tiny window.

Nothing.

He checked his watch. He had been up here for over an hour. If he didn't find something soon, he would have to move downstairs to the crawlspace. The more he thought about it, the more likely his uncle had buried his wealth under the house. It was highly likely the bowels of the old property contained a fortune even Paige didn't know about. Why else would she continue living in this drafty old house and working at the drugstore?

Calvin stepped gingerly onto another ceiling joist to reach the next box. He could tell by the heft of it, it contained dishes or pottery. He almost moved on but something told him to stop and look. Later he attributed it to his sensitive artist's nature. He unfolded each of the four sides of the cardboard lid, his heart sinking as more and more of the box's contents came into view.

Just as he thought, glassware.

He was about to push it aside and give up on the attic when something caught his eye; a heavy linen folder at the bottom of the box. He almost missed it because it was the same color as the box. Again, he attributed it to his artist's sensitivity. He carefully removed quart jars and an old cookie jar, all the while telling himself there was nothing to it. But when his hands touched the heavy packet, he knew it was more than lining for the bottom of the box.

He straightened as much as the low ceiling would allow and opened the folder. He fastened the weak beam of the flashlight onto the print. His heart leaped in his chest. In his hand was Howard Trotter's last Will and Testament. He lifted the corner of the Will and found himself staring at a bank passbook and several titles for property and stocks.

With shaking hands, he flipped back to the first page and studied the paper. He scanned through line after line of legal speech typed neatly on an attorney's letterhead.

I, Howard William Trotter, being of sound mind and body...

So, old Uncle Howard actually had a Will. He had something worth taking the time to hire a lawyer to draw one up for him. Knowing his uncle as he did through stories told around the dinner table and anecdotes from visiting relatives, he would have thought Uncle Howard would have scribbled something on the back of a matchbox to save himself the legal fees.

Nearly the entire first page was dedicated to Howard defending his rights to dispense of his property anyway he saw fit. Finally, at the last paragraph, Howard wrapped up his meanderings to actually name a benefactor. Calvin flipped the page and read the top line of the next page...

To my nephew, Calvin Jeremiah Trotter, I leave the bulk of my estate, including...

Calvin let out a whoop of delight. The page he was reading came loose from the stack and threatened to slide onto the floor. He closed his hand over the sheaf of loose papers to keep them from sliding apart and lost his grip on the flashlight. It clattered to the floor, and the room was plunged into darkness. Calvin closed the folder, clutched it to his chest, and leaned forward to retrieve the flashlight. He needed to get downstairs where he could see what he was reading. He wouldn't even bother repacking the glassware into the box. All he could imagine was his name up in lights at the Grand Ole Opry.

In the darkness, his hand closed over the flashlight. He straightened up and hit the button to turn it back on. Nothing happened. "Aw, great," he hissed. He smacked the flashlight against his leg and tried again; still nothing.

"Who needs you?" he said to the flashlight and turned toward the open hatch. Without thinking, he stepped off the floor joist. The thin plaster gave way under his weight. He heard the splintering of wood and felt an unreal sensation of floating in air. Then his ribs and arms caught the rotten boards on his way through the floor. The folder and flashlight were snatched from his hands. He was barely aware of the hallway floor coming up to meet him. Then his feet touched the unforgiving surface, and his legs folded beneath him. He saw a bright red gash appear on his forearm when a piece of the overhead light fixture glanced soundly off his shoulder and sliced through his flesh. Mason jars dropped around him and shattered on the hardwood floor, reminding him of John Wayne dodging enemy gunfire in the war pictures he watched with his father.

His entire body was in pain, though he couldn't isolate a single wound. He stared up at the gaping hole in the ceiling he had just come through as a shower of broken plaster, dust, and heavy linen paper wafted down around him. He became aware of hurrying feet on the stairs to his left. He half expected to see John Wayne moving across the beach leading a battalion into harm's way. Then he realized it was a greater force than John Wayne coming at him.

He laid his head back onto the floor and let the blackness overtake him.

The first face Calvin saw upon regaining consciousness belonged to a volunteer paramedic who worked with the Jenna's Creek Fire Department. He gripped the young woman's arm and pleaded. "Don't tell my Aunt Paige."

The young woman smiled and pulled away from him. Her face was replaced with that of his aunt. "Don't tell me what, Calvin, dear?" she asked, her smile a feigned mask of concern.

Calvin swiveled his head around until he caught sight of the paramedic again. "Just let me die."

She removed his eyeglasses that had managed to remain in place during the fall, and situated a plastic mask over his face. He slipped into sweet oblivion.

Chapter Nineteen

On Monday afternoon, David Davis and Noel Wyatt were waiting in Noel's den for Noreen's attorney to arrive. That morning David had called Noel to ask him about arranging a meeting with Mr. Bruckner.

The judge was making himself comfortable in Noel's den when the doorbell sounded throughout the house. Noel got up and hastened to the front door. David moved to the bay window that overlooked the backyard. He put his hands in his pockets, turned his back to the window, and gazed idly around the room. Besides the kitchen, this was the only room in the house that looked like someone lived in it. Noel's stamp was on every furnishing. Not like the rest of the house that had been professionally designed and maintained. He wondered if it ever occurred to Noel to move into something smaller. He doubted Noel ever gave the matter a moment's thought.

He looked toward the door at the sound of approaching footsteps. Noel was making introductions before he and the younger man entered the room. "Judge, this is Noreen's lawyer. His daddy, Harrison Bruckner went to school with me about a hundred years ago. You'd never meet a finer litigator. Present company excluded, of course." He slapped the young man on the back and laughed at his own joke. "Young man, this is Judge David Davis. He's retired from the Appellate Court. Before that, he was the county prosecutor here in Auburn County."

David and Jarrod met in the center of the dark paneled room.

"Nice to meet you," David said, pumping the young man's hand. "I'm afraid I didn't get your name."

"Jarrod, Sir. It's a pleasure to meet you too, Judge."

"Sorry about that," Noel said from the doorway. He advanced into the room and put his hand on Jarrod's shoulder. "I never can remember your name, son. You won't hold it against an old timer, will you? Every time I look at you, all I see is your old man forty years ago. You look just like him, except you're not near as ugly."

"Glad to hear it, Sir."

Noel laughed, as much at the joke as Jarrod calling him "sir", then clasped his hands together. "All right, then, let's get started. Everybody have a seat. How about I get us something to drink first?"

After everyone was settled around the den with glasses of iced tea, David began.

"I was reading the files of the Sally Blake case the other day. Came across a few interesting factors." He told them about Connie Noble and her relationship with Sally Blake. "If anyone had a reason to go back to the house and see something she wasn't meant to see, it was Connie. She didn't care for Sally. She made no bones about it in her report. There's a possibility she also wouldn't have seen a need to report what she saw to anyone. Since Sally's remains weren't found for so long, she may have thought it best to let sleeping dogs lie. If she didn't think Noreen had broken any laws, and as long as no charges were filed, she might not have wanted to get involved. From what I could gather, she's lived out west for years and is probably unaware Sally's remains have been found and Noreen charged in her death."

He stopped talking and took a drink of his tea. Noel and Jarrod stared thoughtfully into their own glasses.

"If the witness was Connie, who do you suppose made the phone call to me?" Noel asked. "A husband, maybe?"

"Could have been an ex-husband who she told what she knew before she moved away," David speculated. "If he heard what was going on, he might have felt inclined to help Noreen out."

"But why come forward after she's been in prison for more than two years?" Jarrod pointed out. "If our caller didn't want to get involved twenty-some years ago, why is he willing to now? And why keep Connie's identity a secret? If she didn't do anything except keep quiet about what she saw, he surely wouldn't think she'd be prosecuted after all this time."

Noel spoke up. "Not necessarily. Lots of folks around here are nervous about getting involved in legal matters, regardless of the amount of time that's passed. We've got to assume a lot has changed in this person's life in the past thirty years. Consider this fellow—or lady, for that matter—has matters going on in his own life he doesn't want to jeopardize."

Jarrod set his briefcase on the coffee table in front of him and opened it. He took out a pencil and a yellow steno pad. "At this point we know of three people who could be our witness, the caller, or both. Connie Noble, the woman who was jealous of Sally." He scratched her name on the steno pad. "The alleged married man. And Tim Shelton." He looked up and gazed at each of them. "Anyone else?"

They both thought for a moment and then shook their heads. "I've talked to most of the people on Noreen's list," Judge Davis said, "and read and reread reports. No one else seems to have had a reason to go back to the house. Most of them were just friends of the group and guests at the party."

Jarrod had been studying another paper in his briefcase. "What about James Steele, the man everyone thought killed Sally in the first place? He would've had a reason to hang around. He said he dropped Sally off. What if he waited for her, and then got tired of waiting and walked up to the house?"

Noel shook his head. "The caller talked about the witness in present tense. He had to know James has been dead for three years.

And why bother telling me a dead man had witnessed something to prove Noreen's innocence?"

"Because there's more evidence out there if we know where to look. He didn't want us giving up without pulling out all the stops."

"But why bother unless he has some kind of connection to Noreen?" Noel insisted. "I mean, if Noreen wasn't anything to him, would he care if we go to all this trouble or not?"

"So you're suggesting the caller is either a family member or a close friend?" David clarified.

"It has to be something like that; someone whose conscience is keeping him up at night."

"Someone like Tim Shelton," Jarrod said.

"I didn't say that. But I doubt it's someone Noreen doesn't have at least a passing acquaintance with."

"These are all things we need to keep in mind," David admitted. "It seems like every time there's a new development in this case, it's because of something that was overlooked in the first place."

"James Steele," Jarrod said aloud as he added another name to the short list.

"Well, since it's impossible to question him," Noel said, "what's the likelihood of talking to Connie or the unknown married man?"

"Not good," David replied. "I talked to Connie's uncle, and he and his wife can't even agree what state she's living in. And the married man could easily be a figment of Sally's imagination."

Noel sat back in a black leather chair and put his foot on the corner of the coffee table. "If there was some way of finding out if he actually existed or not..."

"The most likely one to get that information out of would be Tim Shelton," Jarrod said. "But he isn't talking. It's a shame we don't know how to get hold of Miss Noble."

David looked up from his end of the black leather sofa. "I know someone I might speak with who may know something about the situation."

"You do that, Judge, and I'll pay Mr. Shelton another visit tomorrow."

It had been several days since he'd last heard anything from Noel Wyatt. Tim was beginning to hope everything had blown over. Without a witness to come forward, a new trial was out of the question for Noreen. He would not be forced to get involved. What he knew would stay his secret. So why did he feel so rotten?

He knew this was exactly what Joyce and Leslie wanted. They were worried that Mr. Blake would realize Tim was talking to Noel and want to know why. How could Tim continue to work at Blake Realty if he testified on Noreen's behalf? How would he pay for his three youngest sons' education if he were suddenly out of a job? What about Leslie? She would never forgive him if his participation in Noreen's defense cost her her future at the agency.

He held his breath every time his office door opened for fear it was Noel or the attorney with more questions, or worse, accusations that he was hiding something. How long could he avoid them? How long could he avoid the truth?

Every night when he got home, he stayed out of Joyce's way as much as possible. He would almost prefer to face prison himself than her reproving stares. The stares that reminded him of what a failure he was, and if it hadn't been for Ted Blake lifting him out of the dairy stall, he would still be on the farm milking cows with his old man.

A wave of shame washed over him. He couldn't remember the last time he had been home to visit his parents, even though they lived a few miles out of town. About the time the boys were in middle school, Joyce stopped accompanying the family to the farm. She and Leslie stayed home on the odd Sunday when he drove out with the boys to visit his mother. After a while his parents stopped asking about Joyce and their only granddaughter. They knew the truth and hated to hear the excuses Tim made up to appease their feelings as much as he hated making them.

The boys loved the farm as much as Joyce and Leslie hated it. Where else could they gig frogs and chase ponies around the lot beside the barn and wade through the creek? But eventually they outgrew those pursuits, and their other interests kept them too busy to visit their ailing and generally uninteresting grandparents. Without keeping the boys in touch, Tim found it easier and easier to skip the trips himself. What was the point? It was always a battle with Joyce before he left and after he returned, and his parents seemed to understand what was going on.

Tim was never good at sticking up for himself. When his older brothers and sister talked of how they couldn't wait to get away from the farm, Tim joined in their banter. He made fun of the old man behind his back, the way they did. But secretly he loved the open spaces, the freedom of the land, the hills, and the oneness with nature. He loved calving season when he often missed school because he was up late into the night helping Dad with a cow that was having a rough time of it, and the vet was busy elsewhere or Dad couldn't afford to call him.

He certainly couldn't stand up to his friends at school who talked of going into medicine, business, advertising, or something that earned a king's ransom and would get them away from Jenna's Creek. They made fun of his farmer's shoes, farmer's jeans, and the smell of ammonia that clung to everything around him.

Instead of going to agricultural college, which he thought would be interesting, he signed up for business courses.

"There's no money on the farm," he told Noreen, even though the two of them had discussed someday building a little house on the farm and filling it with children. "The only chance of a decent life is out of Jenna's Creek."

By this time, his older siblings had taken their own advice and beat pavement putting as much highway between them and

Auburn County as they could. Dad and Mom never admitted as much, but looking back, Tim was sure they knew how their children looked down on them. Tim was ashamed of the way he felt, but it was too late to change his mind without looking like a fool in front of his friends.

He didn't think Noreen would ridicule him for wanting to stay in the country. She would understand when no one else did. But it wasn't only how she or other people looked at him by then. He had talked himself out of farm life. He liked the idea of a nice house in town, air conditioning, a car instead of a pickup truck, and no more farmer's clothes. He'd get a job where he wore a clean suit to work every day. He wouldn't come home sweaty, sun burned, and dusty. His wife would be proud of him. His kids wouldn't make fun of him behind his back. And even though the old man would be disappointed again, like he had been when the older kids left home and never came back, he would eventually be proud of Tim, too.

Tim never thought of going into real estate. He wasn't much of a salesman. Then he got tangled up with Sally Blake. Three weeks after the one-night tryst he regretted with every fiber of his being, she told him she was "in trouble", as people said in those days. In the next breath, she told him not to worry; she had it all figured out. Tim should have been suspicious, but he was naïve and scared to death.

Just as Sally expected, Ted offered him a position at the agency. The offer was like a gift from heaven to Tim—for about three days. He'd have his office job in an established business. No risk on his part. He'd wear a suit everyday, and eventually he'd learn to talk someone into buying a piece of property they really couldn't afford the way Mr. Blake did.

Unfortunately, the sick feeling in the pit of his stomach wouldn't go away. He knew he couldn't marry Sally Blake. He even realized she didn't really want him. She would grow dissatisfied and cast him aside like she did every other man in her life. She only had eyes for Tim because he belonged to her best friend. Tim had been used. He hated himself.

What could he do? How could he explain to Noreen what he had done while he was engaged to her?

He hated himself. His feelings for Sally were nearly as severe. He thought about running off. He could join the Army. Yes, he would probably never see Noreen again, but she was out of his life anyway. Eventually Sally and her tenacious father would track him down and garnish his paltry military paycheck for child support, but he didn't care. At least he wouldn't have to marry her.

He wondered if the Army was able to force a man to marry a girl he got into trouble. If they tried, he would go AWOL and run away from them, too.

Who was he kidding? He wasn't going anywhere. He was stuck.

He could barely face Noreen while she made plans for their engagement party. Every time he saw her face or heard her voice, he tensed, expecting her to tell him that she'd had a talk with Sally, and Sally had told her some disturbing things; things that couldn't possibly be true, things that involved him. He almost told her the truth a dozen times but every time she looked at him with those trusting blue-green eyes, his nerve deserted him. He couldn't hurt her. He couldn't bear to see her face fill with pain. How could he have been so stupid to throw away the love of such a wonderful, compassionate soul for one moment in Sally Blake's arms?

He thought about ending his own life, but knew he lacked the nerve to do that as well.

Then Sally told him she made a mistake. She laughed and grabbed his hand and said wasn't she just the silliest thing. There was no baby. She had miscalculated. But then she sobered and said nothing had to change. Her parents were already resigned to the fact that she wasn't a virginal bride. They didn't hate him. They didn't even blame him. Daddy would still give him a position in the company. They could still have a very happy life together.

Once again, Tim was too shocked to say anything. All he could think of was he had Noreen back. He was free. He wouldn't be saddled with Sally the rest of his life because of one reckless moment.

Thank you, God, he prayed over and over as Sally prattled on. *I'll never sin again. I'll go to church every Sunday. I'll confess everything to Noreen. I'll never hurt her again.*

Clearing his conscience with God was a lot easier than coming clean with Sally.

When she threw her arms around him and pressed her body to his in celebration, she didn't understand when he pushed her away.

"Sally, please. Don't."

Her arms dropped to her sides. She was unaccustomed to a man's rebuff. "What's the matter? Didn't you hear what I said? There's no baby. We can start our life together with nothing tying us down. We can travel. My parents will send us on a honeymoon wherever we want to go."

He put up his hand to stop her. "Sally, would you shut up for one minute!" he shouted, surprising both of them. He gulped and stared at his feet. He had to say it. For once in his life, he couldn't stand there and let someone else dictate his life.

"I can't go through with it," he said in one breath. "I don't love you. I love Noreen. I'm sorry if I hurt—"

A stinging slap brought his words to a halt. She hissed an oath he had never heard out of a lady's mouth before. "How dare you!" she shrieked. "You used me. You took advantage of my feelings for you. I'll ruin you. I'll tell Nory everything. I'll tell Daddy. You won't get Noreen. You won't work in this county. You'll be sorry you ever met me."

She stormed out. He didn't bother telling her he already regretted having met her.

Nothing was different today than it had been thirty years ago. He never learned how to stand up to anyone. Sometimes he wondered—on the rare occasion he let himself dwell on anything other than his job and his family—if he was somehow punishing himself for the pain he caused everyone who made the mistake of loving him. He continued to hurt his parents with every week that went by without a phone call or token visit. He'd hurt Noreen. She knew about Sally, whether Sally told her or she figured it out on her own, he wasn't sure, but she knew nonetheless. He'd hurt Ted Blake by using what had happened between him and Sally to procure a cushy position for himself in the company. He deserved to be punished.

When Linda buzzed and told him Noel Wyatt was on line one, he pasted a smile on his face as if Noel could see through the phone lines, and picked up the extension.

"Noel," he said expansively. He had been living the life of Tim Shelton—salesman, for so long, it was often hard to shut off. "What can I do you for?"

Noel chuckled. "Tim, how are you? I was wondering if I might hop over there sometime this afternoon before heading home. Are you going to have a free minute before the end of the day?"

"I'm sure I can squeeze you in," he said, even though the knot in his stomach made it harder and harder to maintain the air of levity. He checked his calendar. "How about four or thereabouts."

A pause on Noel's end and then, "Sounds good. See you then."

Tim hung up the phone and reached reflexively for the cigarette in his shirt pocket that was no longer there.

Mark Eisinger hadn't been out of bed in three days. He couldn't keep anything down. He had avoided calling Brenda until the last possible minute. He would have rather called Mona, but it was a weekday, and he couldn't bear taking her away from her classroom of sixth graders.

Now his daughter stood over him, a grave expression on her face. "I called Dr. Pack," she said, wringing her hands. Even as sick as he was, she braced herself for the reaction.

He could barely close his eyes in response. "Brenda, the man's time is valuable. There's nothing he can do for me. He knows it and I know it. Leave him alone."

Brenda choked out a little sob and sank onto her knees beside the bed. "He said we should bring you in."

He closed his eyes again. It hurt too much to shake his head. "I'm not going anywhere," he whispered.

"Daddy."

Mercifully, her husband appeared behind her.

"Steve," Mark said with a relief in his voice audible to everyone in the room, "call Mark Jr. and Mona. We need to talk to the grandchildren."

Brenda barked out another sob and brought her hand to her mouth. Mark closed his eyes and let the pain medication take effect.

David Davis thought he had dialed the wrong number when a young boy picked up the phone on the first ring.

"Hello, is this Dr. Eisinger's residence?"

"Yeah, just a minute." Then he heard, "Mom, it's for Grandpa."

A moment later, a man picked up. "Hello. This is Steve Broderick, Dr. Eisinger's son-in-law. Can I help you with something?"

"Oh. I was wondering if this is a convenient time to speak with the doctor. This is Judge David Davis. Mark and I are old friends."

"Judge Davis, I hate to tell you this, but Mark isn't doing well. We are trying to talk him into going to the hospital. He can be a stubborn old cuss." Then he chuckled nervously. "I apologize for that. We're all under a lot of strain right now. When he gets to feeling better, I'll tell him you called."

David heard what the son-in-law didn't want to put into words. "I'm really sorry to hear that. If there's anything I can do…"

"Yes, sure. Thanks. I'll tell him you called. That might lift his spirits."

David hung up the phone, a sense of impending doom hanging over him. And not just for the ailing surgeon.

Chapter Twenty

"It isn't often we get an applicant with your qualifications, Miss Blackwood," the librarian said with a wide smile. "And so soon after we put the word out we're looking for someone."

Christy smiled back. She had almost not applied when she read the ad in the paper the day before yesterday. She never considered working at a library before, but in retrospect, it seemed like the perfect placement for her. It was better than waiting tables. She only prayed it paid better. The more she thought about it, the more she realized her mother couldn't afford to keep her forever. She needed a job. She needed a reason to get up in the morning. She needed to get on with her life.

"Thank you, Mrs. Gardner. When I saw the ad, I didn't know how long it had been in the paper. I was afraid the position was already filled."

"Well, we have been considering a few other people, but you are by far the most qualified. You would make an excellent addition to our staff. As long as your references check out, I don't see any reason why you won't find a position here. I should be able to let you know as early as tomorrow."

Christy's lips felt frozen to her teeth. Her references; she might as well leave now. She had been as honest as possible in filling out the application, including her employment history. She had hoped the Janelle Wyatt Memorial Library wouldn't go to all the trouble of making a long distance phone call to check her references at BBW.

"Thank you very much, Mrs. Gardner. I look forward to hearing from you."

Christy left the library with a heavy heart. She had noticed a help wanted sign in a dog groomer's window on the corner of Myles and Munroe Streets. Maybe she could stop by there on her way home and see if the position was still open. With her luck, they would want an extensive work history, too.

When Mrs. Gardner had asked why she had left her position at the firm to come back to Jenna's Creek, she hadn't missed a beat. She explained that since her dad's death, her mom was lonely. Her brother was away at college fulltime, and the family didn't think it was healthy for Abby to be alone at this time.

Christy didn't miss the knowing look on Mrs. Gardner's face. Was there anyone in this town who didn't know about Abby's past with Noel Wyatt? Let the woman believe what she wanted. Christy didn't mention that money issues were a major factor in finding a job as soon as possible, and that neither she nor Abby seemed to have much of it. She didn't care what Mrs. Gardner thought. As soon as she saved enough money, she was out of this town.

Noel was glad to see the outer offices empty when he walked into the real estate agency a few minutes after four that afternoon. He didn't want to fight his way through a pack of vultures on his way to Tim's office. He smiled at the receptionist as he walked past. She nodded and buzzed Tim's office.

"Mr. Wyatt is on his way in," he heard her say behind him as he reached Tim's door. He tapped on the door before opening it to the sound of Tim's voice.

Tim was standing at the other side of the desk when Noel entered. Both men leaned across the scarred top to shake hands before lowering themselves into the matching well-used leather chairs.

"Good to see you again, Tim."

"You too, Noel." Tim's assurance didn't quite meet his eyes.

"I know you're busy, so I won't take a lot of your time. You know why I'm here."

Tim nodded. He folded his hands in front of him and rested them on the desk. "Have you gotten anymore phone calls from the witness?"

Noel shook his head. "We've narrowed the possibilities of who the caller is, or who he was referring to, down to four names. Your name is on that list."

"I figured as much. Why else would you be here?"

"You have to admit, Tim, you had the most logical excuse for coming back that night. You had a relationship with both women. You might have thought Sally was going to tell Noreen what happened between you, and you wanted to be there to defend yourself. Or you didn't know Sally was there, and you went back to break it off with Noreen."

Tim shook his head adamantly. "No way. I never would have done that. All I could think about was how to make it up to Noreen."

"And how were you planning to do that?"

His shoulders sagged. "I don't know. I never got around to it."

"Then help me stop wasting time," Noel snapped, his impatience getting the better of him. "Noreen is in trouble." He leaned forward and glared into Tim's eyes. "If it wasn't you, tell me who was there that night. Was it the girl who caught Sally with her boyfriend? Connie Noble? Was Sally seeing a married man? You know more than you're telling, Tim, and you're wasting everyone's time."

Tim looked like he had shrunk two sizes on the other side of the desk. He spread his hands out plaintively in front of him. "I'm telling you, Noel, I didn't go back to the house. I was the last person to leave the party. I stayed and helped straighten up the house a little, but I had to get up early the next morning to help Pop on the farm, and Noreen insisted I leave. It was around one a.m. I think. I went out to my car, got in, and drove away. I didn't see anyone skulking about."

Noel stared at him for a moment, looking for any clue that he was being less than forthright. "All right, then," he said, satisfied that Tim was telling the truth about leaving the party, but still not convinced he wasn't hiding something. "But come on, Tim. You had to have known what was going on between them that led to an all out brouhaha in Will Trimble's living room. If Noreen says she killed Sally in self-defense, I believe her. I know you do, too."

Tim could well imagine Sally making someone mad enough to want to kill her, to want to silence her mocking, to erase the sneer from her beautiful face. He had seen that sneer more times than he cared to recall, and he had wanted to remove it by force himself. "Their relationship was complicated," he said simply.

Noel wasn't buying it. "Noreen is a dear, loving, compassionate soul. I can't believe for a minute she allowed herself to get into a fight over something petty. Tim, what do you know? You have to think of Noreen. You loved her. You were getting married. You have to still care about what happens to her."

"I do care about her safety, but whatever there was between Noreen and me doesn't matter anymore. I have Joyce. I have to think of what all this will do to her."

"What *what* will do to her? Admitting what you knew about Sally and Noreen's fight can't hurt Joyce twenty-eight years after the fact. She knows you had a life before her."

Tim rubbed his hand across his jaw. "Yes, it will hurt Joyce." He gestured around the office. "I'm not a self-made man like you and Ted Blake. All this was given to me…"

When he didn't continue, Noel cocked his head to one side, feigning ignorance. He didn't tell Tim he already knew through Judge Davis about the baby Sally was supposedly carrying. "Why? What did Ted Blake owe you?"

"He thought I was going to marry Sally."

Noel managed to look confused. "Why would he think that?"

Tim hung his head. When he looked up, defeat was written all over his face. Noel almost felt sorry for him.

"This is what I don't want Joyce to find out," he began in a small voice. "I never wanted anyone to know." He stared at a spot on the paneled wall for a moment before focusing on Noel. "I had a one-night stand with Sally. It was a mistake. I loved Noreen. To this day, I don't know why I did it. Stupid, I guess. But regardless, it happened. A couple of weeks later, Sally came and told me she was in trouble. I couldn't believe it. It was the worst possible thing that could've happened. I was engaged to Noreen. We were already planning this big engagement party. I was hoping against hope Sally would realize what a mistake our affair had been and want to forget it as badly as I did."

He shook his head dismally at the memory. "Instead, she seemed to latch onto it. Like it was what she'd been hoping for. When she told me about the baby, she was already making plans; telling me how her dad would be so mad, but then he'd get used to the idea. He would set me up in the business. I would never have to milk another cow as long as I lived. She loved me, and she was so happy we were having a baby together.

"She kept talking and talking, and I kept getting more and more confused. I didn't know which end was up. Then she said we had to go tell her parents right then. She grabbed my hand and said, 'You have to do the right thing, Tim. You did this to me. You can't turn your back on me now.' I knew she was right. I wasn't brought up to turn my back on my responsibilities. When you got a girl in trouble, you…"

He dropped his head into his hand and rubbed his forehead. His free hand stole to his shirt pocket and then dropped back onto the desk.

Noel was glad Tim had looked away. He wondered if Tim realized how closely his story mirrored Noel's own. Only when Noel found out Abby was "in trouble", he wasn't able to make it right.

Forgive me, Father, he prayed for the ten thousandth time in his life.

After another moment of massaging his forehead, Tim straightened up in the chair. He slid open the narrow center drawer in his desk and rummaged around until he found a piece of candy. He unwrapped it, popped it in his mouth, and proceeded to roll the foil wrapper into a tiny ball between his finger and thumb.

"The next thing I knew, I was on my way to Sally's house to tell her folks. My mind was whirling. I kept thinking we needed to slow down. I couldn't think. All I could see in my head was Noreen and how destroyed she was going to be when she found out. Sally, on the other hand, looked like she was going to a party. It was almost like she wanted to hurt her parents by telling them, especially her mother. She had tried so hard to raise Sally to be a good girl, but Sally thumbed her nose at the whole convention.

"I remember feeling like I was going to throw up. I kept thinking of my own mother and how disappointed she would be...and Noreen. What was I going to tell Noreen? When we got to the Blake's house, I stood there like a block of wood while Sally paraded me inside and did all the talking. I'm sure her parents thought I was about the sorriest excuse for a son-in-law they could have imagined, but she was right about their reactions. Her mom cried at first, and her dad got mad but pretty quickly, they got used to the idea. Before we left, they were even plotting how we would hide the pregnancy from their friends and pretend to have an eight-pound preemie. Mrs. Blake even commented that it happened all the time, but good people didn't talk about it."

Tim stopped talking. He swallowed the candy and flipped the wadded up wrapper into the wastebasket. He laced his fingers together, put his hands behind his head, and leaned back in his chair. He tilted his face up and stared at the ceiling.

Noel watched him for a moment. He felt a respect for Tim he'd never had before because of everything he'd been through. At the same time, he wanted to punch him in the gut for allowing himself to be used by Sally in the first place. Noel was of a mindset that people who claimed to be used by others often put themselves into the position to let it happen.

"That would explain what the fight was about that night," Noel said finally, even though he had known all along.

Tim grunted in agreement. He sat forward in the chair and lowered his hands back to the desk. "After Sally disappeared, me and Noreen fizzled out. She couldn't look me in the face. Of course, I was so eaten up with guilt I couldn't look at her either. I knew I didn't deserve her. It never crossed my mind that she might have had anything to do with Sally's disappearance. I figured Sally told her about the baby, and she didn't know if she should believe it or not."

"Why didn't you just ask her?"

Tim shook his head. "I couldn't. I was a chicken. I believed she knew about the baby, and I was scared to death she'd ask me if it was true."

Noel knew all too well about men who lost the love of their life because of fear of speaking his mind. "You lost the woman you loved because you couldn't bear asking her why she was pulling away from you."

Tim shrugged. "I guess. Noreen was a wonderful woman. She still is. I never loved Sally. I've never loved anyone…"

His voice trailed off. He didn't need to finish his thought; that he had married Joyce Davenport after realizing he could never regain what he once had with Noreen.

He smacked his hands on the table and stood up. He hooked his thumbs in his front pants pockets and took three agitated steps to the back wall of his office. He absently studied a certificate in a cheap plastic frame for a moment and then straightened the frame. Then he turned around and faced the desk.

"I was stupid, Noel. I knew it when I was doing it and believe me, I know it now. But I've never had it in me to confront anyone. I couldn't stand up to Sally. Not that I'm using it as an excuse," he quickly added. "I couldn't tell Noreen what I'd done. I can't even stand up to my own daughter. She wants me to stay out of this. She says it'll ruin what I've built here at the agency. I don't know. Maybe she's right."

Noel watched him in silence for a few moments. He never thought he would empathize with the other man's inner turmoil. But he knew just how he was feeling. He'd been going through plenty of the same emotions since Eric found out he was his father. Two months had gone by since all of Jenna's Creek had found out the truth, and Noel still couldn't face his own son.

He stared at Tim and decided he would not become like him. He needed to talk to Eric. He wanted to apologize to Abby. It was time he stopped fearing what other people thought and face the consequences of his actions.

"Listen, Tim, now you've told me your role in this. I know you blame yourself in part for what happened between Sally and Noreen, but we've got to move past that. Someone called me a couple weeks ago, and if it wasn't you, I've got to know who it was. They claimed to know Noreen didn't kill Sally intentionally. That person has got to go to the judge with what they know. Now..." Noel rested his elbows on the desk between a grouping of pictures of Tim's family and a pencil holder. "You've got to tell me who you think this person might have been. You must have an opinion. If you've even heard hints that Sally was seeing a married man, I need to know who he was. Other than you, Connie Noble or possibly James Steele, who wouldn't do us any good if it was him, the married fellow was the most likely person to have seen something that night."

Tim moved to the desk and lowered himself heavily into the chair with a belabored sigh. He glanced at the group of pictures and then the clock on the desk. Noel followed his eyes. It was nearly five o'clock. The office would be closing soon, and Tim would be going home to his wonderful family on the same privileged side of town as Noel.

"Yes, I heard those rumors, too. But I never heard a name." He gave his head a small shake. "Even if I knew who the guy was, I wouldn't tell you. Listen, Noel, you've got to understand. I owe everything to Ted Blake. I can't stand up in a court of law and tell the whole town that Sally Blake was involved with another woman's husband. I can't tell them she had an affair with me for the sole purpose of hurting her best friend. I knew Sally was mean and manipulative, and she'd walk over anyone to get what she wanted. But you can count on one thing. I won't be testifying to that. I have my family to think of."

Noel stared at him. "You mean at the risk of seeing Noreen Trimble killed in prison, you would sit back and do nothing?"

"That's not how I see it." Tim looked pointedly at the door.

Noel dragged himself to his feet. "You know, Tim, I was starting to see you as another of Sally's victims. But you're nothing more than a self-serving coward. Sally's gone. Her parents and this town will remember her however they choose. But Noreen's still here. You can do something to save her."

Tim straightened the stapler on his desk, unable to meet Noel's gaze. "I'm sorry, Noel. I wish I could help you."

Noel shook his head in wonder and frustration, before turning toward the door. The receptionist smiled brightly as he stormed past.

"Good evening, Mr. Wyatt," she called and then closed her mouth in alarm as the door slammed shut behind him.

Chapter Twenty-one

The next morning Mark Eisinger woke up in the University Hospital in Cincinnati. His throat was parched. When he tried to lift his hand to reach for the cup just out of reach, the needle holding the IV in the back of his hand restricted his movement.

A nurse appeared in his line of vision. "Good morning, Dr. Eisinger. Nice to see you awake. I'm Clarissa, the floor nurse. We weren't properly introduced yesterday when you came in at the end of my shift." She continued chatting away as she circled the bed checking his vitals and making notations on the clipboard she removed from the foot of the bed.

"Do you need anything this morning? Dr. Pack won't be in for another hour or so. He spoke to your family last night. Your daughter and daughter-in-law are lovely. They took such good care of you."

Mark didn't have patience for chatty nurses. The higher they were on the food chain, the harder they were to bear. He looked pointedly at the water glass and opened his mouth.

"Can I get you some ice chips, Doctor?" she asked.

He thought he detected sarcasm in her voice, but told himself he was being paranoid. It was common knowledge that doctors made the worst patients, and he always expected to be treated badly if ever on the receiving end of a nurse's care. Yet another reason he resented Chuck for taking up residence in his brain and putting him at the mercy of an army of people who instinctively disliked him.

It was after two in the afternoon before Dr. Pack bothered to make an appearance. Mark had determined after his morning with Clarissa that he would be an excellent patient and not give the nurses any reason to think lower of doctors than they already did. By ten, that ideal had gone out the window. He could have bought stronger pain medication at the counter of the nearest gas station and wasn't hesitant about saying so to anyone who would listen. His roommate was barely shy of one hundred and forty and hadn't stopped moaning and cussing all morning. The fact that Mark's wing was filled to capacity and no private rooms were available was of no concern to him. He couldn't be expected to remain chipper and amicable under such conditions.

The nurses told him he should exercise a little patience and understanding. He told them that for the amount of money they were billing his insurance company, they should exercise more diligence in finding him a private room. Dr. Pack arrived in time to hear him berate a young nurse's aid named Star for taking too long in answering his page.

"I'm in pain," he growled. "I would think you'd move your skinny behind a little faster if you were the one waiting for relief."

"Now, now," Dr. Pack said with a smile for Mark and a look of encouragement to Star, who looked close to tears. "Surely you can tolerate a little discomfort better than that."

Mark was about to remind him he had no room to talk until he found himself flat on his back at the mercy of incompetents, but decided it took too much effort and only made his head hurt worse.

Besides, Dr. Pack had always been straightforward with him, and he was anxious to hear what he had to say. He eyed the sheath of X-rays in the doctor's hands.

Dr. Pack turned to watch the door swing shut behind Star. Mark found himself watching, too. When the doctor turned back to him, he felt his heart rate increase.

"Mark, would you like for me to come back when your family is in the room with you?" Dr. Pack asked.

Mark's heart leaped to his throat. He took a moment to calm himself so he would hear every word clearly. "N—no, my daughter and son-in-law stepped out to get a bite to eat. They've been in here most of the day driving me crazy."

Dr. Pack's attempt at a smile was less than successful. "I could ask Clarissa to come in—"

"Just get on with it," he snapped. Then he added, "Please."

"All right." Dr. Pack extracted an X-ray from the sheath in his hand. "Mark, we're seeing some rapid progression here." He held the X-ray up to the window so Mark could see for himself.

His heart sank as the neurologist continued. "I'm afraid we were being optimistic when we saw you in the office last month." He lowered the X-ray to his side and stepped between the two beds. Mark's roommate let out an indignant moan. Dr. Pack pulled the curtain partly closed behind him. "Six months was inaccurate. I believe it's closer to six weeks." He lowered his voice respectfully. "Maybe a month."

Mark wished he had allowed Dr. Pack to summon Clarissa to the room.

"Mrs. Gardner from the library called," Abby said when Christy came into the kitchen.

Christy's heart did a little flip in her chest. She hadn't realized how anxiously she had been awaiting the librarian's call. "Did she leave a message?"

"Just for you to call her back. She sounded eager to talk with you."

Christy brightened.

"I didn't know you'd applied for a job at the library."

Christy paused. She didn't know how much she wanted to tell her mother about her life. Should she let her in or keep pushing her aside. "I figured it was about time I start helping out around here."

"Does that mean you'll be here for awhile?"

Christy tried not to notice the hopefulness on Abby's face. She was trying hard to stay angry at her mother. Like her grandmother Laura, Christy could usually hold a grudge like nobody's business. But Abby was her mother, and she had gone out of her way not to intrude on the apparent problems Christy was going through. Christy had to respect her for that. She knew how difficult it was for Abby Blackwood to mind her own business.

When they were teenagers, Abby would grill them about every date and outing with friends that came along. She had to know where they would be for the entire evening, whom they might run into, whose car they were taking, and if she knew everyone's parents. Karen and Elaine didn't seem to mind the third degree, but Christy took offense. She was the one who dated boys her parents didn't approve of, broke curfew, and adamantly resisted the groundings that always resulted. Even then, she was preparing for a career in litigation.

"I think I may have to for awhile," she said. "At least until I get back on my feet. That's not a problem, is it?"

"Oh, no," Abby cried, clearly pleased. Then she took a more sedate tone. "You're welcome to stay here as long as you need to." She paused for a moment, searching for words.

Christy braced herself. Here it came. She was going to butt into her business. It was a miracle she'd held out this long.

"This is your home, Christy. I want you to stay here."

Christy was surprised. "You do."

"Of course. To tell you the truth, it's been incredibly lonely since...well I haven't known what to do with myself since Eric went back to school."

Christy took a deep breath. "Mom, I—I really appreciate these past few weeks. I know after how I acted the last time I was here, it must have been tempting for you to tell me to get myself out of this mess."

Abby smiled gently. "Christy, you're my daughter. I could never tell you that."

Christy was uncomfortable with the way the conversation was going and the nugget of warmth growing in her belly for her mother. "Well, thank you anyway," she said, determined to remain aloof. "It means a lot to me. It means a lot, too, that you haven't grilled me about what happened. I know it must seem odd to you that I ended up in Kentucky, and I'm not doing anything about going back to Columbus."

Abby nodded thoughtfully. "I figured you'd tell me when you're ready."

Christy couldn't keep from laughing. "Boy, you're sure not the woman who raised me. When I was little, you wouldn't have cared when I wanted to talk about whatever mess I had gotten myself into. If Abigail Blackwood wanted to know something, the world better give it up."

Abby smiled. "I was never that bad."

"Okay, whatever you say."

The two women sat quietly for a moment, enjoying the companionship, something Christy once thought would never be possible again after what she'd discovered about her mother's past.

"Christy?" Abby began quietly. "It doesn't matter to me what happened in Columbus to drive you to Kentucky. I'm just thankful to God those animals didn't do anything worse than steal your car. All those things you lost can be replaced." She reached across the table and touched Christy's arm. "You can't. I don't know what I would have done if they'd done something to you. I couldn't bear losing you." Her voice cracked.

Christy stared at her mother's hand on her arm, unable to think of a response.

"It would've been doubly hard losing you with everything between us like it is now," Abby continued. "I know you're hurt. You have every right to be angry. And there's nothing I can say to explain or make it better. But for what it's worth, I love you. I love your sisters and your brother. I never meant to hurt any of you."

Christy continued to stare at her hand. "What about Daddy?" she asked, forcing out the words. "Did you love him?"

Abby was quiet for a moment. Then she let out a long breath. "When Jack first died, I didn't know what I felt. I thought I missed him because I was so used to having him around. I'd been cooking his meals and washing his shirts for so long, I didn't know what to do with myself. And of course, my heart ached for the loss you kids were going through. But after awhile, something I never expected happened. I realized I missed him. Not his keeping me company or giving me a reason to get up in the morning to take care of him, but him. I missed him. I realized I loved him. I'm sorry it took me so long to do that. He was a wonderful man. For a long time, I thought I loved him because he loved me and because he was such a wonderful father. But after he was gone, I realized it was him I loved. I'm only sorry I never let him know how I really felt."

"Then why'd you do it, Mom?" Christy demanded. "I'm sorry you didn't get your first choice, but we loved you. We would have done anything to make you happy if we'd only known how you felt."

Abby's heart broke at the sound of her daughter's pain. "Oh, Christy, it wasn't you. It wasn't any of you. I didn't go looking for anything. I love you so much. I love all of you. I'm sorry I hurt you, Christy. That was never my intention. Yes, I was wrong. But how can I say I wish I hadn't done it when I have your brother? I don't know. I'm as confused as you are. I shouldn't have given into the flesh, but it happened. It can't be taken back. And now that I have Eric, I wouldn't take it back if I could."

The room was quiet. The only sound was the ticking of the clock over the kitchen window.

"I'm sorry, Mom," Christy said, finally breaking the silence, "but I'll never understand. You're a hypocrite. All our lives you told us that good girls didn't do certain things. Fornication was a sin. You dragged us to church every Sunday, knowing you had committed adultery? What gives you the right to tell anyone what is right and wrong when you couldn't keep your hands off another man?"

Abby took a deep breath. Christy wondered if she had said too much, but she deserved an answer. All her life she'd been taught to honor her parents. How could she honor Abby if she couldn't explain what she'd done?

"It wasn't like that, honey," she said in a small voice.

Christy crossed her arms over her chest. "I'm sorry, Mom. I really do want to understand. But I don't. Daddy loved you. We always knew that. We could tell by the way his eyes lit up when you came into the room, the way he was always pulling you into his arms. Now that I think about it, you never initiated the contact." Her voice faltered, but she continued. "It was always Dad. He knew you didn't love him. He tried to make you, but you wouldn't."

"Oh, Christy, please. I wasn't putting him at arm's length on purpose. I didn't choose for things to be this way."

"Maybe not, but you shouldn't have married him if you couldn't make yourself love him. You should've done him a favor and turned him down."

Abby stood up and moved across the kitchen. She looked out the window for a moment before turning back to her daughter. Her eyes brimmed with tears. "I used to think that too. But then I realized I never would have had any of you. My life would have been so empty. And you know what I never realized until last spring? My life would have been empty without Jack." Her eyes took on a faraway look, and Christy knew she was thinking out loud as much as talking. "He was a wonderful husband. More than I ever deserved. Yes, he loved me even though he knew I...I didn't have the same feelings."

She put her hands on her hips and looked Christy in the eye. "Do you realize he could have thrown me out when he found out about Eric? I don't know how long he knew Eric wasn't his, but he knew, and he could have divorced me. He would have gotten custody of all you children, too. Things were rough on women in those days. I guess they still are. If he could've proved to a judge somehow that Eric belonged to another man, he could've walked away and taken you girls with him. He never would've had to pay alimony or a dime of child support. What would I have done then? I haven't had a job in years. How would I have supported Eric and myself? And how would I have looked anyone in the face? I would have been an outcast."

Christy looked at her hands. A couple of months ago, she would've thought it was exactly what Abby deserved. Now she knew she wouldn't want any woman to suffer that way.

"How would I have lived without you, Karen, and Elaine in my life? I couldn't have stood it." Abby took a deep breath, swallowing her tears. "I used to feel sorry for myself that my life didn't turn out the way I wanted. But now I realize it wouldn't have been worth living if Jack Blackwood had thrown me out like most people in this town probably thought I deserved. He might not have been what I thought I wanted, but he saved my life. Because of the decent man he was, he made my life worth living."

Christy's eyes stung with tears. She looked at her mother standing at the window and felt like she was seeing her for the first time. Had Abby ever been happy? Was any married woman? Did they all fantasize about life with the one who got away?

Abby wasn't exactly telling the truth. If Jack had thrown her out, she wouldn't have been penniless, pounding the pavement to find a job. She had to have known Noel would've taken her and Eric into his fancy house on Bryton Avenue in a heartbeat, but where would that have left her, Karen, and Elaine? Their mother and half-brother would be living well on the other side of town, but what would've become of them? Would Jack have remarried? Would a stepmother have been able to love them and care for them the same way Abby did? And what about Eric, what would Eric's life have been like without Jack Blackwood in it? Would Eric have grown up to be the young man of integrity and faith he was now?

Had Abby sacrificed her own happiness to keep her family together when she would have been so much better off if she hadn't? Christy didn't want to sympathize with her or think she had done the right thing. She wanted to nurse her anger a little longer, but it was getting harder and harder to do all the time.

With a start, she realized she wanted her mother to be happy.

"I think I'll return Mrs. Gardner's call upstairs," she said.

"Sure thing, dear. Let me know if it's good news."

"Oh, I will." Christy headed for the stairs.

"Christy."

Christy stopped with one hand on the banister and looked back at Abby. "Yeah?"

"If someone had to beat me out of that job, I'm glad it was you."

"What?"

Abby grinned. "I applied for that job last week. I can't really blame Mrs. Gardner. I guess someone more qualified applied."

Chapter Twenty-two

On Friday, Mark was discharged against his doctor's advice. "I'm feeling better, and it's too much of a hardship on my family to drive back and forth from Jenna's Creek. I can hire a nurse from my local hospital to come in and do what I'm paying these people for."

Dr. Pack wasn't happy with the situation, but Mark was right; they had reached the point where the hospital could do little more for him. If he was more comfortable spending his last days at home, so be it. Out of Mark's hearing, the doctor told the family it was important that the nurse be on duty at all times. At this stage it was impossible to predict when he would get bad again and need to be rushed back to the hospital, or worse, he would slip away. It would be better if a trained professional were present when the time came.

The grandchildren knew Grandpa was dying. They took it better than the adults had expected. They didn't even act overly surprised when they were told. It was generally impossible to keep youngsters from picking up on things, regardless of how badly adults wanted to shield them.

"I forgot to tell you," Steve said to Mark as he plumped the pillow of Mark's own bed Friday evening. "An old friend of yours called the other day. Judge Davis. Remember him?"

"Yes, I remember him. I have a tumor. I'm not senile."

Steve ignored the chastening. "He said he wanted to talk to you."

Mark was thoughtful for a moment. "I haven't heard from him in years."

"Wonder what he wants."

Mark eyed the younger man for a moment. For all his present aggravation, Steve was a good enough son-in-law. It took a strong man to live with Brenda. Mark knew firsthand having spent thirty years with her mother. "Bring me the phone book, Steve," he said, emotion warming his voice. "And stretch the phone over here would you?"

Steve eyed him uncertainly for a moment before hurrying to comply.

David settled into the narrow occasional chair beside Mark Eisinger's bed. Mark was propped up on pillows and feeling better than he had in weeks. He hated to admit it but being home, even if it meant he couldn't escape Brenda's ministrations, was good for him.

"I'm glad to see you looking so well," David told him. "When I called last week, Steve didn't make it sound good." He knew he could be honest with Mark. The doctor had seen everything and knew what to expect.

"To tell you the truth, Judge, I didn't know if I'd be coming home."

Both men nodded respectively as they contemplated the depth of his words.

"So how long's it been, David," Mark asked. "I was surprised to hear you'd called."

"A long time, I'm afraid. When I stepped down from the bench, I thought I would have all this free time to do what I never got done before. Turns out I'm busier than ever. You know about Bernice, of course, and we have the horses. They're a lot of work."

"Bernice or the horses?"

Both men smiled.

"I have to tell you, David, it's good to have someone in the room who's not poking or prodding one end or another of me, looking for a sample of something I don't want to give."

The sound of their laughter helped dispel the gloom in the room.

"I am so sorry about all this, Mark," David said sincerely after the laughter died away. "I don't even know what to say. I've been dealing with Bernice's condition for so long, but at least we know she probably has lots of time left. This has to be rough on your family."

"Yes, it is. I feel bad for the grandkids. But they seem to be adapting to everything better than the rest of us." Mark straightened up against the pillows. "But David, please, let's not talk about this. I know you didn't call out of the blue last week. Whatever it is, it's got to be an improvement over what's going on inside my head."

David paused for a moment, unsure of how to proceed. If his suspicions were accurate, he didn't want to upset the patient. Mark didn't look like he could tolerate much upheaval. "I'm sure you remember Noreen Trimble."

Mark seemed to pale a shade against the white pillowcase.

"I don't know if you heard, but she was injured in prison about a month ago. Her family and friends are understandably concerned for her safety and have redoubled their efforts to get her a new trial."

"Didn't she plead guilty to her role in the Blake girl's death?"

David nodded. "Yes, she did, but those of us who know her believe she never would have killed Sally intentionally. She has maintained all along she acted in self-defense."

"Then why didn't she let it go to trial?"

"Because in her mind, even though it was self-defense, she was guilty of taking another person's life."

"What changed her mind?"

David folded his hands and leaned forward in the chair. "The morning after her attack in Marysville, Noel got a strange phone call."

Mark coughed into a handkerchief. His face whitened even further.

"This caller told Noel he had a friend who knew Noreen was only defending herself against Sally," David continued. "According to the caller, the friend saw everything but was afraid to come forward."

"Who..." Mark swallowed and reached feebly for a water glass beside the bed. David grabbed it first and handed it to him. Mark took a sip with a shaky hand and let David set it back on the table. "Does Noel know who the caller was?"

The judge shook his head. "No, but he was sure he had heard the man's voice before. He's not as concerned with the man's identity as he is to whether he was telling the truth or not."

David wouldn't stay much longer. It wasn't fair to wear the man out after the week he had. "I've been reading over the police reports on Sally's case the last few weeks. Noel and Noreen's lawyer had her make a list of people she remembered from the party or anyone who may have come back to the house that night and seen what went on between her and Sally. On that list was a young woman named Connie Noble."

Mark's face remained blank.

"She's your niece, isn't she?"

Mark nodded slightly. "By marriage. She was Betty's sister's girl."

David exhaled, relieved. "It would help us immensely if we could talk to her. We know she caught Sally with her boyfriend at one time. She didn't know who Sally was until she saw her at the party. We don't suspect her of anything," he said quickly before the doctor could think of a reason not to help him. "We just want to talk to her. Maybe she came back to have it out with Sally and saw what happened. Anything she knows might be enough to convince the judge to grant Noreen a new trial. We are confident once we get Noreen in front of a jury to plead her case, she would be acquitted."

"I hate to be the one to tell you this, David, but Connie died of leukemia when she was twenty-eight. She had moved to San Jose and none of us even knew she was sick until a funeral home called wanting to send her remains home."

David's shoulders slumped. "Oh, Mark, I am so sorry to hear that. And I'm sorry to have taken up so much of your time." He started to rise. "Your nurse will probably be in here to run me off in a few minutes anyway."

Mark reached out and snagged his wrist with surprising strength. "I don't want people to think Connie had anything to do with Sally's death or Noreen going to prison."

"Is that why you called Noel Wyatt's house?"

Mark released his hold on him and let his hand drop to his lap. "How did you know it was me?"

David lowered himself back into the chair. "I really thought Connie was the eye witness the caller was talking about. When I remembered your wife was Connie's aunt, I suspected you made the call. Noel said he was sure he recognized the voice on the other end. He's talked to every doctor in town at least once or twice over the phone at the pharmacy."

"Connie wouldn't have had any information to give you."

The judge's eyes darkened. "You were the married man Sally Blake was seeing."

Mark stared toward the door for a moment. Then he inhaled deeply and blew it out through parted lips. "Connie told me she knew, and if I didn't do something about it, she would tell Betty the truth." He paused again. A tear welled up in his eye. "I didn't care. Sally had stopped seeing me, and I was determined to get her back. I followed James Steele's car that night and waited until he dropped Sally off at the house. I waited a while in my car for her to come back out. She never did, so I got tired of waiting and went to the door to see if she was spending the night. I had to talk to her. I didn't care if Betty found out or not. I didn't care that my professional career would be finished in this town when folks found out about us. I just had to have Sally."

He stopped to draw a fatigued breath. Then he looked apologetically at David. "I was a fool. I risked everything. But I couldn't stop thinking about her. I didn't want her to be with anyone else. At first I thought the man she loved was James Steele. I followed them on a couple of their dates. They were heavily involved, but after some time, I realized it wasn't James Steele she was after. She was using him, the same way she'd done me. I went to talk to her that night. I saw everything. I even heard the lie she told Noreen Trimble."

Chapter Twenty-three

C alvin Trotter awoke in the middle of the night in the hospital tethered to an IV. A cast encased his right leg from his upper thigh to his toes. He buzzed for the nurse and discovered forty-eight hours had passed since he landed on the hallway floor of his aunt's house, breaking his left ankle, his right femur and tibia, and receiving a deep gash on his right arm that required eighteen stitches. He also had black and blue marks all over him and a significant knot on his head.

He tried to follow the nurse's explanation of his injuries as best he could in his muddled state. She told him his parents had finally gone home to get some rest after staying by his bedside for two days. It gave him great satisfaction to know Aunt Paige had also been here nearly the entire time.

After the nurse left, Calvin didn't drift off to sleep, even with all the pain medication coursing through his veins. Surely Aunt Paige knew about the Will. Why else had she hung around the hospital? It surely wasn't due to her concern for his well-being. She must have found the Will on the floor beside him. Had she destroyed it? Was there anything he could do to protect himself? If she got rid of the Will after the paramedics left, what proof would he have that it ever existed? It was her word against his. The family would believe him since none of them liked Paige and believed she had been lying all along about Uncle Howard's fortune. But what good would their belief do? He needed legal proof.

He vaguely remembered the attorney's letterhead at the top of the page. If it had been drawn up by a lawyer, there was another copy in an office somewhere, waiting for him to come forward and claim his inheritance, but he didn't know where to look. He couldn't start calling every law firm in a hundred mile radius and ask if they once had a client named Howard Trotter who had left his estate to his nephew. Wasn't the firm responsible for contacting him? But what if they didn't know Howard was dead? Or what if they had been trying to contact him for years, only to be sidetracked by Paige who didn't want them to find him? What if Uncle Howard, in his quest to save a nickel, had hired an attorney out of the back of a comic book? As soon as he turned his back, the crooked law firm took his money and disappeared.

Calvin groaned and put the heel of his hand against his forehead. Just his luck, he was the main beneficiary to a substantial inheritance with no way of claiming it.

He closed his eyes and concentrated on the name on the letterhead. He had only seen it for a moment, but he thought he would recognize it if he saw it again. *Think, Calvin, think,* he ordered himself. *You can't let that old bat cheat you out of your money.*

There was always the possibility Aunt Paige would do the right thing and bring the Will to him as soon as she knew he had regained consciousness. She might be as happy for him as he was over his newfound wealth. Now he could fund his writing career. He could go to Nashville in style to meet the singer who wanted to produce his song, as soon as his leg healed of course.

"Who are you kidding?" he asked aloud in the empty room. Aunt Paige would not freely hand over the Will if it still existed, and she certainly wouldn't celebrate his good fortune.

He had to remember the name on that letterhead.

A picture of Mike Conners, the actor who played the private investigator, Joe Mannix, on TV flashed through his mind. It was one of Malcolm's favorite shows. Calvin had little interest in television and couldn't understand why Mannix was going through his head now. It had to be the medication. He needed to stop thinking nonsense and focus on remembering the name of the law firm that prepared Uncle Howard's Will. Without the name, he was just as poor as he was two days ago.

He finally fell into a drug induced stupor with the show's theme music playing in his head. *Mannix. Mannix. Mannix.*

Paige Trotter didn't know what she'd done to deserve such torment. Three months ago she thought she had the remainder of a pitiful life mapped out. Out of the kindness of her heart, she planned to get her nephew a job as Noel's assistant by threatening to tell the fine people of Jenna's Creek of his dalliance with Jack Blackwood's widow if he refused to cooperate. That plan went awry when Noel and Abby made it public knowledge without giving her the chance to blackmail him.

At the same time—again out of the kindness of her heart—she opened her home to her wayward nephew while he finished his pharmaceutical classes. She never cared for Howard's scheming brother, Malcolm, but she didn't want to hold it against poor Calvin. The boy wasn't the sharpest tool in the shed, and if she didn't give him a hand up, he was going to amount to a whole lot of nothing like his daddy.

What had all her good deeds brought her? Nothing but heartache, that's what; heartache and betrayal for trying to be a good person.

Scatterbrained Eudora got the dates mixed up for their reservations at the dinner theater. The performance they were supposed to see had been the night before. There were no empty seats when they arrived. Paige was livid. The last thing she had wanted to do with her Saturday night was drive all the way to Lebanon, Ohio with Eudora and Malcolm. Malcolm had tried to make it up to her by taking the women somewhere else, but every other decent restaurant in town was booked. They ended up having dinner at one of those all-you-can-eat steakhouses cheapskates like Malcolm frequented and then driving back to Jenna's Creek straight after.

She climbed out of Malcolm's brand new Chrysler—to think he and Eudora were always complaining they had been shafted when Jeremiah left his fortune to Howard—and was putting her keys in the lock when she heard a horrible crash from upstairs. Her first thought was a prowler had broken in and that sissy Calvin had locked himself into one of the bedrooms where the thief was currently busting down the door. She would skin that boy alive if he let some crook come in and damage her house and furniture.

Malcolm and Eudora had already backed out of the driveway and were speeding down her street, so there was no point in yelling for their assistance. She went inside, almost hoping for a prowler on whom she could take out her frustration for eating in an overcrowded low class dive with two screaming toddlers at the next table, threw her purse and coat on the back of the sofa, and headed upstairs.

Halfway up, her nostrils filled with dust and plaster. She sneezed. This was going to be worse than she thought. If Calvin knew what was good for him, the prowler had finished him off and saved her the pleasure.

The first thing Paige saw when she reached the top of the stairs was a gaping hole in her ceiling. Under the hole lay Calvin, a ceiling fixture, and rotten boards and plaster. The hallway was filled with a cloud of dust. It was going to take the rest of the night to clean up the mess.

She put her hand on the banister railing when she reached the top of the landing and sneezed again. Then her breath caught in her throat. Calvin was dead. Light from the bathroom winked off the broken glass around him. Blood seemed to be coming from several parts of his body. She took another step closer and saw his chest moving up and down at a pretty fair rate.

So he wasn't dead. She sniffed and took another step. Now that she was close enough to see the extent of his injuries, she could see he was going to have a lot of explaining to do when he came around.

She looked up at her busted ceiling and put the pieces of the puzzle together. Calvin had been snooping around in the attic. He was looking for something; apparently something he had no business looking for or he wouldn't have chosen the one night she was out of the house to go looking for it.

Suspicion clouded her features as she looked back at Calvin on the floor. Then she noticed the sheets of parchment scattered around him. Her breath caught in her throat. She took a step closer. A sheet lay near her left foot. Even with her cataracts, she could make out some type of legal letterhead. Could it be? Was it possible after all these years?

With a sense of impending doom, she knelt down and carefully snatched the paper off the floor.

She recognized it immediately. It was a page from Howard's Will.

At that moment, Calvin let out a groan. She gasped and looked at him like she'd been caught at something. Then she remembered he was the one caught with his hand in the cookie jar, meddling in her business. This is what she got for doing the boy a good turn. When would she learn decency and compassion never paid off?

Still clutching the page of the Will, she turned and went downstairs to the telephone. After calling an ambulance, she returned upstairs and gathered the pages of Howard's Last Will and Testament from around Calvin's prone body. This might not turn out so bad, she kept telling herself. Howard might actually have had a decent bone in his body and done right by his widow.

Just as she figured, she had plenty of time to secure all the pages since it took more than a half hour for the ambulance to arrive. While she waited, she got a rag from the bathroom downstairs and blotted away the blood Calvin had dripped onto the pages. Fortunately his wound wasn't bad enough to render the pages impossible to read. She took a straight back chair out of one of the bedrooms and positioned herself so she could watch out the window for the ambulance in case they didn't have the siren on, and keep an eye on Calvin.

It took a few minutes to gather all the pages and put them in the correct order since many of them were not numbered. Getting through the legalese was another obstacle that slowed her progress. But her precarious position became crystal clear by the time she reached the top of the second page.

Howard left everything to Calvin; the house, properties as far away as Jackson County, stocks and bonds she did not know existed, any monies in his savings and retirement funds—everything to Calvin.

Paige wiped a bead of sweat off her top lip. "Come on, Howard," she mumbled under her breath. "Don't leave me hanging out on the line here. Be a man for once in your life. Do the right thing."

Her heart sank further and further with each turn of the page.

It turned out she had been right all along. Howard did not have a decent bone in his body. After reading through twelve pages of legal drivel, she found an addendum on the last page making provisions for her.

And to my wife, Paige...

No endearments. No touching tributes. Paige turned up her lip and continued reading.

...she shall remain living at my residence on Pendergast Street until she dies. Should she remarry, or if Calvin reaches the age of twenty-five before her death, she must vacate the premises immediately.

After her death, I bequeath to Paige the spot at the Gentle Slumber Cemetery on my left as Mary is already residing in the space to my right. Should Paige remarry, the plot at Gentle Slumber Cemetery is automatically forfeited.

Paige seethed with rage. Clutching the paper between her fists, she pounded her fists on her lap. "I'll show you Gentle Slumber, Howard Trotter," she growled aloud. "After all the years I bought flowers and put them on your marker like a proper grieving widow. I should have stuck them through your pitiful, little heart."

She jumped to her feet, ready to scream when her eyes fell upon Calvin. He had stirred several times. Once his eyes had opened, and he had looked unseeingly around the room through the glasses that sat crookedly on his nose.

Calvin.

She glared upward at the gaping hole in her ceiling. If he had minded his own business and kept his nose out of her attic, these papers never would have been found. At least not until she was dead, and what did she care about what happened after that? Now her life was turned upside down, and he was suddenly king of *her* domain.

If only he had minded his own business...

What could she do?

Lights reflected across the opposite wall. Paige jerked around and looked out the window. An ambulance turned into the driveway. Her eyes flitted from Calvin to the papers in her hands. What to do. What to do. A car door slammed outside and then another. She jumped out of her chair. She couldn't let anyone see this Will. She was banking on the odds that Calvin had not realized what he was holding when he fell through the ceiling. Or if he did know, he hadn't read enough of it to realize his uncle had left him everything. Even if he had seen enough of the Will to know Howard had betrayed his own widow, how would he prove it once he woke up? Who knew how long the Will had been hidden in the attic? The Will had been drawn up by a law office. She could only hope they were now defunct or their offices had burned down sometime in the last twenty years, along with their records.

Oh, if she could only be so fortunate.

Voices from outside drifted up to her. She heard footsteps on the front porch and then a rapping on the front door.

"Paramedics," a female voice called out.

Paige turned in a complete circle, looking for somewhere to put the papers before she went downstairs to show them in.

She heard the knob on the front door rattle and then the door was pushed open. Busybodies; couldn't they wait to be let in like decent folk? Why hadn't she thought to lock the door before coming upstairs?

"Paramedics," the voice said again. "Anyone home?"

"Up..." Paige cleared her throat and started over. "Up here."

For lack of a better opportunity, she opened the closet door and tossed the offending papers inside. She'd go through them more carefully later. Maybe there was a loophole that would keep Calvin from what rightfully belonged to her. It was nearly November. If memory served her correctly, Calvin would turn twenty-five at the first of January. She had barely two months to come up with a rock solid plan to keep him from yanking her home and everything she worked so hard for out from under her feet.

Calvin told his parents he wanted to go home to recuperate after being released from the hospital. Eudora wouldn't have it any other way. By now he knew Aunt Paige had done something with the Will since she hadn't mentioned it to him after he regained consciousness.

He couldn't help but enjoy a bit of power knowing she was wondering when he would ask about it. She couldn't be sure he'd seen it before he fell through the floor. If he did know what it was, had he read enough to know that he was now entitled to the bulk of Howard's estate? She was probably at her position behind the drugstore cash register, biting her nails and wondering how much he knew and when he would act on that knowledge.

Just knowing the torture his aunt was surely going through made the uncertainty over his future much easier to bear.

Had Aunt Paige known about the Will, or was she as surprised as Calvin to find those loose papers all over the hallway floor? He smiled to himself as he imagined her crawling along the baseboards making sure she hadn't missed a page. He wondered if she had climbed the flimsy ladder into the attic before the men could come to repair the ceiling to see if there was anything else incriminating up there. Of course she had. She couldn't take the chance Uncle Howard had hidden another copy.

Calvin didn't tell his parents about the Will either. Unlike Aunt Paige, they would be thrilled at his good fortune, but would insist he do something ridiculous with the money, like go back to school; a good school this time. Not a community college where they didn't even ask for his SAT scores before he registered for classes.

One thing was certain. He wasn't going to waste another precious minute of his life in college. He was going to Nashville. His trip would be delayed now that his leg was busted and he felt like he'd been backed over by a truck…several times. The first chance he got though he was posting a letter to the publishing company in Nashville to tell them he had been involved in an accident but would be on his way as soon as he was able.

When his mother came upstairs to his old bedroom with his breakfast on a tray and a grave look on her face—she was probably calculating how long he would be laid up, thus dependent again on his parents and unable to get a paying job—he asked for a phone book.

"A phone book? Just tell me who you need to call, and I'll take care of it."

Calvin saw this was going to be harder than it needed to be. "Mom, please, could you just get me the phone book? I don't need you to call anyone. I want to look something up. It would be great if you had some phone books from any neighboring counties as well."

She arched her eyebrows until they nearly disappeared into her hairline. "What are you up to, Calvin?"

"I'm looking for places to apply for work," he said, congratulating himself on the sudden inspiration. "I figured while I'm laid up, I could work on putting a resume together and sending it out all over this part of the state."

Her forehead relaxed, and her eyebrows reappeared. "What happened to working for Noel Wyatt? I thought Aunt Paige was going to set you up there."

"I'm just covering all the bases. And Aunt Paige doesn't have the pull at that drugstore like she thinks she does."

This comment definitely pleased his mother. By the end of the day, she had rustled up phone books from three surrounding counties. As soon as she left the room, Calvin grabbed a notebook and went to work.

He searched through the Auburn County phone book first. Nothing rang a bell with the letterhead he saw on Uncle Howard's Will. Maybe he was mistaken and Mannix meant nothing. But he couldn't get it out of his head.

Tomorrow afternoon was his mother's shopping day. She would be out of the house most of the morning. If he didn't find something that sounded like Mannix, he would venture downstairs with his huge cast and start calling the law offices that weren't long distance and see if any of them recognized his name. He wasn't sure if his cast would fit down the staircase, but he was willing to try. He prayed he wouldn't fall and add insult to injury. He imagined it was extremely painful to re-break a bone that had just been set. The thought of more pain added to what he was already going through made his head swim.

By the time Calvin reached the end of the second phone book, his latest dose of pain medication kicked in and he slept until that evening; too late for calling offices anyway. He put off his search until the next morning.

Chapter Twenty-four

Putting off the inevitable wasn't going to do him any favors. He had been doing that his whole life. He needed to face the music. He waited until Friday afternoon after Russ and Butch left the house for an out-of- town football game. They wouldn't be back until after midnight.

Leslie had a date and had stopped by the house to borrow Joyce's suede boots. Tim figured she would be willing to let her date wait once she found out he had something to tell her and Joyce. He doubted she would feel like an evening out after his news.

"Noel Wyatt called me this afternoon before I left the office," he began.

Joyce's face whitened a shade. Leslie stopped toying with her newly shortened hairstyle that she couldn't get used to and turned to face him, her face questioning.

"I want to prepare you before it becomes public knowledge." He steeled himself for their reaction and then plunged in with both feet. "A new witness came forward in Sally Blake's murder case. Judge Ruddock has awarded Noreen Trimble a new trial." Leslie gasped and Joyce's white face went red. Tim fought the instinct for flight and continued against the current. "It could take a few months before they set a date. She'll be moved out of the prison and down here for the trial."

"What's this mean?"

"Who's the witness?"

"He can't be very reliable if he didn't come forward before now."

"Ruddock is a fool. He'll never get reelected after this fiasco."

Tim waited for their comments to die down before he spoke again. He was stunned at the sense of calm washing over him. He was doing the right thing. The women in his family would just have to trust him, and stand behind him.

He prayed they would.

He took a deep breath and dropped his bombshell. "Noel told me to prepare myself for the likelihood that I'll be called to testify."

"Oh, he did, did he?" Joyce cried. "Well, I hope you told him not to count on that happening. It's out of the question."

"Joyce, if I'm subpoenaed, it's not my call to make."

Leslie cried out plaintively from her side of the room. "Daddy, you can't do this to me. My entire future is at stake. It isn't fair. If you go down, you'll take me with you."

Even after all these years, Tim couldn't believe how self-involved the women in his family had become. Maybe they always were, and he had turned a blind eye to it.

"I'm not doing this to you, Leslie. This is our judicial system at work. Any time new evidence surfaces, a defendant has a right to a new trial. If it were one of your brothers in this situation, you would want to see them treated fairly." He paused and looked at each of them in turn. "Wouldn't you?"

Joyce lowered her eyes to the floor.

Leslie lifted her chin in defiance. "If one of my brothers killed somebody, I like to think I would want to see them punished."

"I hope I could be as civic minded as you, dear, were we ever in that situation," Tim said, finding it difficult to keep his tone level. "But the fact of the matter is, things aren't always so cut and dried. According to a witness, she acted in self-defense. If that's the case, she shouldn't have to spend another seventeen years paying for her crime."

Joyce leveled her eyes back at him. "I don't know how you can be so generous. I understand you once had feelings for this woman, but I would think your loyalties would lie with this family. What's going to happen to us if you lose your job, which will most certainly happen if you get up on the stand and testify that Sally Blake got what was coming to her?"

"I would never say that."

"Just what will you say? They wouldn't be considering calling you if they didn't think you'd help the defense. I want to know what you know, Tim. You owe me that much." She looked past him to Leslie. "You owe it to both of us."

"I don't know anything about that night, Joyce. I already told you that. I wasn't there. But I knew how Sally could manipulate people. I knew she was using Noreen to get to me."

Leslie's mouth dropped open.

"You!" Joyce squealed. "What would Sally Blake want with you?"

Tim felt the air go out of his body like an old tire. He lowered himself into an easy chair. "I wish I didn't have to explain it to you."

Joyce realized her mistake. She went over to him and placed a placating hand on his shoulder. "I'm sorry, dear. That's not what I meant. I just don't understand what you mean by Sally was using Noreen to get to you."

"It's exactly what I mean. I had an affair with Sally behind Noreen's back. She told me we were going to have a baby."

Joyce removed her hand from his shoulder.

Leslie glared at him from across the room. "Daddy, no!"

Tim moved his hand through his hair. "I was young and stupid, but it happened. Then she told me there was no baby, but it was too late. We had already told Ted and Donna Blake we were getting married. Ted set me up in business at the agency. I guess you do that for sons-in-law."

"So you have more to lose than we thought." Joyce's voice was full of contempt.

"We're not going to lose anything, Joyce, by doing the right thing."

"Humph. You better hope not."

Believe me, I do, Tim thought grimly.

Bruckner, McManus.

Calvin recognized the name as soon as he saw it.

Mannix.

It was on the bottom of the first page of listings in the Portsmouth City phone book his mother had brought him yesterday. He found it after only a few minutes of looking. Unfortunately it took fifteen more minutes to get out of bed and cross the room. By the time he reached the door, he was sweating profusely, and his leg was throbbing. His dad made a good living working in the loan department at the bank. Why couldn't he get a phone installed upstairs? It was going to take the rest of the morning to get down to the kitchen.

Then Calvin realized he had left the phone book lying on the bed. He leaned against the doorjamb to catch his breath. He lurched back to the bed and fell onto the mattress, crutches and all. The pressure didn't help his leg any but it was better than standing upright. He pulled himself into a more comfortable position and willed his heart to stop pounding. He needed a pain pill, but he didn't know how long it would take to reach the right person at the law office, and he didn't want to get fuzzy and miss some of the details, or worse, fall asleep in the middle of the conversation.

At the top of the stairs, he realized the easiest way down was to sit down and slide one step at a time. Holding his leg out in front of him and lowering himself onto the top stair proved to be the hardest part. He slid one crutch down the stairs in front of him so it would be waiting when he reached the bottom. He gripped the other crutch in his left hand to help take the pressure off his left foot. With his right hand stabilizing the heavy cast on his right leg and his left side doing all the work, he started down the stairs. Halfway down his right leg bumped against the wall and he almost blacked out. Maybe that would be easier, he thought. Then he could roll down the stairs. He should have taken his chances with the pain pills. He should have at least thought to put one in his pocket for after the phone call. But it was too late for second guessing. He waited for the dizziness to pass and continued his descent.

His mother had been gone for over an hour by the time he reached the telephone in the kitchen. He hoped she had plenty of errands to keep her out of the house until he was finished. He wanted to get everything straightened out with the law office before he had to explain to anyone what he was doing.

A secretary at Bruckner, McManus picked up on the first ring.

Calvin wiped his glistening forehead with a pajama sleeve while she introduced herself and asked how she could be of assistance.

"Yes, good morning," he said in a voice that sounded weak to his own ears. "My name is Calvin Trotter. I believe my uncle Howard Trotter was a client of yours some years back. I recently found a Will of his with your name on the letterhead."

"Oh, hello, Mr. Trotter," the secretary sang out. "I'm looking at your file right now. You saved me a telephone call. Bruckner, McManus has been the executors of your uncle's Will for the last twenty-one years. But as of..." Calvin heard the rustle of paper. "...January third, the execution rights will be turned over to you. We would love to set up an appointment with you at your earliest convenience to go over your uncle's Last Will and Testament."

"I...um...I don't exactly have my copy of the Will with me..."

"Not a problem, Mr. Trotter," she said with a laugh. "We have all the necessary copies here on file, along with the activity of your uncle's estate over the past twenty-one years. I think you will be very pleased when you get here. All we require from you is your social security card and two other forms of identification, including a picture ID, so we know you're who you say you are."

Calvin envisioned his name in lights on a Nashville marquee. "Miss, you don't know how happy you've made me."

She giggled again. "Mr. Trotter, you're about to become a whole lot happier. Now, when can we set up an appointment?"

Eudora Trotter came home two hours later to find her son on the living room sofa in a great deal of pain with no explanation as to how or why he came to be downstairs. Nor could he stop laughing. After wrestling him back upstairs and into bed and plying him with pain medication, she called the drugstore with her concerns that the pills he had been prescribed had put him out of his head.

Christy Blackwood had been working at the library for nearly three weeks and was surprised to find she loved the work. It was methodical, similar to what she had done at the law firm, yet at a slower pace; exactly what she needed right now. With each new day, she found she missed her old job at Bennis, Banociac, and Weiss less and less. After two days at the front desk checking out books for patrons, she was moved to the reference section of the library. It saw much less traffic than the rest of the library, but she enjoyed it more than the front desk. Sometimes she could imagine herself doing this the rest of her life.

It turned out that fate had smiled on her when Mrs. Gardner called BBW for a reference. Pamela, one of the secretaries who had been a close friend of hers, had taken the call. She answered truthfully when she told her what an asset Christy had been to the firm. When asked why Christy left her job, Pamela had responded she felt she could better take care of her mother if she was at home. It turned out that wasn't a lie either.

Christy also liked the women she worked with at the library. The only men on staff were the two who came in after closing to clean the floors. Her stress level had dropped dramatically. She no longer jumped out of her skin every time she saw someone approaching in her peripheral vision. She was even in a better mood at home. She and Abby both enjoyed telling people she had stolen the job from her own mother.

Besides laughing about the job situation, they had begun to laugh at other things as well. Christy had even considered attending church with her mother yesterday, but changed her mind at the last minute. She still felt no conviction to attend church, yet she knew it was hard for Abby to occupy a pew alone for the first time in her life when the whole congregation knew of her affair with Noel Wyatt.

Maybe next Sunday, Christy thought as she stamped another book and slid it onto the shelf.

"You're Christy Blackwood, right?"

Christy turned from the stack of books to see a man nearly a head taller than her smiling down at her. A sense of dread welled up inside her the way it always did when she found herself in close proximity of a strange man, but she pushed it down. She refused to let Stanley and his cousin, and her memories of Sean dictate the rest of her life. Besides, this man was not a stranger.

She scratched her temple with her forefinger as if in concentration. "And you're the man I screamed at on Main Street a few weeks ago, right?"

The man's smile widened and a dimple appeared in his left cheek. "That was me. My ears are still ringing."

Christy put her hand against her cheek. "I am so embarrassed about that." She dropped her hand and stopped smiling when she realized what she was doing. The last thing she wanted him to think was that she was flirting with him.

He stuck his hand forward. "Jarrod Bruckner," he said. "In case you forgot."

Keeping her face neutral against the war going on inside her at the infectious smile and deep brown eyes that seemed to pull her in, Christy shook his offered hand. "No, I remember you, Mr. Bruckner. In fact, the two previous times we met, I wasn't exactly at my best," she said, remembering their first encounter at Noel Wyatt's house when she passed him in the driveway on her way out. "I apologize again for that."

"No need. In fact, I have a way you could redeem yourself."

Christy tensed. She seemed to recall the last time they met on the sidewalk, he had asked her out for coffee. No matter how handsome and harmless he looked, she wasn't ready to go anywhere with a man. Her only contact with Stanley had been at a public gas station, and that had ended disastrously.

"If it's all right, I'd like to sit here for an hour or so to finish some work of mine." He raised the briefcase in his left hand to show her. "The courthouse was jammed this morning, and I couldn't find a free room or table anywhere. I don't need to be back until after lunch, and I would love to get this paperwork cleared up."

Her curiosity was piqued in spite of herself. "The courthouse?"

"Yes, I have to meet with some clients at one o'clock to take a deposition, and I don't really have anywhere to wait until then. My office is in Portsmouth, so I'm sort of stuck here."

"Yeah, I know the feeling," she quipped, and then clamped her mouth shut. She hadn't meant to say anything so personal or casual to this man. He was a lawyer, of all things, and an incredibly good-looking one at that. Two of the last things she needed in her life.

He glanced at his watch. "If you don't have plans for lunch, maybe we could kill our lunch hour together."

"I brown bagged it," she said quickly. She hoped she didn't sound rude, but she didn't want to make him think she was desperate for male company simply because he was nice to look at, and they were both stuck in Jenna's Creek.

Disappointment flooded his features. Once again, Christy felt rotten. She considered giving in. What was the worst that could happen? He'd turn out to be another pompous attorney who thought any woman in a small town would fall all over herself to have lunch with him? She squared her shoulders in resolve. She was through with men.

"Okay, then," he said. "Do you mind if I use this table for my work?"

"Oh, sure, go ahead," she said, replacing her hard look with a smile. "That's what they're here for. If you need anything...any help looking for something, just ask." She almost told him she could help in filling out his deposition, too, but stopped herself in time. She was a librarian now, not a paralegal.

He nodded in acknowledgment and set his briefcase on the table between them. He pulled out a chair and sat down so that he was facing her desk. She wondered if it was intentional, and then reminded herself it was the chair he'd been standing next to, and she shouldn't be flattered by every little move he made. She moved to the other side of her desk and went back to work.

It was difficult concentrating on her duties now that he was working less than ten feet away. Every time he moved, she found herself looking up to see if he was going to say something or ask for help. He didn't. A few times she thought she caught him watching her, but decided she was flattering herself again.

As soon as her lunch hour arrived, she grabbed the sack lunch from under the desk and practically ran to the stairs on her way to the kitchen and meeting room downstairs where the library staff ate. By the time she got back, Jarrod Bruckner was gone. She ignored the flutter of disappointment in her stomach.

I'm through with men, she reminded herself as she took her position behind the reference desk. *Worthless beasts; who needs them?*

Chapter Twenty-five

T he Auburn County jail wasn't equipped to house long term female prisoners. In the rare occasion a woman was arrested for something other than drunk and disorderly and housed overnight, she was bussed to a neighboring county. It was under those circumstances that Tim Shelton found himself driving to Scioto County to visit Noreen Trimble.

Tim pulled out the chair and motioned for her to sit down. Noreen slid into the chair and scooted herself in. He stepped around the table and took the seat opposite her. Neither of them spoke for several moments. Tim had been sweating over this moment since the night he told Joyce and Leslie about the new trial. That was when he realized he had to talk to Noreen when she came back to Jenna's Creek. Even if testifying at her trial never became an issue, he had to come clean once and for all concerning his involvement with Sally Blake. The guilt for his role in Sally's death had escalated over the years rather than subsiding. If Noreen had indeed caused Sally's death, it was only because Tim had put her in the situation in the first place.

After telling Noel he had no intention of helping with the case, Tim had gone home to his family. There, he realized so much of Noreen's torment could have been avoided if he had only been honest nearly thirty years ago. So much of their lives could have been different.

Noreen spoke first. "This feels so strange."

He looked up to see her gazing at the green cement walls. He didn't know if he should agree with her or not. Everything he thought to say seemed inappropriate.

"It's so quiet," she said in explanation. "I'm not used to quiet."

Tim smiled back. Words still escaped him. He vaguely remembered a time when he could talk to her about anything.

"I don't mind," she said. "It's kind of nice."

He realized he didn't know what she was talking about. His mind had wandered.

"I'm sorry."

"The quiet," she repeated. "It's nice."

"Oh, yes. We raised four boys. We haven't had a quiet night in our home in twenty years." Immediately, he realized how insensitive his words sounded. Circumstances had cheated Noreen out of a family of her own.

"I'll bet," she said, apparently not offended. "At the drugstore, I could always tell when it was three o'clock without looking at the clock. That's when the kids came in from the high school. The noise level escalated about ten times."

He nodded in understanding though his heart ached for her. It was a shame that something most people found annoying, Noreen remembered as endearing.

"I lived alone most of my life," she continued. "Just me and my cats. I got used to the quiet. I never listened to the radio. I didn't even have a television at home. When I wasn't at work, sometimes the only voice I heard all day was my own." Her face softened into a smile as she remembered. "For the most part, that's how I liked it; solitude. When I got to Marysville, I realized how much I took it for granted. Now I'm never alone. Not even in the shower."

She gave Tim a quick look, and her cheeks colored in embarrassment. "I'm sorry. I'm sure you didn't come here to listen to a list of complaints."

Tim shook his head. "You have more right to complain than anyone I know."

She shook her head. "No, I don't. My life hasn't been perfect, but I had a job I loved. I have a family who loves me. I know my Savior is waiting for me in glory. If I've learned nothing else in the last three years, I know there's a whole world of women who haven't had a fraction of the blessings I've taken for granted."

Tim smiled to himself. It was just like Noreen to sympathize with the other guy and ignore her own pain. She hadn't changed in thirty years. When he looked across the table at her, for a moment, he saw the young woman he knew all those years ago.

"You're a wonderful woman, Noreen. You deserve so much better than you got."

She shook her head again. "None of us are owed anything. Doctor Eisinger didn't owe it to me to come forward and tell what he saw that night, but he has. Because of that, I'm getting a new trial. Because of him, I've been sent here where my father can visit me almost any time he wants. If nothing else, this opportunity has made things easier for him."

Tim shook his head again in wonder at Noreen's eternal self-lessness. Instead of glorying in a second chance to convince a jury—which she most certainly would—to overturn her murder conviction, she saw her stay in the Scioto County jail as an opportunity for her father to visit her without the discomfort of a long drive to Marysville.

After confessing what he knew to Judge Davis, the presiding judge, Herman Ruddock, the prosecuting attorney, several attorneys from Bruckner, McManus, the county sheriff, Noel Wyatt, a few other interested parties, and a court reporter were sent to Mark Eisinger's house to take his statement. No one wanted to risk the possibility that the surgeon wouldn't live long enough to testify in court. As it was, everything was put on a fast track in an effort to beat Dr. Eisinger's brain tumor.

"I'm happy for you, Noreen," Tim said sincerely. "I've consulted with your attorneys about what to expect if I'm called to testify. They're confident you'll walk away with a full acquittal."

Noreen smiled sheepishly. "I talked to Noel about that a few days ago. He said that the last time he talked to you, you weren't exactly thrilled about the possibility of taking the stand."

Tim looked down at his hands and then scratched the back of his neck. He hadn't had a cigarette in sixteen days. He was still eating candy like it was going out of style but reaching into his shirt pocket less and less often.

"I'm sorry about that, Noreen," he said after bringing his eyes up to meet hers again. "As usual, I was thinking of myself. Did Noel tell you he called me a self-serving coward?"

Noreen's eyes widened and her lips twitched as she tried not to smile.

"He was exactly right. I've been a coward my whole life. It wouldn't have been so bad if it only affected me. But it hasn't. It affected your life. It affected Sally's. Now it's affecting Joyce and our kids. But I can't keep hiding things to save my own skin." He placed his hands on the table, palms down, and took a deep breath. "I'm coming clean about everything, and I'm not going to let the fear of repercussions stop me."

Noreen sat back in her chair. The color drained from her face. "Wait a minute, Tim. I don't know if I'm ready to hear you clear your conscience."

Tim swallowed hard. "No, Noreen, that's not what I mean to do," he said, even though it would make him feel better. "I only want to tell you how sorry I am. None of this would have happened if I had acted like a man."

"You can't say that for sure, Tim."

"Maybe not, but if I'd done the right thing, some things could have been avoided. Like all this pain you've been through. Noreen, you were the only innocent person in this whole mess, yet you suffered the most."

"No, Tim. Sally suffered more."

He ducked his head. He couldn't even apologize correctly.

"Yes, I guess that was insensitive," he began again. "But at the risk of sounding like a louse, if Sally hadn't been bent on hurting you, and me too I guess, she never would have confronted you about me and her. She wouldn't have egged you into a fight. I'm not suggesting she didn't pay the ultimate cost, but you were the only one totally innocent in the matter."

Noreen studied her hands for a moment before looking up. "I don't believe there is such a thing as total innocence anymore. I've spent the last thirty years considering my role in all this. Believe me, I've done little else. I believe much of what a person gets out of life depends on what they put in. Deep down, I knew why Sally was such a close friend of mine." She raised her hand to stop Tim's interruption. "I loved her dearly and we had some great times growing up. But I knew she only formed relationships with people who could benefit her somehow. There were plenty of times I closed my eyes to the warning signs she gave out. I didn't want to see she was using me, too.

"I've had plenty of time in the last three years to think about what I may have inadvertently done to end up in Marysville. Everyone in that place will tell you they're innocent. Maybe in some ways they are. Sometimes we are victims of circumstance. Many of them have been used and abused by the men in their lives in ways you or I can't imagine. I'm sure those circumstances contributed to the choices they made that brought them to their present condition.

"So maybe no one is totally guilty or totally innocent; me included. I could have done something years ago, even if it meant just being frank with Sally. I could have told her I didn't appreciate her using me to get close to other people. I could've told her I didn't like it when she talked about girls she didn't even know. I could've told her to stop gossiping about teachers or making up outright lies."

She smiled sadly at Tim. "But I never stood up to her. I was intimidated by her like everyone else, even though I was her closest confidante."

"Noreen, I didn't come here to blame all this on Sally," Tim said. "I can't apologize for her either. All I can apologize for is my role in it. I treated you horribly. You didn't deserve the things I did."

Noreen's eyes filled with pain. Tim wished he could get up and leave without saying another word, but the time for denial and beating around the bush was past. He had to make things right, as right as they could be after all this time.

"When Sally came back to the party, she said she was going to meet you there. The two of you had something to tell me." Noreen looked at Tim, almost wishing him to stop her and tell her it wasn't true. He didn't.

She absently picked at a torn fingernail and continued. "She was acting nervous; jumpy. She stalled around for a while, and then she said you had probably chickened out and she would have to tell me herself. It was like she was enjoying every minute, like she wanted to hurt me."

Tim glanced away. He wanted to throw in some barb about Sally's character, but it wasn't fair. Sally wasn't here to defend herself, and he wouldn't try to distract Noreen from his fault in the matter.

"She told me she was carrying your baby. That's why we got into the fight. I just couldn't believe it. I didn't want to believe it. All these years…"

He touched her hand. "There was no baby."

She looked at his hand on hers and nodded. "I know. Noel told me. He said that Doctor Eisinger said in his statement that Sally told him all about her affair with you. She said she wanted to get pregnant, but it hadn't happened. She told him she didn't want James Steele's baby, so she used him. He didn't bother to tell her he couldn't get a woman pregnant. He'd already had a scare with another woman. When he had emergency gall bladder surgery the year before, he told the surgeon who was a friend of his, to make sure he would never be able to get another woman pregnant. He knew he wasn't going to stop cheating on his wife; he just didn't want to get caught again. Dr. Eisinger was standing on the porch when Sally and I started arguing. He heard her tell me about the baby. He knew she was lying."

Tim shook his head in disbelief. "She told me a couple of days before our engagement party that she had made a mistake. A false alarm. Then she said she still wanted to…she still thought we were going to run away together."

Noreen looked away. She swallowed hard. "Why didn't you?"

He reached across the table and gave her hand another squeeze. "Because I loved you. I didn't want anything to do with Sally. When she told me she thought she was pregnant, I felt like the bottom had fallen out of my world. Not so much that I had gotten caught in a mistake. I could have handled that. What I couldn't bear was losing you. But I couldn't shirk my responsibilities either. Before I could even catch my breath, Sally told me I had to marry her, and we needed to tell her parents right away. I wanted to wait a few days and get my bearings." He attempted a mirthless laugh. "But you know Sally, once she wanted something, you couldn't dissuade her."

Noreen pulled her hand out from under his. "I couldn't figure out why you stopped speaking to me after she disappeared. It was like a wall went up between us."

"I knew her disappearance was somehow my fault. I figured James Steele did something to her because she told him about the two of us, and he went into some sort of jealous rage. Then I thought if she had taken off, that was my fault too. I was pretty full of my own importance back then."

His attempt at a smile died on his lips. "I couldn't look at myself in the mirror. And I certainly couldn't look at you. I wasn't worthy of you. I never had been."

Noreen laced her fingers together and stared at them. "I thought it was my fault; that Sally had been telling the truth about you loving her, and you couldn't go on without her."

He shook his head rapidly. "No, Noreen. It was all me. I was eaten up with my own guilt."

She shrugged. "It doesn't really matter. I decided a long time ago that if you had an affair with Sally, I would forgive you. I couldn't hold it against you or Sally when I knew it had been my fault."

"How could it have been your fault, Noreen? You just believed two people who claimed to love you."

"Because I knew all along what Sally was doing. From the very beginning, I think she latched onto me to gain acceptance. She was ostracized for having money, and it didn't help that she threw it into everyone's face. So she befriended me to fit in with the other girls. She knew she could wrap me around her little finger. She could fit in and still be in charge of things. But I saw another side of Sally. She had a good heart. When no one was around and she didn't think she had to impress me, she could be warm and funny. You want to hear something strange? Most of the time I felt sorry for her. I always wished I could go back in time and tell her she was worth something. She didn't have to work so hard at standing out. I loved her. Her parents loved her. I wish she could have known how to love herself."

"You are either the most gracious person ever born, or incredibly naïve."

"That's the thing about grace, Tim. None of us deserve it. And we certainly can't earn it, no matter how hard we try. We don't deserve a relationship with God. We should be struck down for even daring to enter into His Presence. Instead He tells us to enter into the joy of the Lord." Noreen's eyes shone against the county issue smock she wore. "What a magnificent God we serve, Tim. If He can give us His grace through Jesus' blood, who are we to deny that grace to others?"

Tim shifted uncomfortably in his chair. He didn't know how to respond. He hadn't seen a faith as strong as hers in a long time. "All I know is that neither Sally nor I deserved you," he said finally.

"You need to stop punishing yourself, Tim. My life hasn't been that bad. I try to be content in every situation I'm in. Though I must confess, the last three years haven't exactly been a day at the beach."

They exchanged smiles. Noreen cocked her head and studied his designer polo shirt stretched over his ample stomach. "It looks like you've done pretty well for yourself."

Tim leaned back in his chair and patted his stomach. "Yes, the Good Lord's never denied me a meal."

They both laughed. Tim's face sobered as he studied her. A wave of compassion, heated by unrequited love, washed over him He wanted to take her hand and tell her he had never loved anyone the way he loved her. Then he realized doing so would dishonor Joyce. Regardless of the current state of his marriage, he owed her his loyalty.

"I'm sorry we hurt you, Nory," he said instead.

Tears glistened in the corners of her eyes. He wondered when the last time was anyone called her that.

A deputy sheriff opened the door and stuck his head in. "Time's up, Ms. Trimble."

Noreen turned her head to look at him over her shoulder. "Thank you, Deputy."

Tim was reminded of the Apostle Paul in prison in Rome. He gained favor with his guards and was allowed to have his friends come into the prison to minister to his needs. That's how Noreen was; a blessing everywhere she went, and consequently blessed in return.

"Have they set a date for your trial?" he asked.

She nodded as she rose from her chair, and the deputy stepped forward. "The sixteenth."

Tim stood up too. "Wow, that's fast."

"Actually, I should be out of jail by tonight. My attorney is making the arrangements with a bail bondsman right now."

"Oh, how wonderful. I didn't realize," Tim said, though he was glad he had come to Scioto County anyway. He doubted Joyce would appreciate him visiting Noreen in Jenna's Creek in front of all their friends.

"They don't exactly consider me a flight risk," she said teasingly.

The deputy pushed in Noreen's chair and took hold of her arm. He reminded Tim of an overgrown Boy Scout helping a lady across the street.

"I'll keep praying for you, Noreen," he said, even though he couldn't remember the last time he prayed for anyone. However this time, he would. "And I'll do whatever I can to see you get out of here."

She smiled over her shoulder as the deputy turned her toward the door. "Thank you, Tim. Thanks for coming. Tell everyone hi for me."

Chapter Twenty-six

Christmas day was a somber occasion. The Blackwoods tried to keep their spirits up for the sake of Karen and Roger's little ones, but getting through their first Christmas without Jack was not without tears and heartbreak.

Since Elaine and Leo were expecting their first baby in January, they didn't come home for the holidays, choosing instead to save their trip to the States for after their baby's birth.

Abby felt Jack's absence more than she ever dreamed she would.

For most of her married life, she thought she had missed out on something. She married a man she didn't love after being rejected by the one she did. Since she couldn't have Noel Wyatt, she had sacrificed any fulfillment she might have found with Jack.

But that was all behind her. She wouldn't allow herself to bemoan the past any longer. The pain she caused Jack and the torment she put herself through for the last thirty years couldn't be undone. She was never one for New Year's resolutions, but this year she was making several. In a few days, it would be 1977. The country had just elected a new president; a Democrat. What would Jack have to say about that?

It was time to move on with her life.

She was determined to enter the job force in the new year. She needed a job, but more than that, she wanted one. The only job she applied for thus far, she had lost to Christy, but it hadn't dimmed her enthusiasm. Now that Christy was settled and appeared reasonably satisfied with her job at the library, Abby would enlist her help in the job search. Between the two of them, they should be able to come up with some kind of job resume that made Abby look moderately skilled at something.

In 1977 she would have a new grandchild, a daughter-in-law, and a career. God was so good.

She stared at the Christmas tree that dominated the picture window in the living room the way one had since the first Christmas after the Blackwoods moved onto Mulberry Street. The tree was adorned with a mishmash of hand-me-down bulbs from her mother and ornaments created during every grade of each of the four kids. Even Christopher and Rebecca were sending over ornaments they made in school. Occasionally Abby imagined setting up a tree like those in the department store, decorated with store bought ornaments and garland that hadn't been fashioned from construction paper and glue. But then she would retrieve the box from the attic and begin her annual sorting through thirty years of memories and know it would be some time before she went into a department store to purchase ornaments.

She went to the tree to begin the arduous task of taking it down. She removed a cardboard ornament cut in the shape of a reindeer that one of the kids had made in elementary school. The reindeer's antlers were lopsided and faded. Its nose was missing; only a shiny spot where the glue had held it in place remained. It needed to be thrown out. Maybe this would be its last year to grace a Blackwood family tree. She turned it around. In childish scrawl, written in black crayon, was the year *1961*, followed by the initials *E.B.*

Eric.

Tears tickled her nose as an image of a first grade Eric sprang to mind. Where had the years gone? How had her little man grown up almost without her realizing it? He was graduating from college this year. He and Jamie had finally settled on a wedding date; June fifteenth, she and Jack's anniversary.

"Oh, Jack, you would be so proud of him," Abby said aloud. "He's going to make a wonderful husband. Just like you."

Usually anytime she thought of Jack and spoke his name, she would apologize for all the pain she had caused him. Not this time. The season of blame and regret was over. It was time to forgive herself and move on.

She straightened the reindeer's antlers and carefully wrapped the ornament in a piece of tissue paper. She wouldn't throw it away. It would be hanging on the tree again next year, just like always.

Abby wasn't the only one looking forward to a new year and a new beginning. Last month, she had driven Christy to Louisville to testify against Stanley, the gas station attendant and his wayward cousin. Both men looked much younger and less threatening than they had the night they stormed into her motel room and stolen her belongings. She almost felt sorry for them, dressed in their ill-fitting suits, lined up behind the defendants' table with their attorneys, flanked by their tired, pinched-faced parents.

Christy gave her testimony and left without waiting for the verdict. She didn't care. It didn't matter anymore. Whatever was going to happen would happen with or without her. Her identity would no longer be determined by two lowlife thugs.

She found she loved her job at the library more and more each day. Sometimes she missed the frenetic pace of the law firm, but only for a moment. She had learned in the past weeks, the slower, gentler setting of the library was more her speed. She recognized many of the regular patrons now and knew what they wanted before they asked.

She also got along well with her coworkers. She almost wished she didn't. The closer she got to them, the more she felt like they deserved to know the truth about why she had left her job in Columbus. She doubted she would ever find the nerve to come clean. Instead, she focused on doing her job well and avoiding the men who came into the library. It would be a long time before another one got close enough to her to sneak her keys out of her purse.

A blush crept up her cheeks when an image of Jarrod Bruckner came to mind. He had called twice since running into her at the library. The first time, he asked her out for coffee, an invitation she ultimately declined after spending fifteen minutes chatting with him. The second time, he wished her a merry Christmas and told her he wasn't giving up on her so easily. He would be calling back, though he couldn't guarantee how much abuse from her he was willing to take. He was handsome and funny, and she definitely found him interesting, but she wasn't ready to think about spending time with a man, even if it was just for coffee.

He still wasn't aware she had worked as a paralegal at one of the most prestigious firms in the state. If she let him into her world, she would be forced to omit a significant part of her past or outright lie. She wasn't willing to do either. Nor was she ready to divulge details. Regardless of what she thought of Jarrod Bruckner, she wasn't ready for the complications that would come with spending much time in his presence.

Still, a part of her hoped he was telling the truth and would call back.

Calvin Trotter's twenty-fifth birthday was four days away. The eight weeks following his discovery of Uncle Howard's Will was spent in bed with his leg elevated before he moved downstairs to the couch. He told the people at Bruckner, McManus he'd had a minor accident and would make the trip to their office as soon as he was able. Then he placed a long distance call to the record publishing company in Nashville and gave them the same story. Both had been understanding and said they looked forward to seeing him after the first of the year.

Sitting on his secret hadn't been easy. Every time his old man started hassling him about sending his resume to the drugstore, Calvin bit his tongue. He wanted to tell his parents they'd never see him working behind the counter at that dreadful drugstore. His inheritance had given him what wars had been fought over since the dawn of time, freedom. By spring, he'd be in Nashville, living in style, with no worries about bussing tables until his big break like every other would-be singer/songwriter. He had it made in the shade.

His eight weeks of convalescing had given him plenty of time to think about his family. Regardless of how much he liked the idea of reminding his parents how they refused to pay for music lessons or encourage his dream of becoming a songwriter, they were still his parents. When they hassled him about settling for a boring job that would enable him to support a family, they only had his best interests at heart. They wouldn't have been on his back so much to make something of himself if they didn't love him and want him to have an easier life than they had.

He also had plenty of time to think about how Uncle Howard had cheated Dad out of his fair share of Grandpa Jeremiah's money. Malcolm Trotter deserved the respect and love of his brother and father. Because of their greed, he hadn't received it. And where had their greed gotten them? Jeremiah had lived out his old age in a rundown house, his liver floating in a sea of cheap moonshine and his heart rotting away with bitterness. His money grew moldy in the back yard while his brain turned to mush.

Uncle Howard's life didn't go much better. If he ever loved any of his three wives, he never showed it. The first two women may have been saved from their untimely deaths had he given up a dollar to seek medical attention for them when they needed it. He never had an heir or fond memories to keep him warm in his old age. He had plenty of money and property, but no one to share it with. He was in the ground next to his second wife, with Jeremiah keeping guard two rows south, and nothing to show for his labors on earth.

No matter how badly Calvin wanted to go to Nashville and show his family he did have talent in spite of what they told him when he was little, he didn't want to end up like Jeremiah and Howard before him. The money wasn't more important than having a life worth looking back on.

Aunt Paige still hadn't approached him about the Will. She apparently hoped he didn't know what he was looking at before he fell through her ceiling or his injuries had given him amnesia. He figured she hadn't known about the Will either, or she would have destroyed it long before he had a chance to find it in the attic. Nor was it likely she knew how much Uncle Howard was worth. If she had, she surely wouldn't have hung around the counter at the drugstore all those years. She was probably just as surprised and flummoxed as Calvin to find out the rumors of Grandpa's wealth were true, and the money had been waiting all these years—for Calvin.

The thought of it still gave him a chill. He was rich. All his dreams and aspirations were suddenly within reach.

Between salivating over the sudden change in his financial status and the thrill of telling Malcolm and Eudora he had no intention of ever working in a pharmacy or at any other equally demoralizing job, Calvin nursed his disgust toward his Aunt Paige.

More than once over the past eight weeks, he thought of picking up the phone and calling her. When she answered, he would say, "You've got ten minutes, you old bat, to get out of my house. And don't take a stick of furniture when you go, it's mine."

He imagined the horror on her face, and the anger. Poor Uncle Howard, how wise he had been to die twenty years before his Will was ever found. He wondered if Paige ever thought about going out to the cemetery and digging him up to give him a piece of her mind.

But something inside him wouldn't let him make that phone call. He attributed his charity to his mother's mother, Delores Jefferson. Grandma Jefferson had loved Calvin in that unconditional way usually reserved for grandmothers and dogs; something to which Calvin was unaccustomed. He knew his mother loved him as well, but she was always siding with Malcolm who was too hard on the boy. While his parents were condemning and un-demonstrative, Delores Jefferson offered him love, security, and assurance that his presence was necessary to the betterment of the world.

Grandma's house was the first place Calvin ran to every day after school. She lived one street over from his house, and he had to go right past his street to get there. His first sensation upon entering her small kitchen through the back door was the smell of baking bread. He still thought of those moments every time he walked past a bakery. Grandma would have a couple of fresh slices, still steaming from the oven, waiting for him on a clean plate in the center of the table with a bowl of fresh churned butter and homemade jelly next to it.

Calvin would climb onto a chair and tell her about his day, and she would laugh or express sympathy as the situation warranted, and give him her undivided attention, which was what he desired most. She was the only person in his life who acted as if his dreams were reasonable and attainable. She never acted like he should be anything more than he already was. She loved him dearly.

And she loved Jesus.

She told Calvin stories of Jesus blessing the little children who came to him. She told him how Jesus fed five thousand people with only two fishes and five loaves of bread. Calvin didn't know much about Jesus, but he couldn't imagine those five loaves of bread tasting any better than Grandma's.

Her eyes would grow misty every time she told him how Jesus loved him more than anything, and He wanted Calvin to be with Him in heaven someday. "You have to give your heart to Him, Calvin," she would say, putting her face close to his so he wouldn't miss the gravity of her words. "You'll serve someone, baby, either this old rotten world, which would like nothing more than to see you fall on your face, or your Heavenly Father. It's your choice, boy. No one can make it for you."

Calvin's parents only went to church when Malcolm wanted to impress someone from the bank. They never talked about Jesus or prayed when they sat down to a meal. Calvin respected his grandmother and knew she would never steer him wrong, but it was easy to forget her Jesus anytime he wasn't in her presence. She died when he was fourteen, and his spiritual training came to an end.

But for the past eight weeks while he was lying in bed thinking up acts of vengeance to pour down on Aunt Paige, Grandma Jefferson's words kept playing over and over in his mind.

"You'll serve someone, baby. It's your choice. No one can make it for you."

He felt a little guilty in knowing how badly Paige was sweating over his silence. It was probably worse on her than if he just called and told her to get out of his house. At least then he would put an end to her misery. Grandma Jefferson wouldn't be proud of how much he enjoyed the power he currently wielded over his aunt. But Grandma didn't know Paige.

Still, it wasn't fair to keep her in limbo anymore than it was fair to keep what he knew from his parents. This involved them, too.

The cast up to his thigh was removed a week before Christmas and replaced with a walking cast on his right ankle. His other injuries had healed and gave him no trouble. The walking cast would be removed the first of January, and he would be right as rain, according to the doctor. Nothing would keep him away from Nashville after that.

On New Year's Eve, he called Paige and invited her to dinner at Malcolm and Eudora's house. "I need to talk to you, Mom, and Dad together," he said.

"Now, Calvin, you know you mean the world to me," she said in a trembling voice. "I went to a lot of trouble to get you that job at the drugstore…"

"None of that matters," he replied, amazed at his ability to keep the ire out of his voice. "I appreciate everything you tried to do, but I'm taking things into my own hands."

She laughed nervously. "I don't suppose you'll give me a little hint as to what you mean by that."

"I'll see you tonight, Aunt Paige. Don't be late."

As if she would. For the first time in his life, Calvin held all the cards. It felt great.

Three hours later, Eudora had barely finished setting the last ceramic serving dish on the table and had settled herself into the chair at the opposite end of the table from Malcolm when Calvin burst out; "I'm going to Nashville next week."

The gravy boat in Paige's hand froze halfway to her plate. A dollop of rich brown gravy landed with a silent splash on his mother's clean linen tablecloth.

"You're still recuperating, dear." His mother reminded him, barely noticing Paige as she dabbed frantically at the spot of gravy with her napkin. "You can't go to Nashville."

"What in the world would you want to go there for anyway?" Malcolm grumbled as he shoveled a forkful of pot roast into his mouth.

Calvin couldn't stop the smile that spread all the way across his face. "Because a major publishing company bought a song of mine, and one of the biggest female performers in the business wants to sing it. She says it's the song she's been waiting for her whole career."

Malcolm snorted. "How much money did they get you for?"

Calvin swallowed the disappointment at the way his news had been received. He had hoped someone at the table would celebrate with him. "They didn't get me for anything, Dad. They're paying me."

"Well, this doesn't make any sense," Eudora said. "I don't understand why you have to go all the way to Nashville. I thought when you sold something for publication, you sent them the song and they sent you a check? Then the song was theirs to do with what they wanted."

"That's usually how it's done, Mom. But the singer's agent told the publishing company she was so touched by the song she wants to meet the writer. She wants to see if there are any other projects we can work on together." Calvin knew his voice sounded star struck, but he didn't care. "I've already put her off for too long with this leg thing. I have to get there as soon as possible before she finds someone else. This could lead to a whole new career for me. In a few months, you might be listening to one of my songs on the radio."

"I thought you outgrew writing songs, Calvin," Eudora said.

"Still sounds like racket to me," Malcolm said to no one in particular.

"How are you going to get to Nashville anyway?" his mother asked. "You don't have any money, and you can't drive in that cast. Whatever happened to the job you were supposed to get at Wyatt's Drugstore?"

She and Malcolm turned reproving eyes to Paige. Paige touched the corner of her napkin to her tongue and attacked the spot of gravy on the tablecloth.

"I would starve on the streets before I went to work in that drugstore."

"Don't get fresh, boy," Malcolm said and jabbed the air with his fork. "There's nothing wrong with good honest work. You'd make a lot more money at the drugstore than you would in Nashville peddling songs to some spoiled singer."

Calvin smiled to himself and sat up a little straighter in his chair. "Well, money isn't exactly a problem anymore. They're taking my cast off in three days, so I'll drive down there myself. And as far as the money goes…" He paused and looked around the table. "I've been in touch with an attorney from Bruckner, McManus in Portsmouth."

Malcolm frowned. "Bruckner, McManus? Aren't they the ones that got Noreen Trimble out of prison?"

Eudora rubbed her chin. "I believe so, dear. I heard Noreen is home again." She turned to Calvin. "See. You should've gone over to that drugstore and got that job while you had the chance. Now Noreen will probably go back to work. Then where will you be?"

"Mother, if you would just listen, I'm trying to tell you what I am going to do. And it has nothing to do with that drugstore." He took a calming breath before smiling at his father. "It seems Uncle Howard remembered me in his Will. As of next Wednesday, which for those of you who don't remember is my twenty-fifth birthday, I'm the chief beneficiary of Uncle Howard's estate."

Malcolm choked on his asparagus. "Estate? What estate?"

Eudora slapped the table with her open hands. Coffee splashed out of her cup and off the saucer onto the tablecloth. "I told you he had money," she shrieked at Malcolm, her face purple with rage. "Didn't I tell you that old horse had money?" It couldn't be certain if the old horse she was referring to was Howard or his father, Jeremiah.

Malcolm ignored his wife's tirade and kept his eyes on Calvin. "How did you find out any of this? Did this Bruckner, Mick-whoever just call you out of the blue?"

Paige was nervously twisting her napkin in her hands, anxiously watching Calvin from under lowered eyelids.

"I found some old papers of Uncle Howard's while I was staying at his house," Calvin said, deciding it best to leave out all the gory details. "I saw the name of the law office that drew up the Will and called them. They said they were looking for me, too. Seems they've been handling Uncle Howard's estate for the past twenty-one years. Next Wednesday when I turn twenty-five, all control reverts to me," he ended with a smile.

No one at the table seemed happy for his good fortune.

"What about us?" Malcolm boomed. "We're you're parents. We should have been handling any estate on your behalf until you became of age. Howard knew I was good with investments. This sounds suspicious to me. Those leeches probably mismanaged everything and whittled the estate down to pennies."

Calvin shook his head. "Oh, no. Bruckner, McManus has handled everything in exemplary fashion. I don't know all the details, of course. The man I talked to couldn't tell me much over the phone. I was hoping to go down there Monday after I get my cast removed to prove I'm who I say I am. I thought you might want to go along, Dad. But according to the attorney, Uncle Howard's holdings have done quite well in the past two decades. Grandpa Jeremiah had bought property in three counties. Along with his stocks and bonds, the whole package is going to amount to a fair sum, even after attorneys' fees."

Malcolm stood up fast, sending his chair flying backward across the area rug where it landed with a crash against the hardwood floor. "I knew Howard cheated me out of a fortune. I only wish he was here right now so I could wring his scrawny neck." He held his hands in the air and squeezed an imaginary opponent.

"Malcolm, remember your blood pressure," Eudora advised.

Malcolm suddenly remembered his sister-in-law sitting to his left. "You!" he raged. "You said there was no money. You tried to take what belonged to me." He advanced around the table.

Paige shrank in her chair. Eudora started around her end of the table and reached Paige's chair first. "Malcolm, stop. Think about what you're doing."

"I've never thought more clearly. I'm going to kill her."

Paige whimpered like a wounded animal.

Calvin stood up, put his hands on either side of his plate and leaned across the table. "Stop!" he screamed at all of them.

In a split second, the only sound in the room was Paige's rapid breathing and the clock on the wall. Calvin straightened up and glared at each of them in turn. "Everybody, sit back down and shut up so I can tell you what's going on."

In mute obedience, Malcolm and Eudora turned in opposite directions and returned to their places at the table. Malcolm righted his chair and lowered his girth into it. Paige sniffed one last time, uncertain if her safety had been assured, and fastened grateful eyes on Calvin.

Calvin waited until everyone was seated before taking his own seat. He centered his water glass over his place and smiled. "Now, this is how it's going to be. Aunt Paige..." The smile he directed across the table at her was malice free. "...who I guess it's time I stopped calling that since you are not technically my aunt, did not know anything about Uncle Howard's Will. The law office was in charge of everything and under strictest orders from Uncle Howard not to divulge any information about the estate to anyone until I became of age. Next week, everything Uncle Howard owned will become my property. That's why I'm going to Nashville. I have no desire to spend my life in this town, nor do I want to become a pharmacist. I'm a songwriter, an artist. My talent is finally being recognized, and with my newfound fortune, I can go to Nashville and focus on my career without worrying about bussing tables or going without my dinner."

"Aunt Paige, uh, Paige," he corrected, "you can keep the house you shared with Uncle Howard. You deserve it. I'll deed it over to you free and clear as soon as I take control."

"That house doesn't belong to her—" Malcolm blustered.

Calvin turned to his father. "It does now. Don't worry, Dad. I'm giving you what remains of the property out on the ridge that Grandpa sold off to the government. There's still over two hundred acres of timber and farmland that should bring a good price. I'm also giving you and Mom whatever other properties remain in Auburn County. You can handle them any way you see fit. The properties outside Auburn County, along with the stocks, bonds, and bank accounts, I'm keeping for myself. For the time being, I think I'll let Bruckner, McManus continue to handle the estate. They've made good work of it up to this point. I don't want the hassle. I have my career to see to."

Eudora sniffed loudly and touched Calvin's arm. "Oh, Calvin, I don't know what to think. I guess your uncle saw something good in you the rest of us hadn't taken the time to look for."

"No, Mom. Uncle Howard was a selfish, penny pinching old goat. He only left the money to me because he wanted to hurt you and Dad, and he didn't believe in charities. But it all worked out. You can stay here and keep doing whatever it is you do, and I'll get out of your hair and do what I want with the rest of my life. Now, if you'll excuse me, I'm going upstairs to look through some new car ads. I don't think my old clunker would make it all the way to Nashville."

Malcolm watched him go and then turned back to his cold pot roast and oven-roasted potatoes. "The only thing that doesn't make sense to me is how that boy found Howard's Will in the first place."

Paige lifted her shoulders in a shrug and speared a baby carrot. "I suppose it just takes knowing where to look." She spent the rest of the meal trying to figure out how to submit a higher price to the insurance company for the cost of fixing her ceiling.

Noel spent his Christmas like every other Christmas before it. He ate dinner with his mother, placed calls to his sisters and their far flung offspring and went home early. He stopped by Pastor Trimble's house on the way home for eggnog and cookies with Noreen and her family. Noreen still looked tired and guarded, but Noel knew she would be fine. Her trial had lasted three days. The lien she had used to post bond for herself had been taken off her house now that she was a free woman, and the money repaid to the bank. He was so happy for her family. He couldn't remember Mr. Trimble looking so good. In his eighties, Noel's last thought as he pulled out of the driveway was, the old man could die in peace now that Noreen was back home where she belonged.

He told Noreen her job was waiting for her behind the pharmacy counter anytime she wanted to reclaim it. She had smiled and squeezed his hand, and said, for the time being, she was going to spend some time with her family. She was even thinking of moving back into her father's house for as long as he needed her.

Noel doubted Tim Shelton was faring as well. His testimony had been the icing on the cake for the defense. The whole jury was already in Noreen's corner before he even took the stand; but human nature being what it is, everyone wanted to hear what he had to say about Sally Blake. Without being told, Noel knew Tim's days were numbered at Blake Realty.

He wondered where that would leave Tim and Joyce. He always suspected their marriage was less than amorous. He witnessed for himself the cool reception from her and their daughter when Tim left the witness box and rejoined his family. Noel didn't envy the lump of coal in Tim's stocking this Christmas. For a brief moment, he wondered if there was any hope for Tim and Noreen. Even after all these years, it had been obvious from watching Tim on the stand that he still felt something for Noreen. Would Joyce be angry enough about what he said about Sally to divorce him? If she did, would he turn to Noreen? Did Noreen want him to?

Noel shook his head. He was too old for guessing games in other people's love lives. He couldn't even handle his own. He hadn't known love and fulfillment for over twenty years. What right did he have to speculate on others?

One week later on New Year's Day, he drove through Jenna's Creek's silent streets and let himself in the back door of the drugstore at eight a.m. The store wouldn't open until tomorrow, but he hadn't had anything to do at home. Anytime he got restless and bored, he headed for his home away from home. He could always find some paperwork that needed tending to, a loose screw on a shelf that needed tightening, or a light bulb that needed replacing. He wasn't even above sweeping a floor or emptying a mousetrap in the stockroom. He loved his store and everything concerning it. It was the family he didn't have. He shrugged at knowing some people found the situation pitiful. Such was his life.

Noel climbed the stairs to the crow's nest over the back of the store and let himself into his office. Just as he rounded the oversized mahogany desk, he heard someone at the front door. He smiled to himself as he descended the narrow staircase to see who it was. It reminded him of the old days. Opening up the store bright and early without an employee in the place, handling every little detail himself, relying on nothing but instinct and what the old man had taught him.

He was a half stride from the door, his hand already outstretched to flip the lock when he saw the young man waiting on the other side. His heart skipped a beat. He exhaled past the sudden knot in his throat and pushed open the door.

"Eric. Good morning."

Eric Blackwood paused a moment before stepping over the threshold. His hands were deep in his pockets and his shoulders hunched against the cold. As soon as he was inside, he snatched the toboggan off his head and stuffed it in his pocket. He ran a hand through his thick dark hair, shoving a lock back into place when it promptly fell over his left eyebrow.

Noel pulled the door shut behind him and relocked it. He hadn't seen the young man since last Labor Day weekend when Eric rang his doorbell. He hoped this meeting would end differently.

The two men studied each other in silence, uncertain of what to say or do.

Noel broke the silence. "D'you have a good holiday?"

Eric shrugged. "It was hard on Mom with Dad being gone..."

He stopped talking, and Noel kicked himself for asking. "Yeah, I'm sure," he replied weakly. "Well, um, did you need something? Or, uh..."

They went back to staring at each other for a moment. Eric unzipped his coat and then stuffed his hands back into his pockets. Noel shuffled from one foot to the other. He tried not to stare at the young man before him, but it was hard not to. He wanted to memorize every feature of his face; study every nuance. He couldn't get over the novelty of having another human being on the planet that looked so much like him. He thought of his own father and wished he were here right now so he could introduce him to Eric. They would have so much to talk about. Two scientists, two brains that worked alike, thought alike, were alike.

"You'd have loved to have known your grandfather Wyatt," he wanted to tell Eric. *"And he would've loved to know you. I can see him in you. I always have. Since the first day you walked into this place three years ago. I didn't want to give you a job, you know. Having you around*

scared me to death. I knew you would see it on my face. You'd know you were my son just from the way I couldn't stop staring at you."

"I guess you know Jamie and I are getting married," Eric was saying.

Noel forced himself to pay attention.

"June fifteenth," the young man continued. "Jamie wanted me to ask you...I mean...she really wants you to be there, and your mother, too. But she said it was up to me. Anyway, I guess I want you there, too. If you want, I mean. I don't want you to feel obligated or anything."

It took everything inside Noel not to cry. "Eric, I'm honored. I wouldn't miss it."

Eric nodded and studied his feet.

"Would you like to sit down and talk? We could get something to drink at the lunch counter. I wasn't planning to open the store today."

"Yeah, I know. I've been sitting out front for a while thinking. Then I saw the lights come on in the back." Eric shrugged. "Anyway, I've got to be getting back to the house. Mom doesn't know I'm gone. I just...I wanted to let you know about the wedding." He pulled his toboggan out of his pocket but didn't put it on his head.

"Um, Jamie and I might have kids someday. You know how women are," he added conversationally, but as quickly as a thin smile appeared, it died on his lips. "Well, uh, she thought I should talk to you sometime about...well, about medical history and stuff. I mean with the epilepsy. They say it's hereditary, and I was wondering if you knew anything about what went on with your side of the family."

Noel nodded in understanding. "Sure, sure, that's smart. You'll want to discuss those things before you start a family." As if he'd know what young people discussed before having children. "I'd love to talk to you and Jamie anytime you want. You could come by the house. My mother is anxious to meet you. Oh, I'm sorry. I don't mean to push you or anything, all that is up to you."

Eric nodded along with him. "I appreciate that. I guess I'd like to meet her, too. I've been thinking about her." He brought his eyes up to meet Noel's.

For the first time, Noel realized Eric was an inch or two taller than him. Those deep blue eyes mirrored his own, but he could see a little of Abby around his mouth. His heart ached an old familiar ache.

"I've been thinking about you, too," Eric said. "I suppose it's ridiculous that we keep avoiding each other."

"Hard to do in a town this size," Noel said with a cautious smile.

"Sure is." Eric exhaled a nervous breath and combed his hair away from his face before pulling the hat down over his ears. "Well, I gotta go. Mom'll be wondering where I took off to. Maybe Jamie and I'll come over before we go back to school. We could talk about...things. Then maybe you could take us to meet your mother. Well, I'd meet her, since she and Jamie already know each other."

Noel's spirits soared. "Sure, sure, I'd love that. Mom would too."

"Great. Well, then, I'll call you." Eric turned away, twisted the latch to unlock the door and pushed it open.

"Thanks for stopping in, Eric," Noel said after him. "Happy New Year."

Eric turned halfway around. "Yeah, you too, Noel." He walked out the door.

Noel stared at the closed door for several moments before his feet came unglued from their spot. He wiped a tear from his cheek as he turned toward the back of the store. He'd been invited to his son's wedding. It was a beginning; a beginning of something wonderful, he prayed.

A smile spread over Noel Wyatt's crinkled features. Eric and Jamie were planning to have children. Grandchildren—suddenly his life seemed a lot more interesting than it had fifteen minutes ago. He looked upward as the smile on his face widened. *I don't deserve it, Lord, but thank you.*

The End

Contest

In Book 4, Calvin Trotter heads to Nashville to make his mark in country music. With the name Calvin Trotter around his neck, he won't exactly pack the Grand Ole Opry. He needs a stage name. This is where you come in. Think country music in the 1970's when Merle Haggard, Conway Twitty, and George Jones ruled the airways.

Send your stage name suggestions to:
Tsaba House Publishing
Attention: Jenna's Creek Contest
2252 12th Street
Reedley, CA 93654

All submissions must be received no later than December 31, 2008.

The winning entrant will have a character named after them in a future Jenna's Creek Series novel, be listed on the Acknowledgment page of the book, and receive a free autographed copy.

In the event that more than one entrant sends the perfectly suited stage name for Calvin's character, there will be a random drawing to determine the winner. The winner will be announced on www.teresaslack.com, www.TsabaHouse.com and be contacted by mail.

Have fun and send in those names!

Coming Soon

Look for the fourth book in the Jenna's Creek Series, coming soon to a bookstore near you.

Learn more about the author and her books on her website: www.teresaslack.com

Teresa always enjoys hearing from her readers. You may contact her at: teresa@teresaslack.com